Golden Opportunities

A Woman's Mystery Novel

Joan Mallgrave

PublishAmerica
Baltimore

© 2010 by Joan Mallgrave.
All rights reserved. No part of this book may be reproduced, stored in a retrieval system or transmitted in any form or by any means without the prior written permission of the publishers, except by a reviewer who may quote brief passages in a review to be printed in a newspaper, magazine or journal.

First printing

All characters in this book are fictitious, and any resemblance to real persons, living or dead, is coincidental.

PublishAmerica has allowed this work to remain exactly as the author intended, verbatim, without editorial input.

ISBN: 978-1-4489-7264-7 (softcover)
ISBN: 978-1-4489-6505-2 (hardcover)
PUBLISHED BY PUBLISHAMERICA, LLLP
www.publishamerica.com
Baltimore

Printed in the United States of America

Dedication

To my sons, who will one day understand me…
To my grandchildren, who may not ever understand me…
To my cheerleaders, who are faithful friends despite me…
And to Joan, Carol and Linda, who understand me but helped me anyway…
Thank you so much.
Remember, I may not be Charlie but Charlie doesn't do anything that I wouldn't do.

CHAPTER ONE

He sat two seats behind his mark on the first morning seaplane flight from Charlotte Amalie, St. Thomas to the town of Christiansted, St. Croix. It was too bad she had to die—she was such a delicious pleasure to admire.

The young professional was clad in an attractive short-sleeved light gray suit with tasteful soft ruffles around the neckline. Her black hair had been highlighted, braided and twisted into a crown around her flawless ebony face. The highlighted strands peeked through the braids giving the impression there were long strings of gold chain entwined within the locks. Large gold hoop earrings framed her face. At least five or six fourteen-karat yellow gold chains of various lengths and links glistened around the smooth skin of her long silky neck.

Her height forced her to keep her long legs somewhat in the aisle. Her curvaceous calves were made even shapelier by her four-inch heels. The mirror-cut gold ankle bracelet twinkled and tantalized her onlooker.

The woman would appeal to any man and the person who sat two seats behind her was no exception so he told himself to stay focused—at least for now. As enticing as the woman was, the real object of his affection was the heavy rectangular leather display case next to her in the aisle. Not once did her hand leave the handle. The wide gold omega bracelet on her thin wrist gave a hint of what was encased within.

The onlooker was forty something, medium height with a barrel-sized chest and thick arms. A casual multicolored tropical shirt with a palm tree pattern screamed "tourist." His khaki shorts matched his crocs. The tan floppy-brimmed hat and wrap-around sunglasses camouflaged a balding head. He knew he would blend in with the thousands of visitors who roamed the Virgin Islands every day. He was right.

He knew the woman's zigzag patterns as she went from one jewelry store to another to replace sold inventories. Each time she made her rounds she varied her route. There was a single spot on her trek she repeated week after week. If she hadn't, she would have had to walk four additional blocks in her high heels. He knew where the side alley was on that block.

CHAPTER TWO

A subpoena lay in Charlie Mikkelsen's lap as her plane touched down at the small Caribbean airport on St. Croix. She grabbed her bulging handbag and burrowed to the very bottom before she felt the smooth flat surface of her compact. As much as she didn't want to admit it, she was excited Victor would be at the airport to meet her and she wanted to look good. She scrutinized her make-up.

Fix your lipstick, Ms. Charlie. But use your lip liner first. Your lipstick bleeds into all those little lines around your mouth.

These lines show the world I've aged gracefully.

No, those lines show the world you're old.

As the plane came to a halt and the jets wound down, Charlie stuffed everything into her purse and turned to her son Jeremy. "This horrible boot is large enough to fit **Sasquatch**. I wish I didn't need to wear it."

"It's a monstrosity but it does protect your fancy new ankle replacement," the young man in the next seat replied. "I can picture you tonight as you glide across the dance floor with your boot. You won't trip Chief **Vic**tor with your crutches, will you?" Jeremy sarcastically emphasized the first syllable of Victor's name.

"Watch your tone. Victor and I won't be on the dance floor tonight."

"The plane is half empty. It's time to boogie, mom."

Jeremy, a thirty-six year old bachelor, was almost six feet tall with dark blue eyes and light brown curly hair that skimmed the collar of his tan sports shirt. He was into boats, jet skis and blondes and was interested in a marina for sale near the island town of Christiansted.

He stood and retrieved his backpack stored in the overhead. It was the sole item he brought onboard because he needed to be hands-free to grab his mother if she should teeter a bit too much. Those crutches were problematic getting up and down the aisle of the plane and in and out of airports.

As soon as the last of the passengers cleared, the flight attendant handed Charlie her wooden crutches and she started her awkward trip up the aisle. The airport provided a lift since there was no Jetway. Jeremy stepped onto the lift first and then he and the flight attendant held their collective breaths as Charlie gingerly stepped onto it with her crutches. Success. Once the guardrail was in place, the two travelers were lowered to the tarmac.

"I wouldn't mind living here year-round," Jeremy said with an ear-to-ear grin plastered on his face.

"The warmth and sunshine does feel good."

The duo tunneled their way out of the bright tropical sun and into the airport. The exit passage led them to an exterior baggage claim area protected by a large roof. Charlie no sooner arrived than she heard a voice she recognized.

"Charlie, Charlie, Charlie." Deputy Police Chief Victor Hanneman V practically skipped to where Charlie stood. Jeremy knew the Chief's greeting wasn't for him so he headed for the carousel.

St. Croix's well-known black police chief grabbed, hugged and then kissed the woman with the silver hair. As many times as the Chief's picture had been in the paper and as many times as he had appeared in public over the course of some forty years, he was never known to smile, laugh, giggle or grin. His out-of-character behavior did not go unnoticed by many of the locals who waited for their luggage.

Whether Charlie wanted to admit it or not, she was very happy to see Victor. Very happy—sorta.

He does look good, Ms. Charlie. And he's so excited to see you.

Yes, he does look good.

But you can't forget about his temper tantrums and his insatiable need to control. We don't need foolishness at our age—no matter how good he looks.

The Chief spotted Jeremy, shook his hand and gathered the remaining luggage. The trio squeezed through the crowds and stepped into the sun. As they neared the curb, a cab stopped and a businessman egressed with a handsome leather display case in his hand. With haste, he headed inside the airport. Charlie whispered to Jeremy that she bet the case was filled with jewelry.

"Mom, why would I care?"

"Jeremy," the Chief interrupted, "millions of tourists come to these islands every year in search of jewelry. The gold and gems are discounted plus there is an added advantage of no sales tax. Even Uncle Sam grants the tourists a liberal amount of purchase power before a custom's fee kicks in. Jewelry sales are a huge source of income for our islands."

Jeremy managed a single "Oh," as the cab pulled away and the Chief's car pulled up. Officer Bob Thompson stepped out and opened the rear door for Charlie.

"Hi, Miss Charlie. It's good to see you again." The young officer helped Charlie into the vehicle. Jeremy sat in the front seat because the Chief wanted to sit in the back with his mother.

"That's quite a gadget attached to your leg," Bob said.

"I'm so glad you noticed. A girl my age has to go to extremes to attract attention, you know. Is there any particular reason why you're my chauffeur and I'm in a police vehicle?"

"The first reason is my boss is sitting next to you and the second is we intend to keep an eye on you until after the trial."

"You are a key witness," the Chief added. "James is positive everyone in the drug ring was identified but he's not taking any chances in case he missed someone."

"So I take it the upcoming trial keeps everyone busy?"

"Oh, yes," Bob said. "We go over and over every detail to make sure the good guys win this one."

When Bob pulled onto the main road, Charlie caught her breath for the first couple of turns and told her stomach to settle down. She had forgotten that islanders drive on the opposite side of the road.

"Miss Charlie, where am I to take you?"

"Jeremy and I rented a tiny villa on West End outside of Christiansted. We have it for six weeks. Jeremy wants to take a serious look at a marina and this visit will give both of us a chance to decide what we want to do."

"You mean you might move here?" the Chief asked. He made no effort to hide the enthusiasm or delight in his voice.

"It depends on what I decide," Jeremy said. "If I invest in the marina, I'll live here full time. If so, Mom and I may buy a small house together. Mom would keep her condo in Pennsylvania but stay here in the winter months."

The Chief glowed with approval and added, "I'll be happy to assist you in any way I can, Jeremy."

Did you hear what the Chief said? He wants to be a buddy to your son, Ms. Charlie.

He wants to help him.

No, it means he wants your son to like him. You need to be honest with yourself, missy. You'll be in over your head before you know it. Men the Chief's age don't change their spots and he is a certified egomaniac.

Shush. I can't talk to Victor and myself at the same time.

* * *

Officer Chamaign Benton called headquarters from her squad car. Since the Chief's vehicle was equipped to monitor all incoming calls, everyone in the car listened. The body of a woman was found in an alley off of Strand Street. The location was less than a block from where the Chief's car now sat at a red light.

"Charlie, I've taken unused leave for the last six weeks, but I'm still the official Deputy Police Chief until the end of this shift. I'd like to go to the crime scene. Do you mind? It will be my last."

"Of course not. Go do your police chief thing and I'll go to the villa and nap. I want to be rested for your retirement celebration tonight."

By the time the police vehicle arrived at the site, Officer Benton had taped off the crime scene. The Chief asked Charlie and Jeremy to remain in the car as he slid out and headed toward Chamaign.

"Now, mom, you don't plan to make like a wannabe detective again, do you?"

"Please remember, if I hadn't played detective the last time I was here you wouldn't have seen the marina for sale."

"Marina or no marina, you stay out of this case. Use your time to decide what to do about your over-anxious suitor."

"He's a very nice person. How many times do I need to repeat that?"

"Who do you want to convince, mom? Me or you?"

* * *

The conversation came to an abrupt end when James Kingston, former detective and now Acting Deputy Police Chief, arrived on the scene and tapped on the windshield. Charlie lowered the side window and everyone exchanged greetings.

"Good to see you two again. It looks like you took the Chief's chariot to town."

"I thought the Chief would keep me out of trouble. As my cab driver, that's more than you did the last time I arrived in this town."

The gold cap on James right incisor twinkled in the tropical sun. "Don't forget, I was an undercover detective back then. It looks like I might have another murder here. Do you plan to solve this case for the Virgin Islands Police Department?"

"That's okay," Jeremy said. "I want the police to handle this case. I'm here to see that mom stays away from murderers and drug dealers."

"Then Elin and I will see you tonight, Charlie. And by the way, Elin needs to talk to you about a potential new store. She told me she wants you with her when she goes to a meeting on Thursday in St. Martin."

"Sounds interesting. Anytime clothes or jewelry are involved, I want to be around."

"Got to go now." James left and joined the Chief.

Officer Bob Thompson returned and drove Charlie and Jeremy to the villa. "That's a nasty one. It's a murder and a possible rape. I bet you could solve this case and become famous again, Miss Charlie."

"Bob, never in a million years did I ever think I would be involved in something like murder and drug trafficking. I'd do it again in a heartbeat if I had the chance. It was more fun than twenty years of marketing plans and advertising budgets."

"Did you know James promoted Chamaign to fill his old job? She's our new detective."

"A lady detective—just like Olivia on *Law & Order* and some of the heroines in my mystery novels. I like Chamaign's honest and outspoken style."

"She's great. And that comes from a man almost twice her size," he laughed as he spoke. Bob's six-six rock-solid muscular build filled a doorway. His body fat registered about sixty percentage points below Charlie's. His dark skin and brown penetrating eyes saw right through a suspect and very few bad guys ever tried to keep eye contact with him.

"Can she intimidate a bad guy like you?" Charlie asked.

"In truth, she's better. Suspects underestimate Chamaign because she is so short. She starts out soft and sweet and just when the bad guy thinks he has it made she turns into this vicious Bengal tiger. She's smart, fast and knows how to stalk her prey. She's also physically skilled. And our new boss thinks it's a hoot she can outshoot all of us on the target range, except for Chief Hanneman maybe."

Bob pulled onto West End. "Which villa is it, Miss Charlie?"

"Number Six." Charlie scribbled down the address and her phone number on a piece of paper. "Would you give this to the Chief and ask him to call me so I know what time he'll pick me up this evening?"

Bob agreed and returned to the crime scene.

* * *

Chamaign, the sole female detective in the entire U.S. Virgin Islands Police Department, assessed the crime scene for her new boss. "I suspect her neck was broken since there are no obvious wounds—maybe a cervical spine fracture. The coroner can tell us if she was raped before or after she was killed."

James walked around the body. "The way she is dressed tells me we have a motive—theft. I would take bets she was in the jewelry trade."

Officer Paul Simpson, Bob's counterpart on the police force, walked into the alley and held up a purse in his gloved hand. "Her name is Camelya Brown. She was with Italian Gold Standards, Inc. Her handbag was in the trashcan down the street. Money and cards are still inside. A can of Mace, too."

"Did you find a jewelry display case?" James asked.

"Not yet. I'll dig through a few more trashcans."

"Well James," the Chief said, "I know what will keep you out of trouble. Welcome to the Kingdom of Chiefhood."

"Chiefhood. Is that a word?"

"No, but you got my drift, didn't you?"

"Chief, I got your drift." James knew the Chief was not good at jokes but he wasn't about to tell him when he only had a few hours left of his Chiefhood. James turned toward Chamaign.

"This is your trial by fire, detective. We'll need this case cleaned up as quickly as possible. Our island jewelers and distributors will not be happy when they hear about this."

"It doesn't feel right to be on such a high, boss. This woman's death was vicious and here I'm excited to get my first big case."

"I understand and felt the same way when I was assigned my first important case. We'll go over things when you return to the station. Can you take care of things here?"

"Yes, boss."

"Good. Meanwhile I'll call Italian Gold and then notify police headquarters in Charlotte Amalie. I'll also contact the airlines. Right now we have someone out there who wants off this island."

James and the Chief slid into an overheated police cruiser. "I have bad vibes about this, Chief. Very bad vibes."

CHAPTER THREE

It was less than an hour before the first wave of cruise ship tourists would finish their breakfast and head for the jewelry district. Roy Parkton, a tall black man in an open-collared white shirt and tan linen suit, was led down a narrow walkway between a jewelry store and a small mall off of Main Street in Charlotte Amalie, St. Thomas. A wooden dowel, imitating the barrel of a gun, poked in the small of Roy's back. He didn't question its authenticity.

The jewelry rep had spotted his assailant across the street headed in a different direction. The man had appeared to be another middle-aged, pot-bellied tourist in tan cargo shorts and white polo shirt with sneakers and white socks. Roy dismissed the man because of his dress and because of his quick-paced stride. He held his head up and barreled down the street at an exercise pace. His behavior didn't resemble that of a thief.

Unfortunately for the young Roy Parkton, the tourist was better trained in Karate than he was and the man's thick arms were trained to kill.

The dark leather display case dropped to the ground when Roy's neck cracked. It contained an array of tantalizing tanzanites, most of them with diamond accents. There were rings, pendants, earrings and bracelets all set with the much sought-after gem. The polished stones ranged in size from tiny pinpoints arranged in clusters to prized ten-carat gems. The jewelry seekers could choose from fourteen-karat yellow or white gold but the finer gems were reserved for the eighteen-karat white.

The stones were cut in all the popular designs plus squares, trapezoids and pear-shapes. Some pieces held a combination of two cuts—

marquise and rounds were always a special combination as were rounds accented by baguettes. The classic of all classics were the large ovals surrounded by brilliant diamond rounds. The colors of the gems ranged from light violet to a deep purple but there was an ample sampling of the most enviable—the rich blues to violet blues.

There was a special section in the case that held small bags of individual gems of incredible quality. These were the favorite finds of the small collector who used his or her own 10X loupe to check for depth of color as well as for internal defects.

When the police happened upon the empty black leather case stashed behind a yellow stucco wall, they knew it was time to search for a body. They found it mid-afternoon hidden behind some bushes.

CHAPTER FOUR

Andre Johnson had been the new Deputy Police Chief of St. Thomas for three whole days. Even though he enjoyed his old job in Internal Affairs at headquarters, he relished the opportunity and challenge of his new position. His office was located in the same area as the Virgin Islands Police Department, which monitored police activities in St. Thomas, St. John and St. Croix—all U.S. territories. Located in the Criminal Justice Center complex, Andre knew he was close to all the latest action and key police officials.

Andre was the son of a black serviceman from Tortola and a white British lady. The family later immigrated to St. Thomas. Andre had the tight kinky curls of a black man but the skin of a tanned white man. His eyes were green with brown flecks. He had his mother's straight, narrow nose. He married his college sweetheart after they graduated from the University of Miami. The Johnsons had four children—three boys and a brand new baby daughter. He was pleased with his recent increase in salary and knew a lot of it would be spent on Pampers.

Andre was aware his competition for his new job was James Kingston, but he also knew James applied for the position on both St. Thomas and St. Croix. He was lucky Victor Hanneman was about to retire and just as lucky the gentle-spoken widower James was madly enamored with Miss Elin Mikkelsen of St. Croix. Even though Andre felt he had the edge for the position of Deputy Police Chief on St. Thomas, he was pleased both he and his long-time friend had received the promotions they both wanted.

It was James who identified Deputy Police Chief Eugene Peters of St. Thomas as the head of the drug ring that had permeated both islands. While Andre had been in Internal Affairs, he had been suspicious of Peters for his lifestyle, but he did not have the evidence he needed to investigate deeper until James gave him the lead. Now Andre occupied Peters' old office while Peters sat in jail awaiting trial.

Andre was quite upset when he hung up the phone for the second time in ten minutes and the look on his face spoke volumes. Both times he had spoken with Detective Marlboro Man Carmen, who happened to be the first personnel appointment he made when he became a deputy police chief. Carmen replaced one of the two police victims of Eugene Peters' drug ring.

Man, as Marlboro's friends called him, had told his new boss about a black leather display case found earlier in the day. The second call was about the man with a broken neck. When the phone rang a third time, Andre was sure it was additional information about the murdered man. Andre was pleased and surprised when he recognized James' voice. The pleasantness evaporated after he heard what James had to say. James was equally horrified when he heard how Andre responded.

"We're quite a set, James. We're both brand new in our jobs and both of our detectives are brand new."

"And we have a big problem on our hands," James said. "This thing is well organized and precise. There has to be at least two unidentified suspects. The unsubs have struck twice now and I suspect they will do it again."

"Will you put Chamaign in charge?"

"Yes. This will be a challenge for Man and Chamaign. The retailers and wholesalers will hold more than their feet to the fire on this case—they'll go straight to the Commissioner. I know it will be hard for me to sit back and allow Chamaign do her job. Victor Hanneman drove me crazy so I hope I don't do the same thing to Chamaign."

"Keep me in the loop, James. I'll fill in Chief Phillipe about what happened on your island."

"That's fine. I've already contacted Chief Farrow. Ten minutes from now both your boss and mine will head toward Commissioner Dylan's office. I suspect Dylan will go ballistic. It will take him a single heartbeat to see all the implications with our jewelry trade."

Andre hung up, made a quick call to Man to tell him what happened in Christiansted, took a deep breath and walked to the office of his boss. He found Police Chief Bill Farrow of St. Croix already in Dwayne Philippe's office.

* * *

Chamaign walked into James' new office with her pen and notebook in hand. "Do I still get to call you James tomorrow after your official induction ceremony as our new Deputy Police Chief?"

"When we're alone, you're always welcome to call me by my name. Have a seat."

Chamaign's new boss had friendly, gentle mannerisms and his management style was in sharp contrast to the man soon to retire. This forty-something tall, thin police veteran was sent to St. Croix on loan from the St. Thomas force. His mission was to go undercover to work a drug ring. Chamaign had been amazed at how fast the detective earned the respect of his fellow officers. She was equally amazed when not a single officer misinterpreted his affable style as a lack of work ethic. Of course, the fact that James chose her to fill the empty position of detective earned him a lifetime of devotion.

"Chamaign, I told you this would be a trial by fire. Well, more fuel has been added and a second alarm has been called." He proceeded to tell her about the dead man on Charlotte Amalie.

"This is horrible and it's so well planned and organized. I've started my murder book and prepared a memo for your approval. But now I need to talk to Man so we can update the memo and get it out to the jewelry trade."

James said, "I assigned someone to cover the airport, Skyhigh Seaplanes and the ferry dock. Plus I've notified the Coast Guard to search all vessels leaving our docks. Remind Man to do the same on St. Thomas. What else is on your list, Chamaign?"

"I've requested a list of passengers from our airport and docks—both arrivals and departures. I've started to call the hotels and resorts to gather the guest lists."

"Sounds good. Go on."

"I asked Bob to call Italian Gold and they said the Brown woman carried primarily gold but quite a few pieces were accented with diamonds. They estimated the retail value at well over a hundred grand. Italian Gold said they would notify the woman's husband and make arrangements for a positive ID. Now Man and I need to compare crime scenes."

"Go on."

"We need to send notices to the Puerto Rico PD, too. After that we'll contact the other islands outside the U.S. territories."

"Go on. You're on a roll."

"Once we have our lists, we need to run them against the FBI's automated database system, VICAP. If any known violent criminals are on the list, we'll know where to start. If we're lucky enough to get any kind of print from the crime scenes, then the FBI's electronic fingerprint ID system will come in handy."

"How about you call Man and then put your plans on paper. We'll meet with Bob Thompson and Paul Simpson for a few minutes at around five-thirty. We'll be rushed to get to the Chief's retirement dinner and dance but we can make it."

"Yes sir, Deputy Police Chief James Kingston." Chamaign stood and took a military stance as she shook her new boss's hand. Her round dark face was filled with pride and passion. She took a deep determined breath and headed for her new miniscule office. En route, she stopped in the ladies room to re-pin the bun that held her hair up and out of her face. She paused and added something else to her list—call husband and have him fix dinner for their son and pick up the babysitter.

* * *

Man shook his head at he looked at the dead man's body. "Have you finished with your crime scene pictures?"

The young officer nodded and stepped away. Officer Ben Shore had already checked the man's wallet. "His name is Roy Parkton and he worked for International Tanzanite Gemstones Ltd. And Man, he carried a gun in his belt—he must not have had a chance to go for it."

"Ben, could you give his company a call and tell them what happened. Find out his next of kin. The firm must have an inventory of what he carried so see if you can get a detailed list and pictures, if possible. We should have a value so ask them to fax it to my office ASAP."

"The coroner is here," Officer Sam Watson said. "It shouldn't take us any more than an hour to finish up the crime scene."

"When you finish, go where the walkway intersects with Main Street. Search the path all the way from that point to here. Check every place within an arm's length for prints. Then start to re-trace Parkton's steps this morning."

"Ben, mind if I hitch a ride with you and Danny to headquarters?"

"Be my guest."

Man hopped into the passenger side of the squad car. Rookie Danny Marsten drove.

"I've never been to an actual murder scene before, detective."

"I'm sorry to say it won't be your last, Danny."

As Marsten sat at a traffic light, at least a hundred tourists started to pass the squad car as it sat at the intersection leading to the undisputed jewelry Mecca of the U.S. Virgin Islands. Many headed for the myriad of jewelry stores along Main Street. Others had blown their budgets in the stores earlier and had started to return to their resorts or cruise ships.

"Detective, if you don't mind, may I ask why people call you Man?"

"I was named for the Marlboro Man himself. You know, the rugged good looking guy on the horse."

"I don't think I've heard of him."

"He became famous doing tough-guy ads for cigarettes. Anyway, I was a preemie and my proud dad said I was the toughest three pounds of red meat he'd ever seen—thus the name. I grew to five feet-three inches and was kidded about my name and height all the way through school. I hated the jokes but knew what my dad did was out of love. Believe it or not, I like my name now. I bet I'm the one and only Marlboro Man Carmen on planet Earth."

Danny smiled as he drove toward headquarters.

Man's cell buzzed and he saw that the incoming call was from Chamaign. "Hey lady detective, I understand the two shortest people in the entire police force have the hottest case around."

"Well I've been busy." Chamaign rattled off the list of people she had contacted and what she had accomplished. "What have you done? You know we have to keep in sync on this, Man."

"The Coast Guard—I didn't think about them—do they know about St. Thomas?"

"I called them back. Anything else new over there?"

"It's not official but I'd say our vic's neck was cracked."

"We believe ours was, too. What was your estimated time of death?" Chamaign asked.

"Don't know for sure but it had to be before the tourists arrived in hordes."

"Ours was similar. This isn't good, Man. These crimes were well orchestrated."

"Agree. I'll get a list of air and ferry passengers, too. I hadn't thought of that. Can you fax me the inventory of what your vic carried? I'll send you mine when I get it."

"I'll request it and fax it to you and the Coast Guard. I need to prep for a quick meeting and later the retirement dinner. Keep in touch, Man."

* * *

Chamaign finished the game plan and emailed it to Man. She printed out copies for herself and her cohorts. She realized how the media would spotlight this case and she knew neither she nor Man could afford to make a mistake. She was glad Man was closer to the Police Commissioner's office than she was. He would feel the heat before her.

CHAPTER FIVE

The Chief called Charlie while she napped and Jeremy took the message for his mother.

Victor would pick her up at six.

Once awake, Charlie headed for the shower. The landlord had placed a shower seat in the stall as she had requested. She placed her crutches next to the shower wall and maneuvered her butt onto the seat. She took off the orthopedic boot that went from her knee down to her toes and set it outside the shower. She relaxed for ten minutes as she pampered herself.

After she was half dressed, it was make-up time. No brand of face cream could do a thing about the multitude of wrinkles on her face or her sagging jowls.

Ms. Charlie, you do have one thing in your favor—you don't have a chicken neck.

But what I do have are age spots.

Well, get to work. This effort will take some time.

You make me feel like I'm hopeless.

You know why I do what I do? Because when you listen to me you look great.

Twenty minutes later Charlie picked up her pearl gray silk evening outfit.

Now how am I supposed to put this on while standing on one foot?

The woman in the mirror told her to stand next to the bed and if she lost her balance, she was to dive for the mattress.

Charlie hung the gown over her arm, used the crutches to get to the bed, stood on her right foot and balanced herself as she leaned against the side of the bed. She didn't dare put any weight on her left foot. The top of her two-piece outfit slipped on with ease but she couldn't stand on one foot and zipper the back at the same time. She sat on the bed and slid on the Palazzo pants and put the boot on under the pant leg.

Much to her horror, the Velcro straps on the boot snagged her silk crepe pants. "Crap," she yelled.

Jeremy put his laptop down and went to his mother's room. "What's wrong?"

"The Velcro on the boot snags the material in my new outfit."

"You'll survive, mom. *Victor* won't even notice."

Charlie glared at her son and pointed to the open zipper on her top.

"Now mom, I want you in by eleven and no necking in the back seat of the squad car with Chief *Victor*." Jeremy chuckled as he zipped the back of his mother's dress.

"Don't be cute. You could have gone with us, you know."

"No thanks. I find it difficult to watch an old man drool over my mother in public. TMI."

"TMI? What's that supposed to mean?"

"Mom, TMI—too much information. Get with it—it's a sign of the times."

Charlie dug through her purse for her watch.

"Do you plan to wear your silly watch, mom?"

"So you have a problem with my watch?"

"It's so silly. You're all dressed up and you put on a child's watch."

"And what do you have against Princess Summerfall Winterspring?"

"Aside from the yellow wristband and an Indian girl with fat hands, it looks inane with your outfit."

"And since when did a man who lives in jeans and tee shirts become a fashion critic?"

"Forget it, mom. By the way, don't forget to fix your lipstick before *Victor* gets here."

Jeremy returned to his laptop and continued searching local sites for various marinas on the island. Charlie returned to the mirror.

Fix your lipstick. TMI. Victor! I'll kill him yet.

Now, now, Ms. Charlie. Jeremy hasn't had to share you with another man in a long time.

"Mom!" Jeremy screamed with five explanation points after mom.

Charlie put down her lipstick and made her way to the living room on her crutches.

"Mom, you're on the Internet. There is a picture of Chief *Victor* as he kisses my mother at the airport."

"Ohmagod. Someone must have had a camera phone. I won't hear the end of this from James and Elin. What does the caption say? No, no. Never mind. I don't want to know."

Jeremy hit a couple of keys.

"What did you just do?"

"Sent the link to my brothers."

"Tell me you didn't do that."

"Done, mom, done."

"Run to the store and get the newspaper, please."

"I found a courtesy paper outside but I haven't looked at it yet." Jeremy searched underneath the piles of marina papers on the floor and found it. "Whoa. Front page, mom. Wasn't it Bob who told you a couple of hours ago you could be famous again? Well, you're famous again and you just arrived. Now I need to email the Internet picture to the *York Daily Record*. All of South Central Pennsylvania needs to know how you misbehave in public. Do you think WGAL-TV will be interested?"

"Wipe the grin off your face."

"Mom, go back and fix your lipstick."

"What is the commotion outside? I sure hope we don't have to listen to noisy neighbors for the next six weeks."

"Sounds like a smokin' car to me—gotta be a Mustang." Jeremy peeked through the vertical blinds. Sitting next to Jeremy's blue rental compact was a new Mustang Shelby GT500 V8. "I hope you brought a head scarf. It's a convertible and guess who is behind the wheel?"

"Victor? Victor! At his age?" Charlie swung her crutches as fast as she could to get to the bathroom.

Mustang convertible, Ms. Charlie! You've got yourself a problem. Isn't he a little old for male menopause?

Absolutely. I believe "second childhood" would be a better choice of words.

GOLDEN OPPORTUNITIES: A WOMAN'S MYSTERY NOVEL

Charlie peeked through the bathroom blinds and saw Victor and Jeremy outside as they gushed over two white stripes on a shiny red hood. The Chief, in full dress uniform, stood next to his new toy immersed in total ecstasy. He caressed the front bumper with his white dress gloves. With great ceremony, he allowed Jeremy to sit in the driver's seat and touch the black leather steering wheel. When the two men stood and admired the right rear tail light, Charlie rolled her eyes and tapped her foot.

And its red, no less, Ms. Charlie. He's acting like The Fonz.
Fonzie drove a motorcycle if my memory serves me correctly.
Oh. My brain crashes a lot these days and it doesn't always reboot like it should.
Then get refrigerator stickies like me. I think Victor has reverted to his teens.
Then Ms. Charlie, Jeremy's right. Eleven sounds like a good time to be home.
I don't need you to tell me what to do.
Well, missy. You're the one who will have to keep his sixty-five year old hands off of you.
At my age I can make my own decisions about hands, thank you very much.

* * *

"Charlie, what a delight you are. You look wonderful. In fact, you look delicious. I didn't know what to do about flowers so I brought you a wrist corsage," said the gentleman who was tall and well built but not exactly handsome. He had a full thick head of salt and pepper hair combed with care.

"Thank you, Victor." Charlie had a fixed smile on her face as she slipped on the posies.

Jeremy picked up his mother's camera. "Smile," he grinned, "I'll take your picture."

"Jeremy, this isn't a high school prom. Put the camera down."

"No, Jeremy, don't," the Chief interrupted. "This is a very special celebration and I want a picture of me with my charming date." He winked at Charlie as he spoke. "Take a couple of pictures, son."

Son? He called Jeremy "son." Ms. Charlie, now what?
Go away. I need to figure this out.

Charlie tried her best to smile but wondered what kind of look she had on her face as she posed for the pictures.

"Do you know about the picture taken at the airport, Chief?" Jeremy asked.

"What's this about, son?"

Jeremy went to his laptop and located the picture on the *St. Croix Source*. "The same picture is in the newspaper."

"What an embarrassment—and at my age," the indignant Chief said as he desperately gasped for breath.

Charlie went postal. "How about at our age, *Victor*? I'm the same age as you and I'm embarrassed, too."

"Well, let's hope none of the dinner guests have seen this. Who looks at the Internet anyway? Are you ready? I can't wait to show you my hot new Mustang."

"A lot of people read the paper and a lot more look at the Internet—that's why they have newspapers and the Internet, *Victor*!"

The Chief was uncomfortable and not sure what to do or how to react. Before he could stammer out a reply, Jeremy interrupted.

"Chief, I want my mother home by eleven and no heavy petting in the back seat."

The Chief was startled by Jeremy's unexpected comment. After a speechless few seconds he did his best to laugh. He wasn't very successful.

Charlie scowled at her progeny as she struggled to the door on crutches. She stepped outside, hesitated and looked back at her son. Only an infuriated mother could glare with such precision and perfection. "This isn't exactly a lol moment, son."

* * *

"Mother, look who's on the Internet kissing a woman."

"Is that Chief Hanneman?"

"Yeah. Now look at the woman."

"Is that the woman who helped the detective in the drug case?"

"Yeah. Dad said she was a real troublemaker."

"Tomorrow is visitors day. I'll let your father know she's back on the island. She must be here to testify at his trial."

"Do you want me to do anything or make any calls?"

"I'll take it from here. You keep your nose clean. Remember, the less you know the better."

* * *

"Isn't she great?" Victor asked as he zipped around a series of ogees. Charlie's stomach acid sloshed in four directions at once.

"Would you slow down a bit? You don't want a ticket on your last day on the force."

"But this thing has so much power. And listen to her engine purr. Rubee is sheer enchantment."

"Rubee? You named your car Rubee?"

"Yep. She's a retirement gift to myself."

No, Rubee is a toy car with testosterone in the tank, Ms. Charlie.

You got that right. Did you bring my Tums?

Oh. Fraid not.

"The ride is exhilarating, don't you think?"

"Rubee's a beautiful car, Victor. But why not a Lexus or a Beemer?"

"Don't you like Rubee?"

"I like that you like her. As we said back in the fifties, why don't you take the pedal off the metal?"

"I'll slow down if it makes my girl happy."

He called you his girl, Ms. Charlie. I told you that you were in over your head.

I'm not in over my head and I'm no one's property.

When are you going to tell him?

"Thank you for slowing down. I'm not used to riding on the left side of the road and every curve takes my breath away. I don't mean to put a damper on your evening, Victor, but I suppose this upcoming trial casts a longer shadow than I expected."

"It's hard to believe Eugene Peters was stupid enough to get mixed up with drugs and have his own detective murdered. I sure hope he is convicted."

"Why wouldn't he be?"

"At first he admitted his guilt. Then he recanted. The hard evidence centers on his bank account and offshore accounts. There are a number of emails that imply a few things but no one knows who he hired to kill the detective."

"Could he have done it himself?"

"No, Eugene wouldn't get his hands dirty. The only person who could identify him as the group leader was Rich Myers and as you know he was killed in the shootout with James. If Eugene does get off, the IRS will nail him for taxes on his undeclared income."

"What about Clint Spell and Fred Willard?"

"James has a ton of evidence against them and they'll be in jail for a long time. Willard and Spell will never bother you or Elin again nor will they murder or sell drugs again."

The conversation didn't relieve Charlie's fears. The thought that Peters would not be convicted defied her imagination.

* * *

Maria Peters made a phone call.

"Back, huh. I'll take care of her. Don't worry."

"Her testimony won't hurt Eugene but it will surely put Clint Spell and Fred Willard behind bars."

"Not if she isn't around to testify. The more kinks we can put in this case the less we have to worry."

"Do what you need to do," Maria ordered. "Keep my kids out of it."

CHAPTER SIX

The Chief and Charlie were the two last persons to arrive at the retirement dinner. The Chief helped Charlie out of the Mustang and patiently escorted her to the entrance of the Harbor View Seafood Restaurant. The banquet hall was located on the second floor. The restaurant sat high on a hill and overlooked the town of Christiansted. Before entering they stopped on the terrace to admire the incredible view of the town. The entire scene was an impressive big sparkle from all the stars above as well as the boardwalk lights, which doubled as reflections in the harbor's still waters. There were a dozen or so sailboats anchored in the harbor and several cast thin golden lights through their small portals. Several marinas were visible but Charlie had no idea which one interested Jeremy. It seemed so quiet and peaceful and the panoramic view was beyond exquisite. Charlie had enjoyed the restaurant's awesome scenery, its colorful and creative "island" drinks, and its decadent and delicious dishes on her last trip to the island.

"Beautiful view, beautiful date and a beautiful evening, Charlie."

"Thank you."

"Question, is that a child's watch you have on?"

Charlie nodded.

"Are you making some kind of social statement?"

"Not really. It's my favorite watch."

"Oh." The Chief said a bit confused.

Ms. Charlie, if the Chief can have a car for a toy, you can wear a toy watch. Right?

Right. Except his toy cost about $100,000 more than my toy.

But why do you really wear it?

Because it's the only watch I have that I can read without my glasses.

"It's a shame we have to go inside with a lot of people and noise," the Chief said.

"Now Victor, you know how many times you worked an eighty-hour week to earn tonight. It's yours to enjoy."

Victor led Charlie inside and to the elevator. Upstairs, they exited into a small foyer that led to opened glass double doors. Charlie looked around for a second and her body stiffened as straight as her fifty-year old ironing board. She was ready to turn and run. Her lips became thin and her jaw set hard enough to remove a layer of enamel off her teeth. The Chief was catatonic with an expression of total horror planted on his ruby-red face—not an easy feat for a black man.

Someone, probably James, had a dozen four by six posters made of the now infamous Internet kiss. They were taped on all four walls. Charlie looked around the room for James. When she spotted him in a corner, he was bent over slightly as he held his stomach and hooted. Tears of laughter ran down his face. Elin's composure wasn't any better. Charlie was ready to disown Elin as her island cousin.

The younger officers in the hall tried to hide their smirks—Bob Thompson, Ben Shore and Axel Stevens among them. Police Commissioner Dylan and the St. Croix Chief of Police, Bill Farrow, sat there and grinned like the proverbial Cheshire cats. Not one guest seemed upset that their opinionated and bullheaded deputy police chief, known for his outspoken diatribes and acerbic remarks, seemed uncomfortable.

To make matters worse, the Chief had to escort Charlie all the way across the room to the head table and everyone in the room watched the expressions on their faces.

Smile, Ms. Charlie, smile. You need to pretend this is funny.

I'm smiling. I'm smiling. Can't you tell?

Not really. You best try harder. With that look on your face I wouldn't want to meet you on a dark street unless I had a loaded Uzi in my hands.

Every lady in the room evaluated Charlie's evening garb and there were quite a few obvious whispers about her humongous black boot only partially hidden under her Palazzo pants.

As Victor held the chair for Charlie to sit, he apologized to her for the public kiss. "But at least Jeremy isn't here; my son, daughter and grandchildren are. I'm mortified."

Ms. Charlie, I know you're mortified, too, but you need to watch your tongue now. A lot of people are watching you. Whatever you do, don't say what's on your mind. Smile now.

Why Victor doesn't think I'm not mortified is beyond me.

Now Ms. Charlie, calm down. Smile at everyone. Try real hard to pretend this is funny.

This is not funny.

As I said, smile. Order a stiff drink as soon as you can.

Charlie did as she was told and waved and smiled at the few people she knew in the room. Of course when she spied James again, she gave him a look that could have reversed global warming.

Three little children ran over to their grandfather and kissed him. After three big hugs he introduced Victor the VII, Candy and Aaron. Vick the VI and his wife Kerry laughed and waved. Daughter Kristi and husband Thom waved and grinned, too. The young boy pointed to the pictures on the wall and asked his grandfather why he kissed the lady. The Chief told him to ask his father.

A waiter asked the Chief and Charlie if they would like a drink. Victor ordered two chardonnays.

"*Victor*, I'd rather have a Cruzan Cream."

For the second time that evening, Victor was confused by the tone of Charlie's voice. "But that's more of an after dinner drink."

"Well, I need something a bit stronger than a chardonnay. Right now. Now is a very good time to order me a Cruzan Cream, *Victor*. And make it a double."

The sound of her voice left no doubt in the Chief's mind Charlie had not made a request but gave an order. The hackneyed cliché about light bulbs flashed in the Chief's mind. "Ahh. I get it. James left a cold bottle of Cruzan Cream for us the first time I took you to visit your ancestor's old sugar plantation. It's like an 'our drink,' isn't it?"

Charlie tried hard to hide her look of sheer horror. She considered Cruzan Cream a *my* drink, not an *our* drink. She tried very hard to smile,

"Something like that," was all she could say.

Reverend Moran stood and went to the microphone. Before the invocation, he asked the Chief if he would be asked to perform the wedding ceremony. The room exploded with laughter and Charlie slid down her seat. The sole reason she didn't slink to the floor and crawl under the table was because she knew it would take at least four men to get her upright again. To make matters worse, the Chief tried to bluster out an explanation but gave up mid-sentence. He put his hand over his forehead and covered his eyes. A second round of unconstrained laughter filled the room for what seemed like an endless hour. The minister laughed; the Chief cringed; and Charlie smiled as if she enjoyed the minister's insidious attempt at humor.

After a short invocation, a lavish and decadent dinner was served. A large plate of appetizers was set on each table—codfish fritters accompanied by a hot red sauce, coconut shrimp with a rum and coconut sauce and fried calamari with tartar sauce. A conch salad and rolls followed. The main entrée was grilled tilapia with lemon sauce. Dessert was freshly sliced island fruit with a thick cream sauce over rum cake.

The dinner conversation went well and the food was beyond superb. Afterward there was the litany of prescribed speeches with accompanying plaques, commendations and proclamations. Following, the Chief's peers roasted him. Everyone in the room laughed and Charlie did her best to smile. She conceded this was payback time for the Chief's famous overbearing and caustic nature. She felt a little sorry for him as he tried so hard to smile and pretend he enjoyed himself. She even patted his hands a couple times as encouragement.

Don't feel too sorry for him, Ms. Charlie.

I'm not.

I hope you're not dumb enough to believe the Chief has changed his bad habits.

Go away.

Just another warning, girlfriend. He's bombastic, demanding and self-absorbed. That's a lethal combination in my book.

Since this is my novel, I suggest you turn the page and move on.

After the roast, Charlie encouraged the Chief to walk the room, greet his guests and receive all the appropriate handshakes and adulations.

Charlie made her way over to Victor's children and introduced herself. She joined them and chatted about the roast, the weather, her boot, and all the delays everyone had at the airport. Not once did anyone mention the pictures plastered on the walls. After about a half hour, Charlie excused herself to find James and her island cousin, Elin. By now Charlie was on her third Cruzan Cream. Two was her normal limit.

"Well, James, I see you still have your hand on your stomach. Does it hurt that much from all your laughter?"

"I wish it did, but I believe I might have some kind of bug."

"Well, I think I'll put a curse on your bug and turn it into appendicitis, which would serve you right. I know you're behind these posters."

"Now Charlie, you were fair game at the airport. You have to watch for those camera phones. You never know who has one these days." James laughed and his gold tooth twinkled from the light of the candle centerpiece.

Charlie glared at Elin, "Et tu, Brute?"

"I tried to stop him with the poster bit, honest Charlie, but I must admit I didn't try too hard," Elin said as she giggled. She was exquisite in a silk tangerine cocktail dress with a scooped ruffled neckline. The front hem hit above her knees and dipped to mid-calf in the back.

"Well, some kind of cousin you turned out to be. Isn't blood thicker than water?"

"Not when I look into James' eyes. I actually like this man of mine."

"Terrible excuse," Charlie responded.

Elin grinned at James. Happiness exuded from the radiant owner of the upscale Island Elegant Apparel Shop in Christiansted. Elin oozed sophistication and style; simplicity and significance; subtlety and soul. With her huge black eyes, extravagant high cheekbones, snazzy hairdo, plus hourglass figure, James returned her unconditional adoration.

"Well Kingston, your big induction ceremony is tomorrow. Are you ready?" Charlie asked.

"As ready as I'll ever be. All five ladies in my life will be there—my moder, Aunt Jeanette, Elin, Alyse and you. My mother's anxious to meet you, Charlie."

What's a moder, Ms. Charlie?

It's Danish for mother. Now shush. Can't you see I'm busy?
Why Danish?
These islands were once part of the Danish West Indies.

"We're having a party at my house after the ceremony," Elin said. "It will go well into the evening. You and Jeremy will come, won't you? You'll get a chance to sit and talk to everyone. Even my sister Alyse will be there with her new lawyer friend. Mama and I need your opinion of him. You can even bring the Chief if you want."

"Thank you, but I believe I'll let Jeremy be my escort. Let's not let the Chief know about this. If I bring him he'll want my entire attention. I need a chance to chat with your mother and Jeanette and meet Mrs. Kingston. Then I need to check this lawyer and see if he meets my specifications. Now, tell me about this expansion."

"I need you're advice and want you to go with me. Scandinavian Seven Seas Cruise Line wants to discuss an onboard version of Island Elegant on the five ships sailing the eastern and western Caribbean. They asked me to bring along a sampling of my inventory. Charlie, I've never taken a cruise before, have you?"

"A number of times but only once on Scandinavian Seven Seas. I believe the ship was called *Aqua Lights*. I suppose when you live in the Caribbean, you don't need to take a cruise to the Caribbean, do you?"

"Funny, Charlie," James said. "Your jokes are almost as bad as the Chief's jokes. Are those ships as fancy as the pictures I've seen?"

"My jokes will never be as bad as his. But yes, they are elegant and fancy ships. *Aqua Lights* is sophisticated and adult-orientated with high-end shops. There are other cruise lines that are a bit more casual and children-oriented. But, the bottom line is that sailing from Florida to the Caribbean, there should be a full day at sea—plenty of time to walk around and spend money in the shops onboard."

"With a store, do you think I'd be my own competition once the tourists hit the ground?"

"Probably not. You know yourself that most tourists head for the jewelry district, not the clothing stores. But there are enough adult late night activities onboard where your gowns should do well. There are fancy dinners, dances, lounges, nightclub-style events, and of course there are little alcoves every other ten feet where you can have formal pictures taken. Your gowns should do very well."

"We're supposed to meet Thursday on St. Martin. *Aqua Waters* is in dock that day and we're invited to take the trip back to Miami. If you agree to go, they said they would provide a wheelchair plus fly us back."

"You do understand we will eat well, don't you? Those chocolate fountains are guaranteed to put on five pounds a day. And of course pizza can be ordered twenty-four by seven. A soft ice cream machine will be available, too."

"Not a problem. Let's do it!"

"How long will you be gone?" James asked.

"Aqua Waters leaves late Thursday evening. We dock Sunday morning stateside so that gives up two full days at sea. I'll be back home Sunday evening."

"You really want to leave me for almost four days?" James whined.

"You'll survive, tummy ache and all, poor baby." She turned toward Charlie. "I'll call Carolyn Rodgers, my Island Elegant manager, and tell her to select a sampling of appropriate apparel to show. I'll have her pick out special outfits for us and she can meet us in St. Martin."

"Clothes—this is the type of adventure on which I thrive."

James spoke. "And best yet, Charlie will have no excuse to rescue anyone from a murderer or a drug kingpin. The Chief and I won't have to worry about our wannabe detective while she's on the high seas."

"How disappointed my mystery novel heroines will be. They approve of my adventures, you know, Chief Kingston."

James grinned at Charlie and then looked at Elin. "Honey, your grand opening of the new store is a few days after you get back. Will you have enough time to get ready?"

"Lise Holtzen is the manager and she's very dependable. The new product is in and once the shelves are installed, she'll need to steam a few things and rack them. Charlie has done the marketing end so we are set to go."

"I do plan to help," Charlie said. "Alyse will be there too, won't she?"

"Oh yes. She can put her dental practice aside for two days. Besides, she knows if she doesn't help me she won't get her new wardrobe at cost.

That's a pretty good incentive, don't you think?"

"Cost, huh? Do I get the same deal?"

"Of course. The local marketing agency wanted a fortune to do what you've done for me and you've done twice as much."

"Four days without my girl is a long time," James said as his gold tooth twinkled.

"You're a big boy, lover. Deal with it."

CHAPTER SEVEN

Chamaign approached the table where James, Elin and Charlie sat. She looked chic and classy in a smart black cocktail dress accented with an attractive pin composed of small peacock feathers.

"Your dress is gorgeous!" Charlie said.

Chamaign was a bit embarrassed by the compliment. "Well, three guesses where I purchased it."

Charlie looked at Elin. "Island Elegant Apparel Shop?"

Elin answered, "Where else does a discriminating, savvy woman shop for delightful and well cut clothing?"

"You missed the dinner, Chamaign. Where have you been?" James asked.

Chamaign sat down. "I need to bring you up-to-date. Our victim and the St. Thomas victim both had their necks broken and the time of death was very close. Both medical examiners said our vics didn't fight back so we need to assume they either knew the perp or else they were taken by surprise. Our vic was raped before she was killed. No DNA."

James shook his head. "These guys had this thing planned for months I bet. We need to get a step ahead of them, Chamaign. Do you have anything else?"

"Man and I each have an inventory of both jewelry cases. Our lady carried a retail value of over $140,000. On St. Thomas, the vic carried almost $240,000 in tanzanites and most of those gems were set with diamonds. Gemstone Jewellery had pictures of the larger, more expensive pieces so the Coast Guard has copies of both inventories.

They will stop any boat leaving the islands. May I have permission to ask our water patrol to assist with the smaller vessels?"

"Permission granted. Go ahead and get them involved."

"That will be a big help. I did manage to get the passenger lists from the airport and Skyhigh but I haven't had a chance to crosscheck anything yet. The night clerk on duty has begun to data enter the names into a spreadsheet so we can sort for multiple entries and departures."

"I didn't realize there were two murders," Charlie said. "When you say their necks were broken, do you mean like what the bad guys do on TV—a fast crank of the neck?"

"You got it," Chamaign said. "But it is a lot harder than it looks on TV. Whoever these men are, they are skilled in the art of murder."

"And about the victims. Were they the representatives who carry the gems from store to store or from island to island?"

Chamaign nodded before she spoke. "The wholesalers as well as individual shop owners cornered the commissioner this afternoon. He demanded fast action from both Man and me."

"About what time do these jewelry agents leave the island?"

Chamaign was puzzled by her question. "Charlie, why do I think you know something I don't know?" Both James and Chamaign sat straighter in their chairs and stared at Charlie.

"You helped me solve the case of Elin's abduction," James said, "and helped me identify Eugene Peters as head of the drug ring. Give this puzzle a try, partner."

"I would call what happened a happenstance. While the Chief, Jeremy and I waited for Bob Thompson at the airport, a cab stopped in front of us. A professional-looking man exited and had a large brown leather case that was larger than an attaché case. It looked quite heavy. I told Jeremy I thought it was a jewelry display case. The Chief looked at him and agreed with me and gave Jeremy a short lesson on island economics."

"What time was this?" Chamaign probed.

"Oh, about three minutes after someone took my picture with a camera phone. About eleven-thirty I guess."

"Charlie, what did he look like?" James asked.

"White male. Mid-forties. Five-ten maybe. A little overweight but very solid. Short dark hair. Wrap-around glasses. White shirt and tie. Don't ask me the color of the tie. The Chief and Jeremy saw him, too. They may be able to add to the description."

"James, I need to check with the Transportation Security Administration and the luggage inspector at the airport. I'll see if the TSA knows more about him and where he was headed."

"The inspectors would have demanded his ID with the display case," James said. "See if anyone remembers the name of his company. Also, there should be a security video, too."

"You got it," Chamaign said. "I need to establish if the man Charlie saw was a real rep or a fake. I want to go back to the station. Do you have a problem if I go, boss?"

"Not at all." Chamaign headed for Bob, Paul and Axel. The four of them left the building together.

* * *

Charlie decided it was time to find her own date when James refocused his attention on Elin. Her island cousin didn't seem to mind. When Charlie's exquisitely beautiful cousin batted her thick black eyelashes and then opened them with excruciating slowness, James was ready to drag her under the table despite his bellyache. When the DJ played Tony Bennett's version of Old Black Magic, neither of them could stand it any longer and headed for the dance floor.

Ms. Charlie, would you like to be on the dance floor with the Chief?

Without the boot and crutches, yes. He really is a good man.

You say that a lot. Who do you need to persuade—you or me?

Is there any difference?

Yeah. I keep you honest. Remember, no man the Chief's age is ever going to change.

True. But there are some things about him I wouldn't want to change.

I need to think on it.

While you do, notice that Victor has the best build of any man his age in this room.

Noted. It's nice to see an older gentleman without a pot, isn't it, Ms. Charlie? But I bet he must have a hundred creases ironed into his shirt.

And I bet he ironed the creases in his shirt himself.

Victor was at the table with three little tikes. "Charlie, come over here."

Charlie sat and chatted with Victor's family again. She was intrigued with the strong resemblance between Victor and his son—tall, solid, medium skin tone with fine facial features. Vick VI was a high school math teacher in Charlotte. In addition, he worked on a PhD so he could move to the college level.

Kristi resembled the picture Charlie had seen of her mother. She was tall but much thinner than her brother. She was a second-year surgical resident at a hospital in Raleigh.

Vick and Kristi amused Charlie by many tales of their teenage rebellion years and how their father reacted to each speeding ticket, every car accident and every time they were out after midnight. They both used the term "anal-retentive" several times until little Vic asked what the word meant. Charlie didn't admit that she used the same term when she described Victor to her three sons.

She asked the Chief to get her another Cruzan Cream and was delighted when he returned with a glass for each of them. She remained with Victor's family the rest of the evening until people started to stop by and say their good-buys and good-lucks as they filtered out the door.

James and Elin left a little early and James rubbed his stomach as he disappeared through the double doors. Charlie and the Chief decided he was excited about his induction ceremony the next day.

The hall had cleared by midnight and Victor collected his gifts, his medals and plaques plus an impressive proclamation from the Governor of the U.S. Virgin Islands. Charlie had Vick remove a poster for her. He removed one for his father, too.

Victor and Charlie were the last two out of the banquet hall.

"I survived. For a while there, I didn't think I would," Victor said.

"We both survived, Victor, but you did have to contend with a lot more than I did."

"Did those posters bother you, too?"

"They bothered me more than I wanted to admit."

"Thank God I don't go to Rev. Moran's church."

"Me, too," Charlie replied as Victor helped her into Rubee.

The Chief left the parking lot and pulled onto Restaurant Road. It spiraled its way down the precipitous hill toward the main road to Christiansted. As he approached a particularly tight curve, a dark blue SUV shot out of nowhere, aimed for the Mustang, and hit Rubee twice in the right rear and tried to push the car toward the edge of a steep bank. Victor turned the steering wheel and the Mustang spit gravel as it tried to gain traction on the berm and move back onto the road. The sports car fought back long enough that the SUV driver gave up and moved to the right lane and passed. The dark vehicle sped off with a damaged front grill and left front fender. Victor put on the emergency break and turned the ignition off.

"That was close. I didn't get the tag number, did you?"

"I wasn't looking for a tag number, Victor. What I saw was a missing guardrail and a very steep bank. We could have soared over the edge and been killed."

"Probably some drunk from the restaurant bar decided to play games." Victor turned his damaged Rubee around and drove up the hill.

Once out of the car he checked the front. "Her whole rear bumper and fender will need to be replaced and she has a total of forty-seven miles on her."

"I have a few more miles on me than Rubee and I'm glad I don't need to be replaced, *Victor.*"

"I'm sorry. You stay in the car. If anyone comes near Rubee, you put your hand on the horn and don't let up. I'll be right back." Victor headed into the restaurant.

Nice to meet you, Rubee.

Why doesn't she answer you, Ms. Charlie?

Because she's an inanimate object and can't speak.

The Chief talks to her like she's alive.

That's imbedded in a man's DNA.

Victor found no diners but several employees were there. Neither had seen anyone leave for over an hour. He entered the bar and found six patrons. He walked up to the bartender. "Excuse me, but how long ago did your last customer leave?"

"What's the problem, sir?"

"Excuse me, young man, but you will answer my question first."

The twenty-something bartender looked at the happy boozers on stools and raised his eyebrows and made a what's-with-this-guy-face. A patron leaned over the bar and said something in his ear.

"Excuse me, Chief. I didn't recognize you. Three regulars left about fifteen minutes ago."

"Their names?"

"Bill Morris, his wife Tilley, and his brother Sam. Bill was the designated driver and he didn't drink all evening."

"Thank you." Victor started to leave but turned around. "A drunk almost forced me off the road. Are you sure no other customers have left?"

"No one else has left the bar since them."

Victor returned to Rubee and his date. "Charlie, three people left awhile ago. I saw a single person in the SUV. Did you notice its make?"

"It was a 2003 Highlander—I know because I used to have that model. Do you think this was deliberate?"

"I can't imagine why it would be deliberate." Victor used his cell to call headquarters. He asked the officer on duty to run down any owners of Highlanders.

"I didn't appreciate that close call. You do realize that whoever drove the Highlander wanted to send us flying off into the atmosphere."

"Stupid drunk—he could have killed us both."

Atmosphere? Ms. Charlie, I could have been killed.
Me, too.

Neither Charlie nor the Chief said anything for a good ten minutes.

"Victor, that man waited for you back there. He hit you on purpose."

"But why?"

"Did you send someone to jail years ago who might be out now? You've received a lot of press in the last couple of days. It could have brought back old memories of being convicted."

"That's a possibility. I'll check tomorrow and I won't put you at risk until this is cleared up. I'll call Bob Thompson as soon as I get home."

Victor and Charlie were silent the rest of the way to the villa. Victor didn't turn Rubee's radio down until he turned onto Charlie's street. When he turned off the engine, Victor felt awkward because the lights were on and Jeremy was inside. He didn't linger too long because he worried Jeremy would flick the outside light off and on—something he had done to his own daughter many times. He had had enough embarrassment for a single evening. He did kiss Charlie good night. She didn't mind but she thought for sure Rubee was jealous.

As soon as the Chief arrived home, he called the police station and left a message for Bob to call him in the morning.

* * *

After Charlie locked the door of the villa, she saw her son asleep on the sofa surrounded by piles of papers. His computer was still connected to the Internet. She closed down his open programs and plugged the laptop in to recharge before she headed for her bedroom.

After removing her make-up she applied a cream advertised to reduce the appearance of her fine wrinkles.

Ms. Charlie, you've been using that cream for months but it hasn't worked yet.
Tell me something I don't already know. Better yet, be quiet.
I was scared when that car hit us.
Me too. I now have a dozen new gray hairs.
Does that include the new ones in your eyebrows?

Charlie applied a moisturizer and returned to the bedroom. She sat on the bed and unrolled the poster. She was relieved Jeremy hadn't seen it.

You're smiling, Ms. Charlie.
Go the bed.
Tell me again you don't know how you feel?

CHAPTER EIGHT

The man dressed like a tourist. He knew he was one of the million plus visitors who invade St. Martin yearly. Dark blue shorts, brown leather moccasins with a touch of fringe, and an expensive multi-hued shirt with a design of parrots amidst sultry green branches. His shirt matched the one he bought for his wife the day before on St. Croix. Both shirts had the exclusive Island Elegant label.

He walked the jewelry district before the tourists arrived from the cruise ships. It wasn't hard to pick out his mark last week and he figured it would be just as easy today. He was right.

The Dutch owned this part of St. Martin. The police were fastidious about the jewelry district but there were no officers around at the moment. The town's attention was on its healthy investment in the area's infrastructure. It was important to keep the momentum barreling ahead because of all the new construction occurring every day. The two endless strips of massive white concrete that made up the piers at Pointe Blanche were now complete and could concurrently serve four one thousand foot cruise ships. The island now poured all its energies into the new construction close to the piers.

Sapphire Jewellery International Ltd. dealt with the largest and most high-end jewelry stores around the world. They carried the most desirable of the Columbian emeralds, the finest of the Burmese rubies, the most exquisite of the Zambian and Columbian amethysts and the most stunning of the Ceylon sapphires. Among all the gems they wholesaled, Gemstones Jewellery built its reputation on its array of blue, pink, yellow and green sapphires. They sold the gems in all the standard cuts plus cabochon, baguette, trapezoid, heart, and princess. While the rich, violet-blue Ceylon sapphires were their specialty; the exquisite blue Kanchanaburi sapphires received a lot of attention. Ever so often the company carried a prized cornflower-blue Kashmir sapphire but those stones were rare and hard to find. Needless to say, diamonds enhanced all of the better-grade gems.

The wholesalers handpicked each of their reps. The men and women were well educated about the gems they sold and were well trained in a variety of self-defense techniques. Their leather cases held gems of every color of the rainbow and the cases were worth a fortune.

Mark Andrews was a rep. He was an American who had fought in Afghanistan. His military expertise was extensive and he kept a Glock .45 tucked into his belt. As all reps did, he varied his route that morning. His eyes constantly darted from the left side of the street to the right and from the gutters and manhole covers to the rooftops. As he turned the corner to pass from Front Street to Back Street, he spotted a tourist. There was something familiar about the man who leaned against an alley wall. He searched his memory banks for a few second and then yelled, "Al Bladensburg, is that you?"

"Mark, buddy, you made it back from Afghanistan in one piece. Good to see you."

Mark grinned and relaxed. He was happy to see an old Army friend. "What are you doing here?"

"The stores will open soon. My wife gave me very specific instructions about what she wanted and I'm in for a real challenge. I don't have much time this morning because I'm here at a conference with my company. Tough when you have to fly to the Caribbean to go to work."

"What does you wife want? I might be able to point you to the right store."

"She wants a yellow gold ring with the largest pink sapphire I can afford."

"Well, Only Sapphires is across the street and Pinks to Purples is on Back Street. They would be my choices."

"Thanks. You saved me a couple hours this morning."

"I hope you have time for a drink or two tonight," Mark said as he handed his friend a business card with his private number written on the back.

"Not a problem. Is eight okay?" Al said.

"Yep. The Coral Reef Lounge?"

"Great. And I know right where it is."

The men shook hands and Mark turned his back on his old Army buddy. Mistake.

CHAPTER NINE

Jeremy woke his mother so she wouldn't be late for James' induction ceremony as the new Deputy Police Chief. As she started to dress, the Chief called.

"James was airlifted to Schneider Hospital in St. Thomas about three this morning."

"Why and why didn't he go to the hospital here?"

"His doctors are over there—remember James is from St. Thomas. He told me you put a hex on him and gave him appendicitis. What was that all about?"

"*Oh Victor*! Do I look like a person who is into voodoo? I told James I'd turn his stomach bug into appendicitis because he put those posters up. He knew I was kidding. I don't do voodoo, *Victor*. Thanks for the vote of confidence."

"I didn't mean to sound that way and I'm sorry if I overreacted," Victor said. "But it was a three-ring circus at the helipad. Between his mother, his aunt, Elin and her mother, there were enough tears to drown the man. Needless to say today's ceremony is canceled."

"Would you like to tell me if James is okay?"

"I don't know the whole story but I called Elin's mother this morning and she said it was appendicitis but everything turned out fine."

"Now Victor, please tell me none of these women were serious about the hex or curse or spell or whatever voodoo queens do."

"Elin was okay but I don't know about Mrs. Kingston or her sister Jeanette."

"Did anyone fly to St. Thomas with James?"

"Elin did."

Charlie said, "His mother lives on St. Thomas and I'm sure she stayed here last night with her sister Jeanette. Has anyone made arrangements to take Mrs. Kingston back home this morning?"

"I'm not sure."

"I'll give her a call and I'll keep in touch. And by the way, I had a delightful time last night." Charlie said a quick good-bye and disconnected as Jeremy popped in her room.

"So you had a nice time last night, did you?"

"Watch it, son."

"Mom, what's the problem and you're about to fly where? You don't plan to chase criminals again, do you?"

"Some people on this island think I'm into voodoo."

"Well you could have at least told me. There are a couple of people back at work I'd like to zap. Why would anyone think you're into voodoo? Or maybe I should ask you what you've done now?"

"I need to call Jeanette. Grace Kingston is there." Charlie told Jeremy about James as she searched for her contingency notebook filled with minutiae including reams of phone, cab, medical and police numbers.

Think, Ms. Charlie. You didn't put a curse on James by accident, did you?

Harry Potter is a novel, remember? There are no such things as curses and hexes. Grow up.

How can I grow up—we're the same age.

Don't remind me.

"Good morning, Jeanette. This is Charlie. Is Grace Kingston with you and would she want me to accompany her to St. Thomas today?"

"Honey, please tell me you didn't do anything bad to our James?" asked the short and plump Jeannette.

"No ma'am. Honest."

"Thank God. I didn't think you'd do anything bad. Yes, both Grace and I need to go. We are so worried."

"Have you heard from the hospital?"

"Elin called us earlier. His appendix did burst but the surgery went well. He will be hospitalized for three or four days and is on a ton of antibiotics."

"Let me get tickets," Charlie said, "and I'll have Jeremy take us to Skyhigh or to the airport. Do you have a preference?"

"Whichever will get us there the fastest."

Charlie disconnected and called Skyhigh Seaplanes. There were seats on the ten-fifteen flight.

"Jeremy, get dressed and get ready to go." Charlie packed for two nights, dressed, grabbed her passport and purse, and clunked her way to the car in khaki slacks and a white cotton blouse. She sported her orthopedic boot and crutches.

Jeremy had the three ladies at the airport in time for them to get their tickets and go through security. Jeanette and Grace went right through; Charlie required a thorough pat down because of her multiple replacement parts.

Ms. Charlie, do you ever feel stupid doing this?

Always, but I suppose there are a few sixty-five year old Caucasian grandmothers with gray hair and replacement parts who could be terrorists.

But you look so dumb standing there with your arms out.

Don't think for a moment I don't feel dumb. Everyone in the airport stares at me every time I go through this.

So do I.

Close your eyes and go away. I'm doing my civic duty!

Once boarded on the seaplane, Grace Kingston thanked Charlie for arranging things and called her a nice girl.

What a nice compliment, Ms. Charlie. Grace called you a girl.

Yeah. And I have more wrinkles than she does and she has no replacement parts.

And she doesn't have any age spots like you do either, Ms. Charlie.

Go haunt someone.

Charlie's attention shifted back to the women. "Now ladies, maybe we should combine our mind power. Tell me, everyone who wants to see James and Elin married, raise your hand."

Three hands went in the air as Grace laughed and Jeanette hooted.

"We need to put our minds together and 'will' James to marry Elin."

Jeanette high-fived Charlie and Grace smiled as she spoke. "Elin's such a beauty. She and James do make a beautiful couple, don't they? It is time for James to remarry."

"I agree," Grace said. "I do have a handsome son—of course any woman would be interested in my James and his sweet smile. Besides, Grete Mikkelsen couldn't find a better son-in-law in the whole world. He is my only child, you know, Charlie."

* * *

After Jeremy dropped his mother and the ladies off at the airport, he headed for a tour of the marinas on the island. He examined each and every one to determine what his competition would be if he bought the property for sale. The last marina on his list was the one on the market. Jeremy knew enough of his heritage to know pirates had roamed in and around St. Croix when his great, great, great grandfather arrived on the island in the late 1700s. His mom had shown him the myriad of census reports she had garnered. She showed him, generation by generation, how Elin's family was intertwined with theirs when her great grandfather married a freed slave.

Jeremy's ancestor owned a sugar plantation and had a successful import/export business. He knew those pirate ships hid in various coves and crevices and waited to attack the next merchant ship to appear. He thought maybe the marina's name was a good omen—Pirate's Cove.

The marina's owner was an older gentleman in his late seventies named Gillis Kliver, better known throughout the island as Gil. Jeremy thought Gil reminded him of St. Croix's version of Popeye. Gil had powerful upper arms and a thick chest. He even came equipped with a cap and stubbly chin. Jeremy wondered if Olive Oyl was somewhere in the area.

"Come on in my office for a minute, young fella. I'll show ya around."

The office was a conglomeration of nautical gear from the old days. Glass-front cabinets lined three walls and they held everything from fishing trophies and pictures to a large brass-plated cleat. Gil displayed a series of charcoal drawings of various parts of the town on the upper wall.

"What's with the brass-plated cleat?" Jeremy asked.

"My great grandfather put that big ole cleat on the first pier he built. When my dad replaced the pier the cleat was the one thing he kept. I later sanded it and had it brass-plated."

"Who drew the pictures?"

"I did. It's a lifelong hobby. I git a kick out of it." Gil's pride glowed and his Danish blue eyes sparkled as he told Jeremy about every trophy and picture. Like Jeremy, he had ancestors that went back to the time of the pirates.

Gil showed Jeremy every plank and piling. Pirate's Cove had been substantially rebuilt in 1990. Gil used Hurricane Hugo as an excuse to repair, rebuild and expand the size of the slips to include vessels up to one hundred feet. He told Jeremy his piers were built the "tried-and-true Danish way." Jeremy didn't know what that meant but it seemed important to Gil.

Jeremy decided the "Danish way" was the right way. Jeremy told Gil he was interested in the property and would like an accountant to check the books so he could have a good handle on the income stream. Gil said he didn't mind and made Jeremy an offer he hoped he couldn't resist—he offered to stick around for three months after the sale until Jeremy felt he knew the ropes. Jeremy had spent his high school summers at work on a large marina in Ocean City, Maryland, so felt he knew the ropes but the offer intrigued him.

After he left, Jeremy stopped at a restaurant on the harbor near the armless windmill. He ate a late lunch and admired the harbor's azure waters. Along with his meal, he ordered a mug of the restaurant's home-brewed beer. After feeding the sand crabs his leftovers, he decided to ask *Victor* to recommend a good lawyer, appraiser and structural engineer.

CHAPTER TEN

After the Chief talked to Charlie he called Bob Thompson. "I called in a drunk driving accident last night."

"I saw your report this morning, Chief. We identified the car but haven't found it. It was stolen last evening."

"A theft. That blows my drunken driver theory. It also means it wasn't any accident the car hit Rubee."

"Who's Rubee?"

"She's my new Mustang, Bob."

"Wow, a Mustang. What model?" The Chief described every nut, bolt and piece of chrome on the vehicle.

"I'm jealous, Chief. I'll get me a lean, mean machine like Rubee some day. Anyway, in all probability kids stole the SUV and got drunk."

"I suppose. Can you please make time to meet me on Restaurant Hill in a half hour?"

Bob agreed and hung up. *Wow. The Chief called me by my first name. I didn't think he knew it. He even said please. Has he changed or something?*

* * *

As Grace, Jeanette and Charlie sat in the cramped seaplane headed for Charlotte Amalie, Jeanette asked Charlie about the Chief.

"I don't have 'wedding' written anywhere on my calendar. I enjoy the Chief's company but I don't appreciate a man who orders a lady a drink without asking her what she wants."

"So let me understand this," Jeanette interrupted, "on your last visit, you did genealogy research at the Landmarks Society?"

"Yep. Elin had seen a post I had placed on a message board on a genealogy website. She contacted me with information about my great, great grandfather, some of which I hadn't known. That's why I came to the island in the first place. Elin and I wanted to find out more about him and locate the old plantation."

"Well, I don't know anything about this Internet thing and I don't want to learn," laughed eighty-four year old Grace whose name described her demeanor.

Charlie explained what a message board was and what kind of genealogy information was available on the Internet.

"Is the Chief in any way related to you?"

"Nope. I stumbled across his ancestors in a Danish census report. His ancestors worked for my ancestors on Claudine's Quarters."

"They were slaves?"

"Slavery had been abolished by this time but I am sure they were initially brought to the island as slaves."

"Does this bother the Chief? I mean the fact his ancestors worked for yours?"

"If it did, I don't think he would have asked me to be his date last night."

"We saw the picture in the paper, Charlie," Grace said with a wink.

"Let's not talk about that picture. You do understand, Grace, your son is the person who had the picture reproduced and plastered around the banquet hall."

"Elin told me what he did. He was bad, wasn't he? You know Jeanette, there might be a second wedding we can attend." The two sisters giggled like they did as little girls.

Well, Ms. Charlie. The ladies came to a logical conclusion. You're the one who doesn't see the whole picture. Are you sure you're not leading Chief Peacock on?

* * *

Bob Thompson had already examined the stretch of road with the missing guardrail when the Chief drove up.

"Morning, Chief. I checked on the guardrail before I left the station. It is due to be repaired before the end of the month."

"Well this missing guardrail could have been fatal last night."

"Sorry, sir. So this is Rubee?"

"She was new as of yesterday."

"What a hot babe even with the damage. I'll have to get her sister."

"I hope it doesn't take you forty years like it took me."

"Me, too, Chief." Bob led the way to an area of the road before the bend. "There was a vehicle tucked between the brush and the trees here last night. The tire depression is obvious. And look at the marks the tires made when the man took off after you."

"Have you taken pictures?"

"Done. I believe this person was after you, Chief. Maybe we'll get a break when we find the SUV. We could get lucky and find prints."

"Why on earth would anyone be after me? It's been twenty years since I've put anyone in jail."

"I don't know, sir. On another note, I enjoyed your party last night."

"I suspect you enjoyed it a lot more than I did."

"I understand, sir. Did you see the paper this morning?"

"What! Not more pictures?"

"A couple pictures—you and the commissioner and another of you and Miss Charlie. The article was great. I had no idea what you accomplished throughout your long career."

"I was warned headquarters put out a press release. I guess that's where the reporter got the information. Did George Harris write it?"

"Yes, sir. Georgie Boy gets carried away sometimes but he did a good job on this article. You need to buy a couple of papers for your family. It is upbeat and impressive. You'll feel good about it."

"Thank you, Bob. When you find the car, let me know."

* * *

The silver and green seaplane landed with the slightest of splashes and putted its way toward the pier. There was the gentlest of bounces as waves swept under the floats. Once moored, the co-pilot helped all three ladies exit. They headed down the pier toward the street so they could hail a cab and head for the hospital.

Upon arrival, Grace was the first to find the private room James occupied. After a gentle tap on the door, she and Jeannette burst right in.

"Mother, I hope I didn't scare you. I'm okay now."

James' speech was slurred. His mother decided he still had some anesthesia in him. "Oh my poor baby. You're not quite awake. You did scare me and now I hear you're on a steady diet of antibiotics."

Elin laughed as she patted and then kissed James' hand. "He sure is and will be for some time. He won't be doing any somersaults anytime soon either."

Jeanette rolled her eyes and gave Grace and Charlie an all-knowing glance.

Elin grinned at Charlie. "And what is with this hex?"

"You were there last night and heard what I did. Hexes and curses are something I do in my spare time. James better think twice before he has any more posters printed."

Even James managed to smile while his eyes were half shut.

"Where will you stay tonight, honey?" Grace asked Elin as she kissed her on the cheek. Jeanette rolled her eyes with a second all-knowing glance.

"I don't know. Lise Holtzen brought me some clothes. She is the manager of the new Island Elegant shop on St. Thomas. There is some benefit to owning a dress shop, you know."

"Well then, honey, you, Charlie and Jeanette will stay at my house."

Jeanette whispered into Grace's ear, "Sister, you are so subtle. Why don't you go ahead and mail out the wedding invitations."

While the older ladies gushed over James, Charlie cornered Elin. "Now what about the meeting you have tomorrow on St. Martin. Do you still plan to go?"

Elin nodded. "What about you? Are you in?"

"I'm in. What's the fastest way to get there?"

"Plane." Elin pulled out the tickets she had purchased. "Can you exchange these for us? They're for departure from St. Croix but we have to leave from here."

"No problem. Do you have your passport and everything else you'll need?"

"Yep."

"James, can you survive without Elin and me for a couple of days?" Charlie asked.

"Of course. I have my moder and aunt with me." Grace grinned and kissed her son on his forehead. Jeanette beamed.

"Have you been with James since he came out of surgery, Elin?" Grace asked.

"I sure have, Mrs. Kingston."

"Mrs. Kingston. Darling girl, I'm Grace to you. You could even call me moder."

Jeanette looked at Charlie, rolled her eyes again and winked. James didn't miss the wink and a ray of light bounced off his gold tooth.

"By the way, Andre Johnson, the Deputy Police Chief here, had an officer pick up James' old car at his house. We do have transportation to get around. As soon as James takes his afternoon nap, which will be in about ten minutes, I'll take you ladies to my new shop."

Jeanette and Charlie agreed. Grace wanted to stay at the hospital. After the ladies chatted for a few more minutes, James drifted off. Elin, Jeanette and Charlie left to go to the new shop.

* * *

Grace sat quietly with her son and watched as he slept. Her heart burst with happiness because Elin was now in his life. Two months ago she had told her doctor she would not take chemo again—twice was enough for her aged body. She took comfort now that Elin would look after her James.

Grace opened the drawer to the small chest next to James' bed and reached for the Bible.

CHAPTER ELEVEN

Man waited for Chamaign's plane to land. The detectives needed to spend time to compare notes, talk through scenarios and decide what else to do. Chamaign planned to update James before she flew back in the evening.

Once in town, they crammed themselves into Man's office and double-checked each other's activities. Frustration saturated the faces of both detectives, as neither the Coast Guard nor their own patrol boats had intercepted any of the stolen jewelry. Did this mean the gold and gems had not left St. Thomas? They hoped so.

Chamaign said, "I spoke with the agents at St. Croix's airport and checked their security video."

"Any good shots?"

"Not really. It was obvious the man used the airport before and knew the location of all the security cameras," Chamaign said. "He managed to keep his face either down or in another direction from the cameras. The TSA agent did confirm the man carried a full case of gold jewelry."

"Was the agent suspicious?"

"He had no reason to be suspicious then."

"Well, I had a little more luck," Man said. "I checked the video at our airport and Charlie's description of his clothing was pretty accurate. He knew the location of our cameras, too, but we managed a fairly good shot as he exited the men's room. It was somewhat blurred but better than nothing."

Man explained that while the man was in the men's room, he emptied the display case into a duffle bag and left the leather case in a stall. After a passenger spotted the unattended case, the bomb squad was called to clear it. "I had the case tested for fingerprints and there were none. I tracked down the cab driver who drove him to town. He exited on Post Office Alley and was untraceable from there."

"Do you find it strange he went right to town?"

"I suspect he did that so he could switch cabs. We spoke to many of the other drivers but none of them remembered him. We might get lucky but we need a good picture."

"Did you arrange to have all the outgoing luggage checked?" Chamaign asked as she mentally checked the list in her head.

"Yep—airlines, seaplane and ferry. Nothing so far. Unless our perpetrator slipped off the island before we started the search, the perp and the loot is on St. Thomas."

"What about the security video taken before we tightened the rope?"

"We checked that, too. Nada."

The two detectives prepared to merge the spreadsheets of all travelers in and out of the islands. They color-coded both the departures and arrivals of each passenger for each island. They added the guest lists from all the hotels and the names of as many of the home and car rentals as they could get. After they electronically merged two documents into one, they sorted by name and studied it. Nothing stood out.

"We are still at work on our list of all arrivals and departures for the past month," Chamaign said. "Then we can sort again to look for repeat passengers. These men had to have scoped out the routes the reps took before yesterday."

"That will work providing the travelers didn't use fake ID's," Man said. "I'm not sure it's worth our time and money but we'll do the same."

After the detectives developed a second spreadsheet of names and addresses, Man forwarded it to the FBI to run through their system.

"You know, Man, these men were skilled. They may have been military at some point."

The two detectives discussed the possibility. Both agreed it was possible but they didn't have enough information to request a check by the military.

"Chamaign, what if this is an inside job—meaning what if a local jeweler plotted this?"

"I don't follow."

"What if one of our jewelers hired someone to murder the agents? The jeweler could absorb the gold and gems into his or her own inventory. The jewelry would be almost impossible to trace."

Man and Chamaign walked to Andre's office to run this theory by him. Andre shuddered at the thought this was done by a jeweler and he knew James would be horrified, too.

"I don't know, guys. Jewelers might compete for business on a daily basis but they look out for each other."

"So you don't buy the theory?" Man asked.

"We need every theory we can get right now. Look into it but keep it low-key."

"How do you want us to handle the press?" Chamaign asked Andre.

"We need a press conference. And we don't want to mention the possibility that a jeweler may be involved."

Andre called James and suggested a joint press conference by the two rookie detectives. James agreed and advised the detectives to consult with Charlie for a Media 101 Workshop before they went before the microphones. The two rookie deputy police chiefs hoped the press conference would keep the police commissioner at bay for at least another fifteen minutes.

* * *

Andre worked at his desk when he heard the familiar Outlook ping as an email arrived. It was from the St. Martin Police Department. He read the email and took a deep breath before he walked to Man's office and told the detectives about the latest murder.

* * *

"Trial by fire?" Chamaign exclaimed. "This is a trial by firing squad!"

"We don't have much to placate the jewelers and suppliers, do we?" Man replied as he paced. "And we need to get Charlie to work with our sketch artist and teach us how to deal with the press."

The two made a list of what measures they had taken and called Charlie's cell. She was at Elin's new shop. Man asked rookie Danny Marsten to get her.

* * *

Charlie didn't require a second invitation to visit police headquarters. She had enjoyed the surge of energy and excitement she had when she was there with James on her last visit to the islands.

Man escorted Charlie through the cube farm and introduced her to the sketch artist named Benny. Charlie sat in Benny's cubicle and did her best to describe the man at the airport. She decided Benny must have the patience of Job since she continued to ask him to erase multiple things.

"Let's do this," Charlie suggested after she made Benny redraw the perp's hair for the seventh time. "Email the drawing to my son Jeremy and the Chief." Charlie called both men while the image was scanned and emailed.

Jeremy was the first to reply. He felt the man's hair had to be shorter, more like a military style. The sketch artist made the changes and Charlie felt it was more accurate. It was again scanned and emailed. Jeremy agreed it was better.

The Chief called. "Charlie, the man had very broad shoulders and a thick chest and neck. I'm sure I noticed a wedding ring, too."

Again the changes were made and the sketch was scanned and emailed. The Chief and Jeremy both agreed the modified sketch was the best they had seen. Charlie agreed, too. Man noted the image resembled the suspect in the blurred video.

He then escorted Charlie to his office where Chamaign sorted data on the computer. He asked Charlie if she had time to give Chamaign and him a lesson on press relations. Having been her company's spokesperson before retirement, she agreed. Man joked as he asked her if she would hold the press conference for them. She declined and reminded him his boss wouldn't approve.

Andre, Chamaign and Man hoped for a miracle. Chamaign had watched the press conference James held when he worked the Peters' murder and drug case and she knew Charlie had prepped her boss for it. Now with a third murder, the flames were even higher and a lot hotter.

With an audience of three, Charlie gave them a short lesson. "We need to start with a list of talking points. What exactly do you want the media to know?" She stood in front of a white board with a pen in hand. Charlie wrote the talking points on the board as the detectives verbalized their thoughts. She asked for a list of items they should not discuss and then the detectives complied. Charlie shared a number of suggestions as to how to deal with the press and stressed the importance of control.

"You need to establish yourselves as authority figures. You need to request cooperation and in return you must do your part and keep the media apprised of any updates."

Charlie sat down and held a mock conference. She starred in the roles of Obnoxious Reporter Number One, Pushy Reporter Number Two and Arrogant Reporter Number Three. Chamaign and Man had to deal with negative questions, demands for answers, snotty implications about police competence, and haughty remarks about the lack of progress.

"Whew. I never sweated my police exams like I sweated this," Man said. "Can we go through this again, boss?"

Andre shook his head and the two detectives left to walk down the steps to the main lobby where the media camped.

"Man, it must feel this way when you walk down death row," Chamaign said.

"Frankly, I can't imagine how it could be worse."

The reporters pushed each other to get to the detectives and peppered them with questions. Man held up his hand as Charlie had instructed. He remained silent until everyone quieted down. Charlie and Andre cheered from the sidelines.

"Before I answer your questions, I need to make an announcement," Man said. The room exploded as the detective told the reporters of the murder on St. Martin. "While the details are few, the value of the stolen jewels was far more significant than the first two robberies. We do have a sketch of one suspect when he left St. Croix and arrived at the Cyril E. King Airport this morning. We will pass out DVDs of the sketch in a few minutes."

Man pointed to a former high school classmate, "Georgie, question?"

"I'm George Harris with the Virgin Island Press. How many murderers are there?"

"There has to be at least two. The murders on St. Croix and St. Thomas occurred at about the same time."

"How do you know they are connected?"

"All three victims were jewelry reps. All were attacked early in the morning and all the reps had their necks broken."

A woman yelled out a question at the same time as two others. Man followed his instructions and stood there and said not a word. When the reporters settled down, Man pointed to the woman.

"Three people are dead and over a half million in jewelry has been stolen. What other information do you have other than a sketch?"

Even Man thought the response he gave her sounded lame. "I'm sorry but it would not be prudent to discuss other aspects of the case at this time."

"Detective, you must have more evidence than you shared. Why is this case taking so long to solve?" a second woman asked.

Chamaign took her place at the mike. "Detective Carmen and I developed a list of all plane and ferry passengers and the list is now with the FBI. Since our suspects seemed to be aware of the victims' routes, we suspect they observed the jewelry reps before yesterday. Therefore, we are now compiling a list of people who visited the islands in the past month so we can check for duplications."

"How do you know the jewelry is still around?" George Harris asked.

"As of noon today, the luggage of all departing passengers at the airports and ferries on St. Croix and St. Thomas has been checked. I assume St. Martin will put the same procedure in place."

"Detective Carmen, what if the perps used a boat?"

"The Coast Guard was notified at once. They started to intercept all boats and yachts leaving port."

Several more questions were asked but Chamaign ended the conference as planned. She told her listeners they had no more information they could share but promised she would keep the media in the loop as information evolved. She handed out the DVDs with the sketch of the suspect. The two detectives turned and left.

Charlie and Andre high-fived it. Andre made a mental note of the entire list of Charlie's instructions.

* * *

As Man and Chamaign walked away, George followed. "Man, you gotta give me more than this. I'm your bud, remember?" said the tall, pudgy, blue-eyed reporter with baby-fine brown hair.

"Georgie Boy, there is nothing, and I mean nothing else I can say. Now give it a rest. We have work to do."

"I have another question and the question isn't about the murders."

Both detectives hesitated. "What is it, Georgie?" Man asked.

"Why is the Mikkelsen woman here?"

"Is there a reason she can't be here?" Chamaign asked.

"Did she ID the suspect at the airport?"

"She did. Chief Hanneman saw him, too," she said.

"Ah yes, the Kissing Chief."

"Drop the sarcasm, Georgie Boy," Man said.

"Hey you two, doesn't it make you wonder that whenever this woman is around, there is trouble?"

Chamaign glared at him. "What is that supposed to mean?"

"Why is she so tight with the cops—even the Chief?"

"That's it, Georgie Boy, you're out of line and out of here. Move it."

"I represent the press, you know."

"And we represent the police, you know," Chamaign said. "You're in my line of vision. Now get out of it."

"Okay, okay. I'm out of here for now. I still think it is curious."

The detectives turned and walked toward Man's office. "Jerk. I used to like him," Man said. "Why did he act like such a prick?"

"I don't know but I bet he expected an exclusive. Let's get back to work."

* * *

James and Elin watched the six o'clock news. "It sounds like the department has very little to go on," James commented.

"It sounds to me if Charlie hadn't noticed the man at the airport, they would have nothing to go on. Maybe the police should hire her."

"My love, maybe you two should go to St. Martin tomorrow and stay out of police business."

CHAPTER TWELVE

Elin arrived at Mrs. Kingston's home around seven and the four ladies nibbled on a light snack. Grace and Jeanette spent the evening in guarded whispers about possible wedding plans.

Charlie had spent twenty years of her life in marketing and hadn't missed her old job until that evening. She became a bit nostalgic as she reviewed her press releases and edited copy for a series of print ads—all for Elin's Grand Opening for her new Island Elegant shop. She selected the color pictures that would best translate into black and white for the newspaper. She selected color images that would accompany the releases for the Internet. Elin agreed with her choices.

They discussed the upgrades needed to the shop's website. Elin wanted to include a picture of the second shop. Charlie suggested a map where both stores were located. The ladies agreed the tone of the site must remain the same. Charlie liked the laconic welcome message and captions: At Island Elegant, you'll find a line of clothing specifically designed for those discerning and discriminating women who are addicted to quality, style and deliciously well-cut high fashion.

Charlie suggested she add pictures of the new expanded line of casual wear and a large section for those colorfully wicked bikinis. She suggested a link be provided to the matching accessories—casual necklaces, sun hats, purses and sandals.

The ladies worked on the radio commercials. They role-played the dialogue for the two spots and Charlie used her stopwatch to ensure they could be recorded within the sixty-second time frame. She edited the second commercial so it could air as a thirty-second spot. Lastly, she reviewed Elin's honed objectives for the grand opening and the budget that accompanied it.

Afterward, she and Elin shared a Cruzan banana rum and Diet Pepsi as they discussed the agenda for their meeting with the business development representative from Scandinavian Seven Seas. Tomorrow was the big day and their flight would arrive in the early afternoon.

"On a scale of one to ten, how much do you want to do this?" Charlie asked as she munched on her favorite treat—a Tastykake chocolate-covered bar.

"You need to tell me more about cruise ships first. I can't pull a number out of my head."

"This is not the *Titanic* here. Most Caribbean cruise lines are very casual but Scandinavian Seven Seas is a tad more fanciful. They have two to three formal nights where you will see a handful of tuxedos but most men are in suits. About half of the ladies wear long dresses and the rest are in snazzy cocktail dresses—definitely more urbane. This clientele uses the private upscale restaurant, the nightclubs, and of course, they sit around the gaming tables. They occupy the suites instead of the staterooms and they represent your high-end market."

"And the rest of the markets?"

"I would say the remainder is divided into three or four segments—some of which may overlap. Young singles, newlyweds and professionals would be the second market. There are plenty of opportunities for the ladies to go for the glitz in cocktail dresses or mid-priced gowns. Even your strapless sundresses would appeal to this group."

"Sequined or beaded dresses are my specialty," Elin said.

"Middle-aged persons and retirees would make a third market. This group has enough discretionary income to buy what they want. More sedate possibly—but definitely cultivated. They will make only one or two purchases but will pay well for those items. I would think a nicer outfit with a matching purse would be perfect. And your coordinated costume jewelry would fit right in. These people choose cruising for relaxation and are not interested in the Jewelers of the Caribbean."

"Keep on going, it's sounding better and better, Charlie."

"Now about the parents with kids—forget the kids and concentrate on your men and women's matching big shirts, sundresses and women's bathing suits. The women most likely brought a new suit with them but if one new bathing suit is nice, two is better."

"What other information is available?"

"Before you pick up any pen, we need to get numbers from the cruise line. We will see how cooperative they will be to help you target your markets correctly. Remember, a ship like *Aqua Waters* has over 3,000 passengers and over half of them are woman. We need numbers. I'm sure they could provide an age segmentation and break the groups down even further into estimated spending."

"I must admit I didn't expect this many layers of complexity on a cruise ship."

"Don't worry. These liners are in the water to make money and they have their demographics down pat. I'm sure they can perform database sorts on their passengers' addresses and come up with estimated income figures that are close enough to accurate to be scary. They can predict to the penny which passengers provide the income. Their whole business plan is based on this knowledge."

"Well, if they can provide me with that kind of data I'll need a marketing plan for each segment."

"It won't be hard once we understand the demographics. You can kill two birds with one stone. I bet you would approach the suite dwellers on ship in much the same way you would market your new store to the ladies on those yachts moored in the mega yacht marina here on St. Thomas. We can hand deliver an invitation to shop privately by appointment. Or, you can offer to bring a sampling of your apparel to them."

Elin responded, "I would enjoy a taste of that. We could test it on the ship before we approach the ladies on those yachts."

"And another thing, I forgot to tell you that each cruise ship puts out a mini-newsletter each day with all its activities. How about an ad targeted to the men for a private showing of potential gifts for their ladies or a men-only hour in the shop. Many retail stores do the same before Christmas."

"A men-only hour—every saleswoman's dream. I can sell a man anything—an outfit plus accessories."

"Do you have any feel for your profit margin?"

"Not really. I'm an expert on how to make a buck in a store on terra firma but profit projections on a cruise ship is a huge question mark for me."

The ladies decided they would wait and see what the next day would bring.

* * *

Chamaign changed her plans to return to St. Croix because Detective Larson Fossing arrived from St. Martin. As the three detectives sat and discussed the facts of their cases, a document emerged from the fax. It was from the Royal Bahamas Police Department. The problem was Andre had left his office less than five minutes before so he could be home in time for his son's fourth birthday party.

* * *

As Jeremy entered the villa, the phone rang. His mother wanted to know how his day went.

"Pretty good. I do like this marina. Most of the piers are relatively new but there is a definite need for more cable lines and wi-fi and the marina's small shop, showers and laundry are in dire need of expansion and updating. You know, with the number of high-priced yachts and sailboats moored here, you could help me bring in high-end gourmet meats, vegetables and pastries to sell. We could even have a small restaurant."

"Aren't you a couple of steps ahead of yourself? First of all, son, you should have figured out after some thirty plus years that your mother only cooks on holidays. Secondly, you need the marina appraised; you need a structural engineer to inspect it; and then you need to get some advice from an attorney. And don't forget about a little thing called a loan."

"I haven't forgotten. I spoke with Victor today and..."

"Whoa. Excuse me, son. Did you say *Victor* or Victor? I need to make sure I heard you right."

"You heard me right. Victor. Yes, tongue-sucking *Victor*. The passionate guy in the Internet picture who slobbered over my mother."

"Should I now assume you feel Victor is a human being?"

"Yeah. I suppose. He purchased some property not too long ago and felt he had a good real estate attorney. He gave me the man's name and suggested an appraiser."

Ms. Charlie, did you hear that? The Chief bought some property. What do you think he has in mind?

How should I know? I left my ouija board at home.

You know, Ms. Charlie. Maybe we should have a séance.

Why? So I can talk to my island ancestors?

Well then, how about I pick up some Tarot cards.

You do that.

"What did he say he purchased, Jeremy?"

"He didn't. Why is my mother curious?"

"I'm not curious."

"I suspect otherwise. We need to have a little talk when you get back. Victor may be human but neither of you should rush into a relationship."

"Strange, I wasn't under the impression I rush. Trust me, your mother isn't into stupid."

"Good. By the way, I need to go back to the marina and finish checking the pilings. I told you I'd get plenty of use out of my diving gear. Victor may even come with me."

"Victor, huh. My, this friendship you have with Victor sounds serious. Are you sure you have not rushed into anything?"

"It's time to say good-bye, mom."

Before Charlie let her son off the phone, she told him about St. Martin and the cruise line. She said she would keep him in the loop as to when she would return. After she disconnected, her cell rang as Victor's name appeared on the screen.

Are you sure you want to take this call, Ms. Charlie.

You tell me. You're the one with the tarot cards.

Charlie finished the last bit of her second Tastykake as she took the call.

"How's it going, Victor?"

"Oh. I can't get used to people knowing who I am before they answer the phone."

"Cell phones are here to stay, Victor."

"I know. I know. I have a cell but I don't use it often."

"Do you have my number programmed into it?"

"I haven't figured out how to do it yet."

"Did you read the directions?"

"No need to. I have your number memorized. It is better for an aging brain when you make it work, you know."

"Well I have too many senior moments to trust my aging brain. I trust my refrigerator stickies instead," Charlie said.

"What do you do when you're not around your fridge?"

"That's why I carry a notebook in my purse. It's crammed with information about my universe."

"I can't believe you do that."

"Victor, when you were a patrol cop, didn't you carry a notebook in your shirt pocket?"

"Well, yes. But my facts were important."

"And mine aren't?"

"Okay. Okay. I give up. Your notebook is important, too. Let's move on. Your son called me today. It's hard to believe but I think he likes me."

Charlie decided not to share too much of Jeremy's conversation. "He told me he asked your advice."

"It was so good to have someone seek me out. He's such a nice young man."

"I agree but don't tell him."

"You're back on St. Croix, aren't you?"

"No, I'm at Grace Kingston's house. Elin and I will fly to St. Martin tomorrow. I'm not sure when I'll be back."

"Oh no. I've already made plans for us tomorrow."

"Victor, please don't plan my life unless you speak with me first."

"I guess I've done it again, haven't I?"

"Sorta like that." Charlie proceeded to explain what she and Elin planned to do on St. Martin. She even told him about the cruise.

"Don't stay away too long."

"I'll be back soon. Remember Jeremy and I will be here for six whole weeks. You'll be bored with me by then."

"Somehow I don't think so."

"By the way, what's up with the Restaurant Road accident?" Charlie asked.

"The accident—how could I forget Rubee's dents. The SUV was stolen so Bob Thompson and I met at the site. The car did sit and wait for someone to come down the hill. There were skid marks and everything."

"So a man was after you?"

"I suppose. I'll go to headquarters and look up my old records. I'd feel better if I knew for sure if this was intentional or random. If it was deliberate, the police will at least know where to start."

"I need to go now, Victor. Be good, drive slow and stay safe."

The Chief disconnected. He was anything but thrilled that Charlie wouldn't be around. The only thing he could think about was the surprise he had planned. He was so preoccupied with his own thoughts he forgot to ask about James.

CHAPTER THIRTEEN

Andre arrived at his office a little after eight the next morning. He had a coffee and muffin breakfast with chiefs Phillipe and Farrow, Commissioner Dylan and James. As soon as he saw a fax from the Bahamans Police, he sensed what it was about. He went to his meeting and found James was already on the conference call.

"The Bahamans want to know more about our murders," Andre said. "They had two people killed Monday morning and both men had their necks broken—no thefts involved and no apparent motives."

"Great. More murders," Dylan bellowed, "so to sum it up, all you have so far is a picture—nothing more than a sketch. Gentlemen, I know your detectives are dedicated and determined but we need results and soon."

"Commissioner," James said, "would the jewelry trade consider a reward for the capture of these two men?"

"I'll talk to them. I can't stress how this will tarnish our image if we don't resolve these murders. Right now the public does not have any confidence in us." Dylan rose and stormed out of the room. The body language of the remaining men was anything but confident.

* * *

Andre returned to his office. He wanted to talk face-to-face with all three detectives so he called James and asked about Chamaign. "I'd like to meet with all the detectives together and I'll conference you. Chamaign and Man need their strategy updated."

James agreed and disconnected.

Chamaign looked at Charlie. "You wouldn't want to join me and solve this case, would you?" she kidded.

"I've received orders to stay away from murderers. Besides I need to meet Elin at the airport in a few minutes."

"Send Elin my love," James pleaded. "I miss her already."

"That I can do but I won't look into her eyes and gush and fuss over her like you do."

"Thank God for small favors," James said as he laughed.

Charlie and Chamaign left the hospital room together.

"I think that man's in love," Chamaign said as they walked down the hall.

"I know that man's in love," Charlie responded. "And I know who is in love with him."

***

James was by himself for only a few minutes when his mother popped in the door. "Hey moder, how's my girl?"

"You already have a beautiful girl. I'm still your mother, I believe. But while we're on the topic, I have a few questions for you."

"Mother, you won't try to micromanage my love life, will you? I'm a little old for that."

"Of course not. Would I do that to my favorite son?"

"The answer is 'yes' and I'm your only child."

Grace Kingston smiled and pulled a chair up to James' bed. She reached for his hand. "Honey, how serious are you about Elin?"

"I think it is pretty obvious I care about her."

"Are you in love with her?"

"Mother..."

"This is important to me, James. Are you in love with her?"

"Why is this so important?"

"Because you're so very important to me. I need to know."

"And you need to know right this minute?"

"Right this minute." Grace's voice had become serious and her son sensed the change in her tone. His forehead furrowed.

"I love Elin very much. Why? What's this conversation really about?"

"Do you love her as much as you loved Corrine?"

James took a deep breath. He already had this conversation in his own head several weeks ago. "Mother, it's not quite the same. No woman will ever fill Corrine's place in my heart. Nor should they—she was my wife for many years and she gave me two fine sons. But she's been dead for over three years now. Elin has filled a void inside me I didn't know existed. I'm alive again. And I know now I can love again and that feels good. I didn't think I could ever love another woman but now I can't imagine my life without Elin."

"Does she feel the same way about you?"

"Why these questions?"

"Because it's of utmost importance to me."

"What's wrong, mother?"

"We'll get to me later. You go on."

"Elin loves me."

"Do you think the two of you will get married?"

"We've already broached the topic. She has a birthday in May and I plan to give her a ring. It will be official then. Does that make you happy?"

"Oh my, yes."

"Any particular reason why this is so important, mother?"

Grace hesitated for a second and looked down at her lap. "It's the cancer again."

James' body tensed. "You've beat this twice before and you can do it again, I know."

"No, James. Not this time. It's spread too far. I told the oncologist two months ago I wouldn't undergo chemo again. Chemo will prolong things. This is the way I want it. You're father's been gone almost twenty years and I need to get to him before he finds another girlfriend."

James tried to smile only because his mother made such an effort to smile. He kissed his mother's frail hand. "I'll be there for you, I promise. So will Elin."

"I knew you'd say that. And if you don't, I'll have Charlie put another hex on you."

James tried to laugh but the incision in his lower stomach still burned. "Mother, Elin and I will take care of you. That's a promise."

Grace handed her son a small black velvet box. Inside James found a worn but beautiful sparkling ring—his mother's engagement ring. "Are you sure you want me to give this ring to Elin?"

"Sweetheart, I'm not going to die until I know my son will have a happy life." Grace pulled out the Bible again and sat back in her chair. She began to read scriptures to her son.

CHAPTER FOURTEEN

Jeremy left the accountant's office with a smile on his face. The marina's books were well documented and the marina's income stream was strong and steady ten out of twelve months. He knew he would never become a multi-millionaire as the owner of the marina but he knew he would have a job about which he could be both passionate and happy.

Jeremy called Victor and told him the news. Victor invited him for lunch provided he received a guided tour of the marina afterward.

Delighted with his progress, Jeremy drove to the home of the man he sometimes mocked. As soon as he arrived, he noticed the damaged Mustang. "What happened?"

The Chief explained.

"Was my mother with you?"

"We were on our way back to the villa after the party."

"Was this an accident or was this deliberate?"

"Why do you ask?"

"There isn't a murderer after my mother again is there, Victor?"

"Frankly, that hadn't occurred to me. Anyway, the police are on the lookout for the Highlander. They know it was stolen—probably by some teens. We'll check for prints."

"If this is anything involving my mother, you will tell me, won't you?"

"Of course I will." The Chief didn't tell Jeremy his question triggered a swirling tornado in his gray matter.

Victor's home was not huge but the property was about a half acre and very private. The home was painted an adobe color similar to what is seen throughout the islands. It had a green tin hipped room with no overhang.

There were forest green decorative shutters that matched the trim. Drop-down hurricane shutters neatly lined the top of each jalousie window. Full length, heavy-duty shutters designed to shut tight flanked the mahogany double front doors. Through a few trees Jeremy could see the harbor in a distance.

Victor showed Jeremy his modest but well kept home. He apologized because things were not in their proper place since his family had left for the airport earlier in the morning. Jeremy wished his mother's home looked half as neat. He didn't tell Victor it was against his mother's religion to cook or clean unless it was Christmas, Easter or Thanksgiving. After the tour of the house Victor took him to the sun porch located in the rear. With pride and gusto, he showed off his very large and very expensive telescope.

"Look through this and find the marina so I know where it is."

Jeremy agreed and grinned when he found Pirate's Cove. The Chief peered through the scope and declared that this marina had the best reputation of any marina on the island. He told Jeremy its location made it desirable since it had been dredged so larger yachts and sailboats could easily maneuver into the slips. Jeremy didn't want to get his hopes up too much but he couldn't help but smile inside and out.

The Chief had made lunch for the two of them so they sat on the sun porch and ate. Jeremy updated the Chief. He was now down to five obstacles—the appraiser, real estate lawyer, engineer, sales price and the loan. The back-at-home obstacles included the sale of his rental condos, some land he owned plus his own home.

Both men finished their sandwiches and beer and headed for the harbor. Gil met them on the docks and Jeremy introduced him to the Chief. Gil was visibly surprised when he recognized the Chief's face. He hadn't missed the front-page kiss or the article about the Chief's retirement dinner.

"Chief Hanneman, it's nice to meet ya again. Don't worry, you wouldn't remember me but I did git to shake your hand at a parade once."

"It's nice to meet you, Mr. Kliver. I look forward to an inspection of your marina."

"Do you mind if I ask you who the nice lady was in the paper?"

The Chief started to squirm and he didn't think fast enough to respond.

Jeremy interrupted. "The lady is my mother."

"Oh." Now it was Gil who began to squirm.

"If you looked at the picture closer," Jeremy said, "you would have seen me in the background although I wasn't the center of anyone's attention. Now, show us the marina, Gil."

As they walked, Jeremy told the Chief to relax and it was okay to smile.

"Well, I'm a bit embarrassed, you realize," the Chief whispered, "and I embarrassed your mother. I don't think I'll ever live down that picture."

"Ya gotta watch those cell phones." Jeremy laughed out loud much to Victor's discomfort.

"Did you see yesterday's paper?" the Chief asked.

"Did my mother make front page again?"

"There was a picture of the two of us. It was a very nice article."

"Good. Mom will enjoy that."

The two visitors followed Gil around the marina. Jeremy's chest swelled with pleasure at the thought of ownership. Victor felt much younger than his sixty-five years and as he looked around he wished he had some of Jeremy's youth and enthusiasm.

"What are these doors all about, Gil?" Jeremy asked as they headed back toward the office.

"They are small storage sheds for my yearly renters."

"What are the inside measurements?"

"Not too big—I believe six by eight. You know, one of my renters left a couple of months ago and did not pay me—jist took off without telling me. Sixty-days late on rent means the shed and contents revert to me. Let me get my master key and I'll show you inside. I'm sure it's empty."

While they waited, the Chief and Jeremy discussed the condition of the planking and what repairs needed to be made.

Gil returned with the key. Once the shed was open the men saw miscellaneous items of fishing gear including a half dozen deep-sea fishing rods. "Wow, these are nice rods—expensive, too. I might keep one for myself and sell the rest."

An oversized ice chest sat in the corner. "Well, I wonder what I got me here? I doubt if he left me any booze."

As Gil opened the chest, a hideous odor consumed the air.

"Gross." Jeremy gagged as he walked away from the shed and tried not to vomit. He knew it would be awhile before the image of a half-rotted body left his mind.

"This is not a good omen, Gil," the Chief said.

Gil shut the lid of the box and stood speechless as his jaw rested on his chest. He heard the Chief call the station and ask for an officer and the forensics team. "Honest, Chief. I knew nothing about this. Honest. I had nothing to do with this. I wouldn't have opened the shed fer ya if I had known what was inside."

Jeremy stayed at the edge of the pier and breathed out of his mouth. Even from where he stood the odor was strong enough to make most men regurgitate.

The Chief closed his phone. "Officer Thompson and Officer Simpson are on their way and will want to interview you, Gil. You may want to gather your records for the person or persons who rented the slip and shed. Now, write down everything you can remember as well as a description of the yacht."

"Sure will, Chief." Gil disappeared into his office.

"Victor, I need to take a walk," Jeremy said. "Want to come with me?"

"I'm going to stay here. It's police policy that when we find a corpse we stay at the scene until all the proper authorities are on site. I'm a civilian now but I still have a hell of a lot of cop in me."

"I want to examine the pilings and bracing. Underwater at least I'll breath in oxygen and not rotted air."

* * *

Charlie met Elin at the airport. Both ladies were excited about their meeting with the rep from the cruise line. Charlie didn't notice the man who sat in the rear of their plane. Reporter George Harris wondered why Charlie and Elin were headed for St. Martin.

As the small prop plane left the ground, they both checked their list of questions to ask.

Elin explained she wanted to know if the cruise line charged a flat rent or if they wanted a cut of the sales or both. She also wanted to know how negotiable the rent or percentage was.

"I didn't realize they would do both," Charlie said.

"If they do require a cut of the sales, I need to negotiate a sliding scale."

"Meaning?"

"If you sell over a target range, their percentage goes down," Elin said.

"Gotcha. Why don't we accept their offer and stay onboard for the rest of the trip. James is out of danger and you need to find out if a cruise is for you. And if you like it, you can have James take you on a cruise on your honeymoon to the Mediterranean or Alaska."

"Dreamer. He may be the Deputy Police Chief but he doesn't make that kind of money. Besides, he has to propose first."

"And you would accept, of course."

"Of course." Elin said. "I never felt this way when I was married to old Fred Willard. I was so young and stupid. And of course I never would have thought he would try to have mama and me killed."

"It wasn't a particularly smart thing for an ex-husband to do."

"I'm so grateful you didn't give up on your search for us after Fred abducted mama and me."

"I was one person out of many. Most of the police force was out that night and that included Deputy Police Chief Kingston, then known as Detective Kingston. To be honest, I never expected to find the two of you buried in a crypt in a cemetery."

"I'll give James some credit, but you are the one who forced Clint Spell to tell you where we were. And you are the one who pried the vault's lid open enough for us to breathe. You saved our lives."

"I couldn't have done it if I hadn't used the tire iron to force the imbecilic Clint to talk. Let's forget about all of this until we testify at the trial. We are two ladies on a mission and at least part of our mission is to have fun."

As the plane neared the airport, the ladies could make out four huge cruise ships moored next to the two white concrete mega piers. "I can't read any of their names, but *Aqua Waters* is among them," Charlie said. The exuberant ladies knuckle-bumped each other.

* * *

Once out of the airport, Elin and Charlie grabbed a cab to take them to the pier. George had his cab driver follow them and wondered what would happen. He was sure that wherever Charlie Mikkelsen went trouble followed. He retrieved his camera and snapped a few pictures before he left for his appointment with the mayor. Carolyn Rodgers, manager of Island Elegant in Christiansted, was at the pier with a rack stuffed with clothing. She had come on an earlier flight, stopped at a friend's house, removed the clothing from a box, borrowed a rack, steamed the garments and had them ready for Elin. She even brought an impressive selection of clothing for both ladies to wear.

Two stewards approached Charlie and Elin and asked if they were the Mikkelsens. The ladies nodded. One steward offered Charlie a ride in a wheelchair and the other placed the luggage on a cart. Elin assumed command of the clothing rack and wheeled it to the gangway. George watched them and wondered what was up.

* * *

Charlie and Elin were soon surrounded by a number of happy tourists returning from the town's wall-to-wall jewelry stores. Once the ladies reached the ramp, Elin looked upwards. "Charlie, this ship is a skyscraper. How many floors does it have?"

"To be politically correct, the floors are called decks and the answer to your question is that I don't know. I was on a ship once and it had twelve decks but this one seems even taller."

"I won't have to worry about exercise. This vessel has to be a mile long."

"I believe the newer ones are closer to a thousand feet. Besides plenty of walking space, there will be a full gym and spa at your disposal. You'll be in exercise heaven."

A third steward appeared and helped Elin up the ramp with the clothes rack. Onboard, the ladies showed their passports and had their pictures taken. They were each issued a stateroom keycard, which served as identification. The ladies put their luggage on the conveyor belt so it could be run through the scanner.

Since this was their first time onboard, the ladies each stepped through the metal detector. With no replacement parts, Elin breezed right through.

The attendant escorted Charlie and Elin to the elevator and then up to level nine. Two stewards followed with the rack of clothing and the luggage. Once inside their stateroom the ladies thanked everyone. As soon as the door closed, Elin danced and twirled around the room. Both ladies clasped hands over their mouths to keep sounds of pleasure to a minimum. The accommodations were decadent. Their suite was elegant and it came with a salon flanked by two bedrooms, each with a queen size bed. The end of the salon had sliding glass doors that led to a private balcony on the port side of the liner. Needless to say, neither woman had experienced such opulence in their lifetime. Charlie assured Elin that very few of the other 3,000 passengers had such luxurious accommodations. As if their surroundings weren't snazzy enough, there was a bottle of champagne chilled in a bucket on the end table adjacent to two crystal flutes. A bouquet of fresh roses graced the coffee table.

Elin checked out the bathroom. "It is so small."

"This room is called a head and it's large by cruise line standards. Most have a shower and no tub. We're lucky ladies to have all of this."

The second head had a portable ramp accommodating a wheelchair. "I think this one is for me," Charlie said as she showed Elin the ramp.

Back in the salon, the ladies sat on the plush white couch and grinned and giggled. Elin popped the cork on the champagne and the ladies toasted each other and giggled some more. Finally they unpacked and prepared for their four o'clock meeting.

CHAPTER FIFTEEN

When Jeremy returned with his gear, he used the marina's shower room to change. Officers Bob Thompson and Paul Simpson were deep into an interrogation of Gil inside his office. The forensics team was on its way.

Victor said, "You might want to start as far away as possible and stay around the other piers. Forensics will have the ice chest open for quite a while."

"You don't have to tell me twice. I'll swim over to the far end." Jeremy sighed as he trudged to the empty slip where the former renters had docked. Once his fins were on he flipped into the water. He surfaced to adjust his goggles.

"Is this supposed to be Halloween or something?" Jeremy howled.

Victor rushed to the edge of the pier. Gil, Bob and Ben heard Jeremy and rushed over. "What's wrong?" the Chief said.

Jeremy gasped. "There are two ropes under here and they are attached to a skeleton. Most of it is under the water. I think it's time for me to look for another marina."

Gil pointed out a ladder attached to a nearby piling.

Bob gingerly descended. He wasn't sure the hand-made ladder would hold his two hundred-forty pound frame. It did—barely. "Jeremy's right, Chief. The head is almost under water now. When the tide comes in, it would be completely covered."

Bob used the pier's bracing to monkey his way over to the piling in the rear of the pier. He pulled on the rope. "Guys, part of the torso has detached. We need a search team. Ben, can you call our Dive Unit? It may be easier now since the tide is out."

Jeremy climbed up the ladder after Bob. "Victor, I'm outta here. Too many dead bodies around this place."

"Ya will come back though, won't ya young fella?" an anxious Gil asked.

"I'll be back again when the air is breathable—maybe."

* * *

Elin and Charlie went to work as they inspected various items of clothing on the rack. Elin steamed two outfits before she was satisfied everything was perfect. Charlie tried on the clothes chosen for her. Both ladies disappeared into their respective heads to freshen their make-up. It took Charlie a little longer because she had age spots to hide. She dared the woman in the mirror to make a comment.

You need your foundation, Ms. Charlie.
If you didn't look at me in our ten-X mirror you wouldn't notice my age spots.
I'm looking at your tummy roll, not the mirror. Did you bring your Spanx?
Of course.
I'm glad you have to wiggle your butt into it and not me.
Thanks. I get a lot more support from Spanx than I do from you.

* * *

Promptly at four Karita Lind knocked on the stateroom door. Elin invited the business development representative inside. She introduced her to Charlie and all the ladies agreed to call each other by their first names.

"How do you want to start our meeting, Karita?" Elin asked.

"May I look at your clothing? I love the print you are wearing."

"Then you'll love Island Elegant Apparel."

Elin took two garments off the rack—a sleeveless cotton top with a deep cowl neckline and a tulip-style gored skirt. The items were in a matching print with a pattern of multicolored tropical birds sitting in emerald trees. She produced a pair of solid colored walking shorts of the same cerulean blue as the background in the blouse and skirt. Out of a box, she selected a sun hat in a matching fabric.

"This is what I do to all my separates. I use prints in blouses and skirts or in a dress. My prints are far too strong and busy for pants and slacks. I feel strongly the pattern would emphasize a woman's tummy or derrière."

"Are these stretch garments?" Karita asked.

"Mostly the shorts and slacks. The rest of the items have a very ample cut and are primarily styled to be loose around the waist."

Elin pulled out an orange dress with an empire waistline. "This is what I mean by a loose waistline for a dress. We're in the tropics and it does get hot and sweaty here. See how these tucks under the bodice allow the dress to hang loosely. Comfort is all in the fit."

"You use a lot of bright solid colors, too," Karita observed.

"I do except for a line of linen shorts and slacks. For the bright colors, I tame them a bit with deep necklines or wide contrasting collars or both."

Karita stood and felt the solid cotton prints. "These are so incredibly soft."

"I love all cotton and use it as often as possible."

"Luscious."

"Karita," Charlie said, "notice this sunhat. Since there is a breeze on ship and on the shore, it has an elastic band inside the brim. This helps to prevent the hat from blowing away."

"Clever, very clever," Karita said as she drooled.

"And there is always a selection of matching jewelry," Elin added.

Charlie put together a softly pleated solid tangerine skirt with a matching sleeveless top. She arranged a tangerine print jacket on the same hanger over the skirt and top. There was also a matching purse and sunhat. "Check out this outfit. It is a good example of the feel of Elin's garments."

"Oh! I want one of each," the animated Karita exclaimed. "And Elin, may I see the gown at the end of the rack?"

"I carry two lines of gowns—almost expensive and very expensive. Depending on the cuts of these cotton blends, I would think most of your clientele could afford these. About half of the silks would be in the same price category, but the better gowns are in a silk crepe and they are a much heavier weight. Most of them have sequins or beading and a substantial price tag. Most of the gowns in the high-end category would be appropriate for semi-formal to formal dining, dancing or even a possible spur-of-the-moment onboard wedding. I suspect after we learn more about your clientele, I may want to carry a few of the expensive gowns and add more cocktail dresses."

"I would second the idea and I want one of each, too," Karita said. She made no effort to hide her enthusiasm.

"Elin would be happy to accept your credit card," Charlie said with an inane grin.

Elin presented a few devilish bikinis in vibrant colors and an equal number of swimsuits appropriate for the one-piece bathing suit ladies. She pointed out how the shearing on the suits disguised the control panels across the waist, tummy and hip areas and how the material used in the suits had a higher percentage of spandex than the average swimsuit.

"I've tried a suit like this," Charlie said. "My friends at the Y commented on my weight loss. And note—the larger-sized swimming attire has a bra cup that lifts and supports at the same time."

As Karita was about to gush, the long deep blast of the ship's horn notified passengers on shore to get back onboard toot sweet.

As she rose to leave, Karita said, "Elin, I'd like to have a long discussion with my boss at headquarters. I do hope you and Charlie will stay and enjoy the rest of the cruise."

Elin heartedly replied, "With accommodations like this, we may never leave."

"Good. May we meet upstairs at eight? Charlie, there is a private elevator behind the purser's office. I'll leave a note for the man on duty to have someone escort the two of you to the elevator and into our restricted office areas. This ship is a maze and unless you know where the private elevators are you'll never find them."

The ladies agreed and Karita left a detailed map of the ship's layout, which was normally available to only the crew.

* * *

As soon as Karita shut the door to the stateroom, there was another blast of the horn. "I need to call James before the ship leaves," Elin said.

* * *

While Charlie and Elin met with Karita, James had joined Andre in a meeting room at headquarters. His stomach throbbed.

Chamaign introduced James to Larson Fossing of the St. Martin PD. The men shook hands over the conference room table.

The aroma of fresh coffee escaped from the pot sitting in the middle of the table. "I forgot the cups so I'll be right back," Andre said.

The detectives talked among themselves and none looked happy. Chamaign glanced at James and shook her head. Not one name on their list of tourists and travelers proved productive to date.

Andre returned with the coffee cups in one hand and a piece of paper in the other. "This is the message I told you about, James." He showed his friend the fax and James grimaced.

Andre spoke, "Detectives, the fax is from the Royal Bahamas Police Department. They had two men murdered Monday morning but they weren't jewelry representatives. The police wondered if there was any possible connection because both of the victims had their necks cracked."

Frustrated, Man hit the table with his fist. "I don't believe this. How do these people get from island to island? People have to jump through hoops to get in and out of airports or on or off the ferries."

James' cell buzzed and he took Elin's call. She told him about the suite on *Aqua Waters*. He listened without comment for a minute before he interrupted. "Honey, we've had a jewelry murder on St. Martin today and two on Nassau on Monday. I need to get off the phone." He heard Elin tell Charlie what happened.

Charlie grabbed the phone. "James," she exclaimed, "now you know how these guys get around."

"What do you mean we know how these men get around? We don't have a clue how these men get from island to island."

"Simple. Nassau, St. Thomas and St. Martin. The murderers are on a cruise ship."

"Cruise ship?"

"Many of the cruise lines sailing this part of the Caribbean first stop at San Juan or Nassau or somewhere off the Mexican coast. That would probably be on a Monday. Then they sail to St. Thomas and St. Martin or the other way around. When were the Nassau murders?"

"Monday. The fax said both vics had their necks broken as we described in our bulletin. The difference was that there weren't robberies involved.

"Well, I'll bet three or four cruise liners were there on Monday. Maybe those first two victims were a practice run."

James told the four people at the table what Charlie said. There was total silence for fifteen seconds before Chamaign told James that Charlie's theory didn't include St. Croix. James repeated her message.

"Sure it does. The last cruise I took, the ship arrived in St. Thomas around eight in the morning. I bet one of the men had a morning ticket to fly over; he did his deadly deed and took an early flight out. It works, James. It works. The man came to and went from St. Croix before the searches were put in place."

"Incredible. I see those ships daily but never thought about where they've been or where they were headed. Now what, Charlie? Which cruise lines?"

"Oh come on Deputy Police Chief Kingston. This brilliant AARP member solved the puzzle for you. Do I have to go after the men, too?"

"No, I don't want you to go after any more murderers. You're no longer a wannabe detective."

Charlie chuckled and said, "I understand but I must remind you how my mystery novel heroines were all proud of me because I helped you once before."

"Tell me about your mystery novel heroines later. I need your recommendations now."

"Here is what you need to do, Chief: all of you get online and search which cruise lines come to St. Thomas. Then go through each ship's itinerary and see if there is a match with the days of the murders. There has to be at least a dozen ships docked in Charlotte Amalie over the course of a week. It shouldn't be hard. You can do this without me."

"Thanks, partner."

"James, say goodbye to your honey. We plan to lead a life of decadent luxury for the rest of the week. Oh, by the way, cell phone service is really expensive to use on a cruise ship so I left my cell at your mother's house and Elin plans to turn hers off so she won't be tempted to call you. So, this is your last chance to get mushy."

James walked into the hall as Charlie handed the phone to Elin. Unfortunately, it did not occur to anyone that the alleged murderers might be on *Aqua Waters*.

* * *

When the ship's horn blasted again, the ladies locked their purses in the suite's safe and Elin slipped a keycard in her skirt pocket. They consulted the map and left to find the stern of the ship. Elin pushed Charlie's wheelchair down the long hallway toward a bank of elevators. The happy tourists stood aside and allowed Charlie and Elin to enter the elevator first.

Once on the main deck, the ladies headed for the rear of the ship. There were waiters with trays of pretty pink "island" drinks served in tall glasses and topped with orange or lime slices and a paper umbrella.

"Oh Charlie, I didn't bring any cash with me, did you?"

"You don't need any. This is how it's done." Charlie told the server her room number and he handed the ladies each a drink.

"Doesn't he take cash?"

"Now exactly. All purchases go on your account and there is no cash anywhere. In our case though, we are the guests of Scandinavian Seven Seas and don't need to worry about our bill."

"Well then, we must have two drinks to celebrate."
"Absolutely. But you, not I, have to stay sober for our meeting."

* * *

Victor drove to the police station and used his former office, now James' office, to review his case files from years ago. Of all the arrests he made resulting in convictions, most of the offenders were out of prison and had been for a number of years. There were two men still behind bars. None of the men released had ever threatened him personally. As a knot formed in the pit of his stomach, he decided someone was after Charlie—and that someone must have something to do with the drug ring. Now he had to decide if he should tell Charlie and Jeremy. Before he left the station he wrote Bob a note. He wanted to know about any prints found on the stolen SUV.

* * *

Thirty-plus passengers were on the stern of the ship as Elin and Charlie arrived. All anticipated a beautiful view of the Philipsburg harbor as the ship headed out to sea. Many of the men snuck a quick glance at a new heavy gold ring or fancy new high-end watch. The women flashed sparkly new necklaces, rings or earrings—some even showcased all three.

Charlie and Elin looked over the railing and watched the turquoise water swirl as the ship's engines revved and the enormous propellers began to turn. Shortly after the last blast of the horn the vessel started to move backwards out of its berth. Once clear of the pier, the whole ship vibrated as the engines slowly moved the floating hotel in a half circle so it could face seaward. The two ladies enjoyed the view as they watched the colorful town of Philipsburg slowly fade in a distance.

The crowd on deck was buoyant and everyone seemed happy about their purchases. The tourists knew they had two more days at sea before the liner docked on Sunday morning. The ship's daily newsletter listed a multitude of activities from belly flop contests to an afternoon of bingo.

The evening's entertainment featured two celebrities from *Dancing with the Stars* who boarded in St. Martin.

As Charlie wheeled her way toward the elevators she noticed a man at the railing with a woman and another couple. The man seemed somewhat familiar but she didn't know why. Normally, she would have stopped and spoke to the gentleman but she and Elin had decided to dine early so they would be ready for their meeting. They both were in dire need of a shower and change of clothes.

* * *

"I had no idea how many blasted cruise lines there are out there," Man said. "And I had no idea how many ships each of the cruise lines has."

Chamaign asked a global question. "We eliminated one cruise line. How many more do we have to go?"

Someone answered, "A lot." The room remained quiet as the detectives pounded the keyboards. Andre paced the floor. James sat and held his stomach as he closed his eyes.

"James, I'm going to update our bosses. Is that okay with you?" Andre asked.

"Thank you. Tell Bill I'm sorry I can't make it."

James knew he had a fever and called his doctor. After being reamed out for his unauthorized departure from the hospital, he promised to return within the hour.

"I've got it. I think I've got it," Larson said. "Scandinavian Seven Seas Cruise Line has two ships that come to St. Thomas and St. Martin. One of them has a port of call in Nassau every Monday. In fact, its whole itinerary matches the dates of our murders."

"Is it in St. Martin now?" James asked.

"Yep."

James said, "Detectives, we can't call the captain and expect him not to sail unless we're positive there are no other options. Eliminate all other cruise lines so we know this has to be the ship."

Another fifteen minutes passed. Every other cruise line was eliminated.

"Boss, on which ship did Elin and Charlie sail?" Chamaign asked.

James thought for a minute. "Oh my God. I didn't even think about them. I believe Elin said *Aqua Waters*. Larson, what was the name of the ship you identified?"

"*Aqua Waters.*"

James shivered as chills racked his body. Chamaign called 911. She tried to reassure her boss the ladies would be okay. "It's unlikely Charlie would spot the suspect out of 3,000 tourists. And it is even more unlikely the suspect would recognize her."

"But if the murderer noticed Charlie at the airport with her crutches and that boot, he wouldn't be likely to forget her." He called Elin's number. No answer. "Elin turned her cell phones off and Charlie didn't take hers. Find out what we can do. They must have a satellite setup onboard," James barked seconds before he passed out.

CHAPTER SIXTEEN

Bob called the Chief. "Sir, we found the SUV and eliminated all but a single print but it is not on file."

"What did the mold of the tire tracks tell us?"

"The tires came with the SUV from the factory."

"Well that doesn't help us. Anything on the sample fibers or dirt taken from the vehicle?"

"Nothing. The owner is a helicopter mom who drives her kids from one activity to another."

"Update me every time you have something, Bob."

"Yes, sir." *This was the second time the Chief called me by my first name. I guess my hearing is okay. Was it retirement or love that changed him?*

* * *

James was back in his hospital bed attached to his antibiotic drip when Grace and Jeanette arrived. Grace didn't hesitate to scold her son for his unscheduled absence.

"Don't you understand how much danger you are in? The doctor said you've developed peritonitis caused by all the bacteria from the ruptured appendix. James, this is dangerous."

"Mother, I'm fine."

"No you are not. You could develop organ damage. You could even die if the antibiotics don't kill the bacteria quickly enough. James, this is serious and at your age you're old enough to know better."

It was Jeanette's turn. "I am disappointed in my favorite nephew."

"Aunt Jeanette, you only have one nephew, remember?"

"So I take it you don't like my mango mousse pie?" countered the feisty aunt.

"What does mango mousse pie have to do with this?"

"Well, if you decide to croak, you'll never have it again."

"That's interesting logic, Aunt Jeanette. If I promise to do as I'm told, will you bring me a big piece?"

"Of course." A grin appeared on the face of James' short and plump aunt.

Andre entered. "Well, you look a little bit better than two hours ago."

"Tell that to my mother and aunt. Did you get hold of the security officer or the captain?"

"Yes."

"Hold on, Andre. Mother, would you and Aunt Jeannette mind if I speak to Andre alone?"

"James, you are in the hospital to get well, not work."

"For a few minutes, mother."

The two ladies left the room but not before they gave James a shame-on-you-glare.

"Sorry Andre, go on."

"I asked how we could get the women off the ship. They don't want a copter to land unless it is our last resort. They're very worried about passenger safety."

"Will they do anything?"

"Not yet. They want to know for sure the suspect is onboard. I emailed them the sketch we have."

James was annoyed. "I don't suppose they have facial recognition technology onboard, do they?"

"James, get real. You can't expect a cruise ship to have that type of technology."

"And what will they do—walk around the deck and compare faces with the sketch?"

"Now calm down, buddy. The staff checks passports and takes digital pictures of all passengers who come onboard. Every time they are in port, the passengers have to punch their room keycard both as they leave and return to ship. Staff compares faces with the picture to ensure no guest comes onboard who shouldn't be there."

"So they have a mug file like we do?"

"I don't think they refer to it as a mug file. They probably call it their passenger file."

"Whatever. How long will it take?"

"They will have to compare faces like we do, and it will take as long as it takes us and they have over 3,000 passengers. Let's hope our man's last name begins with an A, B or C," Andre replied.

"Regardless, the ladies are at risk."

"Probably not. I can't believe the man at the airport would recognize Charlie."

"He could recognize the boot, though," a stubborn James insisted.

"The chances are slim," Andre said.

"Has anyone been able to get through to Elin or Charlie since they left?"

Andre shook his head. "I spoke to Officer Dyrby. He is in charge of security and he said Captain Hansen didn't want to alarm anyone until they confirmed the man's presence. It shouldn't take long, James. And he's right. It is possible we could be wrong. Let these ladies enjoy themselves until we have a reason to worry them."

CHAPTER SEVENTEEN

Jeremy was rattled by the discovery of the skeleton and the rotted body. Forensics had cleared the shed and taken prints. They even took the light bulb. Gil had used several cans of Lysol but the odor lingered. The putrid air seemed to settle over the pier and refused to move.

Jeremy knew the divers had removed the body from under the pier, but he was antsy about a plunge into the waters. He stood on the edge of the pier as he tried to decide if he wanted to own the marina. He had another two hours left of daylight.

A soulful Gil looked at Jeremy. "It's safe to go in now, young fella. I'm really sorry about everything. I had no idea. Several of these boats are chartered for deep-sea fishing expeditions and there is sometimes an odor in the air so I never pay any attention to it. I hope this won't change your mind about the marina."

"I'm not sure what I want right now, Gil." He flipped into the water and Gil lowered the heavy-duty waterproof flashlight to him. Jeremy managed to inspect a portion of one pier. He was pleased at what he saw but his mood was in a slump.

* * *

Chamaign knew her old Chief would want to know about Charlie. She called and updated him about the cruise ship and about James.

"Is there anyway I can reach Charlie directly?"

"No, sir. Charlie didn't take her cell and Elin turned hers off because the cost to use the service is so high."

"Have they been told about the man?"

"No, sir. If the man is onboard, security will tell them."

"Knowing how Charlie seems to find trouble, the man is onboard."

"You may be right, Chief. About another matter, sir, I heard from Bob about the marina. I feel sorry for Charlie's son. He must be upset. If you'll give me his number I'll tell him about his mother."

"I can give you Jeremy's number but would you mind if I talked to him, Chamaign. I've become very fond of the young man."

"That's fine. It would be better if you called him. I know you must be worried about Charlie, too. The doctor almost had to tie James to his bed he's so upset."

"I'll give James a call later. For now, tell him I'll keep on top of the murders over here. Chamaign, you're needed where you are."

"Thank you, sir." Chamaign hung up and looked at Man. "Marlboro Man, I had no idea Chief Hanneman even knew my first name let alone he would use it. Has he changed since retirement or something?"

"Maybe it's love," Man hooted.

"What do you mean?"

"Chamaign, we read newspapers and check the Internet on this island, too. We saw the picture where your old Chief smooched with Charlie. It looked like a lip lock to me."

"You should have seen what James did to the walls at the retirement party."

"We heard, Chamaign. You know how gossip travels between our three islands."

Chamaign yelped, "Yep. From rookie to police commissioner there is only a thirty-second delay."

* * *

Victor drove to the villa. He was not looking forward to his conversation with Charlie's son. Jeremy was on his third beer when he heard the bruised Mustang pull in the drive. He answered the door in his bare feet.

"Hey Chief, I'm celebrating my wonderful discoveries this afternoon. Join me in a beer?"

The Chief looked into the refrigerator, "You have a single can left. Want me to pick up another six pack?"

"Tell me first how you get rid of this smell."

"Did you wash your clothes?"

"I trashed them in the dumpster along with my sneakers and socks and underwear. I have no shoes to wear at the moment and I have enough beer in me not to care."

"Did you shower?"

"Three times and I washed my hair each time."

"I believe the odor is deep in your memory. That was pretty horrific and I know how you feel. The first time I had to face something like that it was a child's body and it took me months before I could look at my own children without disintegrating into tears."

"I'll never watch *CSI* again."

"Son, we need to talk about something else." The tone of Victor's voice made Jeremy set his empty beer can on the floor.

"Don't tell me my mother is involved in police work again."

"There is a possibility your mother may be in danger."

"Why? What has she done now?"

"I need to tell you what she did earlier. I can't believe how her mind works."

"Somehow I don't think I'll like what you're about to tell me."

"Your mother managed to figured out how this murder suspect moved from one island to another." The Chief explained how the cruise lines worked. "Here the detectives have spent their time at the airports and the ferry while the suspect has openly sailed from port to port on a cruise ship. After your mother told them where to look, the detectives identified the proper ship by its ports-of-call. We believe your mother and Elin are on the same ship."

"Victor, what have I missed here?" Jeremy kicked the empty beer can on the floor. It skipped a couple of times before it rolled under a chair. "When mom called, she made it sound like a big adventure."

"It sounded like a big adventure and a wonderful opportunity for Elin."

Jeremy's voice notched up two octaves. "My mother finds trouble whenever she steps a foot on these islands. She managed to live a whole sixty-five years stateside without once coming face to face with a murderer. Explain again why she is supposed to be in danger?"

"Remember the work she did with the sketch artist?" The Chief explained the ship's ID system. "We will know in a short while if our suspect is on the same ship."

"Victor, I've had it. I want my mother back and I want both of us to go home and stay there forever. Can't your police department rescue my mother or do I have to do it?"

"There is nothing either of us can do. The detectives are in contact with the officer in charge of security."

"I can't sit here."

"We have no choice. Jeremy, you know how I feel about your mother. I've been on the police force all my adult life and I am as useless as you are right now."

"As soon as I get my mother back, we'll head home, Victor. If you want to pursue her you'll need to pursue her in York, Pennsylvania."

Victor bit his lip. He didn't dare tell Jeremy he thought the car accident was really about his mother and the upcoming trial. But he would go to Pennsylvania, if necessary.

CHAPTER EIGHTEEN

Charlie and Elin's dinner attire was directly off the racks of Island Elegant. An exotic tropical print gown with the tiniest of straps showcased Elin's square shoulders and accented her dark bronze skin. Its skirt draped softly from right to left and seemingly gathered at her left hip, which in turn made a soft, sophisticated hike in the left hem to about mid-calf. Her hair was combed upwards and its highlights glistened. Her makeup and hairstyle highlighted her extraordinary high cheekbones and showcased her huge dark eyes with thick natural lashes. Her amethyst-painted lips begged to be kissed. Elin had panache and knew how to use it.

Charlie wore a light lilac silk crepe gown with a deep neckline. Her sun-protected skin was ivory and she used a subtle blush to give herself some color. A little bit of eye color was visible with her deeply set dark eyes. She added her own touch of flair with a silver faux fox cape around her shoulders and her Princess Summerfall Winterspring watch on her arm.

Both ladies were very aware of the many eyes that followed them as they were led to their table. Charlie knew deep down she was not the one the men watched. Her body was anything but curvaceous.

And you have those cottage cheese thighs, Ms. Charlie.
You're so tactful.
But your boobs haven't gone too far south yet.
It's only a matter of time before gravity takes over.

With shoulders down and backs straight, both ladies chose their dinners. As they ate, they chatted about their upcoming negotiation strategy with the cruise line. To Charlie's surprise, a woman stopped and asked her where she shopped. She introduced her to Elin and explained she was the proprietor of Island Elegant Apparel on St. Croix and she would have a new shop on St. Thomas in less than two weeks. When the woman asked for a catalog, Elin admitted she didn't sell through a catalog but she did give the woman a business card with her website on it. She told the woman she would be able to order that way within a month. Later, an older woman stopped and commented on Charlie's cape; a third woman stopped and asked outright how much her cape cost. A fourth woman stopped and commented on Charlie's watch and said she used to have one like it and wanted to buy Charlie's.

Elin said, "And now I know why you wore that watch—to get attention."

"It worked, didn't it?"

To complete their meal, the ladies declined dessert and instead ordered Charlie's favorite real island drink, Cruzan Cream. They decided to stop after one drink because it was almost time for their meeting.

Across the room, Karita Lind and Captain Hansen compared notes as they watched the two women and saw the amount of traffic flowing past their table. They didn't miss the ladies who stopped as their husbands stood behind them and stared at Elin. At another table, a man stared at Charlie. He couldn't figure out why she looked familiar.

* * *

"Okay," Chamaign said, "we need to get creative and get creative fast."

Man and Larson agreed.

"We can arrest the suspect when the ship docks," Man suggested. "Of course the Miami police would want to be involved and we would need extradition papers."

Larson commented, "There would be a line of people with extradition papers—Bermuda, USVI and St. Martin."

"I wish the cruise line would allow us to copter in to make the arrest," Larson said.

"Too much danger for the other passengers," Chamaign replied.

"I've never been on a cruise," Man said. "Have either of you?"

"Quite a while ago but it was before all the travel restrictions were put in place after nine-eleven," Chamaign said. "I wonder what it's like now. And an even bigger question is can we identify this man while 3,000 other people disembark at the same time?"

"We need to speak with the security officer," Man said. "As soon he verifies the man is onboard, we'll need to negotiate some communications with our inside source."

* * *

Charlie and Elin found the promenade and browsed for a few minutes. They counted six retail stores. They peeked in the perfume shop, examined the windows of the watch shop, skipped the souvenir-type shop, strolled through the high-end jewelry store, and glanced in the window of a shop specializing in handmade silver jewelry. There was an empty store in a prominent location with significant window space. The cruise line currently used it to promote other cruise vacations.

"Some of the gems in the jewelry store were pretty pricey—there were one and two carat diamonds in there," Charlie said. "I'd love to know how well they do. Maybe we should speak to the manager when we get a chance."

"It does seem possible Island Elegant would work after all," Elin said.

The ladies went on a search for the purser's office. The map Karita gave them showed a shortcut and they arrived within minutes. They were led to the elevator and told which button to punch and that someone would meet them at the other end.

"Oh Charlie, I'm nervous. This idea has really grown on me. Now I need to figure out if it is financially feasible."

"Let's get the numbers for now and do the math in our stateroom."

"That's a plan, cousin."

When the elevators doors opened, a gentleman in a white uniform greeted them. He led Charlie and Elin to the meeting room. Karita was alone and the table was covered with papers.

"How did you enjoy your meal?" Karita asked.

"Excellent," Charlie replied.

"And your menu offers such a nice variety," Elin said. "Where do you find your chefs?"

"All our chefs are products of various European cooking schools and they all have their own specialties. The only time we require a change in menu is when the meat or fish isn't readily available in port."

"Your turn-around time is so short to stock the shelves and freezers."

"Oh yes, on this ship alone we require over 20,000 pounds of meat and seafood and that is for a single week. We require more fresh eggs than I want to count. We jump through hoops when a hurricane in Miami interrupts the flow of food from the vendors to the docks."

After a few more minutes of chitchat, the women spent the next thirty minutes discussing the terms of a lease on the store. Charlie was particularly interested in the demographics of the ship's clientele. Karita had chart after chart as to where the guests lived, their average ages and income and how much they spent onboard. Charlie consumed the numbers.

"Where do you get information like this?" Elin asked.

"From credit bureaus," Charlie replied. "The bureaus can even tell you a household's lifestyle and what magazines they probably read and what brands of cars they probably drive."

Captain Hansen stepped into the room. "I'm most sorry to interrupt your meeting, ladies. Are you Ms. Charlie Mikkelsen?" he asked as he looked at Charlie.

"I am."

"I'm Captain Birthe Hansen," he said as he shook Charlie's hand.

"May I introduce you to my cousin Elin Mikkelsen?"

"It's a pleasure to meet both of you. Ms. Mikkelsen, may I speak with you in private?"

"If this is about the shop, Elin needs to be present."

"No, I'm afraid this is about a different matter. Please allow me to push you since we need to maneuver many corners to get where we need to be."

Once the captain and Charlie were out of the room, she made him stop. "What is this about, captain?"

"The island murders. We need you to look at a picture of the suspect."

Ms. Charlie, I'd rather look at the captain.

Me too. Those eyes of his are the same azure blue as the Caribbean.

Men shouldn't be allowed to be so rugged and handsome, Ms. Charlie. How come men with gray hair still look good as they age? You don't even notice their wrinkles.

That's a mystery of life I'll never understand. If you figure it out, let me know.

The captain was an older gentleman somewhere in his early sixties. He had a marked accent and it was obvious his thinning gray hair was once a thick, rich blonde. His tanned face had an overabundance of lines from many years on deck. He had changed from his formal whites into an open-collar white shirt, white slacks and black belt. The epaulets on his shirt held his golden stripes.

The captain took Charlie through a maze of corridors and ended up in a room banked with security monitors. "Do you use a web browser, captain?"

"No, our system is self-contained."

"Your resolution is great. What is your range of motion?"

"Our security officer can answer those questions."

Dyrby stepped forward. "Ms. Mikkelsen, meet Officer Borge Dyrby. He heads our security."

The gentleman shook Charlie's hand. Dyrby was a handsome blond Lapp and Charlie found him very easy on the eyes.

Ms. Charlie, I want one of him, too.

Oh shush. He's thirty years younger than you.

But he's so pretty.

I said to shush; I didn't say you couldn't admire the scenery.

"I'm surprised you know so much about security cameras," Dyrby said.

"On my last visit to St. Thomas, I captured an arrest on security cameras. I was fortunate the software was so intuitive."

"Well, we have an amazing range of motion. May I show you?" Dyrby offered.

Charlie wheeled her chair over to a PC. "May I see if I can manipulate it?"

Dyrby nodded. Charlie adjusted the keyboard and clicked the mouse on a thumbnail shot of the gaming room. She panned left and right and up and down. She zoomed for a close-up shot of a gentleman as he played the dollar slots. After she watched for a minute, she made an observation. "That man is going to need more dollar chips shortly, Officer Dyrby. Can you lend him some money?"

Dyrby and the captain laughed.

"Ms. Mikkelsen, are you for hire?" the captain asked.

"Make me an offer I can't refuse, captain. But first, where is this picture?"

Charlie was pleased with the captain's attention. She thought he was more handsome than Dyrby and his age complimented his looks.

"If you will excuse me," the captain said, "I'm needed on the bridge."

"Of course. Have a good evening."

You stay here, Ms. Charlie. I'm going with the captain.

Good luck if you can do it.

"I need you at another PC," Dyrby said as he maneuvered her wheelchair to another workstation.

"Mug shots. I know this routine, too. I went through this on my last visit to St. Croix."

"Well here's another test for you." Dyrby showed Charlie a series of twenty shots of men who all looked somewhat alike.

Once the mug shot test was over, Charlie looked at Dyrby. "It was the seventh man you showed me. The name below the picture was Alan Bladensburg of Newark, New Jersey. I saw him on deck after we left Philipsburg but I couldn't figure out why he was familiar."

"That's the shot we picked, too."

"Unfortunately, I saw him in the dining room with a woman and another couple. He looked at me like he recognized me but couldn't place where he had seen me. Officer Dyrby, I'm not happy about this. He will figure out where he's seen me sooner or later but I don't see how he would know I know what he did."

"When did you first see him?"

Charlie explained about the airport and how she thought he was a jewelry rep. "I told Detective Benton and she interviewed airport personnel and the TSA agents on duty. The detective determined he used fake credentials. I was the person who sat with the sketch artist."

"I'll contact the officers at the VIPD in a few minutes," Dyrby said.

"May I speak to them, too?"

"Let me arrange a conference call tomorrow for all of you. For now, go back to your meeting and I'll talk with the captain."

* * *

"We've finished our discussion, Charlie," Elin said. "You and I need to do a lot of homework."

Charlie nodded.

"Karita, it's been a pleasure," Elin said. "I have a lot to think about and I need to make some serious decisions."

"Charlie, Elin said you are the marketing guru. Do you have any promotional thoughts?"

"I have a few. I'd be at a disadvantage if I discussed them now because I don't know what the two of you discussed. May we do this after Elin makes a decision? And may I have copies of your demographics?"

"Certainly," Karita said. "And before I sign any contract I will require a marketing proposal. You and Elin make your decision first."

"When I have the information I need, a proposal isn't a problem. I'll even break it down into target markets. Now if you get a free minute, make sure you check Elin's website. It is spectacular."

"I already did. It was one of many reasons why we were interested in a working relationship with her."

Karita escorted the ladies to the elevator and they went on their way. As soon as the two women reached the promenade deck, Elin asked what the captain wanted.

"Bad news, Elin. The man who killed the jewelry rep on St. Croix is on this ship."

"Charlie, don't tell me that."

"I don't believe we need to worry. I've seen the man twice now. I did sense the man recognized me but he would have no idea I know he is the murderer and the thief. I don't see how he can connect the dots."

"I don't want to hear this, Charlie. I still see a counselor twice a week thanks to my ex-husband Fred and that Clinton Spell creep. My psyche is badly bruised and I can't deal with the thought of another dangerous man."

"The murderer wouldn't be interested in you. It's me. I'm the person he may recognize. And more importantly, tell yourself he doesn't know what we know."

Elin started to laugh after a second. "Well, if he saw the picture of your famous Internet kiss he would know it was the Deputy Police Chief who planted the big smooch. That might make him wonder if the Chief told you anything."

"We will not discuss that picture, dear cousin."

"Let's explore the available store," Elin said. "Karita gave me a key."

As Elin walked and Charlie wheeled her way to the shop, a young man pushed his grandmother in a wheelchair through the promenade. She, too, had gray hair and wore a humongous black boot. The ladies stopped, introduced themselves and chatted about their surgeries and compared notes. Her name was Chrissie Robertson.

Afterward, Elin unlocked the door of the shop. The floor space was limited and she knew at a glance the best way to display product was in the windows.

"If you kept your stock in the back of the store, you would have room for mirrors and a dressing room or two."

"I could put up a wall display, also. Anything to give me more floor space."

"That could work. You know, I bet we could arrange a fashion show as one of the ship's activities. You could find a dozen women anxious to volunteer if you gave them a discount on the outfit. Somehow, people on a cruise manage to lose an inhibition or two."

"I like that idea. But I could run out of stock."

"Elin, get real. You consider that a problem? You should be so lucky. If the fashion show was the first day at sea and you sold your merchandise, you could take special orders and bring the items in when the ship docks in St. Thomas. Then, you could re-stock everything with new and different outfits for the ladies to buy on the way back home."

A confident expression enveloped Elin's face as she took measurements with the small roll-up tape she kept in her purse. She made a line drawing of the store's layout and measured window frontage. She estimated she could display five or six mannequins. "Now, let's go back to our stateroom and do the math."

"As long as we find a bar on the way. I need another Cruzan Cream."

"Me, too. I love the creamy taste. Why does it feel like the rum goes down first and then the cream?"

"St. Croix voodoo, I suppose. You and I will have to tour the Cruzan Rum factory when we get back and ask the guide."

CHAPTER NINETEEN

Al Bladensburg watched the two women. The gray-haired lady had risen from the wheelchair and used her crutches to get around inside the shop. He got it. She was the woman on the sidewalk at the airport. He recognized the other woman, too. She was the lady who sold him the matching man and woman's print shirts in Christiansted. *Hum. Two of them.*

Bladensburg walked back toward his stateroom. Halfway there he remembered the ship had a computer room where he could rent time to surf the Internet. He found a steward who directed him to the room. Once he found an empty computer, he googled the island's newspapers. He clicked on the *St. Croix Source* and looked for back issues. There it was—the old lady with the gray hair being kissed while she stood with her crutches. Bladensburg had been pissed at the time he first saw the picture. The smooch story received bigger headlines than his murder, rape and theft.

DEPUTY POLICE CHIEF PLANTS A BIG ONE

ST. CROIX. Deputy Police Chief Victor Hanneman this morning met Ms. Charlie Mikkelsen at the airport after she arrived from her stateside home. An unidentified source said the Chief would escort Mikkelsen to his retirement dinner this evening to celebrate his forty-five year career.

Mikkelsen made headlines several months ago when she saved two lives.

Grete Mikkelsen and daughter Elin were buried alive in a vault in the Mikkelsen family plot. Alleged drug traffickers Fred Willard and Clinton Spell built the crypt to store drugs. Former Deputy Police Chief Gene

Peters is the alleged head of the drug ring. The trial starts in three weeks and the Mikkelsen women are due to testify.

Bladensburg disconnected and left the computer room. *Her lover is the Deputy Police Chief. What does she know and why is she here?*

He headed for his stateroom. Inside his wife Alice and neighbors Jerome and Julie Ambrose sat on the balcony and drank a variety of rum concoctions. "We may have a problem." Al's audience listened as he explained about the women and the police chief.

"What do we do now?" Jerome asked.

Al thought for a few seconds. *Hum. I'll have to kill both of them.*

CHAPTER TWENTY

"This is Officer Dyrby of the Scandinavian Seven Seas Cruise Line. May I speak with Officer Benton?"

"This is Detective Man Carmen. Chamaign is right here. May I put you on speaker phone?"

Dyrby agreed.

"Detective Larson Fossing of St. Martin is also here," Man said. "Have you been able to identify the man in the picture?"

"We did. May I ask why a detective from St. Martin is there? Not another murder, I hope."

"Unfortunately, there was. There were two similar murders in Nassau on Monday but no jewelry theft. It's a good possibility these five murders were committed by our suspect and his accomplice."

"This gets worse by the minute. The man whose picture you sent is aboard. Our staff identified him and we had Ms. Charlie Mikkelsen look at a series of pictures and she identified him without difficulty. Needless to say, we are concerned, detectives."

"What information do you have about the suspect?" Chamaign probed.

"His name is Alan Bladensburg and his wife is named Alice. They are from Newark, New Jersey. Also, there is a Jerome and Julia Ambrose in the stateroom next to the Bladensburgs and both parties requested the rooms be connected. The Ambrose family lives on the same street in Newark as the Bladensburgs. Ambrose could be involved."

"We suspected there were two men but I didn't think it would be this easy to find the second," Man said.

"Would you give me their full addresses?" Chamaign requested. "We'll run this through every database we can."

Dyrby conveyed the requested information. "The men cannot be armed," Dyrby said. "We have most of the same security measures on ship as you do at airports. The men brought no guns onboard this ship."

"The victims all had their necks cracked. No guns; no knives," Man said.

"I can't arrest them, you understand. Neither man has committed a crime on ship so I can't press charges."

"We don't want you to arrest them. We suspect the men have military backgrounds and we consider them very dangerous. Dyrby, I wouldn't go after these men without a full SWAT team behind me," Chamaign said.

"What would you like me to do?"

"We need to get these men when they are back in U.S. territory. Do you know what time you leave international waters?"

"Around seven on Sunday morning."

"Can we board by copter or by boat?"

"A boat would be most inconspicuous but we do have a helipad on ship. Legally, I need to find out what you are allowed to do. The captain may not allow anything because of the danger to other passengers."

"We will need to work something out, Dyrby," Man said. "Meanwhile, we'll get subpoenas and start the process for extradition papers—one set from the VIPD and one set from St. Martin. Bermuda may follow."

"Detectives, we have over 3,000 guests plus 2,500 workers onboard. None of them can be put at risk."

"Understood," Man answered. "We need to flesh out our game plan and get back to you."

"Ms. Charlie Mikkelsen wishes to speak with Detective Benton. May I call you at nine tomorrow morning?"

"Absolutely," Chamaign said. "We will make it a conference call, too. My deputy police chief will want to speak with Elin Mikkelsen. Ms. Charlie's son will want to speak with his mother, I'm sure."

"Then I will have both ladies available tomorrow."

After Man disconnected he looked at Chamaign and Larson. "After we update our bosses, we'll pull an all-nighter. We've got to get on that ship."

* * *

When Chamaign called James, he insisted the security officer assign personnel to protect Elin and Charlie. He was extremely upset he couldn't speak to Elin until the next day. Chamaign updated the Chief and Jeremy. Man updated Andre. He arranged a conference call and included all the key players.

* * *

On the way to his home, the Chief called Officer Thompson with a number of questions. "Anything new on the SUV, Bob?"

"The men haven't touched it. They have their noses to the grindstone with the two dead men at the marina."

"That takes priority. Anything new on those murders?"

"A sketch artist from headquarters will be here tomorrow and will work with Gil Kliver, the marina's owner. Gil is an artist so he should be able to give us a good description. The coroner arrived a few minutes ago. He'll remove the body and then we can check for prints inside the cooler. We have all the specs of the boat since it was registered in Puerto Rico. The police there will check all the marinas, and if necessary, we will request cooperation from our surrounding islands."

"Any motive?"

"Probably drugs—cocaine to be specific. There were trace amounts in the shed."

"Look for any connection to Fred Willard, Clinton Spell and that dead criminology professor—Rich Myers. Also, all the other men arrested on St. Thomas. We need more solid evidence on Eugene Peters if this case is connected to his drug ring."

"I'll show their pictures around the marina as soon as the artist is finished," Bob said.

"Go through the entire case again, especially the records Myers kept on his computer. Peters and Myers may have transported drugs by boat for all we know."

"Yes, sir. And Chief, do you have an update on James?"

"He's not out of the woods yet. He tried to leave the hospital and passed out at headquarters. He felt he had to be at a stupid meeting. I sure hope he didn't set himself back too much."

"Give him my best if you speak with him," Bob asked.

The Chief and Bob hung up. Victor wondered how two drug rings could operate simultaneously on the island. *There has to be a connection. There has to be. I need to go over the file tomorrow. Charlie could be in danger. Oh, I can't believe what I just said—Charlie is already in danger.*

* * *

Once Charlie and Elin were in their salon, Elin decided to call James. *I don't care how much it costs, I want to speak with James.*

Elin used speed dial to reach James but the call didn't go through. She realized her phone needed to be recharged and went into her bedroom to look for the charger. "Charlie, I forgot to bring my charger!"

CHAPTER TWENTY-ONE

By eight-thirty Friday morning, everyone was ready for the conference call. Jeremy and Victor were in James' office on St. Croix. James was in his hospital bed and Andre, Chamaign, Man and Larson sat in Andre's office. At nine, Borge Dyrby called as Charlie and Elin sat with him.

Chamaign began the conversation. "Dyrby, we came up with several scenarios to arrest our suspects, but I'd like to ask you a question first. What is it like when people come off the ship in Miami?"

"I'm afraid it is mass chaos. People are anxious to get off and push and shove their way toward the exit."

Charlie spoke. "On my last two cruises there was a short gangway leading from the ship directly into the third or fourth floor of a building. Most people used escalators to get to the bottom floor. A few, like myself, used the elevators. Most people carried their own luggage if they could so they didn't have to wait at the dock for it to be delivered. Anyway, passengers eventually end up in a hallway leading to a covered exterior area. This is where the custom agents are located. You hand an agent your declaration sheet. If you are over your allowed purchases, you pay your customs fee and go on your merry way."

"Dyrby," Chamaign said, "Can you add anything to what Charlie told us?"

"She did a very good job. We control everything the best we can at the elevators but passengers are always in a hurry."

"I have a question," Man said, "when is the luggage searched?"

Charlie answered. "On my last couple of trips, it wasn't. In fact I didn't see anyone's luggage searched."

"That doesn't make sense. Luggage is not searched?"

"None any I saw," Charlie said.

"Why not?" the Chief asked.

"Ladies and gentlemen," Dyrby said, "the luggage is not searched unless drugs are suspected. Please remember, we do a thorough security check when our guests initially board and again if they exit and re-board at a port-of-call. At the end of the cruise, we need to get everyone off the ship as fast as possible to prepare for the 3,000 plus passengers who will board several hours later."

Man squirmed at the discouraging news. "Is there a single file of people who come off the ship?"

Charlie replied, "People are bunched up in a long line. With thousands of people, I don't see how you can control any kind of arrest."

"Dyrby, this is James Kingston. We must sound a bit stupid about cruising, but like Charlie once said, when you live in the Caribbean you don't have to cruise the Caribbean. Now, here is my question. These two men murdered five people and stole over a half million in jewelry. Can these men simply pack the loot inside their jockey shorts, close their suitcases and walk off the ship?"

"Most probably. The crowd is so large there is no time for searches. It would take hours upon hours to empty the ship if only a single bag in twenty was searched. And remember, there are at least a dozen ships docking at various terminals all at the same time in Ft. Lauderdale as well as around Miami."

"We have two suspects and we have a reason to search their luggage," Man said.

Charlie countered Man's logic. "True, but that would require you to recognize the men among the throngs of passengers. Honestly, the crowd is so anxious to get off the ship that even Dyrby could lose them if he tried to trail them. And once you add the fact that these men are murderers, the men could and would use a passenger as a hostage in a heartbeat."

"Dyrby," Man asked, "how did these men get all this jewelry through your security when they returned to the ship?"

"We discussed this among ourselves yesterday. Even our captain joined in the discussion. There are four people, two men and their wives. They could divide up the jewelry and each could wear quite a bit. Plus, everyone could carry four or five packages back onboard with the jewelry divided among them. If they put the packages through the metal detector one at a time, it probably wouldn't meet the threshold to set off an alarm. Our records show that on St. Thomas, the Ambroses boarded, checked out a half hour later and two hours afterward the Ambroses and Bladensburgs boarded together. That could explain how they got all the jewelry back onboard and not set off an alarm. It is too late to help us now, but the captain had us adjust the metal detector so smaller amounts of metal will set off the alarm. I will check our records and find out how these four boarded yesterday in St. Martin."

"Well," Man replied, "this blows our game plan. It doesn't seem like we could arrest them as they exit."

"Officer Dyrby, this is retired Deputy Police Chief Victor Hanneman. I have a serious concern for the safety of our ladies. Charlie saw this Al Bladensburg at the airport. She even pointed him out to me. Of course neither of us knew he murdered and raped a woman nor did we know he stole hundreds of grams of gold. What I do know is I saw the woman's body and I am well aware of how much skill is involved in such a murder. I respectfully request the Mikkelsen ladies be guarded at all times."

"This is Deputy Police Chief Andre Johnson of St. Thomas. Chief Hanneman is right about how these people were murdered. This isn't the movies or a television show. These men are skilled. Can you tell us how our ladies can be protected?"

"Andre, that's not all," Charlie added. "The man recognized me. I don't know if he remembers where he saw me but he does know he's seen me. And Jeremy, I know you're there but don't you get any ideas about any rescues."

"Mom, don't you get any ideas about making like a wannabe detective again."

"I understand your concerns," Dyrby said. "Ladies and gentlemen, I will speak with my captain. We will ensure the safety of the ladies."

"Elin, are you there?" James asked.

"I'm here."

James didn't need to see Elin to know tears streamed down her cheeks. "Elin, I need you to hold it together. You and Charlie will be fine. Dyrby will see to it. Call me later on your cell."

"I can't, James. My cell is dead and I forgot my charger. Now please tell me you're better and the infection is under control."

"I'm fine, Elin. Really. I'll be out of the hospital Saturday afternoon. I'll meet you in Ft. Lauderdale."

"Ladies and gentlemen, I'm sorry but we must cut this conversation short," Dyrby said. "I promise you I'll make arrangements with my captain."

* * *

After everyone hung up, the Chief made a direct call to James. "I know you're the island's new boss but would you mind if a retired deputy police chief works with Thompson on those murders at the marina? To be honest, James, I've already given him a good deal of direction."

"I don't mind, Chief. Bob doesn't have much to go on until the reports come back. Did I miss someone in Peters' drug ring?"

"I don't know what to think. But I find it hard to believe there were two drug rings operating independent of each other at the same time. If there is a connection, Elin and Charlie are in danger since they are both scheduled to testify. We do need answers and I want to help."

"I think they are at a greater risk right now. What are the odds our ladies would end up on a cruise ship with two alleged murderers?"

"I know Jeremy thinks his mother steps into a quagmire of crap whenever she puts a foot on this island. He's very upset."

"He has good reason to be upset. Chief, I'd prefer not to tell the women about any potential connection to the drug ring. Same for Jeremy. I believe the young man has enough on his mind at the moment."

* * *

Dyrby spoke to his captain about the phone call and recommended protection for the ladies. "The detectives told me they suspect these men are former military."

"Which is all the more reason why we stay out of this. What suggestions did the detectives offer?"

"I believe they might want to place officers onboard during the night so they can arrest the men as soon as we are in U.S. territory. They asked about a helicopter or a boat."

"A boat would attract less attention and wake fewer people. We would lose speed, of course."

"But we could minimize or even eliminate any risk to passengers."

"True. Arrange for the protection of the women."

* * *

An hour later, Man put down his phone at the same time Chamaign did the same. "We have a hit on our suspects," he said. "Both Bladensburg and Ambrose were in the Army's Special Forces in Afghanistan and were indeed trained to kill. No police records and nothing in VICAP. The FBI wants to know how they operate to see if it fits the profile of any of their unsolved murders. What on earth would turn these two men into murderers?"

Chamaign responded, "I just spoke to the Newark Police. The answer to your question is greed, greed, greed! Now hear this, detectives. Take a deep breath and fill your brain cells with fresh oxygen. I want you to absorb this."

The men sat and listened.

"What business would you think our Mr. Bladensburg and Mr. Ambrose run?"

Man and Lawson stared in anticipation.

"Three years ago, Mr. Alan Bladensburg and Mrs. Julia Ambrose inherited a jewelry store from their father."

"My idea was right—I was only about 1,200 miles off," Man said with a grin.

"Correct. It's so easy this way," Chamaign said. "They wouldn't have to worry too much about customs; they wouldn't need to fence the jewelry; and they would never report their profits to the IRS. They'd make a ton of money to boot—I need to call James."

"Andre Johnson will love this. I'll be back in fifteen."

"Don't gloat too long, you two," Larson said. "We need to figure out how to get our butts onboard."

CHAPTER TWENTY-TWO

"I don't have much faith in my math abilities right now, Charlie," Elin said.

"Let's do it anyway and not think about other things."

It took two caffeine-laden Diet Pepsis before Elin was able to focus on her profit analysis. She worked the numbers various ways and used several different scenarios to build a variety of models. Under most circumstances, the bottom line stayed black as opposed to red.

"Let's take a break and sneak up to the promenade and talk to the manager at the jewelry store," Elin said as her excitement level grew.

Charlie put her paperwork down. "Sounds good to me. When will you be finished with the laptop?"

"I'm done now. The marketing plan is up to you."

The ladies peeked out the door and saw an empty hallway. They headed for the elevators. Once on the promenade deck, the ladies made a beeline for the jewelry store. Neither noticed Alice Bladensburg. She had planted herself on a bench with a book and hoped Charlie and her wheelchair would appear. She watched the women disappear inside the store. She changed to another bench and placed a lightweight shawl over her pink tee. What Alice didn't see was the security guard who left the elevator with Charlie and Elin. She didn't see him watch both her and the two cousins as he pretended to clean tables.

* * *

"May I speak with the manager?" Elin asked.

"Ma'am, I can take care of most problems. May I be of assistance? A return item, possibly?"

"This is a business visit but I thank you."

The man picked up a phone and spoke several words. He was not about to leave the floor since there was an anxious couple who peered inside a glass case of engagement rings.

The manager, a well dressed distinguished gentleman, appeared in a back doorway and Elin discussed the potential apparel shop. "I hope you can be candid with me. I need to know if there are enough passengers who have the purchasing power for the clothes I sell."

"As I'm sure you know, Ms. Mikkelsen, jewelry has a much higher mark-up than apparel and I can sell far fewer items and still make a nice profit."

"Do you sell many of these engagement rings?" Charlie said.

"Believe it or not, we sell one to three engagement rings each sailing."

"Do you have problems with people out of credit?" Elin asked.

"On occasion. Most customers simply hand me another credit card."

"What was the largest sale you've ever had?" Charlie asked.

"That was a sale I won't forget—I had purchased a large Kashmir sapphire for my private collection that trip. Later, a gentleman asked specifically for a Kashmir and I mentioned I personally owned one. He paid me well over a quarter mil for it. Of course I requested a wire transfer from his account to mine and he agreed. The last day of the cruise he waltzed out of here with the stone and a woman forty years younger than he."

Elin prodded. "If I was your daughter, would you advise me to sign on the dotted line?"

"Ma'am, I think I would. However, I would insist on a three-month trial before the contract kicked in. That's what I did."

"Now that's the kind of advice I can use. Thank you so much."

The ladies left the store and headed for the ice cream shop across the promenade. Charlie said, "I want a hot fudge sundae since I've not watched my figure for the last twenty years."

"I want one, too, since I allow James to watch my figure now. I bet your buddy Victor wouldn't sit down to an ice cream sundae. It's obvious he watches his weight."

"That's his problem, not mine. I can enjoy a sundae; he can't. Too bad."

I'm glad we can have sundaes, Ms. Charlie.

Me, too. We get to split the fat and calories between us.

Oh goodie. Now I don't have to feel guilty.

After the ladies were served their calorie-laden treats, Elin asked, "So, what is with the two of you anyway?"

"I assume you mean the Chief and me. Good question. I don't know. I haven't encouraged Victor but I haven't discouraged him either."

"But you do enjoy his company, right?"

"I must admit I do. But when he tries to make my decisions for me, I'm not exactly appreciative—I've been independent far too long."

"Can you ever see yourself in a permanent relationship again?" Elin asked.

"I didn't think I ever would until I met Victor. It surprised even me."

"I wanted a man who respects me the way I am and I found a gem," Elin said. "James seems so perfect it scares me. Like he's too good to be true."

"James is exceptional. And he's entered a new phase of his life—not only his new job but his relationship with you."

"I will say 'yes' when he proposes. My mother and sister Alyse are in total agreement."

"Grace and Jeanette would say the same thing, I know."

"But what if this is too good to be true, Charlie? What if the bubble bursts?"

"None of us knows what will happen down the primrose path. James never expected his wife to die so young. You never expected to have your ex-husband try to kill you. Let me tell you something your mother and I know that you don't. When you open your mailbox and see that Medicare card inside, the air around you fills with the aroma of coffee. Smell the coffee now so when your card arrives, it won't be too late. Don't put off your life another day."

"What about you and the Chief? Do you practice what you preach?"

Be careful, Ms. Charlie. Don't say anything I wouldn't say.

Go listen to your I-pod and leave me alone.

"Yes and no. Yes, I've thought about it. No, I've dismissed the thought almost immediately. I can't marry a man who has an insatiable need to control. I've smelled the coffee and I enjoy my life. It remains to be seen if the crystal ball has Victor or some other man in it."

"This conversation has become a bit too deep for me. Let's order a pizza and talk about something simple. I know—we need to discuss if I should invest some $40,000 of my hard-earned money to put a branch of Island Elegant on this ship."

The ladies indulged in a large pepperoni pizza on top of their sundaes while they engaged in shoptalk. When stuffed, Elin pushed Charlie around the promenade six times before they headed for the elevators. "I needed to exercise so I wouldn't end up with heartburn. Maybe we should have had the pizza first followed by the ice cream."

That's the kind of workout I like, Ms. Charlie. We get to sit and Elin gets to push.

Me too.

* * *

Good ole Alice stayed planted on her bench until the ladies headed for the elevators. She was right behind them as the doors slid open. Charlie punched level nine. "Oh, nine is my deck, too," Alice said. The security guard took another elevator and punched nine.

Charlie glanced at the woman in the elevator. "You have an incredibly beautiful sapphire pendant. I somehow think its brand new it's so shiny."

"My husband picked it up for me in St. Martin. I was delighted."

Charlie teeheed as she responded, "Well I need a husband with a taste in jewelry like yours."

The ladies left the elevator and Charlie and Elin barreled away in one direction and the lady in the opposite. Alice stopped and adjusted her sandals so she was able to note which stateroom door they opened. The guard watched Alice watch Charlie.

* * *

The next morning, Jeremy was in a better frame of mind about the marina but his mother's predicament worried him. He had called his brothers and told them. Jason shook his head and wondered how his mother managed to get into trouble again. Jake wondered why only their mother could meet so many murderers face to face in the course of three months. Both brothers agreed to fly to St. Croix or to Miami if the situation got worse.

After the calls, Jeremy picked up the Chief and drove him to the marina. The Chief had the double murder books with him and had agreed to sit on the dock with Jeremy's cell in case he received a call.

Jeremy donned his diving gear and went under to inspect the remaining pilings while Victor studied the police reports. The man who owned the *Columbus* was named Roy Stevens. His address on the boat's registration was a suburb of San Juan. The Puerto Rico police reported he hadn't lived there since 2006.

The *Columbus* was a fifty-eight footer designed for sport fishermen. It was built in 2005 and had twin Caterpillar diesel engines. It was meant for some serious deep-sea fishing and it cost a bundle.

Benny, the same sketch artist who had worked with Charlie, took the ferry to St. Croix to work with Gil. The sketch of Stevens was detailed: dark skin, forty something, short black hair, brown eyes and mustache. Gil decided it was his civic duty to draw a head-to-toe version. Roy weighed around two-ten, height about six feet, sizable pot and his left leg was slightly shorter than the right.

Benny's drawing of the second man, Chuck, was equally detailed thanks to the marina's owner. Gil's full-length sketch showed the man was about five feet ten, around forty years old, weighed one-sixty, medium-dark skin and short hair. When the artist returned to Charlotte Amalie, the VIPD put out an All Points Bulletin to police departments stateside as well as all the neighboring islands.

Bob had updated the murder books. He noted that Stevens had invited Gil to fish on the yacht several times and Gil had said the men were sloppy and didn't keep the craft clean or scrubbed. Gil had stated that the men had trouble with the navigational system and he needed to explain it to them several times. Twice they beached the fishing yacht on an offshore sandbar because they paid no attention to the dials of the depth finder. The Chief wondered how these landlubbers ended up owning a fishing charter service.

The Chief called the coroner's office. The body in the ice chest had been removed and the remains and the clothing were under examination. The coroner wasn't ready to offer a guess about the time of death. The ice chest itself was dusted for prints and there were two different sets. Bob put the prints through the FBI's AIFIS system, an electronic program used to identify fingerprints. There were no matches.

Jeremy surfaced. "There are at least two bad pilings so I'm going to recheck everything. Any calls?"

"No calls, son."

"Do you have time for me to go under again?"

"Take your time and do the job right."

CHAPTER TWENTY-THREE

Dyrby entered Hansen's office. "Captain, Seaman Tier observed Mrs. Bladensburg get off the lift with the Mikkelsen ladies. She went in the opposite direction down the hall but stopped to adjust her shoe as she watched which stateroom the ladies entered. She walked to the end of the hall and circled back to the lifts."

"I don't believe the VIPD will like that."

"Sir, I don't have the staff to cover the ladies plus the two men and their wives if they should split up."

"What are your recommendations, Dyrby?"

"Keep Tier on the ladies. Have Seaman Fog monitor Bladensburg and Ambrose over the security monitors. I will speak with the ladies about Tier."

"Are Tier and Fog former military?"

"Yes, sir."

"You want your men armed. These suspects will figure out soon enough the ladies are under our protection. That might dampen their enthusiasm if they are in the mood to murder. Accompany the ladies to dinner tonight and I'll dine with you. Tell the Mikkelsen ladies to stay together when they leave the stateroom. No separate visits to the ladies room. All three of you watch yourselves and be aware of your surroundings."

"Yes, sir. Captain, I have another suggestion. During dinner tonight, may I make arrangements to move passengers from the rooms surrounding the Bladensburg-Ambrose staterooms? This way we can allow the police to arrest the suspects and not put any passengers in danger."

"Excellent suggestion."

Dyrby left the captain and called the maitre-d' to make dinner arrangements. He headed toward the Mikkelsen suite and brought Tier up to date. He told Tier to leave his station and get his weapon while he was with the ladies. He rapped on the door.

Elin checked the peephole before she invited Dyrby inside. He sat on a sofa amidst a ton of papers neatly stacked. Elin's rack of clothing was covered in a white sheet and sat in the corner. Charlie stopped her marketing analysis and both ladies gave Borge Dyrby their full attention. Neither liked what they heard.

* * *

Chamaign, Man and Larson sat around the table. They had a plan and it needed to be blessed by James and Andre. A conference call was arranged and the Chief was included as a courtesy.

The detectives would fly to the Coast Guard Air Station in Miami on Saturday afternoon and after midnight they would take a Coast Guard cutter to the ship so they could board early in the morning. They would have Dyrby lead them to both staterooms and arrange entry as soon as they were in U.S. territory.

"You need more manpower," James insisted. "These guys can kill with one arm."

"Bob Thompson can go with us," Chamaign said. "May we request that the ship's security accompany us when we head for the brig? There should be someone at both ends of the hallway in case a drunk totters down. Then after the ship docks and the passengers leave, we can ask the Coast Guard to escort us from the brig to a plane for the return flight."

"That's fine," Andre said, "but what about their wives? They have to be involved in these crimes, too."

"I agree, sir. We need to speak with Dyrby to ensure we can do this. May we go ahead?"

"It's fine with me," James said, "but I want you to work out every potential contingency that can occur and have a plan to deal with each."

"I second that," Andre said.

"Man and Chamaign," Victor added. "Have the security officer send you a layout of the ship. It will help you to visualize what you need to do."

Andre said, "James, I'll notify my Chief. Do you want me to update your boss?"

"Thanks. The two of them can go see the Commissioner together. Chamaign, would you see if you can arrange a call tonight with Elin?"

"Will do."

"Both Jeremy and I would also like to talk to Charlie," the Chief said.

* * *

The sun was low when Jeremy surfaced. "There are a few other pilings in need of attention."

"You know you can always have a new piling set next to the old one so you don't have to tear the pier apart."

"I have to get this on paper while I remember it and I'll get several bids to replace the pilings or else double up."

As the men were about to leave, Gil's outboard putted into the marina. He tied his rope to the piling and climbed up the ladder. "Hi young fella, what did you find down there?"

"At least three pilings need attention before the next hurricane season."

"I can have it done or we can adjust the price. Let me pull the papers from the last time. I'm sure the cost has gone up."

"Gil, you did a good job with the sketch artist," the Chief remarked.

"Thank ya. Find the boat yet?"

"The fishing boat hasn't been seen."

"That's a fancy fishing boat, Chief. It's a fisherman's dream. We have a better grade clientele at this marina," Gil boasted.

Jeremy said, "I don't even have a boat anymore, Gil. Do have a three-person Kawasaki Jet Ski. I'm in a ski club and I spend a good bit of time on the Susquehanna River."

"Never been on a jet ski," the Chief said, "Your mom rides the skis?"

"My mom tries everything at least once—even opens up crypts in cemeteries in the middle of the night during a raging storm."

Aghast, Gil asked, "Was it your mom who saved those Mikkelsen ladies last January?"

"Yep."

"Did she really bound that Clint Spell creep with duct tape and use a crowbar on his hands so he would tell her where he buried Miss Elin and her mother?"

"That's my mom, Gil."

"Isn't she supposed to testify at the trial soon?"

"Yep."

"Ohmagosh! Could you git her autograph fer me?" Gil's adrenaline rush caused him to slap his thighs repeatedly out of sheer excitement.

"At the moment she's after two murder suspects."

"Holy moley! You're mom's already famous. And now she's after some more of those bad guys. She's gonna be even more famous. I've gotta git her autograph. Can ya do that fer me, young fella?"

"First I want to get my mom back in one piece and alive, Gil. Then I'll get her autograph for you. Maybe you can trade one of your sketches for an autograph."

"A sketch? I kinda save my sketches. I tell ya what I'll do. I'll do a special one fer her. What do ya think she'll like?"

"How bout a scene of the harbor?"

"Harbor it will be. When she gets back here, do you think I can meet her?" Gil continued to slap his thighs with his hands.

"Sure. I'll introduce you. She'll want to see all your artwork, too, so be prepared."

"You help me git the autograph and I'll reduce the price of the marina a wee bit more. After all, your mom is famous."

* * *

"Captain, I spoke to Man Carmen, the detective from St. Thomas. They wish to board the ship during the night and arrest the suspects early Sunday morning. The Coast Guard will transport them."

"Dyrby, I want this very clear. Your staff will assist as little as possible. Correct?"

"Correct. They've requested a layout of the ship and I emailed it."

"Did you tell the ladies everything?"

"Everything. May I suggest one more thing, captain? I'd like to move the Mikkelsen ladies to another stateroom on another deck since the men know their current location."

"I still want an armed man to shadow them at all times—day and night," the captain replied.

"Absolutely. May I put the Mikkelsens under assumed names?"

"Make that a need-to-know basis only."

"Absolutely. There is one other thing," Dyrby said. "Both ladies wish to speak with their gentlemen friends this evening. One is a deputy police chief and the other is a retired deputy police chief. I believe Ms. Charlie wishes to speak with her son also."

"Fine. Keep the call short."

* * *

"The doc says I can leave the hospital Saturday, mother. I'll fly to Ft. Lauderdale to meet Elin and the Chief and Jeremy will probably go with me."

"I wish you'd come home with me to get better. You need some meat on your bones."

"I promised Elin I'd be there for her. Now, mother, let's discuss the chemo."

"My decision is made. I'm ready to join your father. I've had a full life and I am so proud of you and my grandsons."

"I'm not ready to have you go."

"It is neither your decision nor is it mine. Chemo or no chemo, I will not die one day sooner than the good Lord planned."

"But, mother…"

"James, this is why they call it faith. I'm at peace with myself. Trust me. Your mother knows best."

"As soon as I see Elin I will propose."

"Oh sweetie, that would make me so happy. I know she'll look after you."

"I want us to be married before…"

"No, son. Your woman deserves to have a lovely wedding and lovely weddings take time to plan. If I'm here, I'm here. If I'm not, I'll watch from above. Don't worry. I'll not miss your wedding."

CHAPTER TWENTY-FOUR

Ohmagosh, Ms. Charlie. Look at this stateroom. It's plusher than our last.

I don't know why we need a fifty-two inch flat-screen television. The only thing on it is COX News International and replays of the ship's entertainment from the night before.

"Charlie, I don't believe this room," Elin said. "My furniture at home isn't this plush."

"You don't hear any complaints from me, do you?"

"At least those men and their wives don't know where our stateroom is anymore. My anxiety level is down by seventeen points."

"Other than dinner tonight and our meeting tomorrow," Charlie said, "I don't want my butt to budge from here. We'll let security escort us to and from our meals."

"I agree completely. Now if you would excuse me, I need to freshen up."

Look at your bedroom, Ms. Charlie. You've got a king-size bed. You know, that bed is big enough for you and a man the size of the Chief.

Your imagination is too active today. Here my life is in danger and what do you do—fantasize about my love life.

You should try a little fantasy sometime—if you haven't already, that is.

Well, you stay out of my fantasies. They are none of your business and there will be no thrusting pelvises in this novel.

You think we are in danger, don't you, Ms. Charlie?

We could be but the security team will keep an eye on us.

You won't play a mystery novel heroine and get me killed, will you?

Well, if you die, I'll go with you, okay?

Charlie and Elin joined each other and decided to go through the rack of clothing and decide what they would wear to dinner. Elin chose a sequined red strapless gown—a slinky silk crepe with a straight skirt and a slit up the left side to above the knee.

"I believe Mae West would approve of all that bling," Charlie whooped.

"Think so? Too bad I'm not endowed the way she was."

"You don't need any more up top. You already have that come-up-and-see-me-look the way you are."

"What will you wear, Charlie?"

"How about this aqua gown with the net top. I could wear the faux fur aqua-dyed boa."

"You'd look good in that color and the long skirt would cover your boot."

Charlie returned to her room and took a shower. She dressed and went into the head to apply her makeup.

Work a little harder to cover those age spots. If I'm going to end up dead, I want to look good.

Shush. You're not going to end up dead.

Well if you put your lip liner on correctly this time, I'll shut up.

Charlie finished her makeup.

Does this suit you?

I'd say you look pretty good, Ms. Charlie. I'm definitely aging more gracefully than you.

That doesn't compute. How can you age more gracefully?

Simple, I don't have as many chin hairs as you do.

Elin knocked on Charlie's half-open door. "Cousin, you're gorgeous. No wonder the Chief is so fixated on you. He can't resist your sex appeal."

"Well, he's sorta gorgeous, too, but I can resist. Or at least I have so far. I wouldn't mind if he was here right now with those murderers out there."

"I wish James was here, too."

"Elin, James is of no use to us if he holds his stomach in one hand while he tries to shoot with the other. Besides, Bob Thompson said

Chamaign is the champion sharpshooter of the whole VIPD. We need her."

"Charlie, with all the cruise ships passing through our ports, how did we pick a ship that had two murderers aboard?"

"Luck, I guess."

"Luck? I don't think so. But I do know this—I'm freaked and afraid for my own life. It won't take too much to push me over the edge."

"You're a strong woman, Elin. We both need to be strong right now."

"I hate that strong woman caca, Charlie. I don't want to be strong anymore. Strong almost got me killed once. I want James to be strong for me."

"We all want to have someone to lean on once in a while. That's human nature, but you're not the broken-wing type, Elin. Your strength will prevail whether you like it or not."

"And you know this how?"

"Us birds of a feather will flock together for dinner tonight."

* * *

Officer Dyrby knocked on the door and identified himself. Elin answered. His eyes popped wide when he saw Elin in her scintillating scarlet dress.

Dyrby stood tall and straight—a good six feet four inches. His beautiful Norwegian blond hair was combed smartly back and his robin's egg blue eyes sparkled. His white uniform with shiny brass buttons didn't hurt the overall effect, either. Charlie decided she wanted to be the Queen of Sweden.

Oh Ms. Charlie, I told you before I want him, too.

Elin and I have first dibs.

Officer Dyrby pushed Charlie's wheelchair and both cousins tried hard not to giggle as they were escorted to the main dining room.

* * *

"Okay, all arrangements are made with the Coast Guard down to the smallest detail," Man said. "Larson, any questions?"

"I've reviewed the recommended route from the staterooms to the brig. We have to move past a corridor with a bank of elevators. We pass them and go to the next bank. Right?"

"Right. The men must be cuffed in the staterooms," Man said. "We take one man down the elevator at a time. One man; two officers. We need our hand-held radios to coordinate this."

"What about the wives?" Chamaign asked Man.

"They must be handcuffed, too. We'll leave Bob in the room with the women and ask Dyrby's crew to accompany us. His crew will not be put in any danger. When the men are behind bars, we'll go back for the women. There is a place for all four of us to stay near the brig. At least two of us must be on guard at all times."

"Chamaign, what about the flight back here?" Larson asked. "Did you get the VIPD to approve a private flight?"

"I used my feminine charm to talk Chief Farrow into that."

"Okay, are we done?" Man asked. There were two nods. "Chamaign, would you use your feminine charm to email the plan to our bosses?"

"Not a problem, Man. Now get me a cup of hot coffee, one packet of Splenda, no cream and two donuts."

CHAPTER TWENTY-FIVE

Karita Lind and Captain Hansen watched the security monitors as they followed Elin and Charlie on their way to the dining hall. They wanted to see if the ladies' garments attracted any attention.

"Oh my, did you see what I just saw, captain? The woman in green almost broke her neck she twisted it so far to watch our ladies."

"I was watching the expression on the husband's face," the captain said. "What's the term used in American commercials? Ah yes, 'priceless.' Fits, doesn't it?"

"Do you think it is Elin's figure or the outfit?"

"For the good wife—it is those red sequins. For the good husband, it is her figure, the neckline, the slit in the skirt and the legs."

The seaman clicked on the screen at the lift. Karita said, "Look at the lady to the far side of Charlie. Watch her pet the boa like it is alive. I don't believe this—the other lady wants to feel it, too. And her friend is part of the conversation."

"The older ladies seem to feel free to speak to Charlie—is that because she's older or because she's in a wheelchair?" the captain inquired.

"I'm not sure. I do know the older ladies on our cruises have substantial discretionary income. If an Island Elegant shop were open right now, I'd bet they would head down after dinner. The younger Ms. Mikkelsen is getting her share of attention, too. Watch those women to her right."

"To be honest, Ms. Lind, it's more fun to watch the men peek down her dress and then step back and examine her derriere."

"Captain, I feel an Island Elegant shop would enhance our promenade."

"I think I need to put off my retirement plans and apply for the captain position on a our new flagship, *Aqua Dreams*. If I got the job I could see that Island Elegant would have a larger shop and I'd have a lot more scenery to watch."

"Those two make quite a combination," Karita said.

"Well, don't lose the contract. They could go to a competitor, you know." As the captain headed out the door, he paused. "I can't believe how much attention these women attract."

* * *

As Dyrby rolled Charlie out of the lift, Chrissie Robinson's grandson rolled her out of another one. Her dress was a light turquoise with a print of silver swirls across the bodice. The women stopped again and chatted. After a few pleasantries, each went their way.

The captain arrived at his table as the Mikkelsens were seated. Charlie sat to the captain's right and Elin was seated to Dyrby's right. Also seated at the table were a state senator and his wife, a gray-haired doctor and his twenty-something blonde barbie, and a lady judge and her veterinarian husband.

Ms. Charlie, blondie is half the doctor's age.
Shush, don't stare. Be polite.
I bet he has a daughter older than her.
Stop being catty. I can't take you anywhere.
I bet he traded his first wife in for her.
And I bet he has a supply of those little blue pills, too.
Now who's being catty, Ms. Charlie?

"Ms. Charlie, you're smiling so the wine must be good," Dyrby said.

"The wine is excellent. Thank you for your recommendation."

"It's absolutely divine," the young blonde said in a breathy Marilyn Monroe imitation.

The captain leaned over and whispered in Charlie's ear, "And the wine is older than she is."

Charlie smiled and was surprised and pleased with the captain's sense of humor.

As dinner came to an end, the captain again whispered to Charlie, "Don't tell anyone, but when I took my grandchildren to Disney World, I bought myself a Mickey Mouse watch."

"Do you wear it, captain?"

"Not since my grandchildren have grown up but you've inspired me. That must be Pocahontas on your wrist?"

"No, Princess Summerfall Winterspring. My Indian princess was on television back in the fifties. I found the watch in a yard sale a few years back and haven't been without it since."

"Well, I like the fact I can read the numbers on the dial without my glasses," the captain confessed.

"It is nice to be able to tell time without the aid of the Hubble telescope, isn't it?"

What a dreamboat he is. Ms. Charlie, I love a handsome rugged man with classy brass on his chest.

I was about to say the same thing. Now evaporate so I can continue me private tête-à-tête with our handsome rugged captain.

* * *

Alice Bladensburg spotted Charlie and Elin as they were seated. "Al, how come they get escorted to the dining hall and are seated with the captain? I haven't noticed anyone in uniform offer me his arm."

"Shut up, Alice. If you had a shape like that foxy chick in red, I'd go out and rent a white uniform myself to get your attention."

Julia Ambrose sneered and turned to her husband. "Jerome, I'd kill for the fox boa."

He smirked, "You don't have to, darling, I'll do it for you."

* * *

Much to the captain's pleasure, Charlie and Elin were animated and buoyant and included all the guests in the conversation. At one point,

Elin explained how Charlie and she were related and how their family became biracial in the late 1800's. The story generated a number of questions the ladies answered with grace and charm.

The captain smiled when Charlie ordered a Cruzan Cream as her after dinner drink. "I enjoy a dinner guest with such impeccable taste. We seem to have a number of things in common. Perhaps you would like to visit the bridge tomorrow, Miss Charlie. Miss Elin also, of course."

"We would be honored. Thank you."

"And perhaps you would be my guest at our private dining room tomorrow. Dinner for two?"

"Dinner for two. Sounds good. And thank you again."

Shame on you, Ms. Charlie. What would the Chief say?

He can't say anything because he doesn't know anything now does he?

He'll find out.

No he won't or you're history.

After the five-course meal, Dyrby escorted the ladies to the communication room. Elin called James and they gushed for a few minutes. Her mood and tone changed when James told her about his mother's illness. Elin promised they would have some serious discussions on Sunday when she returned home. She left the room and sat down in the lounge and held back her tears.

Charlie talked to Jeremy and he gave her a brief overview of the marina and told her he was close to a commitment. She suggested he look for small houses until she returned. When questioned about the murder suspects, she assured her son how fastidiously she was guarded. She told him not to call his brothers and worry them. Jeremy admitted he already had.

Charlie repeated the same message to the Chief except Victor was only interested in her safety. Charlie reminded him she would see him on Sunday.

"Charlie, I must tell you something. There is no way to say this but to say it." Victor took a deep breath, "Charlie, I love you."

For the first time in a long time, Charlie was speechless. After a few seconds of silence she regrouped. "I don't know what to say, Victor. I hadn't anticipated this. We need to talk this out. Really talk. You're a couple of steps ahead of me."

"I'm a patient man, you'll see. I love you, Charlie. I'm a very different person from the man you first met and I'll prove it to you."

Before she hung up, Charlie promised she would give their relationship some serious thought.

Oh my, my, my, missy. What have you got yourself into now? And here you're having a private dinner with the captain. Shame.

Shush.

And you know what else—you've have a smile on your face.

Do not.

Do too. Those small lines around your eyes are all crinkled. Your eyes twinkle, too.

Do not.

Admit it, Ms. Charlie. You're pleased with yourself.

Maybe a little bit, but you're jealous. Now go away.

Security Chief Dyrby gallantly escorted the ladies back to their stateroom and bid them adieu.

* * *

After dinner, the Bladensburgs and Ambroses found a small lounge and deposited themselves on two leather sofas. A waitress in a skimpy tropical print sarong appeared and took their drink order. After the drinks were served, the four assessed their situation.

"Those bimbos know something but I can't figure out what," Al said.

"Since we don't know anything for sure, let's not worry about it, honey."

"Alice, if I end up in jail, you end up in jail. I think you should worry a bit since you're the dingdong who planned this whole thing."

"This is so stupid. The old hag saw you at the airport and the younger one sold you two shirts. What else is there for them to know?"

"They can place me on the island when the murder was committed."

"You and how many other people," Alice argued.

"But the old dame kissed the cop at the airport, remember?" Jerome said.

Al replied, "The cop would have known about the murder—that's for sure. If he connected the dead woman to the jewelry business and the broad connected me with the jewelry display case, then the cop could have added two and two together. Then if he checked the airport security videos, he could verify it was me with the display case."

"Then we all end up in jail," Julie said.

"But what doesn't make sense is why the cop would put the women on the ship with us. That's why I don't think they know about us," Al said.

"Maybe they are bait. Maybe the cop is onboard," Jerome said.

Julie scolded her husband. "Cops don't use old ladies in wheelchairs as bait, stupid."

"The day I watched them on the promenade," Alice said, "they first went to visit the jewelry store and spoke for a long time with the manager. They weren't there to look at jewelry, either."

"When I saw them," Al said, "the younger one had a key to an empty store on the promenade. They went in and looked around. She even measured everything and they talked for a long time. What was the name of the shop where I bought our matching shirts on St. Croix?"

"Island Elegant Apparel."

"That's the answer. They're here to rent or lease the empty shop. I bet the younger floozy was the owner of the store and not a saleslady and I bet she has plans to expand. That explains why the ship's officers have singled out the women for so much attention."

"And also why both women are dressed fit to kill," Alice said. "That was a rather clever play on words, wouldn't you say, Al?"

Jerome was too deep in thought to understand Alice's humor. "Now what about the cop?" he said.

"I don't remember what the cop looked like," Al remarked.

"Al, if the ship's officers have fingered us," Jerome replied, "they would have arrested us. Right? Maybe neither the cop nor the ship's officers know what we've done."

It was Alice who offered the ultimate solution to everything. "It doesn't matter why the women are here. If these two are the only people who can place you on the island, what does it matter if you kill two more people?"

"Bright, Alice. Two dead bodies found on ship," Jerome said. "Don't you think someone would notice?"

"This isn't difficult," Alice said. "We get the two after dark, crack their necks and dump the bodies overboard. If there are no bodies to find, no one will know they are gone until someone goes to clean their room after the cruise. By then we'll be in our rented car headed for Jersey. The sharks will take care of the bodies and **voilà**, there isn't anyone to testify."

"Then we have to find them either tonight or tomorrow night," Al said. "Let's split up now. Jerome, you and Julie be a team and Alice and I will be one. We'll meet back in our rooms."

"Sounds good," Jerome said. "What's our plan after we locate them, Al? We had our other murder plans down to a science and everything went off without a hitch."

"We have to make this one up as we go along. If we have an opening, we'll take it. You do the same."

"Make sure to separate the women," Alice said.

"That's why you stay with me and Julie stays with Jerome," Al said.

Alice smirked. "I hope it's you, honey. I want to hear those necks crack."

The couples split to see if they could locate Charlie and Elin.

* * *

"Let's go over this again," Chamaign said. "Larson, I've worked with Bob Thompson and Man has worked with Ben Shore. We will be the two teams. Man and Ben will take the Ambrose room and Bob and I will take the Bladensburg room. Larson, you stay in the hall is case someone tries to get away and you have to keep the ship's crew off to the side."

Man had enlarged the blueprint of the ship's layout and made everyone copies. It showed the outline and furniture layout in the staterooms. "These people have nowhere to go except onto the balcony.

I guess if they want to jump from seven floors up we'll be happy to let them do it."

"Seven decks up, Man," Chamaign teased. "Don't forget, they can try to get to their friends through the adjoining door."

"That's why Larson has to play it by ear," Man said. "We also have to consider the bathroom. One of them can be in there."

Chamaign corrected Man. "Head."

"Head? Okay, okay. Head. I'm the only man in the Caribbean who doesn't have his own boat."

"We could listen outside the room for a few minutes," Larson said. "If they are in the head we should hear them."

"Guys," Man said. "What if the boat's crew used 'port' and 'starboard' instead of 'left' and 'right,' I'm in trouble. I grew up in the middle of a slum and we had rafts, not boats."

"Marlboro Man, port means left and starboard means right. It's simple. Do you know the difference between bow and stern, forward and aft, hotshot?"

"I might be short but I'm not dumb. I saw *Titanic*, too, you know. On what side of the boat are these staterooms located?"

An amused Chamaign pointed to the staterooms on the layout. "First, this is a ship, not a boat. Now, you answer your own question—on which side of the ship are these staterooms?"

"Port?"

"Good. Now show me the brig?"

Man located the brig. "Chamaign, you do understand I'm dyslectic, don't you?"

"You better not be dyslectic Sunday morning," Larson howled.

CHAPTER TWENTY-SIX

Before Dyrby left Charlie and Elin, the women assured the handsome young man they were in for the night and had work to do. Seaman Tier took over the watch dressed as a steward. He fussed around in the supply cabinet while the real steward hovered nearby.

Dyrby headed to the security office. Seaman Fog, seated in front of the main security monitor, watched the Bladensburgs walk the promenade. "They have walked around for the last hour. They've been down the Mikkelsen's old hallway, the gaming room, two bars, the sushi bar and now the promenade."

"What about the other couple?"

"The four suspects left the dining hall together. They sat in the lounge opposite the Mama Bahama Bar. They were there for over a half hour with their heads together in conversation. They broke into couples and headed in opposite directions. I haven't been able to look for the Ambroses because the Bladensburgs are in some sort of marathon race."

"Seaman Fander, power up the other PC and start a search for Jerome Ambrose and his wife," Dyrby said. "I'm headed for my quarters. Call if you see anything suspicious or if either couple goes anywhere near the ladies' new stateroom. The women assured me they are in for the night."

* * *

"I suppose you heard what I told your mother, Jeremy."

Jeremy didn't reply.

"What do you think?" the Chief asked.

"I don't know what I think."

"How do you feel about your mother and me?"

"I don't know how I feel."

"Do you want your mother to be happy?"

"Of course I want my mother to be happy but don't put it like what I think is important. This is not about how I feel, *Victor*. This is about how my mother feels and I don't see my mother doing cartwheels." Jeremy's voice rose two octaves higher than normal.

"Calm down, now. Calm down. How you feel is important—it is important to me and it is important to your mother."

"My mother makes her own decisions and doesn't consult my brothers or me."

"But you mother cares about what you think, doesn't she?"

"My brothers and I would say something only if we thought she was making a mistake."

"Jeremy, I have my own money and a good pension. I'm not interested in what your mother may or may not have in the bank."

Jeremy didn't respond.

"Does it bother you that I'm black?"

"Does it bother your children that my mother is white?"

"Touché. I can't answer your question because I haven't discussed this with my kids. They do know how I feel from the Internet picture."

"Here are some facts as I see them, Victor: You've only known my mother for a couple of months. My mother has been in serious danger both times she has come to the Caribbean. The two of you live over 1,000 miles from each other. And last but not least, you push too hard."

"That's quite a list and you're right on all points, Jeremy."

"Victor, why don't you give her some time?"

"I know you're right."

"Well then, back off a bit. Slow down a little. Let things fall in place."

* * *

Once in her bedroom, Charlie undressed and hung her gown with care. She knew it was a type of garment she could afford to buy maybe once a year. She used her crutches to get to the head where she removed her makeup.

Ms. Charlie, have you thought more about what the Chief said?

Do you see a smile on my face?

Has reality set in?

Fraid so.

Do you like the Chief?

In many different ways.

What if the Chief mentions the M word, missy?

Right now, I'd be angry if he did. I'm not ready for the M word. Crap. I barely know the man—what's it been? Twelve weeks? I'm upset because he used the L word.

Ms. Charlie, may I remind you you're not getting any younger. How many more times will love come along.

Maybe that's the problem—maybe I'm still waiting.

* * *

Elin was in her own room and occupied with her own thoughts. She knew she was in love with James, but she had made such a bad choice with Fred Willard she was afraid of a repeat performance. She thought about how clueless she was when she had married him. The thought that he became involved in drugs and murder was so hard to believe. She wondered if the cruel streak was in him when they were married.

Elin compared Fred Willard with James and decided there was no comparison. James was a respected law-abiding officer. His recent promotion proved it. They had already discussed his marriage to Corrine, and Elin remembered how his eyes welled with tears as he spoke of her death and how it impacted their sons. And now there was Grace's decision to not fight this hideous disease.

* * *

Elin and Charlie ended up in the center salon of their stateroom. "How much work is left on the marketing proposal?" Elin asked.

"Only the executive summary. It's all broken down into target markets based on the information provided. We'll be ready for out meeting with Karita tomorrow. How does everything look to you?"

"Good. Even in a worse case scenario. If my line of clothing is too expensive, I can always switch to a less expensive line."

"It sounds to me like you've made up your mind."

Elin nodded. "Can we put shoptalk aside for a few minutes? I need to tell you something and I need your advice."

"Will this conversation require a Cruzan Mango Rum with Diet Pepsi?"

"Make mine a double." Charlie called the bar and ordered drinks.

"Charlie, tell me everything you know about James."

"What an nice question. I adore him. I've learned he's honest, reliable and caring. He has a delightful sense of humor and he can let out a good belly laugh when it's appropriate. The night everyone searched for you and your mother, he used both logic and common sense to make his decisions. Bob Thompson and Paul Simpson respect him and Chamaign thinks he's God's gift from heaven."

"James said you wanted to introduce us. Is this true?"

"Yep."

"Do you think James is ready for marriage?"

"No question about it. Believe me, he already had his eye on you when I said something. I didn't have to badger him to ask you out."

Elin told Charlie about Grace.

"She is a very strong and determined woman. Now that James has you to fuss over him, maybe Grace feels she can die in peace."

"I know it would make her happy if we would get married soon."

"Marriage—is that what has you upset?" Charlie asked.

"I don't want to make another mistake."

"You didn't make the mistake. Fred did. He chose to betray you while you were married; he chose to get involved in drugs; he chose to murder a man and have Spell dispose of you and your mother. It wasn't your mistake. You know there are no guarantees in any marriage, Elin. Both parties have to work at it. Be sure to do only what makes you comfortable."

Charlie returned to the laptop and Elin went to her bedroom to clear her mind.

Ms. Charlie, you didn't tell Elin about the Chief.

It didn't seem appropriate. I need to follow my own advice and do what makes me comfortable.

And what is that?

Nothing, I think.

* * *

Al and Alice Bladensburg walked all the public decks on the ship a second time. They walked the outside decks even though it was chilly and windy as the ship headed north. Seaman Fog followed them on the security cameras. Finally, they gave up, found an elevator and headed back to their own stateroom.

Seaman Fander wasn't so lucky. He couldn't locate the Ambroses on camera. What he didn't know was Jerome and Julie stopped by their stateroom and changed from dress clothes into jeans and tees. They both carried a lightweight baseball jacket with a cap in the pocket in case they had to go outside.

The couple spent more than an hour and a half as they strolled the various decks. They spotted their mark outside the Galaxy Theatre. A young steward pushed a woman in a wheelchair toward her stateroom. Jerome and Julie followed them from a safe distance.

"Where's the young broad?" Julie asked.

"I don't know. We'll get this crone in her room. It's so dark and cold outside no passengers will be out on their balconies when we dump her so the timing is perfect. The old witch is the one we want the most anyway and we can get the sexpot later. Now listen, there are security cameras all over this place. When we get near the elevators keep your head down. Don't use my name and it's better not to speak at all. Put your jacket and hat on and pull the collar up. Pretend you came in from outside and shiver a little bit. And make sure you don't touch anything once we're in the room."

When the woman in the wheelchair and her steward entered the elevator, the Ambroses stepped in behind them. They exited on the eighth floor. Julie whispered, "Jerome, I thought the women were on the ninth floor."

"Al made a mistake. We have her, Julie. Head down, remember?"

"What about the steward, Al?"

"He'll go overboard, too. There are two security cameras ahead of us so keep your head down. I'll take care of the steward and pull him aside. You have your scarf ready and slip past me. Pull the scarf tight around the old hag's neck so she can't scream. Push her to the balcony if you can. Sit on her if necessary but don't let her scream. Don't say a word, okay? Not a word."

The Ambroses slowed their pace and arrived when the young man opened the stateroom door. Jerome waited for the steward to push the woman inside. Before the door shut closed, he entered and the young man sensed his presence—two seconds too late.

Jerome got the grip he wanted. There was a horrifying loud crack and the man's arms fell to his side as he crumbled into a heap on the floor. The older woman tried to turn her arthritic neck enough to see what happened. She couldn't. Julie slipped the scarf around her neck.

The woman grabbed at the scarf and tried to scream.

Julie's anger erupted. "You ole witch. You're about to get what you deserve."

"Shut up," Jerome reminded her.

Jerome dragged the man's body to the balcony, opened the sliding door and picked up the body. "Bon voyage, stupid." The lifeless body fell eight decks into the black night waters. The roar of the ocean was all that was needed to cover the sound of the splash. The woman gasped in horror.

"Jerome, hurry. This ole crone tried to scratch me."

It was over in a nanosecond. Julie slid the scarf from the broken neck and stuffed it into the pocket of her jeans. Jerome pushed the dead woman's wheelchair onto the balcony and lifted her body up and over the railing.

"Kaput!" he said as he winked at Julie.

"What about the wheelchair?"

"That's gotta go, too." Jerome's strong forearms easily lifted the heavy-duty chair up and over. "Congratulations, little wife, we did good."

Jerome opened the stateroom door an inch and listened for footsteps. Hearing none, he and Julie left with their heads down. They found a side stairwell and descended one deck with their faces lowered. Jerome found a small hallway leading to an emergency exit. It had no security cameras. He pushed Julie in the hall and they removed their jackets and hats. They headed for their stateroom with heads held high. Once safely inside, they pitched their jackets, caps, jeans and tees overboard.

"I want to see the look on Al's face when I tell him what we accomplished," Jerome smirked. With shoulders back and chest out he knocked on the interior door between the staterooms. Alice answered and let them in.

"One bitch down and the cutie-pie to go."

"Meaning?" Alice asked.

"We got the ole hag in the wheelchair. Overboard. There was a steward with her and he's shark food, too."

"What about the other one?" Al asked.

"We'll have to walk around some more tonight. Once we spot her, she'll be history."

"I want her dead, but it was the cop-kissing broad I worried about the most," Al said.

"And if we don't find the other woman tonight?" Alice asked.

"It doesn't matter," Julie replied.

"Why not? Won't the women miss her friend and report it to security?" Al asked.

"The way she honeyed up to the captain, the young woman will think her friend is with him for the evening."

"Well congratulations, you two," Alice said. "I hoped you grabbed the fox boa as a souvenir."

"What in blazes is a boa?" Jerome asked. "It's not a live snake, I assume."

"It's a wrap," Julie said. "You put it around your neck or your shoulders. She had it on at dinner and I pointed it out to you."

"Is that what you told me you wanted?"

Julie glanced at Alice and lowered her head. "I didn't think about the boa. She didn't have it on."

"What happened to it?" Jerome asked.

Al stood and started to pace. "Tell me you got the right broad in the wheelchair. There are two old biddies on this ship who have wheelchairs and they both have gray hair and a boot on their leg."

"Did we get the wrong one, Alice?" Jerome asked.

"I'm not sure now."

Al asked, "Where did this action take place?"

"In the broad's stateroom," Jerome answered.

"And where was this stateroom?"

"I don't know the room number but it was on the eighth deck."

"You two are stupid beyond belief. Jerome, I told you the stateroom was on the ninth deck. You killed the wrong broad."

CHAPTER TWENTY-SEVEN

It was a little after midnight when the phone rang in Dyrby's small but meticulously clean quarters. He forced his tired body out of its bunk.

"Officer Dyrby, this is Fog. There is a Mr. & Mrs. Robertson here. They say their mother and son are not in their staterooms. I'm very concerned—the mother is an older woman in a wheelchair."

"And this has nothing to do with our Miss Mikkelsen, right?"

"I'm not sure, sir, and I don't wish to jump to conclusions. She has a broken ankle and wears a black boot."

"I don't think this is a coincidence, Fog. I'll be right up. Put the Robertson family in our meeting room. Tell Fander to stay on the monitors. I need you to go check the Robertson stateroom. Approach it like a crime scene and wear gloves. Start to take pictures for me."

Dyrby was dressed in less than a minute. His blond facial hair barely showed but his blue eyes betrayed his exhaustion. Four minutes later he sat at a table as a middle-aged couple looked anxiously to him for help.

"Mr. & Mrs. Robertson, I need to make you aware I have sent Seaman Fog to your mother's stateroom as a precautionary measure. Please don't be upset. Now tell me about your mother and your son."

Mr. Robertson spoke first. "My mother is Christine Robertson. Her friends call her Chrissie. Today is mother's seventy-fifth birthday and this cruise is her birthday present."

"What a nice gift. I'm sure your thoughtfulness pleased your mother. Now, I understand she is confined to a wheelchair."

"She broke her ankle about a month ago and she has to wear this orthopedic boot that covers her foot, ankle and calf."

"Which leg?"

"It's on her right leg. There is another woman on the ship in a wheelchair and boot, too. My mother had fretted so about the wheelchair and she was so happy to find another lady who used one."

"Would you describe your mother, please?"

"She has gray hair and blue eyes. She is quite arthritic and doesn't have full use of her hands."

"Thank you, sir. Now please tell me about your son."

"Randy is seventeen although he could pass for twenty-one. He is six-feet and weighs in at about one-eighty. He'll be a senior next year and he has already talked to several college scouts about a football scholarship."

"You must be very proud of him. Would you describe him, please?"

"He's dark complexioned with dark brown hair and eyes."

"Do you feel it is possible your family might be at our all night pizza bar or our gaming room?"

Mrs. Robertson answered. "My mother-in-law was tired and wanted to return to her room and go to bed. I asked Randy to take his grandmom to her stateroom."

"What time was this, ma'am?"

"About eleven-thirty. We all attended the comedy show together."

"And what time did you go down to your room?"

"My husband and I stopped at the bar and picked up a drink. We arrived at our room about twelve-fifteen. We have three staterooms, officer. Ours is in the center, Chrissie's is on our left and Randy and Ralph's room is on our right. I peeked in to see if Chrissie was okay and her bed hadn't been used. The door to the balcony was slightly open and it was chilly inside. I thought it was odd so I checked her closet. Her jacket was there. So was her nightgown. Where could she be? She couldn't have fallen overboard by accident or her wheelchair would be around."

"Your second son, ma'am? When did he go to his room?"

"A little after twelve. We found Ralph on his laptop. He said Randy wasn't there and thought he might be with a girl or something so he didn't want us to know. He knew nothing about his grandmother. Ralph checked the all-night pizza bar and the teen room for us. Then my husband and son walked each and every deck—inside and out."

"I will apprise my captain of the situation and will arrange for a team of men to search the ship. I'm sure we will find your family. Please try not to worry. Seaman Fander will escort you to a small lounge so you may be more comfortable. I will be in contact, I promise."

* * *

As soon as the Robertson's were out of the meeting room, Dyrby called the Mikkelsen suite. "I am so sorry to disturb you, Miss Elin, but I need to ask a favor. Would you please go to Ms. Charlie's room and confirm she's there?"

"Why? What on earth is wrong?"

"I'm not at liberty to discuss it, ma'am. Please confirm Ms. Charlie's presence."

Elin could hear Charlie's snores as soon as she opened her own bedroom door but she still checked Charlie's bedroom. Elin returned to her room and told Dyrby that Charlie was asleep.

"What's happened? I know something has happened, officer."

"Ma'am. I don't know for sure if anything has happened. Please, under no circumstance are you to leave your stateroom without a security escort. Would you assure me of that?"

"Only if you'll answer my questions."

"I'm sorry I woke you, ma'am. I need to go now. Good evening."

Elin set down the phone and sat on her bed. *I hope whatever happened doesn't involve Charlie or me but with our current string of luck...*

* * *

Dyrby returned to his cubicle and called Seaman Fander. "Call our entire search team. We'll meet here at the top of the hour. Who is on the Mikkelsen watch?"

"Seaman Stanford, sir."

"Tell him to be on his guard."

The seaman left to make the calls. Dyrby called Captain Hansen. The men agreed to meet in the Robertson stateroom in five minutes.

* * *

"The balcony door was open, you say?"

"It was ajar, captain," Dyrby said as the men stepped inside the stateroom.

"Captain, good morning, sir," said Fog. "I don't believe I have good news and I need to show you something. Stay right where you are, sir, and study the carpet. There are two faint marks that go from where you stand to the balcony door."

Dyrby stooped down and examined the carpet. "I can see where it was roughed up."

"Sir, this looks to me like the marks were made by a man's heels—like he was dragged across the floor. There are also several small scuffmarks on the balcony."

"Anything else?"

"Afraid so, captain. Mrs. Robertson's purse is on the floor next to the bed. It appears intact."

"Captain," said Dyrby, "I called the Mikkelsen suite. Both ladies are fine. I saw Mrs. Robertson after dinner. She and Miss Charlie Mikkelsen exchanged greetings. They both were in their wheelchairs, both wore similar-colored dresses, both have gray hair and both wore a big boot on their ankle. I fear it's possible the Bladensburgs or Ambroses mistook Mrs. Robertson for Miss Mikkelsen."

"Much to my dismay, I suspect you're right. Secure the room. If your team cannot find the woman, I will need to speak with the family."

* * *

The meeting took five minutes. Dyrby ordered his men to scour the ship from stem to stern. They had predetermined routes and they had practiced this drill many times in the wee hours of the morning. All of the men knew this was no drill. They were given a thirty-minute deadline.

While his men searched, Dyrby went to Fog's workstation to locate the security file. It would show Mrs. Robertson entering her stateroom. He found it and watched as the Robertsons left the elevator followed by the Ambroses. His anxiety built as he watched the Ambroses stalk the grandmother and grandson down the hallway and enter the stateroom door after the young man. He called his captain.

Captain Hansen arrived within minutes and Dyrby reran the scenes taken by the cameras. He had even found the file from the elevator camera.

"Look at this, captain. These people should have worn signs saying 'I killed the old lady and her grandson.' Instead, they wore baseball jackets saying *Newark Bears*. I did say the Bladensburgs and Ambroses are from Newark, New Jersey, didn't I?"

Dyrby allowed the scene to play until the Ambroses exited the room. They kept their faces down as they walked away. "They were inside seven minutes, sir."

"*Newark Bears* and pink sandals. These two are total idiots with empty space between the ears. See if the search party comes up with anything."

Dyrby returned to the meeting room where his staff had gathered. They found nothing. He reported back to his captain.

"I want you to burn a dozen DVDs of what you showed me. Notify the detectives on St. Thomas and tell them we will arrest these people. Now we have the legal right—they committed a crime on our ship—unauthorized entry at the very least."

The captain went to the ship's navigator. He asked for and received the ship's coordinates at eleven-thirty—the time the grandmother and grandson entered the stateroom. As he studied the report he remembered the liner's sister ship, *Aqua Lights,* would soon approach the area where Mrs. Robertson and her grandson were probably pushed overboard. *Since Aqua Lights follows the same shipping lane as we do, it would be best if they performed the search and rescue operation.*

The captain returned to his office, called headquarters in Stockholm and explained the situation. The Chief of Operations authorized *Aqua Lights* to begin its mission. Captain Hansen placed a call to Captain Levin and gave him the appropriate information. Levin put his search and rescue procedures in place.

The captain knew there would be little chance the Robertsons would be found alive in the cold Atlantic waters. He placed a call to the nearest Coast Guard Station and asked them for help if *Aqua Lights* found nothing. *Now I have to explain all this to Mr. & Mrs. Robertson.*

CHAPTER TWENTY-EIGHT

Man and Larson were stretched out on cots in the locker room when the radio dispatcher paged Detective Carmen. Chamaign was asleep on the couch in a small anteroom outside the ladies' room. The page woke her, too. All three merged in Man's office at the same time and Man took the call.

"Dyrby, may I put you on speaker?"

"I assumed you already did so, detective." Dyrby explained what had taken place. "We will arrest all of these people as soon as I get my men organized."

"Dyrby, please don't. We have a plan and are prepared. These men are trained killers. We are in a better position to handle this than you because we wrestle with this kind of trash all the time. We've been trained in SWAT team tactics—exactly what you need right now."

"Detectives, I have no choice. They've committed a crime on ship and I suspect there are two dead bodies afloat in the Atlantic right now. I have a duty to arrest them."

"Dyrby, get your plan organized but please call me before you do anything. We will leave here in a few minutes and will land at the Miami Coast Guard Station around dawn. We can be onboard your ship between seven and eight. Can you call us back?" Man gave Dyrby their cell numbers.

"I will be grateful for your suggestions," Dyrby said.

"Are our ladies okay?" Man asked.

"We moved them to a stateroom on another deck under assumed names. I called their stateroom earlier to check on them and they are fine."

After Man disconnected, both he and Chamaign called their bosses. James left the hospital in a cab and Andre buttoned his shirt on the way out of the door while his baby girl cried in the background.

* * *

Dyrby called his men together. His red eyes and his grim face told his men how serious the situation was.

"We need to arrest these men and their wives before too many passengers start to stir. There is very little time. I must stress the men were in the U.S. Special Forces. Based on what the VIPD had to say, their victims all had their necks broken so we need to be exceptionally cautious when we cuff these men."

Dyrby made several drawings on a white board as to how they would proceed. Three men were assigned to each stateroom but only two would enter. The third would stand in the hall as backup. The team spent twenty minutes on their plans. They ended their discussion with how to get the men to the brig.

* * *

While Dyrby's team planned, Al Bladensburg had been thinking about how he would proceed with his own plan. *Jerome couldn't do anything right if he tried. I'll be the one to survive this mess.*

He dressed and left his stateroom at a little before four and casually walked up two decks. He was at the end of the hallway near the stern of the ship. Starting with the first security camera in the hall, he reached behind the camera and covered it with a sock. He continued down the hall until he came to the last camera at the far end. Unfortunately, the seaman who manned the monitors was in the meeting with Dyrby.

As Bladensburg approached the Mikkelsen door, a steward started down the hallway. Bladensburg stepped aside to let the steward pass and then he turned around. It was all over in a second. Bladensburg relieved the dead man of his master keycard. He was both surprised and pleased the man carried a weapon but he also realized the man wasn't a steward but part of the ship's security. He didn't know the man was sent to pick up the rest of the Mikkelsens' luggage.

Al decided the ship's staff knew about Jerome and him. And that meant it would only be a matter of time before they would be arrested. *I've got to kill these women while we're in international waters. If they catch me, my chances will be better in a foreign court than in a U.S. court.*

Bladensburg stuffed his latest victim into the nearby supply cabinet. *Survival is for the fittest. All I have to do now is to decide how and when to jump ship. The others can do whatever they want.*

* * *

Dyrby called Man on the office phone and told the detective his plans.

After listening and making a couple of suggestions, Man said, "I'm glad the adjoining staterooms are emptied—that's a plus. How good a shot are you?"

"I visit the target range a couple of times a year but that's about it. I don't even normally carry a weapon on ship."

"What about our ladies?" James asked.

"There is an armed member of our team stationed in front of their door."

"Good. What is your plan for the wives?"

Dyrby explained his plan and it was very similar to the detectives' plan.

"Are you sure you can't wait for us?"

"No, I'm under captain's orders."

"Any news on the passengers who went overboard?"

Dyrby told them about *Aqua Lights.*

"Dyrby, five of us will fly to the Coast Guard Air Station in a few minutes. Please inform your navigator we'll call for coordinates when we get there. Please keep us updated with a message on our cells," Chamaign asked.

"Dyrby, when this is over, please have our ladies leave us a message," James asked.

"I'll be happy to do so, sir."

* * *

The cruise line had a long list of procedures for various emergency situations that could occur while on land or at sea. The captain went over the list carefully. Following procedures, he ordered his communication officer to turn off all passenger access to Internet services and cell phone usage.

CHAPTER TWENTY-NINE

Chamaign called the Chief on her way to the airport.

"It's too early for a social call so what's wrong, Chamaign?"

She explained the situation on the ship. "It seems Charlie wasn't the only older lady onboard who was in a wheelchair and wore a black boot."

"It could have been Charlie who was murdered!"

"And Elin, Chief."

"What's been done?"

Chamaign told him about the second cruise liner.

"I would think the Atlantic waters are too cold for the two people to survive, especially the older lady."

"We thought the same thing. On another note, James will go to Miami with us."

"Call me as soon as you know anything, Chamaign. Don't forget."

* * *

The Chief mulled over the situation for ten minutes before he decided to go online and purchase two tickets for the six a.m. flight to Miami. He called James and then drove to the villa to get Jeremy. It was a few minutes before five when he arrived and he had two boarding passes in his hand.

"So let me get this right, Chief. A man killed a woman last night because he thought she was my mother, correct?"

"I'm afraid so."

"So the situation has changed from my mother *may* be in danger to my mother *is* in danger. Correct?"

The Chief nodded.

"Are the detectives still scheduled to fly to Miami?"

"They've left for Miami already and the Coast Guard will copter them to the ship."

"Well *Victor*, I will be on the next plane to Miami. When I find my mother, dead or alive, she and I will be on the first plane back to Pennsylvania never to return here again. I want my mother home where the worst trouble she can get into is to go to a wild Red Hat dinner."

"Son…"

"I'm not your son. Next plane, *Victor*."

"Jeremy, I already have the tickets."

"Leave me alone and leave my mother alone."

"I will not do so unless your mother tells me she no longer wants to see me."

"You are a hard-headed egomaniac. You don't care about what my mother wants; you only care about what you want."

"Get your things, Jeremy. We're on the six o'clock flight. I'll wait for you in the car."

Neither man spoke on the way to the airport. The Chief's whole mind and body stung from what Jeremy said. He wondered how much truth was in his words.

* * *

With keycard in hand, Al went to the door of the suite. He knew if the latch was in place he could shoot it off the door. *How nice of the crew to provide me with such a nice gun—it sure does simplify life. Now I don't have to stand in the hall and pound on the door.*

He slid the keycard into the slot and opened the door a quarter of an inch to see if the latch was in place. It wasn't. *Stupid broads.*

He slipped inside the salon and gawked at the plush surroundings. *The cruise line didn't provide Alice and me with a stateroom this plush.*

He saw the closed doors to the bedroom and entered the one on the right. The room appeared empty and the bed had not been used. He listened at the door of the head. There were no sounds so he opened it. Empty. He slid the door to the closet open and was shocked to see it empty. *These two sleep together—I should have known.*

Al left the room and went to the second bedroom. He peaked in the door and saw a second empty bed. To his dismay the head and closet were empty. *Where are these hags?*

Back in the main salon he spotted two suitcases with the same initials on them—CEM. *These must belong to the old crone.*

He noticed a folded piece of paper half hidden under the couch. He picked it up and much to his delight he found a detailed map of the ship. It took but a second to realize the new home of the Mikkelsen ladies—the suite circled in red on deck ten. *Plan B, huh? How nice of them to leave me a trail of breadcrumbs.*

Al studied the map. The new suite was located in a hallway running from port to starboard. There were eight suites in the hallway and six faced the bow of the ship and had their own balconies with a view of a huge pool flanked by a maze of Jacuzzis. He wondered how they rated such snazzy accommodations. He decided the man he murdered was on his way to get the suitcases and jackets. *Perhaps I mistakenly murdered their guardian angel. Let's hope.*

As Al studied the map further, he realized there were a number of private hallways and rooms used by staff. He followed each deck one by one as he searched for a good place to hunker down with a hostage. He noticed the elevators were marked as lifts. He dug deep inside his mind. *Lifts—I think that's what they call elevators overseas. Well, I guess they can call them what they want.*

He noticed a number of smaller rectangles designated as lifts. He surmised these were the elevators staff used. Upon further scrutiny, he found a smaller lifts around the corner of the Mikkelsen's new suite. *If I use it, staff could be inside. But what's another dead body?*

He studied the other decks and examined the areas around this particular lift from deck one through deck ten. There were staff quarters on the first couple of decks and passenger rooms above. He did the same thing going from deck ten to the top. The lift passed through a lounge, the spa and the chapel. *Bingo.*

    He knew there was a possibility the chapel would have security cameras but if it did there were waiting rooms and dressing rooms behind it and they may not be secured. He was sure he had to go up instead of down. Bladensburg left the suite, found the staircase and went up a deck. He followed the hallways leading toward the bow of the ship. He slowed his pace as he searched for the lift. While he saw no elevator he did see a door marked STAFF ONLY. He used the master keycard to open it. The door camouflaged the elevator. He shut the door and moved forward. He knew time was of the essence if he wanted to escape capture.

* * *

    Dyrby and his men arrived at the hallway in front of the Bladensburg and Ambrose staterooms at almost the same moment in time that Bladensburg stood outside the Mikkelsen stateroom. Dyrby assigned a man to both ends of the hallway to keep passengers out of any potential gunfire.

    Dyrby had assigned Fog to enter one stateroom with Stanford. Fander would be his second man. All the men realized the obvious flaw in the shoot-the-latch scenario. There would be no element of surprise and the suspects would have two or three seconds to react. All the seamen, including those at the end of the hallway, were instructed to shoot first and ask questions later if there was anything remotely resembling trouble. Dyrby and Fog inserted the master keycards at the same time. The Bladensburg door opened and Dyrby and Stanford entered. The latch was in place on the Ambrose door. Fog had to step back and fire into the latch.

    Dyrby found Alice Bladensburg in bed. The shots fired by Fog woke her but she had yet to assimilate the situation. Fander cuffed her wrists behind her and retrieved a washcloth from his pocket to stuff into her mouth. He threw her on the bed face down. Dyrby motioned to Fander to check the closet as he provided backup. Empty. Fander opened the door to the head and found it empty. Dyrby headed for the interior door and unlocked it while his partner stayed with the woman.

Jerome Ambrose had opened the head's door seconds before Fog had fired his weapon. The head's door deflected the two shots that penetrated the stateroom door. He slipped inside the head and made a conscious decision to leave the door slightly ajar. As Fog and Stanford entered, Julie jumped out of bed and attempted to escape through the interior door. Stanford told her to halt. The interior door opened and Julie found herself face to face with Dyrby. He grabbed her and pulled her inside and Fander cuffed her.

As Fog watched Dyrby and Julie, Ambrose crept out of the head and stepped behind Fog. A startled Stanford heard a strange noise and looked at his partner. Ambrose held Fog's lifeless body against him for protection and had managed to grab Fog's gun before it fell to the floor. Stanford stood motionless with his gun frozen in his hand as he stared into his friend's lifeless Swedish blue eyes.

Ambrose anticipated someone entering through the interior door. As Dyrby appeared, he shot. Dyrby pulled back as a bullet clipped his shoulder but it did not incapacitate him.

Ambrose glanced back at Stanford, smirked and said, "You dumb scared klutz. Did you pee your pants?" He didn't wait for an answer and put two bullets in Stanford's forehead.

Ambrose had not anticipated an armed seaman would enter from the hallway behind him. The first of the seaman's bullets lodged in Ambrose's spine; the second went in and out of his gut and into Fog's lifeless body. Jerome Ambrose was all but dead.

CHAPTER THIRTY

Bladensburg peeked around the corner to see if a security guard was outside the Mikkelsen door. The hallway was empty. *Hum, I did indeed kill their guardian angel.*

He was quite pleased with himself. He tried the keycard in the slot and found the latch was in place. He stood back and fired twice into the latch and entered. The salon was empty. He wasted no time and entered the door he found to the right.

The gunshots woke Elin. She slid to the floor to squeeze under the bed but discovered the bottom of the bed was enclosed.

Charlie couldn't sleep so she had risen, showered and dressed. When she heard the nearby shots, she took her crutches and went into the head and locked the door. She searched her cosmetic bag for a weapon. She found a pair of cuticle scissors. *These aren't exactly lethal but if I should be tied up...*

She grabbed a bandage out of her emergency travel kit and taped the scissors on her back. She dug deeper into her bag and found two other potential weapons and slipped them in her pockets.

Inside the first bedroom, Bladensburg found an empty bed with rumpled sheets. He checked the head and the closet and they were both empty. He found Elin curled on the floor in a fetal position on the far side of the bed. Her brown eyes pleaded for mercy as her body quivered in fear. His laugh was deep and ugly and meant to taunt.

"I sure do like those shirts you sold me. Now go visit your ancestors." He shot Elin twice.

When Charlie heard the second set of shots, she forced herself not to vomit. She figured Elin was either injured or dead and she would be next. She stepped into the shower and shivered as she leaned her body against the tan ceramic wall. *Please, God...*

Bladensburg quickly walked to the second bedroom. He entered and saw the empty bed and wheelchair. He checked the closet first followed by the far side of the rumpled bed. He then knocked on the head's door and tried the handle.

"Hey you ole gray-haired bitch, don't worry. I decided not to kill you—not yet anyway. Who knows, you may come in handy as a hostage."

There was no reply. "You know, you stole my headline from me with your smooch picture. You must be desperate and horny. A horny ole floozy—how about that?"

Charlie didn't comment. "Okay cop-kisser, stand away from the door. I want you alive for the time being." He shot twice into the lock and heard it break.

As he pulled the door open, Charlie plunged at him with the tip of her crutch as he stepped up the ramp into the head. She caught him mid-step and he fell back against the closet door and slid to the floor. She went at him again with the crutch but this time she went for his groin. Perfect aim. She did it again. This time he grabbed the end of the crutch and pulled Charlie out the door with it. She deliberately let herself fall on top of him to reduce the impact on her replacement parts.

Way to go, Ms. Charlie. You're on top—get him, gal. Get him. You can do it. One hundred sixty-five pounds of pure blubber might inflict some damage, I hope. Clobber him with your boot, Missy. Go for the jaw if you can.

Charlie did her best to obey and bounced up and down on Bladensburg's stomach as she clobbered his neck and face with her boot. Unfortunately, Bladensburg managed to wrestle himself out from underneath her. She settled down when she felt the barrel of a gun on her forehead. Bladensburg stood and pulled his prey off the floor with his arm around her neck. Angry, he pushed her into the salon toward the hallway.

"A single pathetic whimper and you're dead meat."

For once Charlie was grateful for the size of her boot. Now she had to depend on it to support her weight as she was forced to walk without crutches.

The gunshots woke a number of passengers. Two half-dressed men stood in the hallway and several others stood in the doorways of their staterooms.

Bladensburg peeked around the doorframe, saw the men in the corridor and shot without warning. His aim was deadly accurate. The other passengers slammed their stateroom doors shut. One man no longer had a face and the other had his femoral artery severed by a bullet. Blood spurted out the wound with every beat of his heart as the man died.

Bladensburg forced Charlie into the hallway. Petrified, she retched when she saw the bodies sprawled on the plush blue-green carpet and the dark stains surrounding the men.

"Chill it, ole lady."

Charlie shook convulsively.

"You either chill it or die now."

Bladensburg kept his arm around her neck and used her quavering body as protection. He pulled the keycard out of his pocket and opened the door covering the lift's entrance. He saw several heads pop into the hallway and he fired at them. Doors slammed. The elevator came within seconds and Bladensburg aimed to shoot anyone in the lift as the doors opened. He found the lift empty and pushed Charlie inside.

Once the doors closed, he pushed the stop button. "Worried are ya? You should be. Look—no security cameras."

He released the arm grip around her neck. Charlie wanted to scream but she felt like her voice box had been glued shut. She couldn't utter a sound.

Al removed a pair of Alice's pantyhose from his pocket. He stuffed Charlie's mouth with part of the rump portion, wrapped the legs around her head and knotted it in the back. He removed a second pair of hose. He pushed Charlie against the wall and leaned on her as he tried to rip the pantyhose in half.

Charlie watched in horror and then amusement as the determined psychopath dared to test the strength of a single pair of pantyhose.

"What in the hell do they make this friggin stuff out of?" he mumbled out loud. He pulled in one direction and then in another. He tried to split them at the waist and got nowhere. Finally, he stepped on one end of the hose and pulled with the other end. The seam pulled apart at the crotch. He poked his fingers in the small rip and pulled the hose into two pieces except for the waistband. After another minute of cursing, growling, and spewing spit across the small lift, he gave up on the waistband.

During Bladensburg's comic routine, Charlie pushed her large Princess Summerfall Winterspring watch down to her wrist with the face of the watch turned to the inside of her arm. She anticipated her hands would be tied so she crossed them herself so the watch's large face was covered.

"Only a stupid broad would wear pantyhose. Now turn around."

As Al tied, Charlie angled her wrists as much as possible to allow space for movement. As he tightened the knot, she lost almost all of her flexibility. When he finished, Al let the waistband and the other leg of the pantyhose dangle behind her.

"Now we need to find a nice safe place to hide, you ole bitty."

CHAPTER THIRTY-ONE

Seaman Tier nearly collided into Officer Lindstrom as they both headed for the captain at a record pace.

"What's this?" the annoyed captain asked. "Both of you know you don't run on the bridge."

Tier stood back so Lindstrom could proceed.

"Captain, the desk has received numerous calls about gunfire on decks seven and ten. Two passengers were shot in the hall on ten and a passenger reported he saw a man with a gun escape into a small lift with his arm around the neck of an older woman."

"Miss Charlie," the captain said. He paged officers Sahlin and Ohlssen. The men were in their shared cubicle a few yards away and had overheard the conversation. They were at the captain's side within seconds.

"Both of you get your weapons and return here."

"Captain," Tier said. "Excuse me for the intrusion but you need to know what happened on seven."

"Go on."

"Sir, I man the security cameras and saw Officer Dyrby enter the stateroom with the master keycard and saw Fog shoot the latch on the second door and enter. A few seconds later the seaman stationed in the hallway entered the room Fog had entered. He had his gun cocked and aimed. I don't know what else happened, sir."

The captain called and spoke to the ship's doctor.

When his officers returned with their weapons, the captain finished his orders. "Sahlin, the doctor will meet you on ten. Find Miss Elin—she may be hurt. It sounds like the man used the staff lift to make his escape and took Miss Charlie as a hostage. Ohlssen, the nurse will meet you at the main lifts on deck seven. Make sure it is safe before she enters the Bladensburg and Ambrose staterooms."

"Lindstrom, man your duty station. Seaman Tier, tell Lieutenant Simonsen to come here and then check all the monitors for the man who has the Mikkelsen lady."

Lindstrom left and gave the captain's message to Simonsen before he returned to his duty station.

Officer Simonsen arrived at the captain's side. "Sir, how may I help?"

"Assign someone to assist Tier with the monitors. If the Mikkelsen woman is not seen, put a new person on the monitors and have Tier review the file for the past half hour."

"Right away, sir. May I ask if there is any word from Dyrby?"

"Not yet. There has been two shootings though." He explained where the doctor and the nurse had headed.

* * *

Officer Erik Sahlin and Dr. Clive Reinfeldt arrived on deck ten within five minutes of the captain's orders. There were a dozen passengers who stood in the hallway and gawked at the bodies. The doctor who had sat at the captain's dinner table the night before had taken the men's pulses. He was in his pajamas as he introduced himself.

"I am Dr. Adams. Both men are quite dead, I can assure you."

"Thank you for your help. I'm Dr. Reinfeldt. Did you by any chance check the stateroom to see if we have a wounded occupant?"

"No, I didn't."

"Doctor," Sahlin said, "I need to clear the stateroom before you enter. Please wait until I signal you." He guardedly approached the Mikkelsen stateroom.

"Dr. Adams. There were shots on deck seven too. May I ask for your help?"

"Of course."

"What is your specialty?"

"I work in the ER at the Prince Georges Hospital Center in Maryland. I tend to bullet wounds several times a week."

Sahlin appeared. "Dr. Reinfeldt, the younger Miss Mikkelsen requires your immediate attention."

Both doctors rushed inside and found Elin unconscious on the floor next to her bed. Blood had seeped from her torso. Her red hands rested on top of her stomach like she had tried to stop the bleeding. Reinfeldt moved her hands and saw the two bullet entry points. He turned her over to look for exit wounds. There was a single hole. Reinfeldt searched his bag for a role of bandages and vinyl gloves for both men.

"Please, let me," Adams said. He applied pressure bandages over Elin's wounds as tight as possible.

Reinfeldt used his stethoscope to listen to Elin's heart and took her blood pressure. "We have no idea what the extent of her internal damage is and her pulse is weak; the blood pressure is past critical. Let's get her downstairs."

Reinfeldt called for six seamen and three stretchers.

"Dr. Adams, this young woman is Miss Elin Mikkelsen. Would you accompany her to the medical center and do whatever you can for her while I go to deck seven and assess the damage?"

"I met Ms. Mikkelsen last night at dinner. I'll do what I can. Do you have blood onboard?"

"No, the best I can do is an IV with a saline solution."

"She will require more help than we can provide."

"I know. I know. Unfortunately, I know," Reinfeldt fretted. Before he left he asked Sahlin to update the captain.

It took only minutes before the seamen appeared. They placed Elin on the stretcher and rushed her to the Medical Center. Dr. Adams stayed in close pursuit as his blonde chickie threw him a robe. A few minutes after Sahlin roped off the hallway, he directed the seamen to take pictures of the dead men from all angles, cover them with a sheet and carry them to the center.

* * *

Al reviewed the ship's map again. As Charlie watched, she realized how he found her new suite. He pushed the elevator button for deck twelve. When the door opened, he checked the hall. He didn't see anyone but did hear a crewman as he spoke into his hand-held device. Al pushed Charlie in a front corner of the elevator and he stood inside the open door. The crewmember came around a corner and from a distance he could see the lift's door was open. *This is my lucky day.*

A millisecond later the officer noticed the man in the elevator and hesitated. "Excuse me, sir, are you a passenger?"

"I visited the chapel this morning and now I want to get back to my stateroom."

"And your deck, sir?"

"Seven."

"Do you have your keycard, sir?"

Al gave the crewmember his card. The man looked confused but returned the card and stepped inside. The young crewman's eyes grew wide when he saw a woman with her mouth stuffed with something. Unfortunately, Al's arm was already around the man's neck. Charlie scrunched her eyes tight but she still heard the hideous crack as the man's neck broke. Today wasn't his lucky day.

* * *

Dr. Reinfeldt headed for the Bladensburg-Ambrose staterooms. The doctor spotted Dyrby first.

"I'll be okay, doc. Your nurse is in the Ambrose stateroom. Please go in there."

Reinfeldt entered through the interior door. He saw Fog and Stanford sprawled on the floor.

"I checked our men, doctor," the nurse said. "They are quite dead. This is Mr. Ambrose. He has two entry wounds and one exit and is the man who killed Fog and Stanford."

"Let's get him to the medical center. Call for seamen and stretchers."

The doctor walked back to Dyrby. "Let me see your injury."

Reinfeldt checked Dyrby's shoulder. "You're lucky. The bullet grazed your shoulder blade. Let's be grateful it didn't sever any major arteries. I'll probe for bone fragments downstairs but I believe your main worry is infection."

"He killed my men. I believe Fog had his neck broken; Stanford has two bullets through the forehead. Did they suffer?"

"Both deaths were immediate. That's my honest assessment, Dyrby. Who shot Ambrose?"

"I wish it were me but it was a guard in the hallway. I heard there were shots on ten and I'm afraid to ask about our ladies."

"There was a young woman in the suite who took two bullets in the stomach."

"Miss Elin. What is her condition?"

"It doesn't look good."

"And Miss Charlie?"

The doctor told Dyrby about Charlie and the dead passengers.

"What a fiasco I organized."

"You did everything you could. Now, can you walk to the medical center or do you want a ride downstairs?"

"Neither. I need to call the captain and then escort the wives to the brig."

"As soon as you're done, you get to the medical center."

* * *

Dyrby called his captain. "Fog and Stanford are dead. Ambrose has significant injuries and is not expected to live. I know about the Mikkelsen ladies. I don't begin to know how to apologize, sir."

"We have no time for apologies. Are you hurt?"

"I took a bullet in the shoulder but it's minor. Fander and I need to take the wives to the brig."

"From there get yourself to the medical center. Captain's orders."

Fander pulled the women off the bed. Both kicked and struggled. Dyrby called for two guards in the corridor. With four men, each took an arm and marched the women down the long hall. They wore their nightgowns with a robe thrown over their shoulders. The washcloths were in their mouths and neither woman had on shoes. Another guard walked ahead of Alice and Julie to keep the horde of passengers out of the way. The voyeurs recorded the event on their cell phones, cameras and cam recorders.

* * *

Sahlin reported to the captain and explained the situation he found. "I don't understand how this man obtained a weapon and a master keycard."

"I suspect from one of our own," the captain replied. "We have another dead crewmember somewhere."

* * *

Al pushed Charlie out the elevator. He relieved the man of his keycard and left the man's body inside but pushed the button to keep the elevator door open. He forced his prey down the hall with his arm around her neck.

Ms. Charlie, you're not exactly a fashion statement right now. You look pretty stupid.

Why is it stupid to be petrified?

Your hands are tied with one leg of those pantyhose but the other leg is attached at the waistband. It drags on the floor behind you as you walk.

I have more important things to worry about right now.

You're right. It could be toilet paper.

Aren't you a little old for potty talk?

Bladensburg and Charlie came to a second short hallway. He used the newly purloined keycard to get through the door and into the next hallway. They went through a second secured door and Al saw the chapel but he noticed a security camera. He shut the door and retraced his steps. He opened an unsecured door off the hallway. Inside it were mirrors, a bench and a closet. He opened the closet and found three wedding gowns. He realized it was a bride's dressing room.

Lady Luck is still with me.

Al tied Charlie to a chair with the second leg of the pantyhose. "Don't try to get away now. I have to get the dead sailor boy in the elevator to keep you company."

He left the room and hurried toward the elevator. He lifted the crewmember over his shoulder and pushed the elevator button to go to deck three. When the doors closed Al listened for a gentle whir to assure the elevator descended. Within another minute he was back in the changing room. The dead body was deposited in a hump on the closet floor against a backdrop of fluffy white wedding gowns.

He studied the map again and looked at Charlie, "If you get bored you can talk to your new dead friend."

Al left the room laughing to himself and went down two hallways and through a series of secured doors. He spotted a door that interested him. It was all steel and had a heavy-duty industrial lock instead of a keycard pad. Bladensburg wasn't deterred. From the center city streets of Newark, he learned how to pick a lock when he was nine-years old; by twelve, he had graduated to warehouse locks. Even now he carried what he needed in his wallet. He extracted a short, thin metal pick and a small tension wrench. The items had come in handy several times when Alice had changed the locks on their home doors after they had an argument.

With the skill of a petty thief with a practiced hand, the door was open in less than fifteen seconds. It was a small room about five by six. The walls were lined with electrical junction boxes and miles of wire fed into them. Once he ensured the door could be locked and unlocked from the inside, he left his wallet between the door and the frame so he wouldn't have to pick the lock again.

He went back for Charlie. "Guess what, girlie? I found us a nice quiet place to relax and get to know each other." He untied Charlie from the chair and forced her down the hallway to the electric closet. He put the light on and pushed her inside. He shut the door and sat down. Charlie slid down the walls in the far corner of the closet with her hands tied behind her.

CHAPTER THIRTY-TWO

"Captain, sir."

"Where did he take the woman, Tier?"

"I haven't found her, sir. I reviewed the video from deck ten and below and didn't see anything." Tier updated his captain in graphic detail about what he saw on deck ten.

"How on earth did he know where to look for the lift?"

"Sir, he had a piece of paper in his hand. I enlarged and enhanced the picture and it looked like one of our staff maps of the ship."

"Where did he get it?"

"I don't know, sir."

"Wasn't there a security guard stationed on ten?"

"There was, sir. I saw Wessen stationed outside the suite. He left his station and walked down to staff lift three. I can't find him on any video so he could have gone to nine. Remember, the cameras on deck nine are down."

"Was there a camera in lift three?"

"No, sir."

"What about decks eleven through fourteen?"

"Sir, this lift only goes to staff areas on those decks. We have no cameras there."

"Continue on and see if you can determine where they went. Don't leave your station."

Tier returned.

"Sahlin, go down to deck nine. Sift through all the storage and service closets in the hallway. I suspect you'll find Wessen. Also, determine what is wrong with our security cameras."

Sahlin acknowledged the captain's orders and left.

The captain calculated the dead and injured. There were the grandmother and grandson and the two passengers in the hallway on deck ten. Then there were his two dead seamen plus a missing third man. The captain put his next in command on the bridge and headed for the Medical Center. *Five or six dead plus Miss Elin is injured and Miss Charlie is probably a hostage.*

* * *

"How bad is it?" the captain asked Dyrby.

"I'm fine, sir. Dr. Adams extracted a few bone fragments so my only possible complication is an infection and the doctor already put me on antibiotics."

"Is Doctor Adams the man that sat with us last night?"

"Yes, and he offered to assist Dr. Reinfeldt."

"What happened on seven?"

Dyrby told his captain what happened in the Ambrose stateroom.

The captain shook his head in disbelief. "Wesson can't be located. Do you know about him?"

"He was on duty on ten, sir."

"Tier reviewed the security files and saw him leave his post and head for the lift."

"It's my fault, sir. I told him to pick up the women's personal items in their old suite. I thought the women would be safe since we would be at the suspects' staterooms. The gun Ambrose used must have belonged to Wesson."

"Sahlin is looking for him on nine."

"Sir, I know Miss Charlie is a hostage so I must organize and begin a search. I have Fander and two other guards."

"Are you up to it? I can put Sahlin in charge."

"Sir, I was responsible for the ladies. I will do this."

"Very well but work with Sahlin and Ohlssen."

Dyrby left the medical center and headed toward the bridge while the captain went to find the doctor.

* * *

"Doctor Reinfeldt, an update," the captain asked.

"Ambrose died a few minutes ago. We've done all we can do for Miss Mikkelsen. She is stabilized but I suspect she has internal bleeding. She has a bullet in her and she requires immediate surgery."

"You're not a surgeon, doctor. How can you do that?"

"I can't. She would not survive without several liters of blood. Something has to be done soon or we'll lose her."

"I'll make some calls," the captain said as he made a beeline for the bridge.

* * *

"I wonder what happened," Man said to Chamaign as he peered out the plane's windows.

"My gut tells me it isn't good. We're almost in Miami so we'll know soon enough," she replied.

James heard what the detectives said but felt so ill he sat with his eyes closed. For a brief minute, he thought about his IV bottle with its life-saving antibiotics. He returned to his prayers for Elin and Charlie.

* * *

Five seconds after Charlie settled in the corner of the small room, she tested the tightness of the pantyhose wrapped around her wrists. She had the tiniest amount of slack after Bladensburg had tied them. She forced the fingers on her right hand to push her large Princess Summerfall Winterspring watch up her arm to give her a bit more wiggle room at the wrists.

What time is it, Ms. Charlie?

I'm not exactly psychic, you know. I can't see behind my back.

How is our rescue going?

With the watch out of the way I have enough room to maneuver my scissors, I think.

Where can I get a Princess Summerfall Winterspring watch?

Call Howdy Doody.

Charlie stretched the pantyhose enough to wiggle her tiny cuticle scissors out from the bandage. She informed her crooked arthritic fingers that it was a dire necessity for them to work and that clumsiness was not an option. It took her a minute to get her thumb and the first finger of her right hand into the small round circles of the chrome handles. She used the strength in her arm muscles to stretch the hose as far as she could and she managed to move her hands from a crossed position to a position where one hand was over the wrist of the other—all thanks to the sliver of space left by her watch. The pantyhose cut into her wrists but she again forced her hands apart in order to poke the open scissors into the top layer of the hose.

Ms. Charlie, does it hurt?

My shoulder joints aren't happy, my muscles are spastic and my crooked fingers are screaming obscenities that would make the captain blush.

You got me into this mess, now you get me out of it, hear?

I'll make a deal—if I get to live, so do you.

Charlie started to snip away thread-by-thread with a microscopic cut each time. She flexed her arm muscles for less than fifteen seconds before she had to stop to give them a rest. She repeated the process over and over and over.

I said a prayer, Ms. Charlie.

Good. Say another one.

It's bad?

It's bad.

* * *

By satellite phone, Lindstrom connected the captain to the Coast Guard Air Station in Miami.

"Seaman, I need to speak to someone with decision-making authority. This is Captain Birthe Hansen of the Scandinavian Seven Seas Cruise Line. My ship is *Aqua Waters* and this is a request for immediate medical assistance."

Twenty-two seconds later, Captain Peter West spoke, "Captain Hansen, how may I assist?"

Captain Hansen explained Elin's condition and her immediate needs.

"What on earth happened, captain?"

The captain explained the deaths and injuries. "I request immediate transportation for Ms. Elin Mikkelsen." He gave Captain West the ship's coordinates.

"I understand your position, Captain Hansen. Does your injured security officer require help?"

"I believe his injury is minor. He has organized a search for a second woman who is held hostage."

"Captain, I will see if there are any Navy ships in the area that can get to you faster than I can. I'll get back to you ASAP."

After Captain Hansen disconnected, he walked to the communication officer's cubicle.

"Lindstrom, please open all channels for a public announcement." He wrote a short statement for Lindstrom to read.

A few moments later the public address system blared. "All officers report to the bridge. All remaining staff leaders report to the Galaxy Theatre." Lindstrom repeated the message twice.

More than a few passengers paid attention to the announcement. Some who were asleep woke; most of those who were awake had heard about the gunfire; a few were aware of the absent grandmother and grandson; and several had seen the dead bodies in the hallway. Quite a few picked up their cell or logged onto their computer only to realize there was no service.

* * *

Lindstrom informed his captain the Coast Guard was on the line.

"Captain West, can you help us?"

"We can but the Navy can do it better. There is an aircraft carrier close to you on its way to Norfolk. They've sent a copter with a medic onboard and he will start a transfusion. You can expect him in fifteen minutes. It will be another fifteen-minute ride back to the carrier so your passenger will be in surgery as soon as the copter sets down."

"Thank you, captain. I'll relay the message."

"I understand there are some detectives on their way to our air station and they will require a lift from us."

"Four officers are with the VIPD and one is with the St. Martin PD. We need their help since my men are not trained for shootouts."

"If I may ask, why did you opt for the VIPD instead of the Miami police? Miami could get to you sooner."

"The VIPD left early this morning and they will be on your doorstep shortly. There were three other murders on the islands and the police want the suspects back there for the trial. Of course all of these plans were made before our lady was injured and the other taken hostage. I hope my decision was one I don't live to regret."

* * *

The captain called the Medical Center. Dr. Reinfeldt was relieved to hear the Navy was on its way. He rushed to prepare Elin for transport.

* * *

Lindstrom reported. "Sir, there is a call for you from *Aqua Lights*."

Hansen took the call. "Levin, did you find my passengers?"

"And good morning to you, too, Hansen."

"I apologize for my abruptness. All hell has broken loose around here. I have two more dead passengers, two or three dead crewmen, a seriously injured passenger, plus one held hostage. I need to restrict my other passengers to their staterooms in a few minutes."

"And I thought search and rescue was hard. Since we've lost a little less than an hour, only a few of my passengers will miss their flights out of Miami."

"Did you find the bodies?"

"Because of the darkness the crew had to use their searchlights and they did find the grandson's body. I hope this is of some consolation to the family."

"Could you determine how he died?"

"It appears his neck was broken."

The two captains spoke for a few minutes before they disconnected.

CHAPTER THIRTY-THREE

Dyrby, Sahlin, Ohlssen and Lieutenant Commander Hasse Simonsen met with the captain in a private room.

"Sir, our search team is ready," Dyrby said.

"Are your men prepared?"

"Tier and Fander are well trained but I need to keep Tier on the monitors. I would appreciate it if you would appoint several people to assist him."

"Done."

"Captain, I would like to help Dyrby," Ohlssen said. "I'm former navy but I'm not in his league."

"I would like to assist, too," Sahlin offered.

"The three of you will work as a team. Dyrby, how many others do you need?"

"Respectfully," Dyrby said, "I hesitate to put anyone else at risk who is not trained. My concern is Bladensburg may be in an empty stateroom."

"Recommendation?"

"Sir, would you announce all passengers must stay in their staterooms?"

"Absolutely. I completely agree."

"I request the four of us check each and every stateroom, occupied or not, and clear one deck at a time. I'll call you as we clear each deck. This is the only way we can ensure passenger safety."

"Excellent. Before you start, call the VIPD and tell them what has happened. Inform them a Navy copter will be here within minutes and

Miss Mikkelsen will be in surgery within a half hour. The carrier will dock in Norfolk."

"This is the first good news I've heard all day," Dyrby said.

"Sir," Sahlin interrupted, "We have enough empty staterooms that we can move the passengers in the hallway on deck ten where the men died. I only need your approval."

"Proceed. What about the passengers adjacent to the Bladensburgs and the Ambroses? If we can move them we can cordon off the whole area."

Dyrby replied. "Sir, the eight immediate staterooms were emptied last evening. There are four staterooms left in the hallway."

Sahlin said, "I'd be happy to arrange for those passengers, too. It will require a quick call."

The captain nodded and Sahlin left.

The captain said, "In a few minutes I will announce that all passengers are to stay in their staterooms. I spoke to all officers a few minutes ago and they will look for guests in the exercise room, spas, pools and breakfast areas. After our men validate the passenger's identification, the officers will escort the passengers to the theatre. I've asked the maitre d' to organize meals so they can be served in the staterooms. All kitchen and dining staff are reassigned."

* * *

When the captain dismissed the meeting, Dyrby returned to his desk and called Chamaign. He left a message and explained everything that had happened and what was planned. He understood too well how upset they would be about the women. Immediately after the call, the team headed for the lowest passenger deck.

* * *

The captain took the microphone and read from the statement he prepared. It was a bit past dawn.

Good morning Ladies and Gentlemen. This is Captain Birthe Hansen. I have a very unusual request for you but I must ask you to listen and do as instructed. For those of you in your stateroom you must remain in your stateroom. Officers will inspect every stateroom on every floor for a missing passenger. Do not open your stateroom door unless you check the peephole. The person who knocks must be in uniform and show you photo identification. After each deck is cleared, breakfast will be served to you in your rooms. For passengers who have left their staterooms, please stay where you are and a staff person will escort each of you to the theatre.

Your safety is my responsibility. Therefore, your cooperation is expected and required. Anyone who does not comply with this announcement will be arrested. Officers and staff will be available to assist you in every way we can.

As some of you know, there were guns fired on two decks this morning and there have been several deaths. A U.S. Navy helicopter will arrive shortly to transport an injured passenger. Additionally, the Virgin Island Police Department will land by helicopter. You are required to stay in your room as a safety precaution.

As a representative of the Scandinavian Seven Seas Cruise Line and as your captain, I apologize for this inconvenience. I sincerely thank you for your full cooperation.

The captain repeated his message.

* * *

The captain stood a safe distance from the helipad located at the bow of the ship. He wasn't the only person who watched. Passengers with suites that faced foreword stood on their balconies and watched. Most took pictures of one kind or another. Dr. Reinfeldt had Elin on deck but kept her safely out of the wind and sun. She had regained consciousness and was aware of what was about to happen. She was too weak to ask anyone to tell James.

As soon as the copter's rotors stopped, four seamen rushed her stretcher to the copter. Reinfeldt kept up with them as he held Elin's IV bag in the air. Once the transfer was complete the rotors started to whirl and pick up speed. Dr. Reinfeldt had placed a pick in Elin's vein and an IV fed into it. The medic removed the saline solution from the pick and attached a liter of blood. Lift off.

* * *

As soon as the tires hit the runway of the U.S. Coast Guard Air Station in Miami, everyone on the plane turned on their cell. Chamaign had a message from Dyrby. As she listened, every eye on the plane focused on her.

When she closed her cell, she looked at James and chose her words carefully. "Elin's been shot and is seriously injured—that's part of the bad news. On a more positive note, a Navy copter flew her to the deck of an aircraft carrier and she is in surgery."

James kept it together until Chamaign finished the update. "What is the rest of the bad news?"

"Bladensburg has Charlie. Dyrby doesn't know where they are on the ship but a search crew is in place. Dyrby should have waited for us."

James listened to the voice mail from the Chief and told the detectives what he said. He knew his fever had returned so he sat and stared out the window while Man, Bob and Ben gathered all the required tactical gear they brought—helmets, Kevlar vests, automatic rifles and ammo. Everyone left the plane together.

"Boss, there is no point in you being in Miami if Elin will arrive in Norfolk. Why don't you grab a cab and head for the airport?"

James nodded.

"You will see a doctor when you get there. Promise?"

"I have no other choice."

"Good. We'll keep in touch." Chamaign started to leave but stopped. "What about Elin's mother and sister?"

"I'll give Alyse a call."

"And your mother?"

"I'll call my mother, too. Thanks for your concern. Now all of you get to that blasted ship."

"Boss, will you call the Chief and Jeremy and update them?"

***

Before she boarded the Coast Guard helicopter, Chamaign called her husband and told him where she was and where she was headed.

"Honey, this man is a psychopath and kills everyone in sight."

"I know. I'll be protected with all the proper gear so I don't want you to worry. Remember, I'm the best sharpshooter on the force."

"Please be careful. I love you."

"I love you, too. Kiss our little boy for me." Chamaign did not allow herself to think of how much she wanted to kiss her son.

After the five officers were in the air, they studied the ship's layout again. Chamaign was sure of one thing: Bladensburg had found a very good cubbyhole in which to hide.

***

A feverish James arrived at the airport and purchased a ticket to Norfolk. With boarding pass and ID in hand he patiently endured the long lines that snaked toward security. As he headed toward terminal C, chills started to rack his body. He stopped at a multi-purpose shop along his route and purchased four small containers of aspirin, four bottles of water, four energy bars and a gray sweatshirt that said "Miami Moonlight." Under the large colorful letters, there was a moon and the outline of a beach with two lovers who cuddled in the sand. He wished the lovers were he and Elin. He stopped at an ATM and withdrew five hundred before he plopped himself on an end seat in the area reserved for boarding passengers at Gate 14.

He placed the shirt across his back and tied the arms around his neck in an effort to tame the chills. Four aspirin and one empty bottle of water later, he removed his cell and stared at it with glassy eyes. He dreaded the calls he had to make.

"Alyse, this is James. I need to tell you about your sister."

"I already heard she decided to cruise. Lucky lady."

"Not so lucky. Elin and Charlie are on the same ship as the men who murdered the jewelry reps. Your sister was shot and is in serious condition."

"How serious is serious?"

"She required surgery."

"Do they do that on a cruise ship?"

"A Navy helicopter airlifted her onboard an aircraft carrier. Hopefully, she's in surgery by now."

"I'm afraid to ask, but what is her prognosis?"

"I don't know anything more than what I told you. It must be bad for the Navy to intervene."

"How did you find this out?"

"Ship security left a message on Chamaign's cell while we were on the flight to Miami. The detectives are headed for the ship by Coast Guard copter."

"You're in Miami and not the hospital?"

"I'm afraid so."

"Can't they get you on the Navy ship?"

"All this happened before we arrived. I'm stalled in Miami until my flight leaves for Norfolk. The carrier will dock there and I want to welcome Elin."

"James, are you okay? Your words are slurred."

"My fever is back and my antibiotics are in my hospital room. I'll see a doctor as soon as I get to Norfolk."

"You'll call me as soon as you know something?"

"As soon as I know something—promise. Will you tell your mother for me?"

"I guess I need to, don't I?"

"You need to. I'll call my mother while you take care of your mom."

James walked to the men's room and splashed cold water on his face. He couldn't figure out how he could be hot and cold at the same time. He took some wet paper towels with him and returned to his seat. With the towels on his forehead, he dialed his mother's number.

"James, why did you leave the hospital?" his aunt scolded.

"I need to talk to my mother, Aunt Jeanette."

"You don't sound well, James. What's wrong?"

"Let me speak with my mother. Now."

"That's not how you speak to your aunt, James."

"Aunt Jeanette, right now," he shouted into the phone.

When Grace Kingston picked up the phone she knew there was a serious problem. Her forty-five year old son wept as he told his mother what happened.

* * *

James called Jeremy's cell and left a message. He told Jeremy where he was in the airport and asked him to find C-14 as soon as possible. Then he called Andre. When done, James rested his elbows on his knees and put his head between his hands. He closed his eyes and tried to pray. His mind was so muddled he couldn't remember the words of a single prayer.

CHAPTER THIRTY-FOUR

Al and Charlie each sat in their corner of the electric room. Because of the boot she had to extend her legs straight in front of her. Al had his knees bent.

"You heard the captain's announcement. I bet my wife is dead like your buddy. Tit for tat—a bitch for a bitch."

Charlie couldn't respond with the pantyhose in her mouth. Al pulled the hose out. She wondered if she could save her own life if she engaged Bladensburg in a personal conversation.

"I'm sorry about your wife. She didn't do anything wrong."

"Sure she did. She planned this whole operation from start to finish. If she hadn't played games with our jewelry store business, the IRS would never have investigated us. If they hadn't investigated us we wouldn't have had to pay those fines. If we hadn't had to pay the fines, we wouldn't have needed to rob anyone. Good ole dependable Alice—until death do us part."

"What did she do?"

"She kept a set of books for her and a second set for the IRS. She got caught. She even thought we didn't know what she did. My sister and I could have ended up in jail."

"How could the IRS put you in jail if she kept the books? There had to be a paper trail a mile long somewhere with her handwriting on it."

"Oh there was. The IRS knew it was Alice but they only wanted their money plus interest plus a fine. The State of New Jersey wanted a cut, too."

"But why did you have to murder? Robbery I can see, but not murder."

"Alice said it was the only way there would be no witnesses. She wasn't even right about that. You spotted me at the airport and the shop owner could have recognized me, too. I was trained to kill so I killed. Jerome, too."

"Who did Jerome kill?"

"The jewelry rep on St. Thomas. But he and Julie killed the ole lady in the wheelchair and her steward by mistake."

Charlie sat horrified for a minute before she said, "Do you mean Chrissie Robertson?"

"Overboard. Both of them."

Charlie was both stunned and horrified. "He killed Chrissie because he thought she was me?"

"Jerome made the mistake—he's as dumb as Julie."

Charlie was speechless as she digested the news that Chrissie died instead of her. Finally she asked, "Why don't you surrender so you won't risk your own life? Haven't there been enough senseless deaths?"

"I've killed five people and you will be my sixth. I think it is time for you to shut up."

"Who else died?"

"A jewelry rep on St. Martin and your buddy."

"Elin's dead?"

"Yep."

Al reached across to stuff Charlie's mouth again. "Please don't. I won't scream. Did you think of this—if you get yourself killed, Alice would get away with everything? Remember, the captain said a passenger was injured but we don't know who it is. I'm not sure the Navy would bother to rescue a murderer or a murderer's wife, but they would rescue an innocent injured passenger like my cousin. You will take the wrap for all of this if you don't write down the part your wife played and what you did and didn't do."

Al thought hard for a few minutes. He had a glimmer of hope he could jump ship before it docked but he realistically knew deep inside he was a dead man sooner or later—and most likely sooner. He saw an empty pad of notepaper used for inspections on the wall. A pencil on a string dangled next to it. He grabbed the pencil and broke the string. Al started to write a long message on the lower wall of the small electrical room.

After what amounted to a full confession with a descriptive account of Alice's actions, he sat frozen in his stuffy corner with his eyes half closed. His mind raced in such tight circles he was almost nauseous. He wondered who was dead. He knew Jerome didn't have a gun so a crewman must have killed him. *Why do I care? Alice has been a noose around my neck for years. She planned this fiasco and she should have her rump in a jail cell for years to come. What a moron. If only I can get out of here...*

* * *

Alice Bladensburg and Julie Ambrose each sat on their bench. Their cells were side by side and they each scooted to the inside edges so they could talk.

"Where is Al?" Julie asked.

"How do I know? He was upset last night when he found out you two jerks killed the wrong woman."

"Who are you calling jerks, Alice?"

"You and your mindless husband. You're a matched set of deranged dolts."

"Don't be so high and mighty. You're the idiot who planned this whole disaster. Jerome said you're the one who should end up in jail."

"Look around you, stupid. Like you didn't notice the bars around us?"

"This is temporary. They can't hold me because they can't prove a thing."

"What about the security cameras in the hallways?"

"We hid our faces."

"Julie, you're dumber than I thought. The cameras can track you throughout the whole ship."

"No, Jerome is smarter than that. When we left the room, we hid in a short hallway and it had no cameras so we took our outer clothes off. We might be on a camera but they can't prove who it was who entered the old woman's stateroom. We threw our stuff overboard when we returned to our stateroom. See? No clothing and no dead bodies."

"Well I don't believe for a second a jury will buy your story."

"What jury? We're in international waters."

"There will be a jury someplace. You can bet on it. Now tell me this—you didn't happen to wear those blue jackets—the ones that say *Newark Bears* on the back, did you?"

"Oh."

* * *

"Hey there, Georgie Boy. What's up?" Andre asked as the reporter entered his office.

"What's going on, Chief? Scuttlebutt has it that a squad car left here this morning loaded with officers and tactical gear."

"Have a seat, George. Let me finish the notes for my report and then we'll talk." Andre wanted to make a list like Charlie suggested. After a few minutes he placed his pen and paper next to his computer where his guest couldn't sneak a peak. "George, there are some developments on the murders and thefts."

Andre identified the men and told the reporter how the men moved from island to island on a cruise ship. Then he identified the detectives who went to arrest them.

"How did the detectives figure out how the men got around?"

"The detectives looked up the itinerary of all the cruise ships that come to St. Thomas and St. Martin. The ship's security officer verified the men were aboard."

"What does Charlie Mikkelsen have to do with it?"

"Why do you ask that?"

"She seems to be around a lot and she seems to know a lot."

"She is the person who suggested the itineraries be checked."

"So she is involved? Why didn't you tell me in the first place? What are you hiding, Chief Johnson?" George thought he sensed a sensational story in the works.

"George, you're a good reporter but you must understand there are things about each and every case we don't share with the press. And we do that for a very good reason whether you like it or not."

"You want to protect her, don't you?" Georgie sat forward in his chair with his elbows on Andre's desk.

Andre sat there and stared George down until he squirmed in his seat and removed his elbows.

"You seem to have a real hang-up about this woman, Georgie. Tell me what you mean."

"She seems to be around whenever there is trouble."

"Do you stalk her, George? You seem to spend a lot of your energy on her."

"Don't be absurd."

"And your implications are equally absurd," Andre said as he sat back in his chair and folded his arms across his chest.

"Where are the officers who left this morning?"

"The last I heard they had arrived in Miami and were on the way to the ship courtesy of a Coast Guard helicopter."

"Is Kingston with them?"

"He left with them."

"Where is Hanneman? He's disappeared into thin air."

"He didn't go with the officers. Now why don't you draw an assumption from that? This meeting is over, George. When there is significant progress I'll call a press conference." Andre stood and leaned over his desk in George's direction. Both hands were flat on the desktop and his jaw was set tight. He glared at George.

"What ship are they on?"

"We did our research, George; you do yours."

"*Aqua Waters?*"

"Why did you ask if you knew?"

"I saw both the women get on it with a huge rolling rack of clothes. They planned to have a good time."

Andre said no more and opened his office door. Georgie Boy left with a smirk on his face. He was sure this story would make his career.

CHAPTER THIRTY-FIVE

Ladies and Gentlemen: This is Captain Hansen. As many of you have heard, the Navy has airlifted our injured passenger. Within minutes, the Virgin Island Police Department will land. I have been informed by the ship's security team that many of you feel you are unnecessarily detained. Ladies and gentlemen, you are in your staterooms for your own safety. Unfortunately, we have a murderer loose on this ship. All passenger decks are now cleared, so searches will commence elsewhere. It is imperative you remain where you are until this man is captured. On another note, our food staff is doing their best to serve all of you as soon as possible. Please be patient. Thank you.

* * *

"Jerome is really dead, isn't he? I can't believe they killed my Jerome," Julie said as she began to wail.

"They haven't caught Al, though. He'll come get me. He must have shot the injured passenger."

"It's you two who should be dead. You planned the whole thing and Al is the one who talked my Jerome into this mess."

"Oh shut up or we'll both end up on death row. Don't you realize not one single person can link us to anyone's death unless you have diarrhea of the mouth."

"You think we'll go free?"

"Of course a lot depends on how clearly the security cameras picked up *Newark Bears*," Alice said as spittle tainted with sarcasm flew between the black iron bars.

"We'll keep our mouths shut. I can run the jewelry store alone. We're not bankrupt and we still have those diamonds stashed away when we staged that fake robbery last year."

"When I say shut up, I mean to shut your mouth, Julie."

"They've arrested us. We'll be questioned. What can I say?"

"Be yourself—look stupid. It's quite simple. Our husbands treated us to a cruise. That's all we know. We didn't know what they were up to or what they did. We had no idea about the jewelry thefts or murders. Got it, Julie?"

"That's all we say. Are you sure?"

"I'm sure. The less said the better."

"I can do that. I will do that. I want to get home to my kids," Julie whined.

"Let's make a deal. You won't rat on me and I won't rat on you. Remember, friends don't rat on friends."

* * *

Captain Hansen went to the Robertson stateroom and knocked. The husband answered and motioned the captain inside.

"May we speak, please?"

"This isn't good, is it?"

"No, sir. Our sister ship found your son's body. His neck was broken so he did not suffer. Your mother's body was not found. Perhaps the weight of the boot took her down."

The family stood in numbed silence for a few minutes.

"Are you sure it is my son?" the mother asked.

"His wallet was in his pants, ma'am." The captain gave the Robertsons a printout of the description of the clothing the young man wore. "Please accept my personal condolences and those of my company. An autopsy will be needed and the cruise line will arrange for shipment of your son's body back to your hometown and cover all expenses and memorials for both your family members. I realize this is little consolation for such massive grief."

"Do you know who murdered my family, captain?" Mrs. Robertson asked.

"We do, ma'am." The captain described what was on the security cameras.

* * *

Charlie snipped away at the pantyhose as she and Al listened to the captain's announcement.

"You know as well as I do I'm your ticket out of here, Al. You did notice, didn't you, the captain didn't mention me. He did that on purpose. It sounds to me like they have a plan up there on the bridge. It's standard police procedure—never tell everything you know. Always hold back a critical piece of information."

"Do you want your mouth stuffed again?"

Charlie was smart enough to shut up.

Ms. Charlie, Ms. Elin must be alive. I bet it was her who the Navy rescued.

I hope so. I sure do hope so. Say a couple of prayers.

Is it true what you told Al? Do the police really hold things back?

That's what they do on Law & Order. All my mystery novel heroines do the same thing, too.

Wow. What about the real police?

Charlie didn't answer but rested her fingers for a few minutes. Her wrists no longer stung when she forced them apart.

* * *

"Captain," Dyrby said, "I sent Fander and two seamen to search staff's quarters. I can't imagine Bladensburg would go among staff but we need to make sure."

The captain nodded as he watched Ohlssen and Sahlin unroll blueprints of decks eleven through fourteen.

"The three of us agree we should take one deck at a time. When we start we will leave a crewmember at each exit."

"Excellent. But I don't want anyone else dead or injured," the captain said. "What are your plans?"

"Sir, we plan to stay together at all times. We used the detailed blueprints to identify small places where someone could hide. We highlighted those areas in yellow on our staff maps to ensure we don't miss them. We designed the path for each deck in red."

"When is the VIPD due?" Hansen asked.

"Soon. Captain, I feel responsible for all of this and don't want to waste another minute. I need to start now."

"All right, the three of you start. When I hear the helicopter, I'll contact you through your hand-held radio."

The men headed for deck eleven.

* * *

The Coast Guard radioed the ship it was about to land. The captain notified Dyrby.

Passengers on the port side of the ship peered through their windows as the large helicopter passed. Many of the voyagers grabbed their cam recorders, cameras or cells. For the second time, the passengers who faced the bow watched a copter bank and land. One by one, five people in full tactical gear and firearms exited the copter. Dyrby rushed to greet them.

Chamaign was easy to pick out. "Officer Benton, it's a pleasure."

Chamaign shook his hand and introduced Man, Larson, Bob Thompson and Ben Shore. The officers were led up the lift to the bridge.

"Whoa. Look at the view from up here," Man exclaimed.

Dyrby walked them over to the window with its floor to ceiling glass. "It is exciting to be here. You won't believe the sky at night."

"I bet the bikinis during the day aren't hard to look at either," Man said with a Grand Canyon wide smile.

"True enough." The tall Swede smiled as he looked down at Chamaign and Man. Somehow his six feet-four inch height seemed inadequate next to the confident and determined demeanor of the two short detectives. "It's time to meet the captain." The officers followed Dyrby to where the captain stood and introduced them.

"It's a pleasure to meet you, officers. I believe it is safe to say we can use your help." He introduced Nicklas Ohlssen and Erik Sahlin.

"Sir, has there been any update on Elin Mikkelsen?" Chamaign asked.

"The carrier's surgeon contacted me a few moments ago. Her surgery went better than expected. She required six liters of blood and had to have several organs repaired. She is on some serious antibiotics."

"When will the carrier reach Norfolk?"

"Monday, I believe."

"That's great. My boss will be a happy man. Thank you, captain."

"Dyrby, we're ready to start if you are," Man said.

"Come right this way." Dyrby led the five-member team toward a meeting room in the rear of the bridge. They passed thirty or so consoles filled with dials, switches, meters and gauges and the crew that monitored them.

A large set of ship blueprints filled the entire long tabletop.

"None of us had any idea this ship would be so complex. Help us get orientated," Chamaign said.

"Our crew's quarters have been checked thoroughly as have all passenger decks. We are left with parts of decks eleven and twelve through fourteen. They are the most complicated decks because they include the promenade, pools, nightclubs, kitchens—the list is almost endless."

"Where was Bladensburg the last time he appeared on the security cameras?" Larson asked.

The security officer pointed to Charlie's suite and showed them the hallway where lift number three was located.

"Dyrby," Man asked, "at the risk of sounding stupid, a lift is an elevator, right?"

Dyrby nodded. He tried hard to smile but the strain on his face prevailed.

"And port is right or left, Man?" Chamaign teased.

"You guessed it, Dyrby. I've never been on a ship before. Two or three times on twenty footers maybe, but that's it."

"But you are a fast learner, right?" Dyrby said. This time a hint of a smile was on Dyrby's face.

"Back to deck eleven," Chamaign said.

Everyone studied the blueprints to devise a strategy.

* * *

Both Jeremy and the Chief turned on their cell phones as their plane touched down. Jeremy had a message. He listened and let out a deep, angry breath. "Things are bad. James didn't go into any detail but he told us to meet him at C-14. He's on a flight to somewhere so we need to hurry."

"He didn't tell you where?"

"He only said to hurry."

The plane sat on the tarmac as another plane prepared to back out twenty-two minutes late for departure. After the annoying wait, their plane pulled in. Upon exit into the terminal, the men walked as quickly as they could. It took them almost fifteen minutes to find the right terminal and gate. Passengers already stood in line as they waited to board flight two-six-two to Norfolk.

"Jeremy, over here," James called.

Both men spotted James at the same time. He looked exhausted and his polo shirt was wet from sweat. His shoulders drooped and the look on his face was of defeat.

"You look bad, James. Are you okay?" the Chief said.

"I took four aspirins a half hour ago. I'll feel better soon."

"What's happened?" Jeremy asked.

"Sit down for a second." Once the men were seated, James looked directly at Jeremy. "Things have not gone well on the ship. Bladensburg went after Elin and your mother. Elin was shot; your mother is held hostage."

Jeremy sat motionless. The Chief stood and paced. He asked James if he knew anything about Elin's condition. James told him what he knew about the Navy and Elin's surgery.

"So that's why you're on your way to Norfolk," Jeremy said as he stared at the floor.

The Chief said, "I'm sorry about your mother, Jeremy. Five of our officers should be on the ship by now. They have much more experience than the ship's crew. Chamaign and Man will find your mother. That's a promise."

"What do you suggest I do, James?"

"Rent a car and get a hotel room. Afterward, locate the Scandinavian Seven Seas Cruise Line office and go there. You might have to get in their faces but get in their faces. The Miami people may not know the details but headquarters in Stockholm does. Insist you talk to them. Demand they update you on any activity on the ship."

"Will they let me go onboard?"

"Probably not. They have over 3,000 passengers to deal with at the moment."

"What if something happens to my mother?"

"Jeremy, it's all I can do to keep positive about Elin. It isn't easy and I haven't been very successful. You have to keep positive and you have to push the cruise line to keep you informed. I can't stress that enough."

"Is the Navy in contact with you?" the Chief asked.

"Things happened so fast they don't even know about me. As soon as I get to Norfolk I'll take a cab to the base. I will insist on some form of communication."

"You need a doctor, James."

"I know. I'll get one in Norfolk."

"When is the ship due to dock?" Jeremy asked.

"Well, it wasn't too far from *Aqua Waters* so I don't see how it will make Norfolk tomorrow. I suspect it is due on Monday."

"James, I'm sorry. After I get Mom we'll fly to Norfolk. I can ask one of my brothers to meet us there or else I'll rent a car and drive us home."

"That would be good, Jeremy. Very good. We have to stay positive. Very positive."

FINAL CALL FOR FLIGHT TWO-SIX-TWO TO NORFOLK.
"I have to go."

Jeremy and the Chief watched James shuffle his way to the gate. He didn't appear to be positive about anything.

* * *

Georgie worked at a feverish pace with a fiendish grin planted on his face. His urge to brag became too intense so he rushed upstairs to his editor. "Sam, I've got something you have to hear. We have a story for the wires that I know will explode world-wide."

"Have a seat, Georgie. It's that good, huh?"

Georgie sat and read what he had written so far and told his boss the rest.

The editor immediately saw the possibilities and composed the headline in his mind:

TWO MURDERERS LOOSE ON CRUISE SHIP

"Scandinavian Seven Seas, huh? Georgie, this is big. Get it on paper. I'll call Johnson to verify the facts when you are done. You're right—this will make news across the globe."

An excited George returned to his desk and pounded his keyboard. He decided he was either in for a big raise or an important job at another newspaper. *Who knows—maybe a television offer. I might even get a book deal out of it. Go Georgie Boy, go. When you got it, you got it. I'll show 'em!*

George almost finished his story when a thought occurred. He logged onto the cruise line's website and found the address and phone number for the home office in Sweden. With a diabolical look on his face, he dialed the number.

A woman answered in Swedish but George plowed ahead in English. "This is George Harris from the Virgin Island Press. Put me through to your media people."

"May I ask what this is about?"

"I need details about your ship that left St. Martin with two murderers onboard. I have a story about to break over the international wires."

George was asked to hold, which he did for seven minutes.

"Britta Swensen."

Georgie immediately conjured up a picture of a tall, curvaceous Swede with long, flowing blonde hair and turquoise blue eyes.

"Miss Swensen, George Harris from the Virgin Island Press. I'm on a deadline and need detailed information about your ship that left the Caribbean with two murderers onboard."

"What kind of information?"

"Let's start with the name of the ship."

"I find it strange you believe there are two murderers loose but you don't know the ship's name, Mr. Harris."

"*Aqua Waters.*"

Swensen hesitated a few seconds before she spoke. "There are some difficulties aboard the ship, Mr. Harris."

"Would you confirm the alleged murderers are Alan Bladensburg and Jerome Ambrose?"

"Those are the names."

"Have they been captured?"

Britta hesitated again and then cautiously spoke. "Mr. Ambrose is dead."

George realized the story was far bigger than he thought. "Britta…"

"Miss Swensen, please." Britta's tone changed from professional to iceberg cold.

"Miss Swensen, has Mr. Bladensburg been taken into custody?"

"No."

"Have any other passengers been involved?" There was silence on the phone for a good fifteen seconds. George decided to trust his gut despite what Deputy Chief Johnson said. "Miss Swensen, I know Charlie Mikkelsen and Elin Mikkelsen are on your ship."

"I will not confirm the names of any passengers."

"Are there other passengers involved?"

"It is not prudent to divulge any other information, Mr. Harris."

"Miss Swensen, I have the ability to make your cruise line look good in this article or to make it look bad. How do you want the story to go?"

"Mr. Harris, there are over 3,000 passengers on the ship. I will not discuss this because some 3,000 families around the world will think the worst has happened to their loved ones."

"Do you want your company to look good or bad?"

"We will not compromise the concern we have because you threaten us, Mr. Harris. I need to go now."

"Please, Miss Swensen. I understand your job is to protect the passengers and families. I do. Please tell me if the two women are okay?"

"I must go, Mr. Harris."

Georgie knew if he kept the woman on the phone long enough, he might get a sliver of information. "Miss Swensen, I appreciate your patience, but since your ship is in international waters, why did your staff get involved with the two men?"

"Mr. Harris, we had a legal right and obligation to make the arrests."

"Miss Swensen, is there anything you can tell me you wouldn't consider confidential?"

Britta relented a bit. "I can tell you one thing because the family knows what happened." Britta told him about the invalid grandmother and her grandson and explained how *Aqua Lights* became a part of the drama.

George was stunned into total silence for a half minute. "Was the grandmother Charlie Mikkelsen?"

"No."

"Did the murderers have wives or other women with them?"

"Julie Ambrose and Alice Bladensburg are in the ship's brig."

George decided to take a long shot. "Miss Swensen, I am truly distressed by this nightmarish situation. One more question. Did Ambrose mistake that poor grandmother for Ms. Charlie Mikkelsen?"

This time Miss Swensen was stunned into silence. "I cannot provide you with any more information, Mr. Harris."

"Ma'am. Was Charlie Mikkelsen the passenger injured?"

"That's enough, Mr. Harris." Britta hung up.

George's phone rang. "When will you be done?" Sam Kentland asked.

"Boy am I good, boss. In fact, I'm better than good—I'm great. There's more, boss, a whole lot more. This is one huge story!"

CHAPTER THIRTY-SIX

Jeremy and the Chief left the terminal and walked downstairs to where the car rental agents had their booths.

"I'll rent the car, Jeremy," the Chief said.

"I'll rent the car, *Victor*. She's my mother."

The Chief ignored Jeremy's contempt and bit his lip as the young man signed the papers. Before Jeremy left the desk he asked to see the phone book. He found the cruise line in the yellow pages and wrote down the number and address. The two men walked to the rental car pick-up area when Jeremy's cell rang.

"Hey young fella, this is Gil."

"I'm in Miami at the moment Gil, what's up?"

"I couldn't find Chief Hanneman anywhere so I called you. I have some info on those two men we found dead. Do you know where the Chief is?"

"He's with me. I'll put him on."

"Jeremy, you'll come back, won't ya?"

"Don't think so, Gil. Here's the Chief."

"Hanneman, here."

"This is Gil, Chief. You know, Gil from the marina."

"What can I do for you?"

"I know you're not the Chief anymore, but Chief Kingston isn't around. I thought I should let someone know what I found."

"No more dead bodies, I hope?"

"No, but those dead guys, ya know the guys we found, Chief?"

"What about them, Gil?"

"I drew my own pictures of them and went into a bar last night and talked to some people. Chief, those guys sold drugs."

"What bar?"

"The Palm Shack."

"Who told you they sold drugs?"

"Burt the Bartender pointed out three people he said he knew bought drugs. I asked how he knew and he told me he saw it."

"Do you know who those people are?"

"Oh yeah. Burt said he saw the two men one night with two guys he didn't know. He said the strangers looked out of place because they wore expensive slacks and shirts instead of casual stuff. That's weird—ya know—the Shack is not one of them classy bars or anything. And ya know what else? They also weren't even high or drunk."

"Gil, I want you to listen to me now. You've stumbled into something in which you should not be involved. I want you to let the police handle this from now on. Do you understand me?"

"Sure, Chief. Okay. I thought you would want to know. When will you be back?"

"Probably late Sunday or Monday. I'll call you. For now I want you to write down the names of those three people and a physical description of each. Draw pictures if you think it will help. Okay?"

"I sure will. Can you tell me if the young fella will be back? I really like him."

"I don't know, Gil. I hope he will."

"Me, too. I like him a lot."

* * *

Bladensburg looked at his watch every five minutes in the hot and stuffy electric closet. He put his ear to the door and heard no sounds or vibrations from someone walking so he opened the door for thirty seconds and swung it back and forth to get fresh air inside.

Whew. We needed fresh air, Ms. Charlie.

You're right. Good ole Al didn't use his Mennen this morning.

How do I smell?

I wasn't aware an alter ego could smell.

Good. Then the stench is you, not me. Your deodorant wore away an hour ago. You smell almost as bad as when you had those hot flashes.

Charlie continued to snip and her fingers continued to ache. She had a ways to go but she no longer had to force her arms apart to give her fingers room to work.

* * *

Georgie went to his editor's office and told him to check the story. It took a few clicks on the keyboard and the story appeared on the editor's monitor. He read it. "This is better than great, Georgie. You have a real scoop here. Now let me handle Andre Johnson. You sit and see how a pro does this."

The editor dialed Chief Johnson. "Andre, this is Sam at the VIP. I'd like to confirm what you told George."

Andre became anxious. He wasn't thrilled to speak with the press again so soon. "I'll be happy to, Sam," he fibbed.

"Why was Charlie Mikkelsen on the cruise?"

"Charlie? Why do you ask about her?"

"We know about the mistaken identity thing, chief."

"Who divulged that information?"

"Now chief, you know a good reporter like George has to protect his source. Sorry, but we won't tell you."

"Scandinavian Seven Seas invited Charlie and Elin to complete the cruise back to Miami. The cruise line wanted to discuss the placement of an Island Elegant Apparel shop onboard."

"Was George correct when he said James Kingston went with the team?"

"Yes."

"But didn't his appendix rupture earlier this week—Tuesday morning, right?"

"Right."

"Should he have traveled?"

"I don't tell James what he should or should not do, Sam. Deputy Chief Kingston went with them."

"Is he in Miami now or on the ship?"

"Sam, this is some mighty sensitive information. You can't print this."

"Andre, I not only can print it but I will print it. It all boils down to whether you want this to look like some kind of police cover-up."

"This is not a cover-up, Sam. We need to protect the identities of the injured parties."

"So was Charlie Mikkelsen injured?"

"I'm not aware that she was."

"We know Ambrose is dead and the wives are in the brig. Where is Bladensburg?"

"They haven't found him."

"So he's hidden someplace?"

Andre didn't respond.

"I take your silence as a yes. Who else is injured?"

"Why do you think there are other persons injured?"

"You just said the words 'injured parties' and that makes it more than one."

"I'll tell you, Sam, but you can't release it now. You have to save it for later. Do I have your word?"

"George won't mention anything you tell me from this point on. You have my word."

"You can't print your second release until after Bladensburg is captured. That has to be part of the deal."

"Agree."

"And I have your word and George's word?"

"Agree."

Andre told Sam about Elin's injury, Charlie's situation and the murdered passengers and crewmembers. He mentioned that the passengers were confined to their staterooms until Bladensburg was found. An exasperated Andre hung up. *God help me. I hope I didn't screw things up.*

* * *

"That was awesome, Sam. Now I have two stories."

"You call Johnson every half hour until he knows that bad-ass Bladensburg is captured. Send the story out like it is and start on the follow-up where we name everyone."

"Are you sure we can't send the whole thing out now, Sam?"

"I'm mature enough to feel a responsibility for the families of those passengers. I gave a man my word. Learn that lesson well, Georgie Boy. A man is only as good as his word. Didn't they teach you that in college?"

"I don't appreciate what you imply, boss."

"Well, you need to earn the right to be called George Harris and not Georgie Boy."

* * *

Jeremy stepped inside the doorway of the cruise line office. It occupied the twentieth floor of a Miami highrise office building. At the reception desk he introduced himself and the Chief.

"My mother, Charlene Mikkelsen, is on *Aqua Waters*. She is the woman held hostage by a murderer. I want to speak with someone who will answer my questions. Don't waste my time with anyone else. Do you understand?"

"Yes, sir," the woman replied as her forehead furrowed. "If you will excuse me a moment, I'll find someone who can help you."

The Chief sat on a very modern and a very hard wooden chair. Jeremy stood with his arms folded tightly in front of him.

"This office is huge," the Chief said. "I bet this is where they purchase all the food that must be hauled into the hulls of their ships every Sunday."

The sneer on Jeremy's face dripped with distain.

"I'm only trying to make conversation, Jeremy," the Chief said as he shifted in the uncomfortable seat.

The Chief sat and Jeremy stood for a good ten minutes before the receptionist slid into the chair at her desk and tried to be invisible. Ten minutes later, a young man entered the area and headed toward Jeremy.

"Good morning, gentlemen. I'm Tom Barrett."

Jeremy and the Chief shook Mr. Barrett's hand and introduced themselves.

"Won't you come into my office?"

They followed Tom through several hallways to a small office. The title on the door silently announced that Thomas M. Barrett, Assistant Vice President of Customer Relations, worked inside.

"Sir, I am sorry about your mother and…"

"Call me Jeremy. His name is Chief. I'm not interested in pleasantries or chitchat. Is my mother okay?" Jeremy said as he glared at the young man behind the shiny new desk.

"Please sit, gentlemen." The Chief sat but Jeremy stood with his arms crossed against his chest. Tom took a deep breath and continued. "Less than an hour ago we were notified there were problems on the ship. We were told to make arrangements to transport a young man's body to his hometown. To be honest, I know little more than what I told you."

"Well," Jeremy said. "You will find out what happened and tell me if my mother is safe and out of danger. You will do this right now while I stand here."

"I appreciate how you must feel, but unfortunately…"

"Unfortunately, Mr. Assistant Vice President of Customer Relations, you don't understand that when I say now I mean right *now*." Jeremy glowered at the young man who looked like he graduated from college three days earlier.

"Please sit down, Jeremy. I can understand how you feel because I have a mother, too. If she were in danger, I would feel the same way and insist on the same information."

Jeremy sat but his jaw remained clenched.

"I need to speak with my boss for a few minutes so he can tell me how I reach the right person at headquarters. I'm new here and do not know the proper line of communication. You may sit here or you may return to the reception room. Your choice."

"I'll stay here," Jeremy said.

The Chief nodded.

"Thanks. I'll be back as soon as possible. You have my personal promise, Jeremy." Tom picked up a notepad in one hand and a pen in the other. Before he left the room he looked back at Jeremy, "I will get you the answers you need."

After Mr. Barrett left, the Chief said, "You came on pretty strong, Jeremy."

"I didn't ask you for an analysis of my interpersonal skills."

"My point is that at times tact can get you further than demands."

"Thanks for the tip, *Victor*. From what I've heard, you know all about how to intimidate peons with your overbearing personality and caustic remarks."

The Chief ignored what Jeremy said. "The cruise line is not at fault here. They are in the midst of a customer relations nightmare they did not precipitate."

"I want to know where my mother is and if she is safe." Jeremy articulated each word slowly and deliberately.

"Treat Mr. Barrett with more respect. The young man empathized with you. He understood how you feel and your concerns."

Jeremy leaned back in the chair and folded his arms tight across his chest. His legs were straight out in front of him and crossed at the ankles. His body language dared the Chief to say another word.

* * *

While Jeremy and the Chief waited for Tom Barrett to return, the Chief's cell rang and it was Andre. He updated the Chief.

"What did good old Georgie Boy want?"

Andre described the dialogue between him and the reporter and told him about his conversation with Sam, the editor. "It will be released over the wires any moment now so you can expect it to be on the air shortly."

"Thanks, Andre. Please keep in touch." The Chief disconnected and turned to Jeremy.

"Son…"

"I-am-not-your-son," Jeremy replied slowly in a deep monotone voice.

"George Harris has this story and its will be released over the wires soon. Andre Johnson expects it will hit the news at any moment."

"The only thing I care about at the moment is my mother's safety."

Tom entered the room. "Jeremy, Chief Hanneman, I spoke with my boss and we called headquarters. There is a lot of trouble on our ship and now news bureaus across the world want to know about it. The phones are ringing non-stop."

"I don't care about news bureaus or your phones. What about my mother?"

"Jeremy, there is no easy way to tell you this. Your mother is held hostage by one of the murderers. I'm so sorry. I can't imagine how much this must distress you."

"We already knew she was a hostage. I need to know what you plan to do about it?"

"Our whole customer relations team and senior management will meet in five minutes. I will tell you afterward what we plan to do."

"Has the VIPD arrived yet on ship?" the Chief asked.

"A few minutes ago. They are in a strategy session as we speak."

"Mr. AVP, I will not leave here until I know my mother is okay."

"I understand. I can let you stay in a small private office across the hall or you are welcome to stay in our employee lounge. I can't let you roam the building though. Which do you prefer?"

"The office."

"Good. I'll have our receptionist bring you coffee and something to eat. There is a small television in there and a private restroom right next door. Here's my key."

Jeremy accepted the key and studied the carpet as the young junior executive led them to the office.

"Mr. Barrett, I apologize for my rudeness," Jeremy said.

"I have a mother, too, remember? Call me Tom. I will exist on coffee the rest of the day so I'll be back to borrow that key."

Jeremy almost smiled at Tom's attempt at humor.

CHAPTER THIRTY-SEVEN

Charlie's joints were stiff and painful. The soft tissue around her replacement knees screamed. She flexed her knees as tight as she could.

"This isn't an exercise class at the YWCA," Al said.

"My knees are stiff. I need to move them a bit, that's all. I'm no threat to you, believe me." Charlie bent her knees three more times.

"That's enough. Stop."

Charlie stopped the leg exercises but continued to snip. She knew she didn't have much more than a dozen snips left before her wrists would be free. She pushed her back into the corner again so Bladensburg wouldn't notice her shoulders twitch as her painful fingers maneuvered the cuticle scissors. "We haven't heard from the captain in a half hour or so," she said.

"No news is good news. I'm not about to move from here until early tomorrow so you get to spend the rest of your life with me."

"I don't understand why you had to kill all those people."

"Because I do what the army taught me to do. Once a killer, always a killer."

"You did have a choice, you know."

"Like that should make a difference now. Shut your mouth or the rag goes back into your trap."

Charlie said nothing more as the last snip freed her hands.

Good job, Ms. Charlie.
My muscles are stiff and achy.
But you did it. That's what's important.
It would help if I could get the handles of the scissors off my swollen fingers.

Now is the time to act like your mystery novel heroines and get the bad guy, missy.

My mystery novel heroines are all thirty-something, have well-defined muscles, zero body fat, jog five miles a day and carry a gun. I'm sixty-five, have three replacement joints, no muscle mass, an overabundance of body fat and I limp. My weapons are cuticle scissors, a small can of hair spray and a bottle of nail polish remover—none of which is lethal.

Charlie massaged her hands in an attempt to circulate the blood. She stifled a scream when she forced the scissor handles over her bulging finger and thumb joints.

That hurt.

Even I felt it, Ms. Charlie. Can you get the hair spray and nail polish remover out of your pockets?

Not until good ole Al here closes his eyes or gets distracted.

* * *

Gil knew the Chief warned him to leave the drug issue alone, but he had enjoyed his role of amateur sleuth and salivated for more adventure. *I survived the last seventy-eight years of my life and expect another thirty or forty. Might as well have some fun so I don't git old and bored.*

Gil returned to the Palm Shack. He found it closed but he figured Burt was inside anyway. After a few raps on the door, Burt appeared.

"Hey Gil, what's up?"

"Have a few minutes?"

"I'm busy right now. Can this wait until I open?" said the unshaven bartender who had just tied last night's filthy apron around his ample waist.

"Now, Burt. It's about Roy Stevens and Chuck Buckley."

Burt allowed Gil inside. "Already told you everything I know."

"Chief Hanneman asked me to ask you a question, Burt."

"Hanneman? Isn't he retired?"

"He's around while Kingston works the murders of those jewelry people."

"So you told Hanneman about me?"

"Told him what you told me. He said he needs your help."

"What's the question?"

"Can you describe those two men who sat at the table with Roy and Chuck? I got me a notepad here."

"Gil, it was months ago. Christmas decorations were up so it had to be around holiday time. How do you expect me to remember way back then?"

"Try hard, Burt. Try."

"I remember the one guy was big. Tall and broad shoulders. He reminded me of a cop."

"White or black?"

"Black."

"Light or dark?"

"Light. The other guy was dark though."

"Now we're getting somewhere. How did the big guy keep his hair?"

"Short. Expensive clothes though—tan slacks and a white short-sleeve shirt. Ya don't see many nice shirts in here—that's why I remember him."

"Was the other guy big, too?"

"About the same as me. Five ten. Average build."

"Did he remind you of a cop, too?"

"Yeah. It was something about the way they held their shoulders. I thought those two didn't match Roy and Chuck's crowd. The second guy was dressed good, too."

"You're on a roll, Burt. Go on."

"Dark skin and a narrow mustache."

"What kind of crowd did Roy and Chuck run with?"

"Loud, noisy—always a bit high on something or drunk on rum or beer."

"And these men weren't like that, right?"

"Right. These guys were here on business. There was serious talk and they kept watchin' so no one came too close. They were up to no good."

"Thanks, Burt. If I drew ya a picture could you help me with their features?"

"Nah. I did the best I can."

"If I can think of some more questions I'll be back. Take care."

GOLDEN OPPORTUNITIES: A WOMAN'S MYSTERY NOVEL

"You do the same. Sold your marina yet?"

"Got me a prospect. Young fella. He was kinda turned off when we found them two dead bodies."

"I can see how that would dampen a deal."

Gil left the bar. He decided he would return later when the people who bought drugs might be around. *If that nice lady can track down criminals, I can too. Might even be famous.*

CHAPTER THIRTY-EIGHT

James left the Norfolk airport, hailed a cab and asked the driver to take him to the Naval base. The eight aspirin he took over the last three hours caused heartburn and the fever barely subsided.

"Where are you from, sir? You have an accent I've never heard before," the driver asked.

"The islands—you know—the Caribbean."

"I hear you get some hurricanes down there."

"We do. You tell me something now. What is the best hospital in Norfolk?"

"Norfolk Regional. My mother had her hip replaced there and she swears by it."

"Have you ever been a patient there?"

"No, but I took my kids there when they needed stitches. Staff took good care of them in the ER."

"Take me there instead, please."

Ten minutes later James entered the emergency room. He registered at the desk and sat down in anticipation of a long wait. He filled out a ton of papers for his health history and insurance. When done, he put the papers down, closed his eyes and agonized about Elin. He must have drifted to sleep because when the nurse called his name, the sound of it jolted him awake. Once inside the curtains the nurse took his temp.

"One hundred and four. Let me get the doctor."

Twenty minutes later the doctor swung the curtains open. He was surrounded by a whole herd of interns. "Give me some background, Chief Kingston. You're from St. Croix?"

James nodded.

"Police?"

"Yes."

"When did the fever start?"

James told his audience about the airlift and the burst appendix.

"Are you on antibiotics?"

"Not since I left the hospital at two this morning and flew stateside. My fiancée was shot and she is due to arrive on the aircraft carrier on Monday. I'm here to meet her."

"Was she shot while on duty?"

"No."

"Accident, huh?"

"No."

"Was she in a cat fight?"

The reaction from James was not what the doctor expected. "No, she wasn't in a cat fight," he bellowed.

Now embarrassed in front of the interns, the doctor dismissed the entourage of eager faces. "Sorry. Sorry. A woman shot on a Navy ship is news. They'll put her in the Naval hospital."

"She's not in the Navy. She was a passenger on another ship. She required immediate surgery so the Navy picked her up and took her to the aircraft carrier."

The doctor's eyes became bigger. "What ship?"

"*Aqua Waters*. It's a cruise ship." James took the cold wet towel the nurse offered and placed it on his forehead. "I need a prescription for antibiotics from you."

"I'll give you a prescription as soon as I see the results from your blood tests." The doctor completed a form and told the nurse to call in a lab technician. "What is your fiancée's name?"

"Elin Mikkelsen."

"Do you want Miss Mikkelsen to be brought to this hospital?"

"If that is possible."

"Double room for the two of you?"

"Don't get smart with me. I'm not in the mood," James growled.

"Calm down, now. Wait here and I'll get back soon."

"Nurse, put him on an IV while he waits and keep cold compresses available." The doctor headed for his computer in his small office. The first thing he did was to log onto www.coxnews.com and then made a phone call.

* * *

The passengers on *Aqua Waters* were frustrated and bored. Their cell phones didn't work; their laptops had no Internet connections; and their requests to call home were denied. Stranded in their rooms, they waited for breakfast. The only source of entertainment was COX where the same news was repeated forty-seven different ways within sixty minutes.

Every passenger grabbed for the remote to turn up the sound when big red letters rolled across the screen: BULLETIN ALERT—MURDER AT SEA. Attention-getting music blared. Even the crawl at the bottom of the screen disappeared.

"This is Karen Wales with COX News International. We're the first to announce this late-breaking news. We have learned that *Aqua Waters*, a ship owned by the Scandinavian Seven Seas Cruise Line, has had several brutal murders while on the high seas. We have with us George Harris, a reporter with the Virgin Island Press, and he is the young man who broke this story and gave us this exclusive interview."

The next shot was of Georgie behind his desk as he stared at his monitor.

"George, what can you tell us?" Karen asked.

With flair and drama, Georgie swung his chair around, brushed his fine brown hair off his forehead and looked straight at the red light as the cameraman twisted his lens for a tight close-up shot.

"Karen, this is one huge story. A murderer is currently loose on a cruise ship that has over 3,000 passengers and each and every passenger is in mortal danger. The ship is now midway between St. Martin and Miami. This story started last night when one of two suspects wanted for murder by the Virgin Island Police Department apparently tossed two passengers overboard. The victim was an older woman in a wheelchair and the other victim was her grandson."

Appropriately outraged, Karen gasped for breath, "George, this is atrocious. Continue, please."

"When the captain verified the grandmother and grandson could not be found, Scandinavian Seven Seas' headquarters in Stockholm immediately ordered a second ship to search for the victims. The grandson's body was recovered but not the grandmother's. When the ship's security force went to arrest the two murder suspects, a shootout occurred. Jerome Ambrose of Newark, New Jersey was killed and his wife was arrested. The wife of the other suspect, Alice Bladensburg, was also arrested."

"Who is the other alleged murderer and where is he?"

"Al Bladensburg is also from Newark. He escaped and is in hiding."

"Your press release said that the Virgin Island PD took a helicopter to the ship. Tell us more."

"The VIPD had identified Ambrose and Bladensburg as the suspects in the murders of three jewelry-trade employees that took place in the Caribbean. Each of these jewelry representatives transported a substantial amount of jewelry from store to store or from island to island. A vicious murder took place on St. Croix, on St. Thomas and on the Dutch side of St. Martin. All victims had their necks broken. The suspects and their wives used the cruise line as a means of transportation between St. Thomas and St. Martin. While the ship was docked in St. Thomas, one of the men, believed to be Al Bladensburg, flew to St. Croix, committed the murder-theft and returned to St. Thomas. Meanwhile, Jerome Ambrose murdered the jewelry rep on St. Thomas. When the ship sailed into port on St. Martin, one of the men murdered a rep there."

"Why on earth was a poor disabled grandmother and her grandson killed, George? That doesn't make sense."

"Karen, this is where this story becomes even more bizarre. That poor woman's horrible death was a case of mistaken identity. Yes, Karen, you heard me right—a case of mistaken identity. Can you believe that? Isn't that outrageous? Doesn't that make your blood boil?"

"Absolutely. Go on, George."

"The police believe Bladensburg must have recognized a woman on the cruise ship who he had noticed in the St. Croix airport. This was an older woman with gray hair and she wore a big black orthopedic boot. So did our poor dead grandmother. Bladensburg must have decided she was a possible witness who could place him on the island at the time of the murder. Apparently, Bladensburg and Ambrose decided to murder her. What they didn't realize was that there were two older women on the ship who had gray hair and an orthopedic boot."

"This is horrible. George, we can't get through to corporate headquarters at Scandinavian Seven Seas. Did you validate this story with the cruise line?"

"Absolutely. I am a true believer of responsible journalism, Karen."

"George, hold on a second. I just received an update from a COX affiliate. An unidentified source in Norfolk said an Elin Mikkelsen was shot onboard *Aqua Waters*. She was in such serious condition the Navy flew to the rescue and transported her to an aircraft carrier for surgery. She is due to arrive in Norfolk on Monday. Do you know anything about this?"

"No, Karen. But I do know who Miss Mikkelsen is. She owns a well-known dress shop on St. Croix. Karen, let me email a picture of her to you right now." George paused as he turned and clicked keys for a second.

"Karen, I took this picture before Elin and her cousin, Charlie Mikkelsen, sailed on *Aqua Waters* yesterday. You'll see the ship in the background."

"Now you have me curious, George. Please tell our viewing audience why you took this picture?"

"Karen, I'll tell you what I can. I can't break confidentiality from a source so I need to be careful. As you know, Karen, a reporter has to protect his or her source."

"Of course," Karen said as she watched George shuffle papers.

"Charlie Mikkelsen is the woman on the right in the wheelchair. I can't confirm this, but she could be the woman who the suspect meant to kill. This is a guess, Karen. I can't confirm it, please understand."

"Why did you take her picture, George?"

"Ms. Mikkelsen flew from her home stateside to St. Croix to testify in an upcoming murder trial. She saved her cousin's life last January when Elin Mikkelsen's ex-husband tried to have her killed."

"The picture has arrived, George." Karen turned to her director and asked for the picture to be put on the television screen. It took but a few seconds before the image appeared. "Now identify the ladies again for us."

"The older lady on the right is Charlie Mikkelsen. The woman on the left is Miss Elin Mikkelsen. Elin was the one who was shot."

"So you think the lady on the right was the real murder target and not the grandmother?"

"That's my theory."

"Anything else, George?"

"One other thing, Karen. From what I was told, all the passengers on *Aqua Waters* are confined to their staterooms for their own safety until the murder suspect is captured."

"Well I bet they aren't too happy. Thank you, George."

Karen didn't wait for George's comment and disconnected. She repeated her story to the people who tuned in five-minutes later.

* * *

Holy Moley! That woman gets more famous each day. If I can figure out the identity of those two men Burt saw, maybe I can be famous, too. Yessiree, I gotta git myself on that Internet thingie.

* * *

Jeremy and the Chief stayed in the private office and watched the small television. Both men simmered inside.

Tom entered the room. "Jeremy, we did not reveal that information about your mother or Elin Mikkelsen. We spoke to the VIPD and they didn't do it either."

The Chief replied, "That information would not have been leaked by an officer, Mr. Barrett. Are you aware Deputy Police Chief James Kingston went to Norfolk to meet the ship."

"Why?"

"He and Elin are pretty much engaged."

"Then I should get in touch with him?"

"You need to contact him. In fact, James should know everything you know. Four of our officers are onboard." The Chief wrote down James' cell number.

"I'll see that we take care of this and I promise you Chief Kingston will be kept up-to-date. Jeremy, we don't know any more about your mother's current situation but she sure seems well known."

"She is, thanks to Chief *Victor* here."

Tom avoided the Chief's eyes. "I want to update you on what we know."

Jeremy shifted in his seat and listened as Tom told the men about the current body count. Neither Jeremy nor the Chief were happy about what they heard.

* * *

"How did Georgie Boy find out about Elin?" Chamaign said in total exasperation. "James wouldn't have told the press."

"Chief Johnson would never have told that twerp about Elin, either," Man said.

"Well hot shot Georgie Boy can't break con-fi-den-ti-al-i-ty, but someone sure did." Chamaign articulated each syllable with undisguised rancor.

"This whole thing is a fiasco," Dyrby said. "May we continue so we can start our search?"

* * *

"Damn, damn, damn," Andre shouted. "What a self-serving mini-God. How did George find out so much?"

Chief Dwayne Phillipe, Andre's boss, said, "I don't want to see Georgie Boy in this building again."

"I can't keep him out, Dwayne. And he did keep his word and did not say Charlie was a hostage."

"Well I'm not about to stand up and cheer George on."

* * *

James could hear the television from his curtained cubicle. "Pissant doctor. There is no way I'll allow Elin to come to this hospital." James rose, wet the towel again, swallowed four more aspirin and started to leave the emergency room.

"Excuse me, sir. You can't leave," the nurse said.

"I will leave or there will be an emergency room doctor without teeth around here," James yelled as he charged out the door.

CHAPTER THIRTY-NINE

"We've got us a plan," Man said.

"It's a good plan, too," Dyrby said. "I see you brought two extra vests and helmets. Could Fander and I borrow the gear?"

"That's why we brought it," Man said.

"Who wants me on their team?" Dyrby asked.

"You go with Team Chamaign and Bob. Fander will go with Team Man and Ben," Chamaign answered. "Larson will track us on our mikes."

The captain entered. "Tier is on his way. He said he knows where Bladensburg is."

A surprised Dyrby responded, "I thought he said he didn't find him on camera."

"That's what I thought, too."

Seaman Henrik Tier entered. "Afternoon, everyone."

"Where did you find him?" Dyrby asked.

"A few minutes ago I remembered to check the reports on our secured door system."

"How does your system work?" Chamaign asked.

Dyrby answered, "I showed you our staff hallways on the blueprints. All entrances and exits to staff facilities have secured doors requiring a special keycard. Our system generates a report by the name of each crewmember who enters and exits a door."

"That's right, ma'am. This way we don't require security cameras in staff areas because we know who comes and goes," Tier said.

"I already checked the system earlier. Wesson never went above deck ten."

Dyrby said, "You're right, sir, but Gottfrid Klinge did. In and out and in and out of various doors."

"I don't understand," the captain said.

"I had him paged, sir," Tier said. "None of our crew has seen Klinge for the last couple hours so I asked his superior to try his hand-held radio but there was no response. I believe he may be missing and Bladensburg may have his keycard."

"Where is Bladensburg?" the captain asked.

"He's hidden on deck twelve in a room off a staff hallway. There are no more than eight rooms to search, sir."

"Whoa," Chamaign exclaimed.

"This also means we have another dead crewmember," the captain said.

Team Chamaign and Team Man scrutinized the blueprints to identify the hall and rooms they needed to search. The way the hallway was designed the two teams could go in from two different directions and sandwich Bladensburg in the middle.

* * *

The cab was on Interstate 64 headed for the Naval base. James tried hard to focus on the anticipated red tape it would take to get onto the base and speak with the right person. He hoped the right person had seen COX News.

"Are you sure you want me to leave you off here, sir? What if they don't let you in?" the cabbie asked.

"I'm not about to leave until I see the person I need to see."

James paid the fare and tip and walked up to the security booth next to the gate. He took out his badge and identification.

"My name is Deputy Police Chief James Kingston from St. Croix, U.S. Virgin Islands."

"Did you come in a car, sir?"

"No, I had a taxi."

"I'm Seaman Watson, sir. How may I help you?"

"Have you heard about the cruise ship in the Caribbean?"

"No, sir."

James explained what happened. "I need to speak with the person who will oversee the transport of Miss Mikkelsen from the ship to an ambulance."

The seaman started to make a series of phone calls. It took almost twenty minutes before he turned to speak to James. "Chief, our commander's aide has sent a car for you so I'll give you a temporary ID badge. Would you please sign in?"

James did as instructed. He happily entered the closed jeep when it arrived. The only thing between James' short sleeve shirt and the chilly weather was the sweatshirt he had picked up in the Miami airport.

Lieutenant Hopkins greeted James as he exited the cab. "Let's go to my office, chief."

"Lieutenant, I hope you can tell me Ms. Mikkelsen is okay."

"She is. While the car picked you up I contacted the carrier's surgeon. She's fine but will require hospitalization."

For the first time in many hours James breathed a sigh of relief. "I can't tell you how much this means to me. Miss Mikkelsen and I plan to marry."

"Congratulations. But right now you look like you could use some sleep, Chief."

"I stopped in the ER at Norfolk Regional and asked for antibiotics. I told the doc why I came to Norfolk and he blabbed to COX. If I hadn't heard it repeated on television myself I wouldn't have believed it."

"I wish we could keep Miss Mikkelsen on a base hospital but we can't. A friend of mine is a doctor at St. Mary's. Would you like me to give her a call? Her name is Ellen, too."

"Lieutenant, you made me a happy man."

A few minutes later James spoke with Dr. Ellen Cowen and made arrangements for an ambulance to arrive at the base on Monday afternoon. He asked Dr. Cowen for an appointment for himself and explained why. She told him that as soon as he arrived at the hospital he should have ER notify her.

The lieutenant called for a ride to the gates and a cab for James.

"I can't express my gratitude enough for how the Navy intervened in this situation. My Elin wouldn't be alive right now if this magic hadn't happened."

"Here is my direct line if you have any questions or you need help in anyway," the lieutenant said.

* * *

Team Chamaign and Team Man took their positions at each end of the hallway. Larson followed Man. Halfway down the corridor there was a right-angle turn so the two teams couldn't see each other. With Kevlar vests and helmets on, they proceeded slowly in SWAT team fashion. At each doorway, one person stayed outside and the other two went in. It was through the second door Chamaign and Borge saw the legs of a man stick out the closet door.

"Here is your missing crewmember," Chamaign whispered.

"I somehow anticipated this," Dyrby responded.

Al's attention perked when he heard the click of a door. He stuffed the pantyhose in Charlie's mouth and turned off the lights in the electric room. He waited for the door to open with his gun aimed to kill. Charlie took the opportunity to extract the potential weapons she had slid in her pockets earlier in the morning—a can of hair spray and a bottle of nail polish remover. She removed the caps of both and sat them in the corner behind her.

You're all set, Ms. Charlie. Do what you have to do.

Let's hope it won't get me killed.

Wrong. Let's hope it won't get us killed.

It was Chamaign who came to the locked door and whispered into her helmet's built-in mike, "We need the key, Dyrby."

"He couldn't be in there. It has a heavy duty lock."

"What's in there?"

"It's an electrical closet. There is one on each floor. All the wiring from each floor feeds into the electrical boxes inside and goes through a conduit to our generator room below."

"Got anything, Chamaign?" Man said.

"I think so. We're around the corner."

As Man and his team rounded the corner, she put her finger in front of her lips in a gesture for them to keep quiet. "Let's move on and check another deck," she said out loud. Both teams moved to an area outside the range of the closet. Ben stationed himself close enough to see Bladensburg if he should open the door.

Once it was safe to speak, Chamaign told the teams about the electrical closet. "If he didn't leave this hallway and he's not in these rooms, there is only one place he can be."

"How would he get inside?" Dyrby asked.

"Didn't you know, Dyrby? Every person in Newark knows how to pick a lock," Chamaign teased.

Teasing or not, Borge took her seriously. "Fander, call for an electrician now. We need that key."

* * *

"Smart, ain't I?" Bladensburg jeered. "How stupid can cops get?" He put the lights on again and pulled the pantyhose out of Charlie's mouth.

"You don't want me to answer that question, do you?"

"Shut up. They won't be back. What's do I smell?"

Charlie grabbed the bottle of nail polish remover and put her thumb over the open top so Bladensburg couldn't smell the solvent in it. "They must have had a can of the stuff you spray to look for fingerprints."

"That's weird." Bladensburg leaned back and relaxed again. *Another deck. Stupid cops.*

* * *

It took the electrician six minutes to get Borge the key.

"We need to assume Charlie is in the closet with him so we can't simply open the door and shoot," Chamaign said.

"Dyrby, you said the door is heavy metal. The person who opens the door is protected, right?" Man asked.

Dyrby nodded.

"That person has to shine a flashlight to temporarily blind Bladensburg. Fander, you're that person," Chamaign said. "He may be couched on the floor so he's less of a target. As long as I see he doesn't have Charlie in front of him, I'll shoot first. If I go down, you take over, Man."

"I'll do it, Chamaign," Man said. "You've got a kid, remember?"

"So we're going to stand here and argue who goes first?"

Man nodded.

"And exactly who is the sharpshooter?"

"I can't argue with that and I'm not a chauvinist either."

Dyrby said, "If Bladensburg is crouched like you think, maybe we need to be on his level. He would aim upward."

"True," Chamaign said. "Dyrby, you're out of this contest. You're so tall you could bend down and still be as tall as Man or me."

"Chamaign, I might be a bit more agile than you," Man said.

"So you think I'm fat, Marlboro Man?" Chamaign deadpanned. "You're right. I can shoot better than you but you can move faster than me."

"Then it's settled?" Man asked.

"No, it's not. Flip a coin and I want heads."

"I want to be in this contest, too," Larson said.

In unison, Chamaign and Man said, "No."

Man won the coin toss. "Fander, you unlock the door but stay behind it. Chamaign, you cover me."

The group silently crept toward the door. Man knelt in place and held his gun with both hands. He motioned to Fander.

CHAPTER FORTY

Bladensburg snapped to attention when he felt the vibrations of footsteps. He only had time to reach up and turn off the light and take aim.

It's now or never, Ms. Charlie. Someone's coming.
I'm on it.

In total darkness, Charlie grabbed the bottle of hair spray and pushed the little white button in the direction of Bladensburg's face. She screamed and kicked him repeatedly with her boot as she continued to press the button. Startled by the spray, he dropped the gun to shelter his stinging eyes. Charlie tried the hair spray once again before she aimed the bottle of nail polish remover and squirted the fluid in the direction of his face. This time he screeched as the solvent splashed into his eyes. His baby blues no longer stung; they burned as the solvent seared his eyeballs.

Charlie aimed her boot at his face and made direct contact with his nose. There was a loud crack. With a last shot of hairspray, she grabbed for the door handle and pushed the door into Fander's face as he turned the key in the lock. She crawled out as Bladensburg found the gun on the floor and took a blind shot.

Man aimed his gun over Charlie's body and fired twice. Bladensburg had two holes in his forehead that matched the set Ambrose had put in Seaman Stanford's head earlier in the morning.

* * *

Before anyone on the team could say anything, Charlie looked at Chamaign. "Is Elin okay?"

Chamaign quickly explained. Charlie remained on the floor as tears of relief streamed down her face. A second later she smiled at Chamaign, "The Navy! She gets to cruise to Norfolk with a boatload of sailors!"

"Yep." Chamaign beamed; Dyrby grinned; Man smiled; Bob and Ben laughed; and Larson studied the woman he had heard so much about but had never met. Fander rubbed his red and very sore nose.

"Where's James?" Charlie asked.

"Norfolk, of course."

"We need to get those two married. Maybe people will stop trying to kill Elin."

In the midst of a belly laugh, Bob said, "She needs to stay away from you, Miss Charlie. Then people will stop trying to kill her."

Now that oxygen again filled Borge's lungs, he laughed uncontrollably. He went to a wall phone and called the captain, described the scene and requested a wheelchair for Charlie.

***

"It's over," the captain announced to his crew. "The Mikkelsen woman is fine; Bladensburg is dead."

The crew clapped and a few let out a hoot.

"They found Klinge's body." The bridge quieted down. "Ohlssen, please arrange for removal of the bodies of Bladensburg and Klinge so we may release the passengers." Ohlssen was on his way before the captain issued his next order. "Sahlin, please arrange for a new stateroom for Ms. Charlie."

The captain went into his private office, shut the door and closed the blinds on the windows facing the bridge. He sat back in his desk chair and took a deep breath and expelled a long sigh of relief. He gave himself those few moments of peace before he sat forward. With elbows on his desk and his hands on his forehead, he remembered the faces of his four crewmen and reflected on the pain he would inflict upon their families. The four passengers had no faces but he dreaded the required phone calls to the two families he still needed to contact. He finally pushed the button on his phone and buzzed Lindstrom. "Connect me to headquarters."

* * *

The wheelchair arrived. Bob put his arms under Charlie's armpits and lifted her. After she planted herself in the chair, Bob pushed her to the elevator and to the bridge. Charlie was on a natural high and chatted away a mile a minute. Her sentence structure was jumbled and phrases poured out in all the wrong places.

"You did fine, Miss Charlie," Bob said. "I told you the day you arrived in St. Croix you could catch the man who killed that lady. Of course I didn't expect all of this to happen."

"Neither did I."

"I'm proud of you, Ms. Charlie."

"Oh hell, Bob, I'm proud of me, too."

So are the heroines in your mystery novels, Ms. Charlie. Even I'm proud of how well you listened to me.

Listened to you?

You shush. Enjoy your notoriety.

"Where is Jeremy? I bet he's fit to be tied."

"He's in Miami. So is the Chief," Chamaign said.

"I need to ask the captain if he will allow me a call all my sons."

"I'm quite sure he will," Dyrby replied.

* * *

"I knew you were a clever woman last night at dinner," the captain said as he hugged Charlie.

"Captain, was that only last night?"

"Only last night, Ms. Charlie. It does seem like a long time ago, doesn't it?"

The captain had a steward pass out champagne glasses filled with the bubbly.

"Ladies and gentlemen, to Ms. Charlie—for creativity beyond the call of duty."

"Hear. Hear."

"Speech. On the other hand, a short speech," Chamaign said.

Charlie hesitated for a second to sort her jumbled thoughts. "A toast: someone on this ship, like the captain, arranged to save Elin's life; others, like Officer Dyrby, put his life on the line to find me; and my friends from the VIPD and the St. Martin PD risked their lives to rescue me. I know there are a lot of other people involved who I don't know about. The only thing I can say is one big thanks to all of you. Salute!"

Charlie's audience clapped. The captain asked her what all had happened and Charlie gave blow-by-blow details from the initial shots in the stateroom to her weapons of choice.

"How on earth did you loosen the ties around your wrists," the captain asked.

"My trusty ole Princess Summerfall Winterspring watch." Charlie explained her wrist maneuvers in detail.

"You do need to write a book about all of this, Miss Charlie," the captain said.

"Not until I take a nap."

"We just happen to have a fresh stateroom all ready for you but I must admit we have now officially run out of empty staterooms," the captain said. "Dr. Reinfeldt will pay you a visit. Someone will bring a few of your personal belongings to you."

"That would be appreciated. After long hours with Bladensburg in a small closed room, I'm in dire need of a shower and clean clothes."

"Officer Chamaign, I know Charlie's room is considered a crime scene but can you pick up some of her things?"

"Of course. We do need to call Chief Johnson to find out what to do about all of the crime scenes."

"Captain, I have to call my sons before I do anything else," Charlie said.

"Of course. I have notified headquarters you are safe. I don't know if the word has filtered down to your son or not. Lindstrom, take Miss Charlie to our communication center."

***

"Jeremy, it's me."

Jeremy's sigh was part out of relief and part out of frustration. "I take it you're in one piece?"

"One piece." Charlie retold the story for the second time in ten minutes.

"Hairspray? That's pretty good, mom."

Charlie continued her saga.

"Congratulations, you really can take care of yourself. Listen, I'll be at the pier when the ship docks and I'll call my brothers. You and I are headed for Norfolk and home."

"Sounds wonderful but I do need to get back for the trial."

"Not without ten armed guards in a nice neat circle around you. I'll hire Secret Service agents if I have to."

"I need to go now. I'll see you tomorrow."

"Hold on, mom, the Chief is here." Jeremy handed the phone to Victor.

"Charlie, I'm so relieved you are safe."

"Me, too. Where are the two of you?"

"In the cruise line office in Miami."

"You sound upset, are you?"

"Relieved is a better word."

"Jeremy will fill in the details. I'll see you tomorrow."

"Wonderful. Tomorrow." Charlie picked up a tone in Victor's voice that didn't compute.

***

As the Chief hung up, Tom entered the room.

"You two know?"

"In graphic detail," Jeremy replied. "Mom called."

"Mom is okay?"

"Okay."

"Would you come up to the meeting room and tell everyone what your mother said?"

The men followed Tom.

* * *

Georgie Boy was squatted in Andre's office when Man called. Andre pushed the conference call button and hoped desperately he wouldn't live to regret his actions. The ambitious young reporter frenetically took notes with a Machiavellian grin on his face as he listened to the conversation.

* * *

Ladies and gentlemen, this is Captain Hansen. The crew and staff thank you for your patience and your concern. I am most pleased to inform you it is now safe to leave your staterooms and enjoy the rest of your cruise home. Lunch will be available in about fifteen minutes in all of our facilities. Free drinks will be available for the rest of the cruise. Scandinavian Seven Seas Cruise Line apologizes for your inconvenience. Thank you.

* * *

James did not hear his cell phone ring. He had passed out in the cab and was now in the emergency room of St. Mary's Hospital.

* * *

"It's over," Julie said.
"Al must be dead or else he'd be in the cell next to us," Alice replied.
"We're on our own."
"It's better that way and not a soul has to know a thing."
"We'll keep quiet, right?"

"We're innocent wives who had no idea what our husbands did," Alice said.

"I'm going to miss Jerome."

"Why on earth would you miss Jerome?"

"I know he was a jerk but he loved me and the kids. Oh, my poor kids."

Alice didn't respond but she already missed Al Bladensburg.

CHAPTER FORTY-ONE

For his second interview, George had taken the time to apply make-up, call his mom and choose his setting. He stood in front of the piers in Charlotte Amalie. Minutes later, music blared and television screens went red. Big black letters against a bright red background commanded viewer attention: COX BULLETIN ALERT. Viewers around the world glanced at their TV screens in breathless anticipation. The interest level for the tragedy junkies was higher than the Empire State Building.

"This is Karen Wales with an exclusive COX News report. We have a special interview with George Harris, the Virgin Island Press reporter who broke the Scandinavian Seven Seas Cruise Line murder story earlier today. George, what has happened?"

"Karen, this story is absolutely unbelievable. And I mean unbelievable. I'll start with the final body count: four *innocent* passengers dead, four *innocent* crewmembers dead and the two murder suspects are dead. Additionally, a woman, Elin Mikkelsen, is injured and aboard a Navy aircraft carrier headed for Norfolk. Charlie Mikkelsen, who was held hostage by the alleged murderer, Al Bladensburg, is now safe. The wives of both men sit in the ship's brig."

"What on earth happened on that ship, George?"

"Karen, I couldn't make this stuff up it is so outlandish. And I mean outlandish. Really far out. Earlier today we knew two passengers had been tossed overboard. We now know it was the alleged murderer, Jerome Ambrose, who did it. What we also didn't know before was that after Al Bladensburg went to the Mikkelsen's stateroom and shot Elin Mikkelsen, he grabbed

Charlie Mikkelsen as hostage. During his escape he barbarically murdered two innocent and defenseless passengers who happened to be in the hallway when he went through. This man was a ruthless killer, Karen. Absolutely ruthless. Unbelievably ruthless."

"The last time we spoke, you told us two security men were killed when they went to arrest Ambrose. What about the other two, George?" Karen asked.

"The two others were murdered at different times. Both of them were unfortunate enough to get in Bladensburg's way and both had their necks savagely broken."

"How did this Mikkelsen woman get away from her captor?"

"Bladensburg found a small electrical closet, picked the lock and hid there for hours with his hostage. Meanwhile the VIPD and the St. Martin PD arrived and worked with the ship's security officer to devise a search plan. The search team narrowed the location down to a single hallway. At this point the horrible became hysterical. As I told you, Karen, I couldn't make up a story this wild! Absolutely wild. Unbelievably wild!"

"Well, don't stop now. Tell us the rest, George."

"When Al Bladensburg blasted the security latch off of her stateroom door, Charlie Mikkelsen heard him. She knew the man was after her so she taped her cuticle scissors to her back and slipped a small can of hair spray and a bottle of nail polish remover into the pockets of her slacks. By the time this Bladensburg character arrived at her bedroom, she had hid in the head with her crutches—remember now, she is the woman with the orthopedic boot who used crutches or the wheelchair to get around. When Bladensburg opened the door to the head she came at him with the tip of her crutch already aimed, well Karen, you need to use your imagination about where she aimed. Anyway, she got him twice before he wrestled her to the floor but she continued to kick him with her boot until he had a gun to her head. Bladensburg forced her out the door, down the hall and into a staff elevator. That's when he stuffed her mouth with a pair of pantyhose and tied her wrists behind her with another pair. To make a long story short, the two of them ended up in the electrical closet. While sitting there with her hands tied behind her, the woman successfully retrieved her tiny scissors and laboriously snipped away at the pantyhose for hours until her hands were free.

"When Ms. Mikkelsen heard footsteps come down the hallway, she pumped hairspray into Bladensburg's face and squirted nail polish remover into his eyes. While he was blinded, she opened the door and crawled out. Bladensburg shot and missed but someone from the VIPD got in a good shot and took him out. Can you believe these incredibly improbable events, Karen? Wild! Absolutely wild!"

"There is an old adage about truth being stranger than fiction, George. Did you confirm this information?"

"Absolutely, Karen. Absolutely! I consider myself a very responsible reporter. I sat in the office of Deputy Police Chief Andre Johnson of St. Thomas when the call came from Detective Marlboro Man Carmen. I heard it with my own ears on a conference call."

"George, how old is this Mikkelsen woman?"

"I'm not sure but she has to be in her sixties."

"Well, I think AARP should hire her as a spokesperson of some sort. She is quite the fighter. Unbelievable. And what an incredibly wonderful ending."

The camera went back to Karen. "Hairspray and nail polish remover. Ladies, we need to store that information in our memory banks. Viewers, this exclusive story was brought to you by COX, the most important news channel on the air. As our logo says, *Important News for Important People*."

* * *

Georgie Boy's mother thought the few strands of boyish sun-bleached hair that blew across her son's forehead looked adorable.

Man's parents sat in their home on the outskirts of San Juan and beamed. "That's *my* three pounds of red meat. What a boy!" Mr. Carmen shouted.

Everyone on the bridge watched the broadcast.

"Georgie Boy disgusts me beyond belief," Man said.

"Frankly, I didn't know there were so many adverbs in the English language," the captain noted. "Isn't that what the Americans call hyperbole?"

"He's nothing more than a contemptible, repugnant, sleazy scumball who specializes in sensationalizing human misery," replied an angry Chamaign. "Boy would I'd like to kick his bahookie to St. Croix and back!"

"Now tell us how you really feel," Larson laughed. "And Man, at least you got your name mentioned on the air."

"Well that part wasn't too sleazy," Man said.

"Buddy, you better believe your boss blew a gasket or two a few minutes ago," Chamaign said.

"No question about it. Let's get back to the DVD Tier made of Jerome and Julie. We need to decide how to handle the women's interrogations."

"Charlie said something about a confession on the wall of the electric room," Chamaign said.

"I took a slew of pictures of it and copied it down," Ben said. "It's a full confession and signed by Bladensburg."

"When do you plan to read it to us, Ben?" Chamaign asked.

To Whom it May Concern: I, Alan Bladensburg, killed the woman jewelry rep on St. Croix and Mark Andrews on St. Martin. Jerome Ambrose killed the man on St. Thomas. Jerome and Julie Ambrose killed the lady in the wheelchair and the man with her. They threw them overboard and were quite proud of themselves.

It was my wife Alice who planned the whole robbery thing.

It was Alice who took two quick trips to the islands last fall and scoped out the routes of the jewelry reps. Our calendar at home will give you the dates. Jerome and I came to the islands last week to see if her plan worked. It was Alice's suggestion to kill the Mikkelsen ladies since they were the only two people who could place me in St. Croix at the time of the murder. It was Alice who said the woman in the wheelchair needed to be killed. I will probably be dead when you read this, so consider this my bedside confession.

Fry Alice—she ain't innocent. Her whole plan is on our computer at home.

You'll have to figure out her password on your own.
Alan E. Bladensburg

"Well his little confession will come in handy. How are we going to proceed?" Larson asked.

"Divide and conquer," Chamaign suggested.

Man knew Chamaign was right.

* * *

The Chief and Jeremy were seated at the conference room table with the cruise line executives. "My mother didn't tell me about the polish remover," Jeremy said.

"She really kept her cool," Tom said. "You're mother is quite creative but George Harris is a colossal creep."

"I can think of quite a few other words that describe him but I better keep them to myself," the Chief commented.

"I need to prepare for a press conference," Tom said. "Do we need to keep the Chief and Jeremy here any longer?"

"Not unless Jeremy would want to join you at the press conference," Tom's boss said.

"No way." Jeremy replied. "I don't want those clowns to put mikes in my face."

Tom walked Jeremy and the Chief through a maze of corridors and cubicles to a back elevator. "The press is staked out front. You don't want to leave that way."

"Thank you for all of your help," Jeremy said both relieved and happy to avoid the press.

"Enjoy your stay in Miami tonight. Remember it is on us. Arrangements are already made. Also, a car will pick you up tomorrow to take you to the pier."

"It will be a media circus and I bet the head clown will be there," Jeremy said.

"Unfortunately, you're probably right. It was good meeting you. Hopefully our paths will cross again under more favorable circumstances."

The men chose to walk the twelve blocks to the hotel.

* * *

"I'll fly back to St. Croix first thing tomorrow morning," the Chief said.

"After all this you won't be here for my mother?"

"This meeting is for the two of you. If your mother wants to talk to me, she'll call. Have a good evening, Jeremy."

Jeremy ate alone that evening and wondered about the Chief's decision. He wondered if his mom would be upset with him since Victor wouldn't be there to greet her.

CHAPTER FORTY-TWO

Charlie turned off the television.
You're famous, Ms. Charlie.
This isn't the kind of fame I need. I bet those TV cameras will be all over us tomorrow.
Well, I won't stick around.
You certainly will. If I have to deal with it, so do you.
That's quite okay. I'm fine if you take all the glory.
I hope I still have my boot if I ever come face to face with Georgie Boy.
What do you think the press will do tomorrow, Ms. Charlie?
I think they'll do anything possible to get viewers to watch their show.
They will want to interview you for sure.
That won't happen.
What if Georgie Boy is there with a microphone?
I'm a lady so I'll walk right past him and not tell him where to put the mike.

* * *

Officer Bob Thompson retrieved clothing and sneakers for both of the women who sat in the ship's brig. Chamaign and Man decided to interrogate Julie first because she didn't appear to be the brighter of the two women. They paraded her in front of Alice to a small room near her cell.

Julie's bleached blond hair was never combed that day nor was makeup applied so every one of her countless freckles showed and her frayed locks resembled a rat's nest. She had on a sleeveless tee over tan walking shorts. Man took a glance at the short, thin woman and thought he could blow her away with his breath.

"Have a nice hard seat, Julie," Chamaign ordered. "We watched how you and Jerome followed Chrissie Robertson into her stateroom."

Man said, "We watched you leave the stateroom in your cute little *Newark Bears* baseball jackets and caps."

"We didn't kill the old lady and the dumb steward."

"Why do you think Chrissie Robertson was an old lady?" Chamaign asked.

"Well I heard someplace an old lady had her neck broken and was thrown overboard."

"Julie, dear. We did not mention the lady's neck was broken or that she was thrown overboard. How would you know that?"

"It was a rumor we heard. One thing I do know is that your precious police department and this cruise line can expect one big wrongful death lawsuit if you killed my Jerome."

"Oh my," Chamaign said. "Are you scared, Man?"

"Sure am."

"Julie, it was you we saw enter the Robertson's room," Chamaign said. "The security camera gave us a real pretty close-up of those cute little lollypop pink sandals you wore. We found them this morning in your closet and they are now evidence in a murder trial."

"Those sandals don't prove anything. We committed no crimes. Show me the bodies, you stupid cops."

"The grandson's body was picked up by another cruise ship."

"Grandson?"

"You and Jerome murdered a grandmother and a grandson. You only thought he was a steward."

"You think I killed them? I couldn't break anyone's neck because I don't have the muscle strength. So there—let your cop brain think about that for a while."

Man spoke, "Let me get this straight. You and Jerome forced your way in, killed two people, threw their bodies overboard, left and strolled down the hall. And you didn't do anything? Chamaign, do you think a jury will believe any of what our friend said?"

"Somehow I don't think so. A poor crippled grandmother in a wheelchair and her high school grandson are brutally murdered and tossed overboard. You know, Man, I know for a fact the jury won't believe our little Julie."

Man said, "Why did you go into the room, Julie?"

"I had to use the bathroom."

"You mean the head," Chamaign said.

"What's a head?"

"A bathroom, Julie. You have to get with the program here. Now, once again, you went to a total stranger to use their head? None of the people I know would do that, Julie."

Julie's eyes widened as her mind probed for a way out of her convoluted story. "We are in international waters and you can't do anything to me so you have to let me go."

Chamaign countered. "You weren't in international waters when the jewelry reps were murdered. We got you on that alone, kiddo."

"Alice and I weren't involved in those murders and we don't know anything about any jewelry reps."

"Julie dear," Man said, "your fingerprints were on the suitcase in your closet and all over the jewelry. There is no juror in the U.S. Virgin Islands dumb enough to believe you weren't involved."

"Well, you can't prove it."

"I suspect she'll get thirty to life, don't you think, Man?" Chamaign said.

"At least. And probably without parole."

Julie tried not to cry as Chamaign pushed harder. "Think real hard about this, Julie dear. You will never hug your children again. I understand you have three."

"Leave my children out of this." A full-fledged spring shower flowed down Julie's cheek.

"Of course, we may get you a deal if you come clean and tell us everything and that includes the part about Alice."

"What kind of deal?" Julie asked hopefully.

"We won't know until we talk to the prosecutor. After all, you were an accessory to two murders."

Julie sat for ten minutes and looked at her hands. Chamaign tapped a pencil on the desk and Man sat and stared at the ceiling.

The silence rattled Julie more than the questions. "I'll tell you if you can get me out of jail. Someone has to raise my children."

"There's jail time, Julie," Man said. "It's a matter of how long. You should have thought about the children before you got involved in theft and murder. I can make no promises."

Another five minutes passed and Julie started to squirm. "It's like this. Al and I inherited this jewelry store but we lost money because Alice kept the books and helped herself. The jewelry stuff was all Alice's idea. She planned the heist from start to finish. She talked Al into it and he talked Jerome into it. Alice is to blame and she's the crook who should be in jail."

"Alice, huh?" Chamaign said. "Well Julie, I have a few questions for you, but think hard before you answer them. If you give me full honest answers we'll talk to the prosecutor."

Julie nodded her head.

"What did Jerome do in the Robertson stateroom?"

Julie described the ugly scene.

"What did you do in the Robertson room?"

Julie told her about the scarf.

"How did you know about Charlie Mikkelsen?"

"Al recognized her from the airport. He figured she and her friend were the only witnesses who could place him on St. Croix that day."

"How did Al know about Elin Mikkelsen?"

"Al bought matching shirts from her shop. He didn't recognize her until he saw her in the empty shop onboard. He realized she could place him on the island, too."

"How did you know Charlie Mikkelsen's stateroom?"

Julie explained about Alice.

"Whose idea was it to kill the ladies?"

"Alice's. She said two more bodies didn't matter."

"Who mistook Chrissie Robertson for Charlie Mikkelsen?"

"Jerome did. I didn't realize the difference either until Alice asked me about her fox boa."

"Did Alice tell you and Jerome to track them down?"

Julie explained.

"Again, who laid out the island murders?"

"Alice. I loved my Jerome, but he wasn't smart enough to do it. In fact he wasn't smart at all. Before my father died he had to give us money all the time so we could feed the kids."

"The plans were precise, Julie. Who is the person who went into such detail?"

"Alice is a CPA. She's all for detail. Al and Jerome were the muscle."

"Who scoped out the rep's routes?"

Julie explained.

"Did you see the murders?"

"Of course not."

"Did the men talk about the murders later?"

"Not a lot. I will tell you something I bet you don't know. Were you aware Al knew the man he killed in St. Martin? They were in Afghanistan together. Can you believe that? He killed his own army buddy. He thought it was funny and bragged because Mark had more kills than he did and yet it was so easy for Al to kill him."

"What about Nassau?"

"Jerome thought he needed the practice."

"How many people were killed there?"

"They told Alice and me they each killed one person. Al and Jerome split up and found their own marks."

"How did you get all the gems and gold back on the ship after the theft?"

Julie detailed their actions.

"Okay, Julie," Chamaign said, "that's enough for now. Someone will type up your statement. If you sign it, I will keep our end of the deal and talk to the prosecutor."

"Don't put me back there with Alice. She'll kill me if she knew I talked."

"Don't go near her side of the cell," Man suggested.

As soon as Julie was in her cell the officers talked with Larson and Dyrby.

"As soon as we get out of international waters, I'll read Ambrose her Miranda rights and have her sign her statement. I'm sure it will end up they will blame each other for what happened."

"Let's get Julie's statement on paper," Man said.

* * *

Gil sauntered into the Palm Shack with the tip of his unlit pipe between his lips. He perched himself on a bar stool and ordered a beer from Burt the Bartender. He faced a large mirror and saw the reflection of the three people who bought drugs from Roy and Chuck.

"Is that them, Bert?"

"Yep."

Gil swung his seat around, took his beer and went over to the table where Tram, Lilia and Steve were seated. He sat down and whispered to Tram, "Since Roy and his pal Chuck are no longer around, where can a guy like me get a small fix?"

"I might be able to arrange something. What are you gonna do for me?" Tram asked.

"I'll be your friend, of course."

"I'm not interested in a shriveled up old fart like you for a friend."

Gil held up his arm and flexed a thick muscle in Tram's face. "I'm not exactly helpless, young fella. I still work out."

"Wow," Lilia said. "This old man has life in him. I'll tell you where to get your stuff if you share it with me."

"Holy Moley. Finally, I've met a pretty lady who understands and appreciates me. You got a deal. You're Lilia, right?"

Lilia nodded.

"And as I said, what are you gonna do for me?" Tram said.

"I'm not here to make enemies but your friend Lilia made this ole guy an offer he can't resist. You're not as pretty as this little lady."

"I don't like you old man."

"That's a shame. I'm a likable old man."

"Look…"

"Come on Tram, drop it," Steve said. "I don't want to be arrested in a bar for a fight over drugs. The old tar isn't worth it. Let Lilia do her thing."

"Do your thing," Tram said as he and Steve rose and headed to the bar.

"Now it's me and you," Lilia said as she batted her eyelashes at Gil.

"My pleasure, pretty lady."

"You meet me tonight at eleven in the rear of the Shack. I'll introduce you to Tommie."

"I'll be there."

Gil left the bar pleased with his progress. He was determined to break this case. *I'll be famous like that young fella's mama.*

* * *

Captain Hansen called Charlie's stateroom.

"Miss Charlie, do you mind if I have dinner sent to your room?"

"Not at all. Vittles from the dining room or pizza shop?"

"Private dining room. There is one catch—I bring the wine and join you."

"I'm honored."

"Instead of dessert, I suggest a platter of various cheeses, a few apple slices and some crackers along with a very special wine."

"Sounds very European."

"How is venison for your entrée?"

"Perfect."

"Seven?"

"Of course, captain."

Ms. Charlie, what was that all about?

I guess we have to wait until seven to find out.

Well, I think he wants dessert.

Well, I think you have a dirty mind. Go read a romance novel.

CHAPTER FORTY-THREE

Charlie tried to take a short nap but her mind whirled in overdrive. She rose and used Elin's laptop to record a blow-by-blow account of what occurred with Al. A little after six, she showered and applied make-up. She couldn't decide what to wear. Chamaign had transferred the rack of Island Elegant's clothing to her suite but most everything was too dressy. There was a lounge coat but she didn't want to give the captain the wrong idea. The snazzy evening gowns were a bit too much. She decided on a casual sundress despite the fact she had no suntan.

You're boot will show, Ms. Charlie.

The captain is well aware of my boot.

Will you use your crutches?

Good ole Al had me walk without them and there was no problem. Haven't you noticed I haven't used them since I've been inside the suite?

Ms. Charlie, what do you think the captain wants?

Maybe the company of a mature woman who is intelligent, gracious and charming.

And what else?

I guess I have to answer the door to find out.

Charlie checked the peephole. The captain carried a bottle of wine in a bucket of ice.

Let me see, Ms. Charlie. How's he dressed?

You don't have to peek. He's my guest, not yours. Now go away.

"Come in, captain. Please have a seat."

The captain stepped inside and placed an ice bucket on a chrome coffee table with a black glass top. He sat next to Charlie on the plush white couch.

"May I ask you to call me by my first name?"

"Certainly. This is a real treat, Birthe."

"The treat is all mine, Charlie. I don't have the pleasure of meeting an interesting person too often."

"I would think there are a lot of women on your cruises."

"Oh don't get me wrong, there are. When and if I decide to have a meal in the main dining room, my staff decides who sits at my table. However, rarely are the women my age interesting and I'm not into chickies."

"Women half your age don't interest you?"

"Charlie, chickies are my granddaughter's age." The captain chuckled as he rose to answer the door.

The server entered with a stainless steel cart covered in white linens. He went to a small narrow closet and removed a heavy-duty fold-up table, set it up in the middle of the room and dressed it with fine linen and gold-plated flatware. A bouquet of pink roses in a crystal vase was set in the center of the table and two tall crystal candlestick holders with gold tapers were placed on either side of the flowers. The server took two handsome white leather side chairs from their place next to the wall and arranged them at the table.

From his linen-covered cart, he removed a silver tray and placed it on the coffee table. In the center of the tray was staged a porcelain bowl of crushed ice containing a second bowl filled with Beluga caviar. A tiny porcelain spoon was arranged in the delicacy. One corner of the tray had a half dozen lightly buttered toast points arranged on a saucer-sized plate. Dry crackers without salt were arranged on a matching plate in the other corner. There were two other small plates—one held spinach puffs and the second contained broiled sea scallops wrapped in bacon. From under the cart appeared a bottle of champagne and two tall crystal champagne flutes. The server opened the champagne and filled the glasses. After leaving small plates and napkins, he left.

"Tell me about this champagne."

"Needless to say it's French and my palate finds it delectable. This is from my own private stock. I've served it to other guests twice in the twenty-seven years I've been a ship captain."

"As tempted as I am, I won't ask about the first or second time."

Birthe grinned, "You don't have to ask, I'll tell you. My wife and I celebrated our twenty-fifth anniversary on my ship. Two years later I served my youngest daughter and her new husband before I left them for the evening."

"How many years have you been at sea?"

"All my adult life. You can't grow up in Sweden and not love the sea."

"How does your wife handle your prolonged absences?"

"She understood my fascination with the sea but never accepted it. I took a six-month leave of absence to help care for her before she died. That was the first time I understood what I missed all those years."

"I'm sorry. That must have been difficult."

"Thank you. I'll retire in several months. I hope to spend more time with my children and grandchildren. Now tell me more about your family on St. Croix."

The two talked their way through the champagne and the appetizers. Charlie could have made the whole meal out of the toast and caviar.

The server arrived an hour later with the entrée. Birthe held the chair for Charlie as she was seated at the table. The server lit the candles and the second bottle of wine was opened. The presentation of the dinner plate was exquisite. The broccoli flowerets fondly surrounded the perfectly cooked venison, which had fancy swirls of a light sauce over the meat and over part of the plate. The baked potato sat smugly amid an array of fresh parsley. It was accented with bits of smoked salmon on top of the sour cream. After the captain sampled the cabernet he poured Charlie a glass.

"Have you ever visited Denmark?"

"No, but I will. I'm not able to research their genealogy records online."

"That would be quite an endeavor. Do you speak or read Danish?"

"Unfortunately not. Luckily, the Danes kept the island's census reports in English. Their legal papers are in Danish though."

"What is life like on St. Croix?"

"I don't know as much as I'd like because I live in Pennsylvania."

"I didn't realize that. I'm embarrassed to say I do not know where Pennsylvania is located. The United States is such a large place."

"It is on the east coast sandwiched between New York and Maryland."

"How wonderful. Maryland is near Washington, correct?"

"Correct. Do you plan to travel when you retire, Birthe?"

"I've already researched New York City, Washington and San Francisco."

"I use a cab to get around NYC but if you need a tour guide for the District, let me know—I grew up there. Whatever you do, don't miss San Francisco."

"If I took you up on your offer, would your friend be upset?"

"My friend?"

"I apologize. I was under the impression you have a gentlemen friend."

"You must mean the Chief. I do see the Chief but we have yet to define our relationship."

"Well, when I do contact you and if you have defined your relationship, I'll understand if you're not available."

After forty-five minutes the server arrived for the third time and removed the plates and a half empty bottle of cabernet. He returned the table and chairs to their proper places and served a platter of cheeses, white grapes and apple slices.

The captain took his bottle of New Zealand wine out of the bucket.

"We never finished the first two bottles," Charlie said.

"True, but this sauvignon blanc will compliment the cheeses and the fruit."

Charlie and Birthe chatted while they nibbled at the cheese. "I have an idea. Are you up to a trip to the bridge?" the captain asked. "There is a spectacular sight I'd like to show you."

"How far will I need to walk?"

"Let's take the wheelchair until we get there." Charlie got into the chair and the captain pushed her a little way down the hall. "Now we will take a staff lift. Will you be okay?"

"Like the elevator Bladensburg used?"

"Very much like it. We can always go down the hall to the main bank of lifts."

"I'll be fine."

Once inside Charlie was a little more uncomfortable than she thought. She brushed her earlier experience aside and concentrated on her conversation with Birthe. After a short ride, Charlie found herself on the bridge.

"Now come over here."

In a heartbeat, Charlie realized why the captain brought her to the bridge. On the port side of *Aqua Waters* Charlie could see two long lines of cruise ships and on the starboard side there was one row. She could make out two ships in front of her. In all, she counted nine cruise vessels, each with thousands of lights that outlined each ship.

"I don't know what to look at first—the stars above or the parade of cruise ships below. Both sights are so marvelous. Are all these ships heading back to Miami and Ft. Lauderdale?"

"They are."

"Are there more behind us?"

"Usually there are two."

"I can't believe you travel in a pack like this. And every ship has thousands and thousands of lights. What a magnificent and breathtaking sight. The whole ocean is one big sparkle. Even Georgie Boy couldn't describe this scene."

"It does humble one, doesn't it?"

"Oh yes. The lights are so majestic and the heaven is ablaze. The stars alone are enough to capture my heart and soul. There must be a million dots of light before me at each and every glance. Humbling? Yes indeed."

"When we don't have fog, the brilliance of the universe shines right through," the captain said. "Now you understand how the sea can crystallize, mesmerize and energize at the same time." The captain refilled Charlie's wine glass. "I thought you might enjoy this scene."

"How do these ships stay so perfectly apart from each other?"

"We each have a lane in which we travel at a designated speed. Our navigators and radar system do the rest."

Charlie said, "As you leave port after dark, do you ever look back to see the lights of the town?"

"Oh yes."

"The lights of St. Thomas are my favorite. Every golden light in the town is reflected in the silent waters of the harbor. Charlotte Amalie is a joy to behold."

The captain nodded.

Neither Charlie nor Birthe was in any hurry for the evening to end. Charlie knew the sight before her was a once in a lifetime opportunity. Finally she said, "You do understand, you are my designated driver."

"I will have you back to your suite within minutes."

Before the captain left Charlie for the evening he explained how she would leave the ship through the exit where food and other products were loaded. A car would await her. "Unless, of course, you want to meet with the press."

"No thank you. I like your way better. Will Jeremy be able to find me?"

"Arrangements are made. He will be in the car that awaits you."

As Birthe went to the door to leave, he kissed Charlie on the cheek. "I want to see your country very much and I would be pleased if you would visit mine."

"That will be something to think about as I try to sleep tonight." Charlie kissed the captain on his cheek and a quick soft kiss on the lips.

Shame, shame on you, Ms. Charlie.

And I don't even look guilty, do I?

CHAPTER FORTY-FOUR

Gil left Lilia in the bar and went to his car. He drove around the block and parked where he could watch the alley that led to the back of the Palm Shack. It was a few minutes before eleven when an old black Chevy entered the alley and parked. A man and a woman sat in the car. Gil left his car and strolled toward the Chevy. He waved at Lilia and the man lowered his window.

"Ya Tommie?" Gil asked.

"One or two bags?"

"One to start. Nice to meet ya."

"Sixty."

"How about two fer a hundred so I can give one to the pretty lady next to you?"

"Only this time, Gil."

Gil rifled through his wallet. He took a tiny key-chain flashlight out of his pocket and shined it into his wallet.

"Get rid of the light."

"It's only so I can see what's in my wallet. Did you know my eyes are seventy-eight years old?"

"Hurry."

Gil removed five twenties and handed them to Tommie and the exchange was made. Tommie and Lilia left.

I can't believe I'm so smart. This little key thing gave me enough light to see his face. I'll draw me a mug shot tonight. I do find it a little funny a drug dealer would have a vanity tag on his car—TURNER—Tommie Turner. I'm gonna be famous like that young fella's mama. I wonder if they'll put my puss on that Internet thingie?

* * *

Julie sat in the corner of her cell as far away from Alice as she could.
"You talked, didn't you?"
"I have kids and you don't, Alice. I don't expect you to understand."
"If you said anything about me, I'll personally kill you."
"You don't scare me anymore, Alice."

* * *

Both women had fallen asleep when *Aqua Lights* entered U.S. territorial waters. Man and Chamaign entered Alice's cell.

"It's time to talk, Alice," Man said. He cuffed her and led her to a small room. Chamaign read Alice her rights but didn't take the cuffs off once she was seated.

"I understand you and Julie are related," Man said.

"We're family, stupid."

"Do you pay the bills at home?"

"That's a dumb question to ask at this time of the morning."

"Do you pay by check?"

"Of course."

"Do you complete the check register?"

"Of course. Your questions don't have much substance do they, detective?"

"Is this your list of jewelry items?" Chamaign showed Alice a plastic bag with a note inside.

"Never saw it before."

"That's interesting. We have this list, your checkbook and several maps. We kinda thought the writing was the same on all of the items. I guess we need a handwriting expert to verify it." She held up another piece of paper in a plastic bag so Alice could see.

"Do you know what this is?"

"Why should I?"

"It's a hand drawn map of the jewelry district. Even the streets are filled in. Let me see here, there is a big 'X' marked on one of the streets.

Your handwriting in the register is the same writing as the streets on this map."

"So what. It shows where the stores were I wanted to visit on St. Martin."

"What is the big 'X', Alice?"

"Al must have put it there."

"The 'X' is where his old Army buddy was murdered."

Chamaign placed another map of St. Martin in front of Alice. "Show me which jewelry stores you visited on the island."

Alice took the map and pointed to six jewelry stores. "Happy now? You haven't proven a thing so far."

"Where did you buy your beautiful sapphire and diamond? Show me the store."

"I don't remember in which store we purchased it."

"We found no receipts for your purchases."

"Al must have lost them."

"Hum. Alice, did you know your pendant was a one-of-a-kind special order?"

"That's what my jeweler said."

"It was listed in Mark's inventory and was a special order for a jewelry store in the area of town you told me you didn't visit."

"Well, I made a mistake."

"You sure did, honey. The store never received their delivery that day. Mark Stevens had it in his display case when your husband murdered him. We know you didn't murder Mark, Alice. But we have hard proof how you planned the operation."

"I am not involved in anything Al might have done."

"It's your handwriting on the St. Martin map as well as on the St. Croix map. You planned both of those heists. And we will get a conviction from both the Virgin Island courts and the St. Martin courts. Our prosecutors will decide the charges. Plus, there will be charges of accepting stolen goods."

"You can't prove I accepted anything."

"We have a pretty picture of you in an elevator when you showed Charlie Mikkelsen your necklace. We have another pretty picture of you as you sat on the promenade and watched the two ladies." Chamaign showed Alice the second picture. "Oh look, Alice, you wore a matching pair of sapphire earrings. I would guess a two-caret stone surrounded by diamonds. This picture blew up quite nicely, wouldn't you say?"

When Alice refused to look at the picture, Chamaign said, "The jewelry will be held as evidence in your trial before it is returned to its rightful owners. The maps will be entered as evidence. Sure you don't have anything to tell me?"

Alice said nothing.

"It's okay if you don't talk. In this list of jewelry items in your notepad, we found every single item in a jewelry pouch in your underwear drawer. Strange as it seems, each item appears on Gemstone Jewellery International's inventory list of the items Mark carried."

"You can't prove a thing."

"We just did. I think you'll get twenty to twenty-five because of the St. Croix heist and murder. Larson thinks you'll get the same on St. Martin. And since we are two separate countries, your sentences won't be concurrent."

"You can't arrest me. We're in international waters."

"Not anymore, honey."

"Look you stupid bitch, I'm a United States citizen. You can't arrest me for anything on St. Croix or St. Thomas or St. Martin."

"Don't think so, Alice. St. Croix and St. Thomas are both U.S. territories and subject to U.S. laws. St. John, too. St. Martin has its own laws and Detective Fossing can and will arrest you, too. The extradition papers are in his pocket."

A shocked Alice blurted out, "I want a deal."

"Deal? We don't need to deal. We have Al's confession," Man said.

"Al? Where is he?"

"Your husband wrote a full confession before he died. He said you planned the heists and your own PC will prove it."

"Al is known for his lies."

"We even know about the jewelry store at home as well as your little IRS adventure."

"It was Al who murdered the woman on St. Croix and the man on St. Martin."

"You still haven't told us anything we didn't already know," Chamaign said.

"Julie helped plan the St. Thomas thing."

"We knew that, too. She told us so. What else do you have on your mind?"

"I want a lawyer."

"You'll get a lawyer when we get back to St. Thomas."

"And when am I going to get my clothes?"

"How about a pretty bright orange jumpsuit? The Miami police will lend us two, I'm sure. The orange will go so well with your fancy stainless steel handcuffs. We'll leave on our own little plane at around three in the afternoon. We got you a direct flight from this brig to the jail in St. Thomas. Enjoy the ship's brig for now. Our jail doesn't serve cruise ship food. Ta. Ta."

Chamaign and Man each took an arm and led a sobbing woman back to her cell.

CHAPTER FORTY-FIVE

It was far worse than Charlie could imagine. She woke up to the whooshes of helicopter rotors. She peeked out her balcony door and retreated in horror. She grabbed for the remote and flipped through channels—one ship channel told passengers how to find the purser's office. Another played the variety show from the night before. A third explained what paperwork was needed to go through Customs. And then there was COX News International.

Hysteria reigned. There was an aerial shot that showed six helicopters as they encircled the ocean liner like a pack of Indian warriors. Instead of arrows they shot visuals of frenetic passengers who waved from their balconies or the main decks. A second copter showed travelers in pajamas, skivvies and a variety of Victoria's Secret underwear. The third showed several balcony scenes of young ladies who thought it was Mardi Gras and bared their bosoms for Planet Earth to enjoy. The world seemed fixated on the ship and its occupants.

Insanity. Total insanity, Ms. Charlie. I'm scared.

We've been OJ'ed!

OJ'd? I didn't have any orange juice!

O.J. Simpson in the SUV chase scene, stupid!

Charlie heard Karen Wales' voice. "This is a shot of the balcony where two passengers were dumped overboard." It was then Charlie realized the passengers were close enough to shore to use their cell phones.

How can these television people be so crude, Ms. Charlie?

There are a lot of idiots in the world so they get a lot of practice.

Karen pointed out the front balcony of the stateroom in which Elin had been shot. Karen warned her viewing audience to send any children out of the room before she showed footage taken with a cell phone. It showed Al Bladensburg as he shot and killed the two passengers in the hallway. Charlie's gut wrenched tight and she ran to the head to vomit.

There were aerial shots of the ship from every angle. With rapidity, Karen Wales repeated the same details over and over and showed the captured pictures over and over. She even showed clips of Georgie Boy as he made his reports the day before.

Charlie took a quick shower and dressed. Chamaign rapped on the door. The detectives and Bob entered.

"Where's Ben?" Charlie asked.

"He's babysitting our ladies," Chamaign answered. "Charlie, you can't go out there. I don't want to go out there. How do you suggest we handle the press?"

Their dialogue was interrupted as Karen Wales announced, "We have new pictures of the two wives led to jail by the ship's officers."

The group watched as Julie and Alice marched down a hallway in their nighties with a robe slung over their shoulders. Their hands were adorned in cuffs.

"Thank goodness Dyrby made them put on robes before he took them to the brig," Chamaign said.

"Did you get any information from them?" Charlie asked.

"Some. The problem is they haven't seen a lawyer but we do have Al's confession."

There was a second rap on the door. Chamaign peeked out and then opened the door for the captain.

"Good morning, officers. And good morning, Charlie. I spoke to headquarters and they are tuned into this lunacy and have a suggestion."

Everyone looked at the captain. "And the suggestion is?" Charlie asked.

The captain was interrupted by Karen's voice on COX.

"Ladies and gentlemen, we reviewed another cell picture. It is quite graphic. If you have young ones around, I would suggest you send them to another room." The picture showed the dead passengers in the hallway surrounded by pools of blood. After thirty seconds, the camera returned to Karen. "I'm sure you'll agree that horrible things took place on that ship. That's all for the moment, ladies and gentlemen. We'll be back after a short break."

"That was truly despicable," the captain said.

"It's about as low as you can go," Man commented with an emphasis on "low."

"What do you suggest, Birthe?" Charlie asked. Chamaign and Man looked at Charlie when she called the captain by his first name.

"Officers, how far are you in your work?" the captain asked.

"Charlie has all of Elin's things and her things. You have the suitcases packed with jewelry in the ship's safe and we packed the personal items of the Ambroses and Bladensburgs. Tier provided DVDs from all the security cameras in which the men and their wives appeared. We have a complete report from your secured doors. Miami forensics will comb for fingerprints and any other evidence. They said it would take about three hours. Miami will send three teams."

"Good. As soon as the passengers leave we will clean all the other staterooms. We have a company in Miami that will clean and disinfect the hallway where the passengers were killed. We have reassigned passenger staterooms so our new guests won't interfere with the officers or the work of the clean-up crew."

"Thank you, captain," Man said.

"We decided to have a number of people arrive by limo at our loading area and later exit by limo with their faces shielded. This will occur throughout the day. We fenced the entire area so the press can't enter and there are guards at the gates. We can bring the limo right up to the ramp so people can come and go in relative peace. The Robertsons and the wives of the two other passenger victims plus Dr. Myers will be interviewed first by our corporate lawyers. They will exit into limos. Then corporate will want to meet with Charlie, followed by Detectives Benton, Carmen and Larson."

"What about the bodies?"

"Vans will be at the loading area when we dock. Someone will come onboard and put all the deceased into body bags and they will then go to the medical examiner's office. Later, they will be shipped home."

"What about the press conference?" Chamaign asked.

"Instead of a conference at our offices in Miami, we thought we should do it at the passenger's exit after the passengers leave. While the detectives hold the conference, Dyrby and Fander will assist your other two officers when they escort the wives to the airport. Charlie could exit then. What do you think?"

"That's a plan." Chamaign said. "Charlie, you have to prep us for this conference."

"I have a better idea. You decide what you want to say and I'll write a statement you can read. Allow no questions. That should take Georgie Boy down a peg or two."

Everyone laughed, including the captain.

"Please excuse me, ladies and gentlemen. I must get to the bridge."

"Will I see you before I leave?" Charlie asked.

"Most certainly. You're not allowed to leave until after I say my personal good-byes."

* * *

After several commercials, Karen Wales reappeared.

"Good morning, viewers. This is Karen Wales of COX News. We have some live shots of the area where *Aqua Waters* will soon dock. The building next to the pier provides passageways, escalators and elevators so passengers can leave. As you can see, there are a dozen or more TV trucks set up. George Harris, the reporter from St. Thomas, is at the dock now. George, tell us when you flew in and what you see."

"Morning, Karen. I flew into Puerto Rico last night and arranged a special flight here this morning. This is one busy place. It is buzzing with camera crews and reporters. I spoke with customs officials to find out how the passengers leave the area. I was told the last thing passengers do is to go through customs. If they owe Uncle Sam, this is where they pay up. After that they can take a bus or cab to go to the airport or wherever they plan to stay."

"Have you spoken to anyone on ship?"

"No. Personnel refused to allow this reporter to speak to anyone. I find it curious behavior and I can't help but wonder if there is something they know that they don't want the media to know, Karen. It is very suspicious no official will speak with me."

"Did you ask to speak with Ms. Mikkelsen?"

"I tried to get a call through to her, Karen and was told she was unavailable."

"In other words, we don't know anything more."

"I'm ahead of the curve on this, Karen. I spoke with a representative of Scandinavian Seven Seas Cruise Line. He said Detective Marlboro Carmen of St. Thomas, Detective Chamaign Benton of St. Croix and Detective Larson Fossing of St. Martin would conduct a short press conference at noon right here."

"George, will Ms. Mikkelsen be there?"

"No, Karen, I was told she wouldn't. Therefore, I plan to stay here until she exits the area."

"Good for you, George."

"I do my best, Karen. And let us not forget, there are all those bodies that need to be removed from the ship and the two wives that need to be escorted back to St. Thomas."

"Have these women be extradited from Miami?"

"Karen, I have already checked with the Miami police. Detectives from both the VIPD and the St. Martin PD came onboard with warrants and extradition papers."

"Do you know how the wives were involved in the murders?"

"Karen, that is the first question on my list. I personally know Detective Marlboro Man Carmen and I fully expect an exclusive from him."

"Where did he get a name like Marlboro Man?"

"I'm not sure but his good friends call him that and I'm a good friend."

"George, we expect a good interview. We'll get back with you."

"One more thing, Karen. I want you to put my cell number on the screen. I would like to speak with any passenger who saw something the press should know."

* * *

Andre sat in Dwayne Phillipe's office on St. Thomas along with the police commissioner and Bill Farrow. Andre turned off the television.

"That nitwit will never sit in my office again," Andre said.

"How strong is our case?" the commissioner asked.

"Pretty strong, I believe. Man said they have two maps drawn by Alice Bladensburg. They detailed where Al Bladensburg killed the woman on St. Croix and the man on St. Martin. Julie Ambrose confessed her part and implicated Alice. And, of course, they have Bladensburg's confession and all the stolen jewelry. Of course neither lady has seen a lawyer."

"With eight people dead on ship and three dead on our islands, I don't want to see these women walk," the commissioner said.

"At least we don't need to put Bladensburg and Ambrose on trial. When the detectives get here we'll talk with the prosecutor."

There was a rap on Andre's door and his administrative assistant entered. "Sir, Chief Kingston is on the phone."

"Put him through."

"James, you're on speaker and the commissioner and our chiefs are here. We turned the cartoons off the TV. What's up?"

"I woke up in St. Mary's Hospital in Norfolk yesterday afternoon. I passed out in the cab and here I am. I saw Georgie Boy on TV."

"You and a zillion other people," Farrow said.

"Charlie is okay?" James asked.

Andre answered, "She's better than fine. The cruise line will provide transportation so she can leave the ship after a debriefing by the lawyers. They'll take her and her son to Ft. Lauderdale for a flight to Norfolk to see you. Chamaign, Man and Larson will be debriefed also. Have you heard anything about Elin?"

"My Naval liaison spoke to the ship's surgeon. She is doing well. I have arranged for transportation for her from the ship to here. She'll get in tomorrow afternoon. My mother and aunt plus Elin's mother and sister are due this evening. If Elin will have me, we'll get married tomorrow. I talked to the hospital chaplain yesterday and he obtained a marriage license and talked to a judge to get the waiting period suspended."

"Why so quick?" Farrow asked.

"I don't want Elin out of my sight again. It's that simple. The only thing I have left to do is to propose."

The officers all offered their congratulations.

"Where is the Chief?" James asked.

"He called this morning. He's headed for St. Croix to work on those murders at the marina. He said the murder cases couldn't wait any longer."

CHAPTER FORTY-SIX

Gil loved to take his rowboat around Christiansted harbor early in the morning. The daily ritual allowed his mind to be mesmerized by the beauty of the early dawn and his lungs to be energized by deep breaths of the dewy midst. The quiet and peace revived the young man who still lived inside him. After a half hour on the oars he sat and completed the second part of his morning ritual. He allowed the boat to drift while he enjoyed a cup of hot coffee from his Thermos. As he sipped, he took indescribable pleasure in the silence of the harbor. With pencil and sketchbook in hand, he captured the light's first rays in yet another version of his sleepy little town with its red and white roofs. This time his focus was the cross of the Lutheran Church steeple in the heart of town. Once he was satisfied with his sketch, he repacked his sketchbook and put his hands on his oars. With his arm muscles still warm and fresh oxygen instilled in his lungs, he headed back.

He tied up his boat and climbed the ladder to the pier above. That's when he smelled a slight hint of smoke and saw a man in a green sleeveless tee and dirty cargo pants run out of the marina office.

"Fire! Fire!" Gil yelled as he ran after the man.

Since fire and yachts don't mix, men with fire extinguishers appeared like magic off their yachts. "My office, my office," Gil screamed as he ran after the arsonist. He watched in vain as the man put distance between them, jumped into an old Chevy and sped away. *Tommie Turner. How stupid can you get?*

The fire was out by the time Gil returned. He thanked the three men who responded to his call and invited them to share a cup of coffee. They declined. Ashes from four old newspapers smoldered on the floor of Gil's office so he stomped them into oblivion. He opened his desk drawer and took out the charcoal sketch he drew of Tommie Turner. *I guess I have to find the Chief today.*

Gil turned on COX and watched the shenanigans for a few minutes. *Holy Moley. There's Georgie Boy. What a baboon!*

* * *

James called Lieutenant Hopkins at the base. "Lieutenant, I have a favor to ask."

"I heard you ended up in the hospital, Chief Kingston."

"Yeah. I passed out in the cab with a fever of one hundred and five. I'm down and out and on a ton of antibiotics but I'll be okay."

"What may the Navy do for you today?"

"Could I get a message to Elin? It's important."

"No problem. What's the message?"

"I have a marriage license and rings in my pocket and the chaplain is waiting for us in the hospital chapel. Our mothers are on their way. Will you marry me?"

"I'll send this on one condition, Chief. You invite me."

"You're invited."

* * *

Charlie had breakfast with Bob and Ben. Man, Chamaign and Larson were too nervous to eat. Charlie split the officers' statement into three parts so each detective would have a part to read and a crack at their fifteen minutes of fame.

"Man, after Larson finishes up, what are you going to do?" Charlie asked.

"I'll step in front of the mike and thank everyone. Then we'll all turn around and run like hell."

"My cell's dead," Larson said. "Can someone lend me theirs so I can call home and have my wife tape this."

"Here, use mine. I've already hustled my husband out of bed," Chamaign said.

"Man, what about your mom and dad?" Larson asked.

Man grinned. "Done."

* * *

Aqua Waters left its sailing lane and glided into the deep-water channel leading to miles of concrete piers. It snaked its way up the channel to its designated mooring place. The huge engines slowed. With the aid of the bow thrusters and a nudge or two from a tugboat, the ship wiggled sideways so it was flush with the pier. It took a good twenty minutes for the ship to tether its thick lines to the heavy white concrete bollards. It wasn't until the ship seemed motionless that the gangways were lowered. Passengers started to disembark and they pushed, pulled and shoved themselves through the maze leading to asphalt.

The media had a field day. Many passengers, loaded down by overstuffed luggage, filed past reporters and cameras and hurried to find the buses that would take them where they needed to go. Others stopped and answered every question the reporters asked whether they knew the answer or not.

A couple dozen passengers sold their camera or cam recorder's memory card to the highest bidder. Each left with a wad of cash in their pocket.

Each cameraman captured a half dozen interviews plus dozens of shots of the ship and passengers. They knew most of their work would be edited and only the best would make it to ten-second clips for the nightly news. The crowds dissipated faster than the media expected.

All major networks and papers had their own reporters and TV crews at the dock so they had little use for George. He was miffed when he realized he would not be the center of anyone's attention but he didn't accept his fate without a fight. He interviewed one passenger after another as he tried to watch what went on at the loading dock at the far end of the ship. He saw half a dozen limos appear at intervals and men and women walk up and down the ramp. He missed the long dark vans parked to the side.

Fortunately or unfortunately, depending on a person's perspective, the cameramen in the helicopters captured the footage of the bodies carried to the vans. They knew their shots would be played and replayed until a better story took its place. The stations wasted no time and aired live shots of the parade of black body bags.

More limos came and others left. None of the reporters and cameramen could distinguish the families of the victims because of the steady number of people who came and went.

Tom Barrett, the cruise line's spokesperson, had a microphone set up on a raised podium at the passenger exit. A sign stated a press conference would be held at noon. The press waited.

Tom Barrett stepped in front of the mike and read a five-minute statement from the cruise line expressing sympathy for the families of those murdered and described how patient and understanding the passengers were while they were restricted to their staterooms. He introduced the detectives and identified where they worked.

Man spoke first. He gave the reporters a myriad of insignificant details so the facts could be blown out of proportion with little harm to the real investigation. Chamaign spoke about how easy it was for the men to chose their murder victims—even the elderly and disabled grandmother and her grandson. She listed the names of those murdered in the sequence in which they lost their lives. Larson gave an overview of how Jerome Ambrose and Al Bladensburg stalked the Mikkelsen ladies and how bravely Ms. Mikkelsen defended herself and defeated a psychopathic Goliath with a can of hairspray. Somewhere between the murdered victim's names and the hairspray, Julie and Alice were led to a waiting vehicle. Even Georgie got a glimpse of their bright orange suits and cuffs.

After the van left, a limo appeared. Captain Hansen led Charlie to her vehicle and she disappeared inside with a wrapped gift in her hand. Captain Birthe Hansen leaned into the car and planted a big smackeroo on Charlie's lips. This time there were no cell phones or photographers around.

As Man thanked everyone for their attention, a large van appeared and the officers were whisked away. Georgie Boy's big story evaporated.

* * *

"Mom, why do men feel they have to kiss you while I watch?"

"How would I know? I'm not a man."

"Well I get a bit agitated when I have to watch an old man slobber on you."

"Son, no one slobbered on me, thank you very much."

"What all happened on the ship?"

"You can say you're glad to see me and happy I'm in one piece, you know."

"I'm glad to see you and happy you're in one piece and what else happened on the ship?"

Charlie again went through the whole scenario for her son on their way to the airport.

"I can't believe the part about the hairspray!"

* * *

Gil found the Chief in the hallway of the police station. "Hey Chief, how ya been?"

"Fine. I came back to work the murder cases."

"How's that famous lady of yours?"

"She's fine I'm pleased to say."

"A can of hairspray—she is something else. Do you think she'd let me have the can and autograph it for me?"

"Right now I suspect the can is part of the evidence box. I don't believe anyone will get to autograph it anytime soon. But yes, Charlie is a smart lady. Now Gil, did you do as I said and stay out of this murder case?"

"Not exactly. If that lady can use her smarts, I can too."

With relish and pride, Gil proceeded to tell the Chief about the bar and the druggies and his late night drug purchase. He pulled a small plastic bag from his pocket. Inside was cocaine. "See, I saved it for prints. You take it now so you can arrest the man."

"That was very smart but very dangerous, Gil. You could have been killed."

"But I wasn't was I, Chief?"

"No you weren't but that's not an excuse. Now all the VIPD has to do is to identify this man by his prints."

"Oh I know who he is, Chief. I even drew his picture for you." Gil described how he used his penlight to see the man's face.

The Chief looked at Gil's picture. "This is excellent work. This man won't be hard to find."

"You're right, Chief. The man drives around with his last name on a vanity tag."

"You wouldn't kid an old cop, would you, Gil?"

"Not me, Chief. Honest. You'll find Tommie Turner's prints on that there little bag."

"To use you very own words, Gil, Ho-ly Mo-ley!"

"Chief, you can get him on arson charges. He tried to burn me down this morning. Even got me some witnesses."

Gil colorfully described the burning newspapers and his pursuit of the man in the green tee who entered the old Chevy with TURNER on the tag, but not until after he told the Chief about his morning rituals and showed him his charcoal sketch of the church steeple.

* * *

Jeremy had said nothing about Victor so Charlie decided it was time she asked. "What happened between you and the Chief?"

"Before I tell you what happened, will you tell me how you feel about him?"

"I thought about it last night on the ship's bridge."

"You were on the bridge?"

Charlie nodded.

"Last night?"

She nodded again and smiled.

"They don't let passengers on the bridge, mom."
"Well the captain did last night after we had dinner."
"You had dinner with the captain?"
"Twice. It was the captain who kissed me."
And you didn't mind either, Ms. Charlie. Shame.
You're jealous.
Am not.
Are, too.

Jeremy was stunned. He was even impressed. He asked his mother to answer his question.

"As much as I enjoyed the captain's company, I enjoy Victor's more. There. That's it. That's all I know, which is about fifty percent more than I knew before last evening."

"So you may be in love with the Chief?"

"I believe I only said I enjoyed his company more than the captain's."

"So you still don't know how you feel?"

Charlie stared at her son. "Never mind, mom. I get it. You enjoy Victor's company more than the captain's."

"Now tell me what happened between you and Victor. The last I heard you asked for his advice."

Jeremy reluctantly explained what else transpired between them.

"And that's it?"

"I wasn't nice about it. I know, mom, so don't say it. I screwed around with your personal life."

"And when do you plan to apologize?"

CHAPTER FORTY-SEVEN

Two planes landed in Norfolk within minutes of each other. One was from Ft. Lauderdale and the other from Miami. Grete Mikkelsen, her daughter Alyse, Grace Kingston and her sister Jeanette waited at baggage claim for their luggage at the same time that Jeremy pushed his mother's wheelchair to the adjoining carousel.

"You're all here!" a delighted Charlie exclaimed.

All the women exchanged hugs and kisses. Jeremy stood aside and hoped he wouldn't be mobbed.

"Jeremy! Get over here and give me a hug," Jeanette demanded.

"Only if you have a piece of mango mousse pie in your luggage," he responded.

"No, but I'll make you a pie as soon as I'm able," she said as she stretched her five-foot frame to kiss the young man's cheek. "You remembered how good my mango mousse pie was from your first visit to St. Croix, didn't you. Grace, isn't he a nice boy?"

"I've heard about you, Jeremy. It's nice to meet you," Grace said.

"My mother denied it, but I hear she put a spell on James and he's in the hospital."

Grace and Jeanette laughed. "I do believe you mother did just that."

"At least she didn't have a can of hairspray with her." Jeanette hooted.

"Whether she did or didn't, James proposed to Elin," Grace said as she hugged Charlie.

"Did he get to speak with her?" Charlie asked.

"He told me last night he was going to ask the Navy to give her a message. He asked me to bring the engagement ring with me."

"Well it's about time. See ladies, it was about combined mind power after all, wasn't it?"

Jeanette decided to chastise Charlie. "Now young lady, there is a lesson to be learned here. James waited until it was almost too late before he realized how much he loved Elin. You need to decide about the Chief. You might be younger than me, but you ain't no spring chicken."

Charlie decided to change the subject. "Is there a wedding in Norfolk?"

"Yes!" Jeanette screamed.

The ladies pointed out their luggage and Jeremy salvaged it along with his mother's.

He said, "While you ladies stand here, I'm going to get a porter to handle our luggage while I go rent a nice big van."

The ladies discussed the hospital chapel, flowers and what they wanted to wear while they waited for Jeremy to chauffer them to the hotel.

* * *

Charlie asked Jeremy to take the ladies to the hospital to see James. She was far more tired than she expected and wanted a hotel room. Once registered, she relaxed with a quiet bath and crawled in bed a little after nine. She knew it would be after ten in St. Croix but she called Victor anyway.

"Jeremy needs to call you."

"He already did."

"Were you upset with him Saturday?"

"In a way but at the same time I knew I upset him when I told him of your situation. Tell me you really are okay."

"Tired, very tired, but okay. When did you know I was a hostage?"

"James left a message on Jeremy's cell. We found James while he waited for his flight to Norfolk. Jeremy was so worried."

"It's been a tough couple of days for a number of people. Those men caused a lot of grief."

"They did but it's over now. On a lighter note, I can't believe you used hairspray."

"Hey, a girl does what she has to do. I also used a bottle of nail polish remover. I think the chemicals in it are what damaged his sight. He started to shoot but even blind bullets can kill so Man took him out. I was half out of the closet at the time and I didn't look back."

"How is James?"

Charlie told Victor about the ladies in the airport and the big wedding plans for later that evening.

"That's wonderful. They make a beautiful couple."

"Jeremy will fly back on Monday. He decided he wanted the marina. Maybe I should come back with him."

"You go home until the trial. Gil did some mighty good police work on his own and I have a good lead on the man who may have murdered those men at the marina. I'll see Bob Thompson first thing tomorrow and we'll go over the case. You stay at home so I know you're safe."

"Why don't you think I'm safe?"

"I'm convinced my bruised little *Rubee* was about you, not me."

* * *

At breakfast, Charlie thanked her son for his call to Victor. He apologized for being a jerk and promised to stay out of her personal life. He later escorted Grete, Alyse, Grace and Jeanette to the nearest mall and then he headed for a tour of the Battleship Wisconsin.

* * *

"What do you think, James?" the Chief asked.

"I agree. If there had been two separate drug rings we would have known. This has to be connected to Rich Myers and we know the now-deceased Rich Myers was connected to Eugene Peters."

"Paul Simpson ran across this Tommie Turner's car this morning before we even put out an APB. There are prints galore. We already checked out his address and he wasn't there. He has an apartment a couple of houses down the street from where Myers lived. Bob and Paul will track down the three perps Gil identified at the bar."

"Chief, put someone at the airports and ferry so Turner can't get off the island."

"Done—first thing this morning before there were any flights or ferries anywhere. I faxed the sketch Gil did, too. Now you give me an update about Elin. I hear you're to be married."

"The Navy lieutenant called me this morning. Elin responded to my message and agreed. My mother is thrilled, Mrs. Mikkelsen and Alyse are ecstatic, Aunt Jeanette, well Aunt Jeanette is Aunt Jeanette," he laughed. "Chief, I haven't seen Charlie. Did she really use hairspray?"

"Hairspray and nail polish remover. That murdering fool didn't have a chance against her."

"Do you know when she plans to return to St. Croix?" James asked.

The Chief told James about Rubee and the accident on the Restaurant Road and his conclusions.

"Shelby 500GT, huh? I'd like to get me a goddess like her."

"She's a beaut. It will be a month before she'll be fixed though. On another note, Charlie is going to her condo in Pennsylvania. You might want to send Elin there, too. Since they will both testify at the trial, they both could be in danger."

* * *

"That's one big boat!" Alyse said as she and her mother sat in Jeremy's car near the naval dock as the colossal aircraft carrier maneuvered it way to the concrete pier. An ambulance sat next to them.

Grete was upset. "Do you think those reporters over there will bother Elin?"

"I hope not. I watched enough stupid reporters yesterday. I suspect the air space over the base is restricted so there should be only Navy helicopters around," Jeremy said.

The three watched as Navy officers and seamen outlined the decks of the ship while they stood at attention. The Navy band welcomed the arrival of the mighty ship and its crew. A horde of spouses, children and significant others cheered and waved while the ship was secured. Flags flew everywhere. Almost every child had one. After the ramp was lowered, men and women began to leave the ship and either headed for their loved ones or headed for transportation that would get them home.

Grete searched the whole area for Elin. She spotted her daughter among a group of uniformed women who accompanied a gurney down another gangway. The gurney was decorated with ribbons and silver wedding bells. The women carried boxes of gifts.

Grete shed tears as she kissed her eldest daughter.

"Mama, meet my new friends. They gave me a bridal shower!" Elin introduced each woman and they shook her mother's hand. "Mama, the ladies scoured the whole ship and put these gifts together. There are no mixers in those boxes but the gifts mean more to me than you can imagine. I now have a table centerpiece made of a bedpan and filled with pink tissue flowers." Grete and Alyse laughed and Jeremy smiled.

"Your chariot awaits, ma'am," said the EMT with the ambulance. The women kissed Elin and wished her the best of luck. She was loaded into the ambulance.

Jeremy followed at a safe distance. So did Georgie Boy.

* * *

The Chief, Bob and Ben left the station to interview Burt the Bartender and determine the last names of the three persons who Gil described. They sat in the back of the Palm Shack and waited for the overweight and unshaven Burt to appear.

"Morning Burt," Bob said as he and Ben got out of the cruiser.

"What can I do for you, officers?"

The Chief joined Bob and Ben.

"Chief Hanneman, is that you?"

"Sure is, Burt. It's been a number of years since I've run you in."

"I straightened out, Chief, honest."

"Well how about an honest answer. What are the last names and addresses of Tram, Lilia and Sam?"

"I don't know, Chief."

"Are you sure you don't know, Burt," Bob said.

"Honest."

"Chief, if we came back at two when this bar opens, do you think we could find enough violations to shut the bar down for a nice long time?" Bob asked.

"I'm sure we could."

"Look guys, this bar is my livelihood. You can't close me down," Burt said.

The Chief replied, "We can, Burt. I bet I could find a reason to arrest almost everyone in your bar. I'm also sure the Health Department can find a reason or two to make you wash your dirty apron."

"Look, if I told you their names they would come back and get me. Gil put you up to this, didn't he?"

"Leave Gil out of this. You've watched drug deals come down. Last names and addresses," Bob said.

"You won't tell them I told you?"

"Not if you don't mislead us."

Burt gave the Chief and Bob the names. He didn't know the exact addresses but he could give directions to their apartments.

"Now tell me everything you know about Tommie Turner," the Chief said.

"He's bad news. He sells. I don't know where he lives."

"That doesn't matter—I do. Where does he get his stuff?"

"I'm not sure anymore."

"What do you mean by anymore?"

"I didn't tell Gil this but do you remember the man who killed the cop and Chief Kingston killed him?"

"Rich Myers?"

"He came in a couple of times with Tommie. The paper said Myers distributed. I think Tommie got his stuff from him."

"Myers has been dead since January. Turner must get his stuff from someone else now."

"I don't know."

"Have you seen him with anyone else?"

"One time another guy was with Myers. I didn't recognize him."

"What did he look like, Burt?" the Chief asked.

Burt told the Chief what he had told Gil.

"We've never been here. Know what that means?"

"It means I don't say anything about your visit."

"Right. You keep quiet and we keep your name out of it."

* * *

James sat in his wheelchair and squirmed as he waited for Elin. After Charlie took Grace and Jeanette down to the cafeteria, she went downstairs to the Emergency Room to wait for the ambulance. A few seconds later, Elin was pushed into the ER on a gurney. As the aid prepared to take Elin to her room, Charlie put her arm around Grete. "Let's give Elin and James a private few minutes to themselves."

"Charlie's right, mama. We'll give them five whole minutes and then we'll march right in." Alyse giggled from excitement as she spoke.

"Oh you two. We'll give them fifteen minutes alone and then we'll go to the room. Grace and Jeanette are not in Elin's room, are they? That wouldn't be fair," Grete said.

"They're in the cafeteria. Why don't we go there?"

Charlie showed them the way to the cafeteria and left to intercept Jeremy before he interrupted James and Elin.

CHAPTER FORTY-EIGHT

"Oh what a sight you are for these sore eyes. You're luscious," James said after Elin was transferred from her gurney to her bed. "I didn't expect you to make an appearance with make-up on."

"The make-up is so you wouldn't see how I really look. Now hush up and give me a kiss, lover."

"Only if you say out loud you'll marry me."

"You better believe I'll marry you. There are no second thoughts on my part."

James slipped the antique engagement ring on her finger.

"It's so beautiful, James. So beautiful. It's your mother's, isn't it?"

"She wanted you to have it."

"I hope she knows I'll cherish it."

"She knows you will."

"My mom said she's here at the hospital."

"Charlie took mom and Jeanette to the cafeteria so we'd have some time alone. She was supposed to corral your mother and Alyse, too."

"Where's your room."

"Right here."

"They'll let us share a hospital room?"

"We'll be married this evening at seven."

"Tonight!"

"Alyse and your mother chose your wedding gown. The flowers are already in the chapel and my mother and Jeanette will be dressed fit to kill with new hats, fancy dresses and gloves. Your mother and Alyse have new outfits, too."

"I can't believe all this," she exclaimed as happy tears channeled down her face.

"Elin, our mother's have nailed this whole thing down. They decorated a wheelchair for you and me; they bought our wedding rings; they picked out the flowers; and they paid the chaplain. Alyse is your maid of honor and will push you up the aisle and your mother will give you away. If my sons get here in time, the oldest will be my best man. If they don't make it, Jeremy will be by my side."

"But we need a license and blood tests."

"The chaplain arranged for the license and the Navy provided the results of your blood tests. Oh yes, Charlie told me to tell you she is your flower girl."

"Don't make me laugh, James. My stomach still hurts."

"What did Bladensburg do to you? I only know you were shot."

"He shot me twice in the stomach. You know those surgeries where people have their stomachs made smaller?"

"You mean to lose weight?"

"You got it. Well, two bullets destroyed part of my stomach and I lost about half of it. There was a lot of other damage but the surgeons patched me up."

"So we both now have stomach cavities filled with bacteria?"

"Yep. And it sounds like our wedding bands and our antibiotics will match, too."

* * *

"Gil, this is Jeremy. I plan to fly back tomorrow so we need a serious talk about the price of the marina."

"Ohmagosh! That's wonderful. Is your pretty mom coming, too? I need to git her autograph. She is so famous. You should see the papers down here. Famous. She's an absolute legend."

"Would you save us copies of the newspapers? My mom's big on scrapbooking."

"Sure will. I'll git myself to the store before they all sell out."

"The Chief gave me the name of a real estate appraiser and a lawyer so I need to meet with them."

"When will your mother be back?"

"She'll return before the trial."

"Is it true? Did she really use hairspray on the guy?"

"Hairspray and some nail polish remover."

"Holy Moley."

* * *

Jim and Mark Kingston interrupted their father as he kissed Elin for the fourth time.

"Enough smooch stuff until after the wedding," Jim said.

James introduced his sons to Elin and she managed to get a hug out of both of the boys. As they chatted with their father, Elin examined their features. Jim looked a lot like his father but Mark had lighter skin with almond-shaped eyes and a narrower nose. Elin thought he looked like the picture of Corrine that James had showed her.

Dr. Cowen entered the room and shooed the sons outside. She instructed James to get back in bed and she closed the curtain between Elin and him.

"I reviewed your charts from the carrier. Those bullets did a lot of damage but your prognosis is good as long as you stick to antibiotics and don't misbehave like your roommate."

"I promise I won't. I can't be mad at him though. He left the hospital because of me."

"Well it is up to you now to see that he behaves. And the wedding is what time this evening?"

"Seven," James yelled.

"Well don't tell James, but a very handsome Navy lieutenant is my escort to your wedding, Elin."

"A lieutenant, huh?"

"He's the officer James spoke to at the base."

"Oh good." Elin proceeded to tell Dr. Cowen all about the gifts the nurses on the aircraft carrier made her.

"I must move on now but one more thing. No sex stuff until both of you can stand up and walk, talk and laugh without pain."

"Did you hear, James?" Elin said as she giggled.

"Oh, I heard." The gold tooth twinkled.

* * *

Bob and the Chief sat in a conference room at police headquarters and reviewed the entire murder and drug case. They used both a bulletin board and a white board to see if they could connect some dots. There was a clear line between the deceased Rich Myers to Fred Willard and Clint Spell and now Tommie Turner. There were no direct connections to former Deputy Police Chief Eugene Peters except through Myers. They knew Myers orchestrated the drug deals and drug movement on St. Croix and Peters did the same on St. Thomas. The Chief was desperate to find more solid evidence against Peters.

The Chief and Bob reviewed the murder books for Roy Stevens and Chuck Buckley.

"Nothing. Absolutely nothing," the Chief said. "We don't have any idea where we can find their families."

"True, but we'll find Tommie sooner or later. Maybe he'll know."

The Chief's cell rang and it was Charlie. She spoke for a few moments.

"James told me he was about to marry but I didn't think it was today," the Chief said.

"I guess he figured since he had a couple of more days in a hospital bed he might as well have her for a roommate."

"Well, good for them. Sorry I'm not there for the ceremony. Congratulate the groom for me and give the bride my best wishes."

"Will do. How is your murder case?"

"We're stumped. We have a good lead named Tommie Turner but we can't find him. We still don't have a positive ID on Stevens and Buckley and won't have one until we can find out where they lived and get dental records or something."

"So they lived on their boat all the time on St. Croix?"

"They lived on the *Columbus*. Very appropriate name for the boat because good old Christopher stopped here before he landed on the mainland."

"Does the murder book mention Rich Myers was from Columbus, Ohio? Did you look for them there?"

"Holy Moley!"

"Holy Moley? I've never heard you say anything like that before, Victor."

"I've been around Gil Kliver too much."

* * *

Grete had chosen a pale green silk dress with sequins around the collar. She didn't have time to get shoes dyed so she wore white satin ones with white accessories. Her small green hat had a velvet bow on the top and netting over her face. Alyse donned an ecru dress with a sateen finish. The color complimented her skin tones. She wore a single white rose in her raven hair. With her short and curvaceous body, she looked great in five-inch tan heels. Grace wore a pale blue silk dress with an empire waistline. She wanted to hide how much weight she had lost the past month. Her hat was one Queen Elizabeth could have borrowed. Jeanette had on a solid purple dress with a wide-brimmed red hat with purple feathers. She decided that at her age a multi-purpose dress and hat was smart. Her outfit was fit for a wedding or a Red Hat luncheon. Charlie was elegant in the outfit she had worn on the ship.

The chapel was small and personal. Light filtered through a series of amber and amethyst stained panels on the right wall. The altar was made of tan marble with creamy swirls through it. It was appropriate for any religious denomination. The solid oak panels in back of the altar matched the three oak pews that sat on each side of the aisle. Grete and Grace had arranged for vases of long-stem white roses on both sides of the altar and a small display attached to the end of each pew.

When the bride arrived, James squirmed in his wheelchair near the altar. Mark placed Aunt Jeanette's arm on his arm and led her to the modest oak piano on the left side of the chapel. Jim escorted his grandmother up the aisle while he looked down upon her with an engaging grin on his face. Mark led Grete to her pew and patted the hand of the tiny thin woman who he would soon learn to love.

When Jeanette played Mendelssohn's **Wedding March**, Alyse pushed the bride up the aisle. Elin's sister and mother had purchased her an ivory satin gown with a gored skirt gracefully covering her legs. The strapless bodice was covered in seed pearls. Her bouquet was a mixture of white roses and Baby's Breath. A short veil, attached to a crown of white roses, covered her face. Elin glowed and James beamed.

I love weddings, Ms. Charlie.
They are wonderful, aren't they?
I need to get you married.
Only if it is right.
But weddings touch the soul and are so romantic.
Yes, they do touch the soul.
And then there is the sex.
Shame on you—you're in a chapel. Reboot your conscience.

The ceremony was beautiful. The chaplain preached about commitment and trust. He advised the bride and groom to lean on each other in times of adversities. Both Elin and James felt they had overcome enough adversities to last them forever but they knew a few more were bound to come their way.

A small wedding cake and snacks were in the borrowed nurses lounge. After the new bride and groom cut the cake, it was shared with the nurses and patients on the floor. Afterward the bride and groom returned to their shared hospital room.

Jeremy snapped several dozen pictures of the evening's highlights and so did the uninvited Georgie Boy.

* * *

Bob Thompson had called Lieutenant Coale in Columbus. It was Coale who had visited the parents of Rich Myers after he was killed. Bob explained to Coale he felt there might be a connection between the original drug case and the murder of the marina men. He sent the officer the picture of the two men taken in the bar and the two sets of unidentified prints found in the storage shed.

"Chief, Jerry Coale said he recognized one of the men in the pictures and he knew he had seen him some time in the past and would go through his old records."

"Let's go back and talk to Burt the Bartender. Tommie must have had a girlfriend somewhere along the way."

* * *

Gil headed for the Palm Shack to see if he could find out anything more about Tommie Turner. When he saw the Chief and Bob Thompson get out of a banged-up Mustang, he scooted back to his office.

Locals started to fill up the Palm Shack along with a smattering of tourists in brightly colored shirts, shorts and sneakers. Burt was busy so Bob and the Chief sat in the back to see who came and went. They had brought a picture of Turner from their mug file is case he should be there.

Bob recognized a half dozen faces from arrests or speeding tickets. They saw Lilia come in by herself and Bob asked her to sit with them for a while. She asked Bob if he would buy her a rum and Coke and he did.

The Chief let Bob handle the conversation.

"Lilia, when you went to find Tommie Turner to tell him about Gil, where did you find him?"

"No one finds Tommie. He finds you. I know which corners he scouts every night and sure enough, he turned up."

"I hope this is the truth, Lilia. You know he tried to burn down Gil's office, don't you."

Lilia lowered her big black eyes. "I don't know nothing."

"Well if you did and you didn't tell us, we'll have a special cell set aside for you."

"I wasn't involved but I did hear about it."

"Who told you?"

"Tram. He told Tommie he thought Gil set him up and Tommie got real mad."

"Go on, Lilia. Don't stop now."

"Tram said Tommie told him he was going to burn Gil out of business."

"Have you seen Tommie?"

"Not in two nights."

"If I wanted to find Tommie, on which corner should I be?"

"Far side of Monroe."

The Chief and Bob left. "I'll put plain clothes officers there tonight. If they spot Tommie they will need to follow," the Chief told Bob.

* * *

Gil picked up the morning paper and read the banner headline. The byline was by George Harris.

WOMAN SHOT ON CRUISE SHIP WEDS

NORFOLK. Elin Mikkelsen of St. Croix yesterday wed St. Croix Deputy Police James Kingston in St. Mary's Hospital Chapel in Norfolk.

The U.S. Navy airlifted Mikkelsen from the Scandinavian Seven Seas Cruise Line's ship *Aqua Waters*. She had been shot and seriously wounded. Navy surgeons operated on Mikkelsen on the aircraft carrier and she remained onboard.

Upon the carrier's arrival yesterday, Ms. Mikkelsen was transported to the hospital where her fiancé waited. Chief Kingston left his hospital bed on St. Thomas and traveled to Norfolk to meet his bride-to-be. He was admitted as a patient for complications of appendicitis.

Charlie Mikkelsen, who was held hostage by the same man who shot Mrs. Kingston, was a guest at the wedding.

* * *

There was a plethora of "oohs" and "ahs" as Gil and the rest of the island community examined the large front-page above-the-fold picture of the beautiful bride and her handsome groom as they sat in their matching wheelchairs and held hands. Both chairs were decorated with silver velvet bows and the attached IV poles resembled Maypoles. Another picture showed Grace, Jeanette, Grete and Alyse as they posed behind the bride and groom.

Maybe I shouldn't have stayed a bachelor all these years. I gotta git me famous and find me a woman. The little lady in the picture named Jeanette looks like a cutie.

* * *

Sam Kentland, Editor of the Virgin Island Press, allowed Georgie to put his story and pictures on the wires. The Associated Press and Reuters picked up the story without hesitation, as did COX. Georgie surreptitiously sold similar pictures to several weekly tabloids on the sly and pocketed the money. His boss wasn't too happy when he found out.

CHAPTER FORTY-NINE

Since Jeremy was returning to the islands, Charlie asked him to escort Grace, Jeanette, Grete and Alyse home. Charlie's oldest son Jason arrived from his home in York and he drove his mother home. They made a short stop in Baltimore to have her joints X-rayed followed by a visit with her orthopedic surgeon. She hoped she had not damaged any parts of the erector sets in her knees or her ankle.

* * *

The next morning Bob called the Chief. "Jerry Coale called. He visited the Myers family and they recognized Roy Stevens, who is actually Roy Myers, cousin to Rich Myers. The parents knew Chuck Buckley, too. He then visited the Buckley family and they identified their son. He forwarded dental records on both men."

"Do these men have police records?"

"There are no prints on file."

"Did you ask about Turner?"

"I didn't think about that because he was born on St. Thomas. I'll do it right away, Chief."

* * *

St. Mary's Hospital phone system went into overdrive because so many media outlets had seen George's news story and wanted an interview with the bride and groom. Karen Walsh was one of the reporters who made a call. James asked the receptionist to take everyone's name and phone number. He and Elin were due to be released over the weekend and he wanted no hassles as they left the hospital. He had no plans to return any calls.

When James saw the Chief had tried to reach him, he called.

"So I did miss someone," James said. "Since this Roy is related to Rich, there has to be a connection with this Turner. But we can't use any of this as evidence against Eugene Peters."

"True. You're much closer to this than I am, any thoughts?" the Chief asked.

"Get Eugene's file and talk to Andre. I suggest we put Eugene's home under surveillance."

"When will you be back?"

"We both will be released in three days. I think I'll give Charlie a call and see if Elin can go to her home. I don't want either one of our ladies back on the island until they are due to testify."

"Do you want me to call Charlie for you?" the Chief offered.

"If you would be so kind. Are things okay between the two of you?"

"Things became strained between Jeremy and me but I believe Charlie figured everything out. Jeremy called and apologized and later Charlie called. I was relieved to hear her voice."

"Well I didn't expect to get married like I did but it was a nice alternative. If we had been home Grete and my mother would have rented the entire Botanical Gardens to hold a wedding and reception for the entire population of the island."

"Well Georgie Boy made your wedding available to a zillion tabloid-reading people instead."

"So that's why we've received so many calls from the press."

"I'll save the papers for you."

* * *

First thing Tuesday morning Jeremy was on the phone with an appraiser and a lawyer. He wanted to know if Gil's asking price was realistic and if the property was free and clear of liens. He checked the

Internet for the local tides and instead found the wedding pictures taken in Norfolk. He was in a picture along with his mother. He thanked God his face was partially obscured.

He found the tide chart and headed for the pier with his diver's gear to inspect more pilings. Gil wasn't around so he changed into his gear in the car. He went toward the end of the first pier where Gil had his little ladder. He brought rope with him and tied it to a piling. He tied his oversized waterproof flashlight to the other end and left the rope loosely coiled on the planks.

The sun was so bright and the water so clear that Jeremy discovered he could examine the pilings and cross bracings without the flashlight so he let it sit on the pier. After a good thirty minutes he decided to take a break and chow down some breakfast. He felt confident that with a few replacement pilings, the piers were strong and safe—at least until another Hurricane Hugo.

Jeremy realized he had not thought about insurance for the pier and reminded himself to do so as he climbed up Gil's ladder. He removed his flippers and headed for his rented car where he had stashed a jug of hot coffee and some local pastries.

While Jeremy was in his car, Gil returned from his extra long early morning ritual. This morning he did three sketches—all of various island structures as seen from the harbor's water. He had exactly eleven more scenes to capture before his collection was a massive collage of the entire town. If Jeremy bought his marina, Gil wanted to make sure he had completed his self-appointed task. He tied up his boat and climbed the ladder.

Once in his office, Gil lounged in his chair and admired his work. He glanced up when someone walked past the open blinds of his office window. "Well if it ain't Tommie Turner. Did ya come to burn me down again?"

"Sure did. This time I came prepared with a can of gas. Isn't it nice you're inside and I'm outside."

"Tommie, don't do anything stupid. The police already know it was you the last time."

"The cops have to find me first. They haven't yet. That says a lot about their stupidity."

Tommie unscrewed the top of the can and opened his cigarette lighter. Gil stood up and approached him.

"Back up, Popeye," Turner said. "I brought a gun this time."

Tommie bent over to set the can down to reach for his gun. As Tommie started to stand up he had the lighter in one hand and his gun in the other. Gil chose that second to plow into his waist like a tackler for the Patriots. He pushed Tommie out on the pier and landed on top of him. The can tipped and gas began to seep out in narrow rivulets spreading along the planks before it dripped down between them. The rivulets widened.

Jeremy had locked the car and stepped back on the pier when he saw Gil land on top of Tommie. He ran to help as Tommie managed to flip Gil into a puddle of gas. Now Tommie was on top. He flicked his lighter again and leaned toward the gas above Gil's head. Jeremy blindsided Tommie and tackled him. Tommie fell to the far side of the gas can and the container pivoted with the can's funnel toward him. Unfortunately, his lighter still had an open flame. The gas on Tommie's clothing ignited at the same moment Jeremy kicked the can off the edge of the pier.

A flaming Tommie jumped up. Jeremy used one of his flippers in an effort to beat the flames but Tommie ran to the edge of the pier to jump. As he did his foot caught in the coil of rope Jeremy had left near the edge. Tommie and the rope went over the pier but his foot was entangled and he hung upside down in flames.

Jeremy jumped off the pier and tried to splash water on Tommie from below. Gil pulled a hose down the pier and aimed it at Tommie. When the flames were extinguished, Tommie Turner wiggled upside down and screeched obscenities.

An owner of a nearby sailboat had heard the commotion and had come on deck. He saw the man in flames and called the police and fire department.

Jeremy and Gil tried to hoist Tommie up to the edge of the pier. Bob Thompson appeared out of nowhere and took the rope. When Tommie was within reach, Jeremy and Gil each grabbed a leg and pulled. Bob grabbed Tommie by the back of his belt and pulled him on the pier. An ambulance arrived and the EMS staff put Tommie Turner on the gurney. After being handcuffed, he was whisked away.

"You're a hero, Gil," Jeremy said.

"Me? A hero?"

"The way you tackled the man was something else. Where did you play football?"

"Never did," Gil replied in total amazement. As he spoke, George Harris snapped his last in a series of pictures.

"You're famous, Gil, famous."

"Holy Moley! I'm finally famous. Do you think ya mom would want my autograph?"

"Absolutely."

"Well, now I jist need me a gal. Tell me what you know about that Jeanette lady…"

***

Charlie powered up her computer to check her email as soon as she arrived home. Most were from her Red Hat friends. Four contained Maxine cartoons—her favorite. She checked the news on the Internet and found the wedding pictures on COX's website.

Ms. Charlie, isn't that dear?

It's beautiful, I must admit. As obnoxious as Georgie Boy is he does take good pictures.

We need to get married.

Well you go right ahead.

Charlie checked the online St. Croix news sites and found several other wedding pictures. Jeremy and she were in one. The news story accompanying the pictures told about the wedding and regurgitated what had happened to Elin and her on the ship. Out of curiosity she went to the York Daily Record's site and several wedding pictures appeared along with the story about York's most notorious resident and Red Hat lady. Charlie downloaded the pictures and saved them for Elin.

The next morning Charlie called the hospital and Elin answered.

"How are you this morning?"

"Married despite the fact we're in two different beds."

"Well you're all over the Internet and you made quite a splash in all the island papers."

"Did that creep Georgie Boy take the pictures?"

"Yep. He's the one COX had on air. The online pictures are great. I haven't looked at the ones Jeremy took. When I do I'll make nice copies for you."

"We received an envelope and a box from Borge Dyrby."

"Ah, our handsome young Swede. What did he send?"

"Two tickets for a cruise of Scandinavia with stops in Norway, Sweden, Denmark and Finland. The literature is gorgeous. Those fiords must be something else."

"What a nice honeymoon that would be. What was in the box?"

"An incredible piece of modern Swedish art glass. It's all these colors swirled into a design. James said if we go on the cruise I'm not allowed in any crystal or art glass shops."

"Tell your bossy husband I give you permission to go."

"I'm not sure about another cruise, Charlie. The last one didn't go too well."

"But this cruise will be with your beloved new husband and not me."

* * *

Bob Thompson explained the scene on the pier to the Chief.

"How bad are his burns?"

"Not as bad as expected. Jeremy put out most of the flames with his fins and Gil doused him with water. The doctor did arrange to have him airlifted to the burn center in St. Thomas."

"He's getting better treatment than he deserves," the Chief growled.

"We should have a positive ID by tomorrow because Lt. Cole sent Myers and Buckley's dental records."

"Anything new on Turner back in Ohio?"

"Unfortunately not."

Bob left to complete his report on Turner and the pier incident. The Chief picked up the phone and arranged a conference call between Andre and James. "Gentlemen, we need a connection with Eugene if we want that conviction."

"I'll get Marlboro Man to interview Turner today if the doctor doesn't have him on pain killers," Andre said.

James said, "I've been thinking about the *Columbus*. It is the perfect size boat to run drugs. I don't think the killer would sink it so I bet it is around somewhere close."

"Our men have been to every marina on our islands. I instructed them to assume the boat's name had been changed so they searched for brand name and size," the Chief replied. "The islands outside of U.S. territories are next on our list."

"Did you put someone on the Peters' house?" James asked.

"I did and nothing so far. When will you fly back here?"

"Friday. Charlie will drive down and take Elin to Pennsylvania with her. They should be safe there."

Andre joked, "You do realize your wedding made the evening television news, the papers and the Internet, don't you?"

"Yeah. Elin was elated, our mothers were giddy, and I pulled the covers over my face. Georgie Boy is a real trip—Elin hates him one minute and loves him the next. I want him as far away from me as possible."

"I share you sentiments exactly," Andre said.

CHAPTER FIFTY

Jeremy negotiated hard and he and Gil agreed on a price. He spent the rest of the week with the appraiser, his lawyer and the local banker. He called home and had his investment property put on the market. He knew his undeveloped forty acres in Lancaster County would sell within a few days at full asking price. His home and the rental properties were in good condition and up to code so he expected them to sell. With things looking good, he started to research homes in need of TLC in and around Christiansted.

* * *

Charlie and Elin spent a quiet week at Charlie's condo in York. It was still painful for Elin to move around so they rented every movie they had never seen. The rest of the time Charlie drove Elin around Pennsylvania Dutch country. They planned to return to St. Croix two days before the trial.

* * *

"I have a positive ID on both corpses," the coroner said. "I can release the bodies for shipment and burial."

"Thanks," the Chief said. "I'll have Bob contact Officer Coale in Columbus so the parents can be told." The Chief hung up and called Bob.

"This will be tough on the Myers family," Bob said. "They've lost two family members within months of each other. Coale said they seemed like nice people."

"These men had the gift of free will and neither used it wisely."

* * *

Charlie and Elin returned to St. Croix from Pennsylvania. James and Jeremy waited for them at the airport. Elin and James headed for her home and Charlie and Jeremy returned to the villa. There were officers stationed outside both dwellings twenty-four by seven.

Later, Jeremy took his mother to a small two-bedroom house he found that was in dire need of some attention. The house was situated on the side of a hill. Two other homeowners shared the long precipitous driveway. The home's foundation was concrete reinforced with rebar and the walls were block filled with rebar and cement, both of which explained why a house thirty-years old survived so many storms—including Hurricane Hugo. A cistern was below the first level and had recently undergone major repairs.

A new roof was needed but the rafters, collar beam and ceiling joists were heavy duty, properly spaced, and met current building codes for areas prone to hurricanes. The windows and doors were in sad shape and the house required new ones both inside and out. The kitchen and bath required a major overhaul but it was something that could be postponed for some time. The strong selling point, according to Jeremy, was a delightful glimpse of the Salt River where it met the Caribbean. Mother and son agreed to look around a little bit more.

Charlie had no sooner arrived back at the rented villa than the Chief called.

"Jeremy took me to see the house last week. It's a little too much work for a man my age but to be honest, my first purchase was in about the same condition. Your son is an ambitious young man."

"I can see its potential but a new metal roof would be the first thing on the list followed closely by AC, new windows and doors and hurricane blinds."

"Remind him to calculate the price of the improvements to determine the actual cost. I have to admit the sales price looks pretty good on the surface."

"He's already investigated the cost of materials. He hadn't realized the materials have to be shipped in."

"Ah yes—those expensive little hidden cost. On another note, I know its too late tonight but how about dinner tomorrow?"

"That would be nice. James said we weren't scheduled to testify until Tuesday so Elin and I plan to fly to St. Thomas on Monday and spend the night at James' old home."

"I'll be there Tuesday myself. Andre will see that you two have plenty of protection."

"Any breaks on the Eugene Peters case?"

"I'm stumped."

"Did you read today's paper? Georgie Boy interviewed Mrs. Peters and she claims that her husband is innocent and he was set up by Andre Johnson."

"That didn't happen. He was arrested fair and square. I look forward to his explanation of why he had almost two mil in an off-shore bank account."

"There was a picture of his sons," Charlie said. "Did you know any of them?"

"I knew Gene, Jr. but Turner and Casey were youngsters the last time I visited his home."

"Turner? Like in Tommie Turner?" Charlie asked.

"A coincidence, I'm sure. But…"

"Did Eugene always live on the islands?"

"I'm not sure."

"Is his wife a native or a statesider?"

"Not sure, either. I'll follow up on everything," the Chief said.

"What's with Alice and Julie?"

"Chamaign and Man have spent hours watching the DVDs from the ship's security files. They feel they have a strong case for aiding and abetting. The detectives don't know how Bladensburg's confession will play at the trial. Anyway, both women saw a lawyer and they both clamed up."

"Do you think I'll have to testify?"

"From what I've been told the only thing you witnessed was Alice in the elevator. If these were murder charges, I would say you would be required to testify but not for aiding and abetting. I'm sure this will result in a plea bargain. On another note, I'll pick you up about three tomorrow."

And while you have dinner with the Chief, Ms. Charlie, whom will you think about—the captain or the Chief?

Good question. I guess I'll find out.

* * *

The Chief went back to a set of blueprints he had on his dining room table but his mind was elsewhere. He was pensive for a few minutes before he picked up the phone.

"Bob, can you call your buddy in Columbus and see if there are any Turners in the family?"

"I'll ask Cole to go to the Myers' home today and do a family tree."

"It will be interesting to see if there are any branches named Turner."

* * *

Man paid Tommie Turner a visit that evening in the hospital. "How's the pain?"

"Who in the hell are you, Shorty?"

"Marlboro Carmen, VIPD."

"Why does a cop care about my pain?"

"I'm part human I believe."

"What is the rest of you, Squirt?"

"Police detective."

"And you act like you're proud?"

"We ID'd the bodies at the pier."

"What's that got to do with me?"

"They sold drugs for your buddy Rich Myers."

Tommie tensed up. "Get outta my face, man."

"You're in enough trouble for arson. If you help me, maybe I can help you."

"Out of here."

"Think about it, Tommie. I'll drop in for a friendly visit tomorrow."

* * *

Just before the tropical sunset, the Chief and Charlie went to the edge of the boardwalk and took a short boat ride to the cay located in the harbor. There was a hotel, restaurant and outside bar on the cay. That night there was a special outdoor buffet with dinner tables and chairs set in the sand amidst palm trees. There was Calypso music and entertainment as the mocko jumbies pranced and danced around on their tall stilts in glittery costumes.

"Now, Charlie Mikkelsen, would you like a Cruzan Cream to start our meal?"

"White wine for me."

"That's interesting. You got mad at me at my retirement dinner when I ordered wine. Now you want me to order wine for you. Can you tell me when I can or cannot order you a drink without a consultation?"

"Victor, you know both of us were upset that night with all those kissing posters on the wall. But to answer your question, ask. Now, has anyone looked for the boat in the British Virgin Islands?"

"I'm on top of it. I know the Chief of Police on Tortola and requested permission to send Bob there. He'll leave early tomorrow."

The Chief and Charlie enjoyed their dinner. It was difficult for the Chief to cut his meat and hold Charlie's hand at the same time.

* * *

The Chief arrived home a little before midnight. There was a message from Bob on his answering machine. The next morning Bob called the Chief again.

"Jerry Coale did what I asked. I need you to sit down, Chief."

"I'm in bed."

"Better yet in case you decide to have a heart attack brought on by a huge sigh of relief. Eugene Peters is a twin. His sister Estelle married one Michael Casey Turner in Columbus. The Turners had one son named Tommie."

"Great work, Bob. Please forward the name of Jerry's boss. I'll write a letter of appreciation for his services. The bottom line is the VIPD needs to hire Charlie."

"Did she put you on to the Turners in Ohio?"

"Of course. Who else? I mentioned the names of Eugene's children. His middle son is Turner and his youngest is Casey. Did you get your flight to Tortola tomorrow?"

* * *

James, Elin, Jeremy and Charlie flew from St. Croix to Charlotte Amalie. James made sure everyone was comfortable at his old home before he went to police headquarters. He sat in a meeting with the prosecutor along with his boss, Bill Farrow, and Andre and his boss, Dwayne Phillips. Emerik Nielsen, the prosecuting attorney, was there.

When the Chief called, Andre put him on the speakerphone.

"We need to prove Tommie worked with Eugene," Nielsen said.

Andre said, "Man will go back to the hospital today. What kind of deal can we cut?"

"You have him on drugs and arson but you need to get a plea bargain out of him and quick. He needs to discuss his uncle."

"I'll go," Andre said.

"Don't do that. We don't want him to think we're desperate," Nielsen said.

"Turner is also the one who hit Rubee," the Chief said. "His prints matched those in the SUV he stole to run Charlie and me off the road."

"You decide how you want to approach Tommie," the prosecutor said. "I need to get to court for the opening statement."

***

The courtroom was filled with spectators and Georgie Boy had a front row seat although he was not allowed to take pictures in the room. The center of everyone's attention was Eugene Peters. The other men on trial were part of the drug ring—Fred Willard and Clint Spell from St. Croix and two from St. Thomas. They would all be tried together.

After the opening statements the judge dismissed the jurors for the day. Testimony would begin Tuesday.

***

The Chief was the houseguest of the Farrow family. He invited Bill and his wife Terri to join Charlie and him for dinner. He had reservations for a restaurant snuggled among the trees on the hill behind Charlotte Amalie. The entire front of the two-floor restaurant was glass.

At this time of the evening, most tourists were back on their cruise ships prepared to sail. The restaurant's clientele came from the various resorts and rented villas and condos or else were locals. The men were dressed mostly in tan slacks with opened collar shirts and the women in sundresses or linen slacks with linen or cotton knit blouses. It cost the Chief several significant bills to encourage the maitre-d' to seat them in front of the main window overlooking the harbor.

"What a view," Charlie said. "I've never seen a ship leave port after dark. The lights are wonderful." She proceeded to tell everyone what it was like to see the town's lights from the ship.

"Am I to order you a drink this evening?" Victor asked. Before Charlie could answer he explained to Bill and Terri why it was necessary to ask.

"Don't mind him. He likes to embarrass me in public."

"Oh you mean like the airport kiss?" Terri laughed.

Charlie twisted her lips to the side and said nothing.

"Do you plan to tell me sometime tonight what to order?"

"White wine, Victor."

While everyone enjoyed their drinks and waited for dinner, Charlie told Victor, Bill and Terri about the lights she saw from the bridge of *Aqua Waters*.

"How did you get on the bridge?" Victor asked.

"I think maybe the captain felt sorry for me. Elin had been airlifted and I was alone so he invited me to dinner."

"Is that something I should be worried about?"

"Not really."

Ms. Charlie, that's what I call a little fib.

Not really.

Then why do you look so guilty?

I'm not guilty.

You're not sorry either.

Throughout dinner, Terri wanted to know all the details about what happened on the ship. Somewhere between the elevator and the electrical closet Victor's cell buzzed. He excused himself and left to answer it.

"We got him, Chief. We got him!" Bob yelled into the phone.

"You sound very pleased with yourself. Did you find the yacht?"

"Yep! The Tortola police took prints for me. The prints on the helm belonged to Peters. His were on top of Stevens, AKA Roy Myers."

"I'll notify the prosecutor. When he is ready we'll ask someone from Tortola to come over and testify."

After the Chief hung up he called Andre and James. He returned to his guests and happily told them what Bob found.

"Congratulations, Victor. Would you wish to rejoin the force as a detective?"

"No, but you may want to hire Charlie."

* * *

"Evening, Tommie. How did it go today?" Marlboro Man asked.

"Get lost. I need my pain medication."

"I asked the nurse to hold up the pain meds until we finish our little talk. This gentleman here is Henry Dank. He is your court-appointed attorney."

"I don't need a lawyer."

"Oh, I think you do," Man said.

"Tommie, you're not to say a word unless I tell you, hear me?" Dank ordered.

"We found the yacht on Tortola," Man said.

"And why do I care?"

"Do you care your uncle's prints were all over the helm of the yacht?"

Tommie didn't respond.

"He's going down, Tommie, and Uncle Eugene plans to take you down with him."

"You can't prove a thing."

"We found your prints in an SUV that tried to run Chief Hanneman off the road."

"Tommie, it's time to be quiet," Dank said. "Let me do the talking."

"I don't need a lawyer. Are you deaf?"

"I can prove you're related to Peters," Man said. "I can prove you sold drugs, I can prove your prints were in the SUV, and I can prove you tried to commit arson twice. Plus, I can call Aunt Estelle to testify."

"You can't get her to testify."

"I can't make her testify against Eugene but I can force her to testify against you. It's that or jail for her."

"What kinda deal are you talking about?"

"Tommie, you let me handle this from here on," Dank said.

Man looked at Dank. "Tell your client that any deal depends on how valuable his information is."

"Man shifted his glance to Tommie. Who murdered Roy and Chuck?"

"Before you answer, are those terms okay with you, Tommie?" Dank asked.

"Shut up, Dank. Uncle Eugene killed both of them."

"Why did he murder them?"

"Roy called my uncle and told him he was taking over the drug ring in St. Croix."

"What did your uncle do?"

"Uncle Eugene piloted his boat to St. Croix that evening and took care of Roy and Chuck."

"How do you know this?"

"I was with Roy and Chuck. He shot and killed Chuck and stuffed Roy's mouth with a rag and hung him under the pier so the incoming tide would kill him. He told me that's what happens when people play games with him."

"Detective, if you want my client to testify he does no jail time."

"Oh, he does jail time and he will testify. But I'll try to get the time cut."

"Tommie? Do you agree to the offer?" Dank said.

Tommie nodded.

"What happened next?" Man asked.

"Uncle Eugene stayed until the tide was in and Roy was dead."

CHAPTER FIFTY-ONE

Since both Elin and Charlie had to testify, neither was allowed to sit in the courtroom.

When Elin was called she answered the questions the district attorney asked with dignity. When defense questioned her about Willard's alleged sexual advances, she sat through some ugly implications in regard to her ex-husband. She was reduced to tears and the judge called for a ten-minute break. Afterward, Elin was asked about Spell and the cemetery. She described the scene at the crypt and the terror that overcame her when she and her mother were forced into it and the lid was slid in place. The DA watched the reaction of the jury. Two the women jurors had tears in their eyes; several of the men shook their heads in dismay.

The DA asked the judge and the defense attorney if it was necessary to bring Mrs. Grete Mikkelsen in to testify. She mentioned Grete's age. The defense attorney said he felt it would not be necessary.

The court adjourned for lunch. Georgie rushed outside and snapped some pictures of Elin as she was ushered into James' car and taken home. Poor Georgie Boy didn't know a reporter from COX was also there.

Victor took Charlie to lunch but she did no more than nibble.

"Nervous?"

"I've never done anything like this before."

"It will all be over soon. I have something I want you to wear this afternoon."

Victor handed Charlie a black, flat square box. Inside was a 14K gold bracelet with a hook design.

"I must warn you there is folklore about how the bracelet is worn."

"Would you like to tell me so I know how it goes?"

"If the hook faces you and your heart, it means you are taken. If it faces outward it means you have no commitment."

"And if I wear it facing me, exactly what is my commitment?"

"Only that you are no longer on the market."

"Market? I'm not a package of meat!"

Victor laughed, "Sorry. I don't want any ole cruise ship captain to think you are available for the taking."

Charlie looked puzzled as she wondered how much Victor knew and worse yet, how he knew it.

I didn't tell the Chief anything, Ms. Charlie. Honest.
Who else would do it?

"Charlie, I saw the two cruise ship tickets the other night when I went to pick you up for dinner. They sat in a fancy new wine glass in the foyer of the villa."

"And you thought what?"

"I thought I'd better not take any chances. You spent an evening on the bridge with him—this bothers me."

"Well an evening on the bridge was lovely but there were at least twenty other people around in consoles filled with green dials and blips and bleeps."

"And that's the whole story?"

Charlie smiled and said not a word. Victor did take note that Charlie put on the bracelet with the hook facing her heart.

* * *

Charlie's testimony took on a circus atmosphere as soon as she described how her stainless steel prosthetic knee jerk disabled Spell in the cemetery. She described what she did after she tied him up with gray duct tape and he still refused to tell her Elin's location. The defense lawyer asked her why she needed to use the four-foot long crow bar on Spell's anatomy. He showed it to the jurors. That didn't deter Charlie as she repeated what he said about how he buried Elin and Grete. "I had one thought and one thought only—I had to get to them and I would have done anything necessary to find them in time."

The district attorney was smart enough not to ask many questions. The defense lawyer wasn't that smart. With each question, Charlie's responses created laughter in the courtroom. The judge told the lawyer to move on and Charlie was dismissed.

* * *

Testimony went on for the next four days as the DA unfolded the role that each of the four small-time drug dealers played. It was time to nail Peters.

The deceased Rich Myers had kept a spreadsheet and it showed how the drug money was divided and the percentages everyone received. The spreadsheet was displayed on a fifty-inch flat screen TV. The DA pointed to the acronym COP, Peters' code name.

Nielsen called on Andre and asked what Internal Affairs knew about Peters' lifestyle. Andre, who was in charge of Internal Affairs at that time, told him about the Lexus, his other woman, the tux and the fancy hotel.

Statements from Peters' offshore bank account were entered into evidence. Finally, the DA played the video of Tommie Tucker as he spoke about his uncle killing Roy Myers and Chuck Buckley. The Rich Myers family tree was shown on the TV with each line leading to family members involved in the drug ring.

The defense attorney questioned everything everyone said but in the end his efforts were not effective. The jury was out less than two hours. Eugene received life without parole, Willard and Spell each received twenty but with the possibility of parole. The two mules on St. Thomas received ten years each. Tommie Tucker's plea bargain got him five years with the possibility of parole after three.

With the verdict in, the Kingstons, Mikkelsens, Johnsons and the Chief had a huge celebration at the Ritz-Carlton. Without her boot, Charlie was finally able to dance with Victor. Meanwhile, Jeremy spied a pretty blonde in the hotel's bar.

GOLDEN OPPORTUNITIES: A WOMAN'S MYSTERY NOVEL

The next morning everyone headed to the airport to return to St. Croix and found Georgie Boy had pictures of everyone in the paper. There was even a shot of the Chief and Charlie on the dance floor.

"Does that man sleep?" the Chief asked.

As they sat and watched COX News on the airport terminal's television, they watched themselves again in front of the Criminal Justice Center. Georgie Boy fumed.

* * *

Georgie Boy didn't get a book deal or a new job. His editor gave him a stern lecture about media ethics instead.

Charlie received several offers to write a book about the events on the cruise ship. She decided to think about it. Victor thought the book was a good idea and would keep her out of trouble.

* * *

The next couple of days Charlie followed Jeremy around as he spoke with his lawyer, the engineer, the insurance agent, and the real estate agent. Victor accompanied Charlie and Jeremy to Gil's office.

"Gil, I hear you need my autograph," Charlie said.

"Holy Moley, it's you. It's really you. May I git your autograph, ma'am, please?"

"Well, I understand you're famous, too, Gil. So I'll give you my autograph if you give me yours."

"You got it." Jeremy took several pictures of Gil and his mother before he and Gil signed a sales agreement.

* * *

Victor and Charlie left Jeremy and Gil and walked toward Rubee. "Now it's about time for me to show you my surprise," the Chief said. "I have something you must see."

He drove to the northwest part of the island. Charlie recognized the area immediately. "We're going to my ancestor's old sugar plantation, aren't we?"

Victor pulled onto what was once an old rutted road. It had been smoothed out and gravel had been pounded into the earth. "Who did this? Did you do this Victor?"

At the top of the road was construction. "You bought this land, didn't you? That's a huge home!"

"I bought the whole plantation named after your great, great grandmother—Claudine's Quarters. Your ancestors may have owned these grounds but it was my ancestors that worked these grounds. They were freed slaves but they worked very hard in the very hot sun for very little return. It was almost like slavery. That isn't a house, Charlie. It's a dormitory for young teens who have not yet decided to take responsibility for their behavior. I provide the land, the accommodations and some guidance. I'm confident I have a grant to provide personnel to oversee the teens. They will work this ground to provide food for themselves and sell the rest to earn money. Each young man will have his own savings account. The school system will provide instruction for their diplomas."

Charlie was speechless, which was very unusual.

What does this mean for you, Ms. Charlie?

I have no idea.

You'll never see the Chief he'll be so busy.

Don't say that. See how I wear his bracelet with the hook toward my heart.

"Charlie, I'll spend a lot of time up here. But the rest of my time will be with you if you'll have me." The Chief got out of Rubee, pulled an ice chest out of the trunk, and took out a cold bottle of Cruzan Cream. He poured drinks into two glasses. "To all our ancestors who walked and worked this land."

There was a clink of the glasses and a silent "Hear, hear!"

Where does this leave me, Ms. Charlie?

With me.

And where exactly are you and the Chief?

Almost there, maybe.